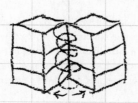

TIMOTHY TAYLOR

STORY HOUSE

VINTAGE CANADA

Published in Canada by Vintage Canada, a division of Random House
of Canada Limited, Toronto, in 2007. First published in hardcover in
Canada by Alfred A. Knopf Canada, a division of Random House of
Canada Limited, Toronto, in 2006. Distributed by Random House
of Canada Limited, Toronto.

www.randomhouse.ca

Vintage Canada and colophon are registered trademarks of Random
House of Canada Limited.

LIBRARY AND ARCHIVES CANADA CATALOGUING IN PUBLICATION

Taylor, Timothy L., 1963–
      Story house / Timothy Taylor.

ISBN 978-0-676-97765-3

            I. Title.

PS8589.A975S86 2007   C813'.6   C2006-904710-3

Text design: CS Richardson

Printed and bound in the United States of America

10 9 8 7 6 5 4 3 2 1

For Jane

And for my parents,
Richard and Ursula Taylor

Harrow the house of the dead; look shining at
New styles of architecture, a change of heart.

W.H. AUDEN

CONTENTS

MARY STREET

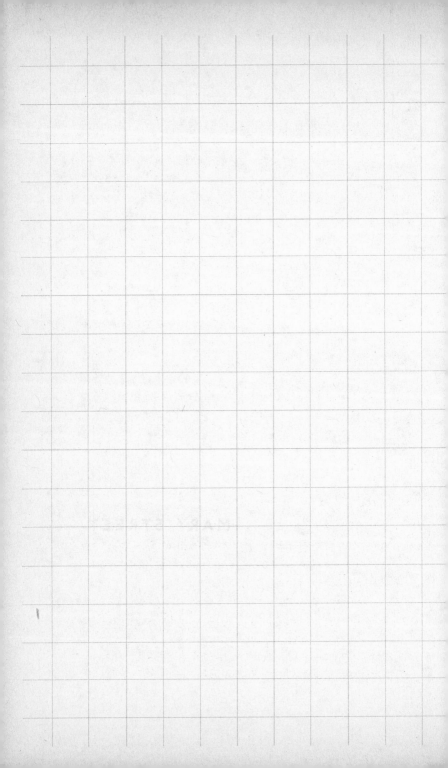

17 years before the beginning

POGEY REMEMBERED THEM APPEARING FROM
nowhere. Ghosting into view. He remembered them like
a punch he hadn't seen coming: only later, when consciousness had returned.

He didn't hear the car arrive on the street above, didn't
hear the gym door open up top, or feet on the stairs. He
was working target mitts with one of the neighbourhood
kids. *One-two. One-two-hook. One-two-hook with an
uppercut. Again.* Gloves slapping home in the basement

air. The bell marked the round. Pogey turned. And there they were.

"Hey," said the blond one. Chunky, with the colouring of indulgence, of a life spent on pleasure boats: light tan, sun-bleached crewcut. Easy on the feet too, as if he'd been in the room before. As if he knew its dimensions and possibilities.

Pogey crossed over to the ropes. "Lessons are five an hour. Drop-in fee is a buck."

"We're here to fight," the kid said. "Each other."

Fourteen, fifteen years old. Not train, not spar. Fight.

"You got a name, killer?" Pogey asked him.

Graham Gordon.

"And you?" Pogey said to the other. A different sort altogether, this one. Asian maybe. Lean, bony-shouldered with long dark hair and hard eyes. With insolence etched in the smirk lines, in the bad posture. And yet that same quality, unhurried possession of his particular space such that Pogey found he did not dispute the claim.

"Elliot," Graham said. "My brother."

Which elicited a snort from the dark-haired one as he dropped his gym bag and squinted around the room like a dubious matchmaker. "Half-brother," he said.

Pogey took the stairs in twos. He found the third party to this transaction leaning against the front fender of a late-model Lincoln Town Car, scanning the facade of the building. A six-footer. Older than Pogey expected, maybe seventy, with a faintly squandered feel about him. Houndstooth jacket, ascot, white shirt, cufflinks like Scrabble tiles: one G, one E. Cigarette-stained fingers and all-concealing sunglasses intended for the unforgiving light of glaciers. These lenses lowered heavily on Pogey as he emerged, affording him the special discomfort of seeing, in reflection, precisely what was under hard appraisal.

"You're Nealon," the man said.

Pogey nodded. Squinted.

"Packer Gordon," he said finally, lifting himself from the car and extending a hand. "I take it you've met my boys."

First thing Gordon wanted to know was why there were clamshells littering the front steps and sidewalk in front of the building. The detail seemed to annoy him.

Crows, Pogey said. Crows that for reasons he couldn't explain favoured 55 East Mary Street over all other buildings in the neighbourhood. For strutting and making a racket, yes. But also for the killing of dozens of razor clams daily, which they dropped from the eaves to shatter on the steps below. "But are we talking birds here, or about your two warriors downstairs?"

They had boxing experience, apparently. The younger one, Graham, boxed intramural at some fancy boys' school in the hills. "Elliot," Packer Gordon volunteered, "takes a more or less self-taught approach to life."

Decisive first instincts came naturally to Pogey. Still a flint-hard welter in these his middle years, with 117 amateur fights behind him, he knew how to assess incoming risk. He knew about pulling the trigger. "Sorry, but I'm full up with kids," he said. "We're busy in the summer."

Gordon motioned him close, dropping his voice. And Pogey, leaning forward, now caught sight of himself again, this time in the car's side mirror, the white front of his own building, where he lived, where he'd run his gym for thirty years, sweeping upward and into the blue sky behind him like a temple, serene and attendant. Taut with judgment.

"They box," Gordon said. "The problem is they prefer fighting."

"Everyone prefers fighting," Pogey said, still leaning in, voice low. "It's easier."

Which provoked a laugh. Packer Gordon liked that. "I'm an architect," he said. "I'm aware of how much easier it is to release force than restrain it."

Pogey straightened up, blinking. He remembered losing himself in the resumption of gym noise below. Someone rang the bell to start another round. Shoes shuffled on the concrete floors. The heavy bags began to groan on their turnbuckles. The speedbag winding out. All the machinery of fight school reeling again into motion. And, missing the moment for escape cleanly, he heard himself say only, "How'd you ever hear of Nealon's Gym?"

Gordon blew past that question, on to terms, money and others. He wanted a closed gym. He wanted Pogey's undivided attention paid to just these two. He wanted to set up a camera and film three rounds, the outcome of which would apparently settle all matters between the boys.

"I'm not letting a couple kids in my ring I've never even seen before."

So they would train. So Pogey could assess them for however long he needed. So they would prove themselves.

Now a money clip was out. Bills peeled off in a way that suggested impulsive spending, often beyond available means. And Pogey was nodding as the cash whispered into his palm, nodding until Gordon had forked over more than Pogey could have hoped to collect in two months running.

"You're telling me you want to rent my gym for the entire summer?"

———

Thursdays. Eight Thursdays. Pogey remembered they trained hard. He had them skip five rounds, do callisthenics five more, stretch, go for a jog. They didn't pull on bag gloves until the second week, by which point he'd withheld the true business of boxing for long enough that they wanted nothing more than to curl their hands into fists, to feel canvas under the balls of their feet. All this while hardly a word of argument passed between them, no revealed schism. Only opposing energy that polarized everything within their field.

Did he acquire polarity of his own? Pogey knew he had tried not to but also that he'd been interested by the cascade of difference between them. Graham's ongoing mention of his father, whose buildings were apparently known around the world. His crested training gear, his graceless, uncomplaining effort to do anything Pogey demanded of them, walking off the skipping rounds, eyes averted to the roof beams or the front windows, taking long, slow whistling breaths or asking earnest, technical questions. He worked out with a war face. He hit hard, his only skill. Cursed to be a puncher. Cursed to have the work ethic most kids lacked entirely, to be devoted and yet unable to master.

Elliot lived in the contrast. A kid with lean muscularity he did nothing to deserve. Who had a sneeze of derision for any instruction. Who worked the bags and mitts, playing bored. Stopping between combinations not to catch his breath (he had plenty) but to talk to Pogey as if this hired coach were a friend just slightly junior in the schoolyard pecking order.

"I'm older by six months," he told Pogey during the second week. "Meaning six months each year we're the same age, six months he spends trying to catch up. It's never-ending."

"One-two," Pogey barked at him from behind the mitts. And the kid jumped back in with a hard and tight combination. Balanced. Impossibly natural.

Graham asked, week three, "So when I throw that hook low, how do I—"

"Why don't we just fight and get it over with?" Elliot called from the ropes, where he was hanging, bouncing, long arms spread out to either side.

"Just because you two been down here a few weeks and are dying to get in there . . ." Pogey yelled, losing his temper for the first time, "don't mean jack shit to me. Pumped-up beginners are the worst for thumbing, lacing, detaching retinas and rupturing freaking kidneys, and that goes double for a couple west-side wannabes getting chauffeured down here by their daddy."

Graham looked hurt by the outburst. Elliot, highly amused.

Pogey relented the following week. They would spar one round. A mid-term test. A look-see. A chance for Pogey to judge if they were learning anything. "Spar weight is maybe 50 per cent," Pogey barked. "I see you go heavy, I stop it. Understood?"

Surprising seriousness between them. They even touched gloves.

Pogey triggered the bell, then turned to see Elliot overwhelm his brother with punches. Graham slugging away, useless while Elliot calmly flicked the jab, countered and moved. It was a mauling at half speed. An outcome so predetermined that when the bell rang, those three minutes passed into history as if they'd never been in the future at all.

Pogey iced the welt under Graham's right eye. He sent Elliot upstairs to wait in the car.

"You okay?" Pogey asked Graham.

He'd cry if he spoke, so Graham said nothing.

"You weren't so bad."

Graham shook his head. He'd been bad.

"You hit like a freight train. But you gotta back off the power and use pace instead."

Deep breaths.

It wasn't pity Pogey felt. Both less and more than that. He saw a tough predicament in the appropriate light. The kid was a puncher. His brother was a boxer. The boxer beat the puncher. It was the arrangement of things unless changes were introduced.

"What sort of changes?" Graham asked.

Had he been speaking aloud? Pogey hadn't noticed. Well then.

He took a breath. "You know rock, paper, scissors?" he began.

Packer Gordon made a practice of waiting topside in the car. Half sleeping, half listening to the radio. Pogey invited him down only once and got a short reply: "Whenever you say they're ready, coach," nodding toward the trunk where his camera gear was stored.

Fine. Pogey left the great man alone, although from time to time he saw through the high front windows as Gordon levered his long limbs from the car and paced the sidewalk, kicking shells, stopping with his legs spread, feet planted. Pogey could see only to the man's knees, but the posture suggested Gordon with his hands on his hips, scanning the building, the neighbourhood.

A week after the practice spar, Pogey had them do ring drills and watched Graham get popped with so many half-weight jabs his nose finally started to bleed.

"Can we do this every day?" Elliot asked.

Pogey went up while the boys were changing. Gordon looked up through the smoked glass, then buzzed the window down. Pogey looked into the face of the man he'd finally gone to the library to read about for himself. A man who'd built his own home on a rock outcropping in the western reaches of the city. Pogey squinted at the pictures and shook his head at the captions. "Unresolved tension at the very lip of the ocean." "As close to plunging into the deep and destroying itself as architecture is legally allowed."

"That was half a grand I gave you," Packer Gordon said out the window.

"This isn't about money," Pogey answered. "This is about calling it off."

TIMOTHY
TAYLOR

Gordon looked Pogey over for several seconds. Then said, "Beautiful morning, though."

Which it was. And perhaps that was good enough reason to proceed with the matter as planned. Settle all

differences between them while sun shone benignly overhead. Only Pogey could not ignore the boxing truth of the matter.

"And what is that truth, Mr. Nealon?" Gordon asked.

The truth, he told Gordon, was that the insolent smart mouth would win. The dogged be-gooder, as devoted and hard-working as he might be, would lose. And not just because the one was angry and the other only disrespectful.

"Anger is bad in the ring?" Gordon asked.

"Lose your temper, lose the fight," Pogey told him. "You can't box when you're pissed."

"And why else is this outcome so sure?"

Because I can feel it. Because you put your wife's kid in against your mistress's kid and the bastard is always more committed to winning. "Because that's what the style triangle tells us," he said to Gordon.

Now here was something that interested the architect. Gordon leaned forward and turned off the radio. He removed the sunglasses, fixing Pogey with the first unmediated eye contact their relationship had enjoyed. He was fascinated, pleased enormously.

"There's a *triangle?*" he asked.

Pogey plunged onward. Boxing was a triangle, yes. Three corners, three fighting styles. The boxer, the puncher and the swarmer. Boxers fought with finesse, fluidity and movement. Punchers with power. Swarmers with volume and intensity. And just like rock, paper, scissors, Pogey explained, these styles were locked in relation to one another. Rock beat scissors, which beat paper, which beat rock. So boxers beat punchers who beat swarmers who beat boxers. The only way to change that reality was to reposition the fighters on the surface of the triangle. And to accomplish that, you either moved yourself to a better position relative to your opponent's or forced your opponent to a worse one relative to yours.

"If you're a puncher facing a boxer," Pogey said, "you either become a swarmer right quick or you turn the other guy into one. It's as simple and as hard as that."

"And because of his temper," Gordon said, "Graham cannot either transform his own style or chase Elliot away from his."

Pogey held his hands up. "Exactly," he said.

"And why is it," Gordon asked, "that you wish to withhold this lesson from them?"

Pogey shifted on his feet, clamshells crunching underfoot. He had no word of an answer.

Packer Gordon set up his camera ringside. Framed his square shot and disappeared behind the viewfinder as if that might reveal the truth to him better than his own famous eyes.

Three rounds, three minutes each.

"I gotta be in there, meaning you're timekeeper," Pogey said to Gordon, who raised his wrist to display the chronograph with stopwatch that would be used.

"Five, four, three, two . . ."

"Box!" said Pogey and waved them together.

Round one: two fighters and their basic instincts. They felt each other out just as Pogey would have predicted. Graham stalking. Elliot dancing and moving, lashing out a jab into his brother's face and staying away. Untouched by the round's end. His brother, Graham, gasping.

"Time," called Gordon Sr. And Pogey leaned in to put an arm between the boys, pushing them apart to their opposite corners, looking over to catch the father's eye, to see if there might be words of advice for either of them.

But Packer Gordon was back behind his camera already.

"You see that?" Pogey said to Graham in his corner, voice low. "You try to punch with him, he boxes you. What happens?"

The boy grunted. He was furious, but his eyes flickered up to Pogey's. He heard.

"Keep them up," Pogey said to Elliot as they both moved toward the centre of the ring. "Don't be prancing around with your gloves down here."

"Time," said Packer Gordon.

"Box!" said Pogey.

Round two: two fighters and the changes one tries to impose. Graham naturally, who could feel himself losing. Who could feel the sting of that jab, the humiliation of that camera humming from just over the ropes. Graham who then did pick up the pace, keeping his hands in motion, bulling in, working beyond anything Pogey had seen before. And landing too. Starting to thud home hooks to the body. Elliot trapped in a corner, bobbing, weaving. Breathing calmly, still, but more curious. More interested by recent developments than by anything Pogey had seen him face previously.

"Okay move," Pogey said to him. "Move, move."

And Graham finally finding him with a hard, high right just then. A punch that crushed Elliot's ear flat, froze him for an instant. But didn't stop him. The boxer spun out and reset. Graham turned to fire again. And Elliot, not allowing himself to be hurried, calmly put one down the pipe. Caught Graham moving, unbalanced on his feet. Put him hard against the ropes from where he went straight down to the canvas, face first. There was blood in the ring. There was blood on Pogey's shirt.

"Time!" called Packer Gordon.

"You okay?" Pogey asked, leaning in. "You sure you want to do one more? Three more minutes. Talk to me."

Graham breathed, he steadied himself. He said, "Gotta do one more, Mr. Nealon. I just got him where I wanted him."

Round three, three minutes. Two fighters and a merciless clock. It ticked up to the top of the dial on Packer Gordon's wrist and at his nod, Pogey triggered the bell ushering in final events that couldn't be avoided. The first knockdown was ugly. Graham bulled in and cut off the ring. He trapped Elliot in the corner. He swarmed, did as he was told. And Pogey, against practice, found himself pleased for one kid over another.

"All right, move, move," Pogey said from a position just out of harm's way. And Elliot did twist free. Missed getting creamed by a short overhand right, dipped down and low and out he went. Graham reset, moved his feet. He bobbed low. Elliot launched the left hook down at him and Graham came up right into it. He took it on the cheek flush and went back into the ropes. Still upright, but Elliot was on him, slapping home a right to the forehead that put Graham onto his knee.

Pogey went to him and knelt down. He took Graham's face in his hand and looked for cuts. None. He didn't ask the question. He stood up and waved them in.

The second knockdown, by contrast, undeniably pretty. Nice to look at because it gave evidence of something Pogey prized very highly in a fighter: an improvement on the last thing that worked. Elliot was tiring himself, breathing through an open mouth, but he was refining tactics on the fly. He slipped another right. Sidestepped and launched his own short left while Graham reset. This hook started low just as before, but now as Graham dipped to catch it, Elliot reeled it in. Up and over the guard.

Jawbone. On the button.

Graham was on his back, then his front. He pushed himself up to his feet, arms along the ropes.

"How much time?" Pogey yelled across to Packer Gordon, who scrambled to fold back a French cuff and find that wristwatch. Who then held up one finger.

"One minute," Pogey barked at both of them. Thinking, Sixty seconds left, both crazy mad, yes, but they'd make it out. He'd declare the match a draw. There would be much pissing and moaning about this, naturally enough, but old man Gordon would then pack up his warring offspring and take them home.

Pogey waved them in a final time.

They met in the middle as the end of the fight collapsed down toward them all. Elliot pawing for an opening. Graham making an audible noise as he swung in the shots, a keening, moaning sound that spiked to a gasp of relief with the effort of each punch. Elliot backed away, circling the ring. But as his defence fell away, Elliot continued to hunt for that last left hook. His right hand idle now as he launched again and again. Graham taking them off the forehead and the shoulder. On the ear. But not the chin, which he had tucked firmly down as he swarmed his way toward the bell.

Pogey counted off what he calculated to be the last ten seconds and prepared to jump between them.

He counted another ten while the clubbing continued and Elliot's left kept pouring through and bouncing away.

He counted another ten, then thought to look over for his timekeeper. In Packer Gordon's unmoving, unblinking frame, this would take the form of a quick glance directly at the camera. Then another glance, anger rising in his features.

"Time! Time! Time!"

While the climax unfolded directly behind him. A punch captured in full. A hook. Routine but square. A punch that broke the third rib up the cage, Pogey calculated later. Pogey who had heard ribs break in the ring before, nothing like the snapping fence post you might imagine, a subtler, wetter sound altogether.

Pogey was still yelling, "Time, goddammit. Time! Time!"

And Elliot was falling straight backward from the pain. Not even wobbly before this punch landed, just getting a second wind. But there was a pain point, Pogey knew, beyond which your body would only tolerate being horizontal. A point you knew you'd reached because your brain cramped around a single thought: all this must now immediately end. A death of kinds, very closely embraced.

Elliot fell that way. Straight back, laid out. And doing so, the back of his neck hit the bottom ring rope, strung taut as it could be. His head snapped forward, hard. His chin driven into his chest, neck folding for an instant into an impossible shape.

And then he bounced free. He rolled over on one shoulder, not quite on his back or his side. His hand moving, all of it from the wrist downwards folding tightly inward. Curling, curling, as if it would disappear. And when the hand relaxed, Elliot Gordon rolled gently to his back and exhaled a very long, very full breath.

one year before the beginning

"RILEY, YOU READY?"

Riley shifted in his seat, causing the springs of his rust-pocked Chevy Funcraft to cringe and squeak. He sat with his feet planted, hands still on the wheel. A big guy, with big guy ways. A tendency to stand close, to laugh with excessive force, to sulk upon encountering obstacles.

"Deirdre," he said. "I think we're having a professional disagreement."

She breathed deeply. Bright blue above, no cloud.

Magic Hour approaching. They had ninety minutes, after which it would merely be dusk and they would be—as a team, from the standpoint of shooting film and capturing the building, in terms of passing the freaking course—well and truly hooped.

"What kind of professional disagreement?" she asked.

Group assignments were difficult. Partnered ones oddly more so. But partnered final assignments, ill defined in scope and worth 75 per cent of your mark, were surely the worst of all unless you slept with your partner in a moment of madness and then, Deirdre supposed, you had achieved the true worst-case assignment scenario.

Now Riley gripped the steering wheel tightly while he spoke. "Analyze a contemporary urban housing project. Discuss the tensions between light and shadow, as well as the relationship between form, function, occupant and structure. *Contemporary*," Riley said. "That's like, I don't know, Gehry. Look at this place. It's old. It looks like a prison."

"The wall apparently came later."

"A wall with barbed wire on top. What is that?"

"Well, that's something we could ask the occupant about the structure."

"Is he a dealer? Is the function of this particular form the distribution of crack?"

"The man is in his seventies, Riley. Crack I doubt. Listen . . ." She leaned into the door, she made eye contact. "My Aunt Cleo knows him. He's a nice, harmless old man."

Riley looked over her shoulder at 55 East Mary Street, dubious.

"Look up, above the wall," she tried. "Smooth white

finishing, stucco of some kind. Box design. Curtain wall. Everything thinned right out."

His eyes narrowed, signalling computation. "Like a 1930s knockoff," he said.

She had to turn away to conceal her exasperation. What had been the attraction? The van. Not for itself, for the idea of it. Eyeglasses were the thing for architecture students that year. Rectangular steel. Clear plastic. The clean line, the sharp corner. Slate grey crewnecks, short hair and retro 1980s music. Riley's van with its Steve Earle stickers and rattling quarter-panels was what counted for high aesthetic rebellion in their school. He wore jungle boots and grew his hair. He proposed a building made of hemp brick. Three in the morning working on their model of a redesign of the entire east side of the city (Mary Street included), Riley was humming while he trimmed down the roofline on a teepee-shaped town hall, surrounded by the requisite sidewalk cafés, galleries and skateboarding bowls. She was tired maybe, but his uncritical self-belief got to her. Gluing in place a mosque minaret, they brushed elbows. They created a kind of wee-hours energy that shuffled aside better judgment. They piled out to his van and did it right there in the back, her hips grinding into the flat weave of a rolled-up kilim.

Now she said, "Riley, if it weren't a knockoff, then what would it be?"

Riley said, "Okay. So real."

1939, according to the title search, although after that it got complicated. Built by a construction company nobody had heard of since. No plans filed with the city. Nothing bearing any kind of architectural stamp at all. Flood loss, went one story. Or just plain lost. Or maybe they were misfiled somewhere never to be located again but for a top-to-bottom tearing apart of the planning registry that probably wasn't happening any time soon. As for the architect behind it, they could only speculate. Maybe someone working for a middling firm that didn't give him credit. Maybe the developer had designed it.

"So this is about authorship," Riley tried.

"Sure. If you want. But look at the building, please."

Already the hues in the street had gone auburn. She turned back to the van to find Riley hadn't been looking at the building at all. He said, "You rock in this light."

She waited ten full seconds until his gaze drifted over her shoulder and onto the building. "Late-afternoon light and shadow," she said. "Light flooding the building, creating a space that glows with promise despite the decay of the neighbourhood. What was 'modern' in the conception still able to remind us of a time before irony, cynicism, consumerism and addiction, even as these forces consume the world around the structure. So does the building, its elevations and the grid of its interior, create a sciagraphical machine telling a story in light and shadow, the daily one of the occupant's life and the longer one of the structure itself."

The van springs complained as he heaved himself out. He gathered up his camera gear and joined her on the passenger side. He said, "Sciagraphical machine?"

"A clock, Riley. Fancy architecture word for a clock. We ready to cross the street now?"

Riley put his hand on her shoulder. She shook it off. They crossed the street.

Pogey had doubts. Not about kids shooting film of Mary Street, however screwball an idea that might be. More about the letter they had sent with its list of sample inter-view questions.

For whom and for what use do you think the architect originally designed the structure?

"You see, how the hell would I know that?" he asked Cleo, who was leaning over the counter of the Postum Diner, topping up his coffee. "My old man dies and leaves it to me. I don't pretend to understand these things, I just live there."

Cleo said, "My niece is in the university." As if that explained everything. Architecture school. It made the request yet more crazy. Structure. Is that what they called it? Two floors up. One down, half below grade. A spiral staircase coring up the middle capped by a leaky skylight.

"I got it," Pogey said. "The architect *designed the struc-ture* for the goddamn crows."

Cleo aimed a familiar expression at him, one that involved a combination of brow scrunching and gaze intensifying. A look indicating that he was either talking nonsense or aloud to himself. Or both at once. Cleo said, "She's a good girl. Very smart."

"Must be," Pogey said. "She thinks that old box is architecture."

But Cleo only waved a hand toward the window, as if in the grime of Hastings Street, with the stingy sunlight that seemed always to gather there, lay all the answers required. Then she said, "Architects. Who knows what they see?"

Which was a good question, Pogey thought an hour later, having heard the firm knock on his front door (buzzer long crapped out). Having made his way down the stairs to inspect this young niece of Cleo's through the spy hole. She had red hair spilling down across cream skin Pogey couldn't immediately place. Cleo was Greek. Her sister too, presumably. What sort of father produced this girl, then? Irish. Norwegian. From a winter-green clime of some variety. She had a finely bridged nose, square jawline, wide mouth. And those eyes, he acknowledged, remembering Cleo's question. Who knew what they saw? Very sharp eyes, dark blue. Very steady eyes, which didn't shift from the door after knocking. She stood there breathing calmly and waiting, nicely balanced on her feet. While behind her, the young man with the camera shifted nervously, kicking clamshells and looking down the street to their left and right.

How has the Mary Street area changed since you first moved here?

Jackson, Mary, Heatley, Columbia. The Terminal, as Pogey called the area on account of the low roar of harbour that filled the air: immense and close, just over the railway yards, tons moved against tons. Railcars, shipping containers, plates of steel and creaking jetties.

Changes. Well, there never used to be blocks of dead street front, boarded shops and abandoned hotels, lobbies and hallways filling with pigeon guano. Never used to be drifts of tired humanity at Main and Hastings each afternoon, colour struggling in weak light. Palm-to-palm exchanges of vials and crumpled bills, the gutters full of waste. No bedclothes strewn on the awning above the Timberman Hotel Bar, someone screaming up to a window above. No woman in the alley mouth shooting heroin into the corner of her eye.

"Come on in," Pogey said to them, swinging open the front door.

They went about the business of having first reactions. The one called Riley confirmed with every glance some conclusion he'd already reached outside. Nodding at wall alignment and commenting on the absence of mouldings. Noting the stairs, which apparently brought to mind some more famous set at a place called Bexhill-on-Sea. He pointed the camera up the shaft and filmed a drip of water working its way free of the metal crossbar that split the round skylight into four panels overhead. When the water flashed down in front of the lens en route to the basement slab below—*platt*, the teardrop atomized—he came out from behind the viewfinder. He said, "Sweet."

She was thinking the space through, some estimate of volume and area coming out wrong. She paced the distance from the stairs to the east wall of the foyer, frowning.

"Ten years ago," Pogey told her. He had no other income at that point, so he walled off half the main floor east of the stairwell. Punched an exterior door through the east wall. Warehouse rent covered property taxes and groceries. Flower wholesaler, bike courier company, movie props storage. He'd used it to store his own papers more recently.

Deirdre disappeared into the darkness of that side room. Pogey watched from the door frame as she ran a finger along the glass bricks that had made up the original exterior wall.

"Painted over," he heard Riley say. "Who'd do a thing like that? Oh, look, mushrooms."

Riley saw the plaster cracks. He saw the sag in a door frame, the fungal shoots spreading along the baseboards of that east exterior wall. "Like enoki only bigger," he said.

Riley couldn't see beyond the water stains, the leaky skylight. He couldn't see past the bankers boxes stacked down every available length of wall. Leaning, sagging, spilling open to reveal handwritten pages, notes, charts, books. They'd been inside thirty minutes and Riley had shot enough footage of structural and personal decay that Deirdre felt they should move on to other narratives trapped within these walls.

"What about the light?" she asked him. "High windows up top, then glass brick."

"What about the fact that it's falling down?" Riley countered. "Or is that what you liked about the place? Like we're trying to capture structure just as it stops being structure at all?"

Not quite that. "I was thinking more about original form and function," she said, as Riley raised the lens. "How they seem to have split away from one another at some point."

Because chaos and order leaned against one another in Mary Street, didn't they? Deirdre saw that the lines of the structure were simple. Three open floors linked by a curling strand of staircase. It was the sort of idea she imagined arriving in one white flash of insight, waking the architect from near sleep. The kind of idea—whole and iconic—that would have driven the architect from bed, downstairs, to a drafting desk, to frantic scribbling. She imagined the form shaping itself on paper, the architect watching an idea revealed.

Inside this revealed form, of course, was all the disorder Riley had noticed. The mould and the slump lines. The boxes, leaning stacks of newspapers and magazines. The accumulated wilderness of words. Alone in a side hall off the top-floor landing, she made her way along a wall lined to the ceiling with stored written idea, and from a box crushed open by the weight of those stacked above it, she managed to pull out a single sheet. On it, dozens of names minutely scratched into some kind of arcane hierarchy, squares linked by lines into webs and spirals. A complexly charted notion that, in contrast to the building itself, seeming to outstrip the holding capacity of the brain into which it had spawned. Deirdre considered the bold capital letters at the head of that page, raggedly underlined. A single word: SWARMERS.

She came and found him. He was reading *Best Fights of Fact and Fiction Quarterly* back issues, halfway through Cribb and Molineaux, round twenty-six, when she rapped at the frame of the open doorway into his room. "Both the combatants trying to recruit their wind and strength by scientific efforts . . ."

"Those questions, in our letter," she said. "I have to ask them."

"Fine," he said. "Me answering will be the hard part."

"If not you, though, who?"

He said to her, "You remind me of your aunt. Even with that red hair."

They set him up in a chair on the top-floor landing, framed by the skylight overhead. Amber light spilled down, rippled by water pooling on the glass above. Pogey stared up through this water at circling crows as Riley jigged a spindly lamp stand into place next to his camera.

How did you come to own the building?

Had you ever heard of Bauhaus? Were you aware of the building as a progressive idea?

Pogey could see her losing confidence in the words they had thought so hard over, used textbooks to devise, consulted professors about. He wanted to help, but simply didn't have much for them. He'd inherited the place, never heard of Bauhaus. His primary sense of the building was surprise that his old man had willed him anything at all.

Tell me how your reaction to the original idea . . .

She dropped her arms and looked over at Riley.

"I think what we're saying here, Mr. Nealon . . ." Riley tried. "Is the architect. What you thought, thinking about him. The architect."

Pogey stared, considering, but then Deirdre scrunched her brow and intensified her focus and read right through him to the answer.

"Mr. Nealon never really thought about there *being* an architect at all."

"No," he said. "I didn't, honestly. I thought it was probably built by an amateur and never finished."

"Because of which features, which elements of the building?"

"Well, the first thing I noticed was the place had no kitchen."

They wouldn't have known that he'd spent the past forty-five years boiling water on a hot plate and taking his meals on Hastings Street, lately favouring the diner owned by the girl's aunt. And now, with the troubling detail revealed, Pogey watched them split in different directions toward conclusion. Deirdre raised her eyebrows, as if the puzzle pleased her. Riley backed away from his gear and began coughing like he'd inhaled a handful of dust mites.

"This isn't even a *house?*" he managed, red-faced.

They took a sidebar over at the window, at which Riley apparently decided he should lead the interrogation for awhile. Pogey enjoyed watching him step forward while Deirdre dipped behind the camera with an apologetic smile. He had all the resolve of a person sparring for the first time, a wildly misplaced belief that it couldn't be all that hard.

"What about your father?" Riley started. "Did he commission the work?"

Pogey said, "My old man commissioned bartenders to make him drinks."

"How did he come to own it then?"

Here was a half-lie Pogey had planned in advance. An inheritance he didn't mind acknowledging. The inheritance of something his father won at a poker table reportedly full of hand-picked marks—eights and fives, no less, not exactly a boasting hand—wasn't a story he wanted to spread around. "My father played cards for a living," Pogey said. "To my surprise, he invested his winnings."

"When did he die?"

"1943," Pogey said. "I got a telegram from a lawyer."

"Where were you living then?"

"There was a war on at the time," Pogey said. "That's where I was living."

"Okay, so after. What did you think? You walk in, your first impression was . . ."

The lights were hot. Pogey didn't think he had hours of this performance in him. It reminded him of his one pro fight. A dinner club show, fat guys squeezed into tuxedos, kludge lights trained on the canvas. He handled his man into the third round, then lost spectacularly. Showboating for an instant and frozen with an overhand right. Then falling, falling. Down toward water, the sensation he remembered on recovery. The sensation of having been *under*.

"Listen," Pogey said. "I'm sorry, but I never noticed much about it. It never occurred to me the stairs were shaped like . . . what?"

"A strand of DNA," Riley said.

"I just thought it was big," Pogey said. "And unfinished."

"Did you like it?" Deirdre said.

Pogey sighed. "Not exactly," he said.

"Hate it?"

Okay, he thought, here we go. "Not quite hate. Distrust."

He'd refused to pick up the keys from the lawyer, having looked the building over once on returning home. This place he was supposed to own, brand new reportedly, just off Hastings, which was a happening strip in those days, a neon river—the Lux, the White Lunch, the Orwell and the Smiling Buddha—and here he found this box that not only didn't look like a new house but looked strangely pre-decayed. Weed-ready. Soliciting pests and squatters.

"I couldn't explain the feeling," Pogey said. "Then I see the door is open, crack it a couple inches and find a hobo taking a sponge bath inside. Got attacked by a racoon leaving."

A worthless inheritance, he decided, was worse than none at all. So he drifted, pointless and angry. Hanging out in the neighbourhood clubs, where he'd hunch into a booth trying to disappear entirely. Avoiding anybody

who might ask him for a signature on a deed, or for a war story, or about his plans, or about anything that would force him to continue the life he'd left behind when he went away and to which he no longer felt any connection.

The lawyer finally tracked him down when the estate was about to revert to the government. Pogey was in the Postum, shaking with hangover and pretending to read the local paper. The man slid in opposite, smacking down the page with one fat hand, staring deep into

Pogey's bleary eyes. "He said to me, *Kill the body and the head will die.*"

Which brought Deirdre out from behind the camera, curiosity flickering across her features.

"Meaning?" Riley asked.

"Meaning Mr. Nealon was a boxer," she said to him.

Nice, Pogey thought. Well done, Cleo's niece.

Riley's brow furrowed. "As in . . ."

As in punching people, sure. One hundred and seventeen amateur fights. "Only one pro. I learned quickly."

"So . . ." Now Riley was casting around for some familiar point from which to re-enter the discussion. "So what's with the wall and barbed wire outside?"

"You may have noticed the neighbourhood's gone downhill," Pogey answered.

"Wait," she said. "So you quit boxing. What then?"

"Were you concerned about protecting the architectural object?" Riley asked.

"More about junkies heaving bricks through the glass downstairs."

"Kill the body and the head will die," she pressed.
"That's advice."

"Sure it is," Pogey said to her.

"Deirdre," Riley said.

"So you followed this advice?"

"I did. I moved in."

Deirdre, getting closer: "That's it? Move in. That's all he was telling you?"

"He was also suggesting I get my shit together. Straighten up. Choose a life and live it. The body's just mechanics. The head is what you do with it."

She took the time to think here, but only for a moment. She turned away a quarter-turn, then back.

Coiling and releasing. "So it was too big to be a house, had no kitchen, was probably unfinished. So you never cared whether the stairs were Bexhill-on-Sea or Eileen Gray, or whether someone was ripping off Maison de Verre or Walter Gropius with the glass bricks. So, years later, you'd wall off some warehouse space to rent. But what did you decide to do with it first?"

She stood with her hand resting on the stair rail, waiting for her answer. A rail that dropped away from a perfect cylinder, lathed and lacquered, down through roughening layers until by the lowest stair you could pick up splinters from the unfinished cedar band to which it had reverted. And maybe she was just now awakening, as Pogey had himself, to details of contradiction, of built-in flaw that could not be explained. Details that cascaded down from the serenity of these upstairs rooms, down through the smooth wood of the main floor and into that most important room, half below grade, where the walls were rough concrete and, at the base of cedar pillars, traces of some primitive carving could be found. Indian or some such, he was no expert. After fifty years, as he'd been trying to tell them in his own way, you noticed only that the details offered nothing in return for your curiosity.

She lifted her eyes from the spiral of descending stairs. She found his.

Pogey said, "Well, if you want to know about all that, we'll have to continue this conversation in the basement."

Riley didn't wait for her to say *cut*. At some point he'd apparently had enough and simply split. She had to run after him. She had to scramble into the van or risk missing her ride.

"What are you doing?" she yelled at him. "We're shooting."

Riley cranked the ignition, the van coughing, shuddering. "Damn it!" he yelled. Then the engine caught and fired, and he stomped the accelerator so hard they lurched from the curb opposite 55 East Mary Street with a squelch, a whiff of gasoline and rubber, her door still open.

"Just tell me you got that," Deirdre said, pulling shut the door.

"Shit! We are so—"

"Tell me you kept that camera rolling out there."

"—so fucked!" he said.

She should have seen it coming. He hadn't said a word in the basement. He'd looked a little sickly down there in the low light, a little distressed by the variety of chaos around them. The sagging ring ropes, the leaning corner posts. All the scattered evidence of something interrupted and never resumed. Toppled stools, scattered gloves and headgear, handwraps, buckets. In the corner of the room there was a pile of heavy bags slumped against a mirror. At the corner of the eye they looked quite a lot like dead bodies. And then the library. Shelves and shelves of 8mm film cans. Miles and miles, hours and hours of recorded fight history.

Jack Johnson on up, he told her, proud of the accomplishment. Not seeing the unsettling effect it had by demonstrating that the darkened room—the sagging couch, the dusty film projector, the torn screen—for all the cobwebs and the rat droppings, was actually in regular use. Then he spooled up some film through the projector and that didn't improve matters for Riley, whose rattling quarter-panels, whose goat beard and cargo shorts full of rolling papers and weed didn't, in the end, prove him any less fastidious than any other architecture student she'd ever met. Riley watched the film through the lens of the video camera, recording the old footage as she had insisted, but flinched when anything in the way of a punch landed.

She took him to a coffee shop to calm him down. Not the Postum, because the situation apparently demanded steamed almond milk. So a place uptown on an intersection flying with the early-evening rush. And only here did Riley climb down from the mountaintop of his righteous anger, carrying the earnest lesson he had learned there.

"Deirdre," he said, lacing his fingers in the way one did with kids: *Here is the church; here is the steeple.* "Deirdre, I know I come across as a bit of a radical, a rule breaker . . ."

She didn't smile. She didn't laugh.

But he had a serious side too, Riley wanted her to know.

Open the doors and see all the people.

Meaning: accomplishment was still important to him. Grades. Reputation. "Meaning I don't think that cutting together a bunch of tape of some lunatic old man talking about—"

"Riley, honey." Was she really doing this? Reaching out to touch his cheek and console him, to remind him that he used to trust her? "Riley, this is good. We have something surprising."

He made the gesture of the reasonable person under some time constraint. He raised hands and eyebrows to welcome incoming comment, then dropped these both sharply, hands falling listless to his lap. "Go," he said. "Surprising."

So she gave it to him, in one long, useless rush. The place had flow, it had direction. Remember the colours. White and pale blue on the top floor. High light. Then polished wood on the main floor. The light more forested. Slate grey in the basement, like a cave. The staircase too, changed from top to bottom. The treads got thicker going down. And that pillar running vertically through each floor? Upstairs, it was a smooth white cylinder. Main floor, it was thicker and lacquered to expose the wood grain. Downstairs, it was unfinished. "There were strips of bark hanging off the timber, Riley. Somebody built the place to draw our attention to the layers. To draw our attention *downward*."

But her case was over and had been rejected, she could see immediately with these words. Because Riley was fully recovered. Rejuvenated by almond milk and disappearing fast into the cluster of self-secure mannerisms that had, incredibly, unbelievably, attracted her to him in the first place. He looked at her with an angled glance that slipped off her face and down toward her chest and her waist. A glance that remembered the mistake between them but would never have any clue that it *had* been a mistake.

He could get them into the Patkau place on Point Grey Road, he was telling her now. "Or homeless people," he said, warming up. "We take the camera down to Stanley Park and shoot one of those shopping cart lean-tos in the bush all layered over with garbage and shit. Bang together something about the inherent tensions of transient structure and we *ace* this thing."

Which they probably would. But a nice, clear irrationalism gripped Deirdre just then, and she surrendered to it. She had her story of occupant and structure. Light, shadow, form and function. And leaving Riley, and eating dinner alone, and falling asleep that night, drifting away into an oddly spare dreamscape, waking the next morning, a shaft of sunlight finding her eyes through a crack in the curtains of her tiny rented Kitsilano apartment, that feeling still held her. 55 East Mary Street was the best story of its kind she'd ever heard, and that truth would be unaffected by whether or not she ever repeated it.

Pogey slept in an oddly spare dreamscape himself: a familiar three floors connected by a coil of staircase, only every room, every hall was empty. He walked these spaces considering that the distance between what he was seeing and the place as he actually remembered it represented roughly the entire contents of his life.

In the dream, part of him argued with another part. His red corner and his blue corner. The blue corner said, *You see? Now here is what happens when you tell everything to strangers. You core yourself out. You end up living in a white cube.*

To which the red corner replied, *You miss the boxes maybe? The film? You miss poring over it all, night after night? Looking for clues as to how you could have been so wrong?*

Blue: *So the truth doesn't matter any more?*

Red: *Truth. Rock, paper, scissors was supposed to be true.*

Blue: *Where have you been for the past decade and a half? My analysis clearly shows that the boxing triangle is true. Those brothers simply presented a different kind of problem.*

Red: *Uh-huh. Sure. Oh and, by the way, did you notice that the water stains on the walls are gone? No mushrooms in the east room? The place looks all right when it's cleaned up.*

He woke on the couch in the basement, a shaft of light dropping down the skylight and bouncing through the building to find him. He blinked awake, out of a clean, spare, white vision of his own surroundings into the wilderness he had allowed to grow there.

"I knew you'd like her," Cleo told him, pouring coffee. Leaning in close. "Though, you don't look so good this morning."

But he was good. He was more than good. He had ideas, which the girl had inspired. Cleo scrunched her brows and examined him intensely, but that didn't shake his conviction of the new day. He'd pushed himself up off the couch that morning, he told Cleo. He'd stumbled to the bottom of the stairs to find that shaft of light coming down to him.

Cleo's entire brow was heading toward the tight knot between her eyes.

"So I'm standing there, looking up," Pogey told her, leaning his head back to show her just how the inspiration had been delivered. "And splat!"

Water from above. Eyes closed, head back, Pogey got nailed by a drip from the skylight.

Cleo consented to nod, some small portion of his point becoming clear. She said, "You're not going up on a ladder, are you, Pogey?"

Indeed he was. In the morning sunshine and with a stomach full of Cheez Whiz omelette, that was Pogey Nealon climbing every one of twenty-five rungs up out of the needle-strewn alley and onto the gravel roof. That was Pogey Nealon standing in the breeze off the harbour, smiling at the circling crows.

He'd said to the girl and her lunkhead friend (whose name had now flittered away into the permanent grey part of memory), "Just watch this one."

"What is it?" she'd asked.

"This one fight. Nobody famous unless you count the guy filming. But it just happens to be the last fight we ever had here." Fifteen, sixteen years ago. And Pogey was glad for the opportunity to relive it. To remember it frame by frame. To see again how those ten minutes of its duration toppled the whole rickety structure of his understanding to that point.

Now the crows were trying to land, swooping in with shells in their beaks. Strafing Pogey with irritable looks and wheeling away. Pogey waved them off, walking around the skylight, caulking gun in hand. There was a bit of business that needed attention first. He dragged one boot after him, as he walked. He traced a large triangle into the gravel. Three long furrows. Rock, paper, scissors. Boxer, Puncher, Swarmer. Fine. So that was it and there it would remain. In the meantime: "Go somewhere else!" he yelled at the birds. "Only my roof will do?"

The bowl of sky brightening above him. Another yawning below as he worked his way out onto the surface of the skylight examining the glass. A twelve-foot circle in four panes, the skylight made a shape like a wheel with four spokes. Pogey gingerly shifted his weight, one palm to the thick glass, one knee on the metal of the frame. And leaning out this way, he began to apply the sealant in a long bead along the edges of each metal member.

Above him the black shapes were wheeling, waiting. Pogey finished one seal and shuffled his weight a quarter of the way around the skylight to begin another. One crow just now peeling free of the others as he watched in reflection, then swinging so close that he swivelled around, glanced up as it skimmed by.

One black eye on him. One oversized shell in its beak, not a razor clam. Too big for that. Pogey squinted as the bird laboured upward and away. It looked about the size of Pogey's fist, whatever it was, which made him laugh. Leaning out again, setting the nozzle of the gun against the metal bar, pulling it back toward him, dropping a long bead of sealant. It was a morning for ambitious projects, new commitments. His own relating to long-standing leaks. This crow here committed to nothing less than the killing of something bigger and heavier than any one of them had taken on before.

Pogey finished the second seal and moved around the skylight another quarter to do the third. Above him the crow mounted into the sky, carving to the top of a long parabola, where it seemed to float in place, to think.

Pogey too, for that instant, watching the bird in the glass. Seeing it poised there. Imagining the two of them linked in some shared anticipation. A suspended moment then brought to perfect conclusion by the sounding of a horn in the harbour.

Something enormous was now moving astern. And the pulse of that warning blast shivered through the air and found them both. Pogey felt it on his skin. And above him, the crow felt it too. Pogey watched the bird startle, in place. Then, more oddly, he watched as it seemed to split in two. One part fluttering away, weightless, while another part broke free and began to plummet. Down and down. Straight toward him. Ghosting in, an object he couldn't identify just a moment before now arriving with terrific, silent speed. An object fully understood only the instant before it hit the glass, when Pogey saw it clearly, poised above its own reflection.

An oyster. Beach. Bad eating at that size if you weren't a crow. Too meaty. Too heavy. Heavy enough to sit uncomfortably in the stomach, to cause indigestion.

Heavy enough to explode the glass pane under his left palm into a cloud of shards. To pitch him forward on the pivot of his knee.

Pogey swiped free a length of still-wet caulking with his shoulder.

Pogey rotated out into emptiness, falling now in the shaft of his own stairs. Down through the double helix. Unspooling the DNA of upper and main floors, frames and treads spinning around him, gears of an enormous clock some core mechanism of which had snapped, unleashing all the energy built up by its rotation to that point, causing the entire machinery to jump into animated reverse, spiralling chaotically back to the beginning, irreversibly, to the bottom of things, the basement.

And still falling even there. Still falling through the dwindling seconds he remained alive. Only stopping much later. Some distance past Mary Street, into water, through the water, then on into some other kind of structure altogether.

an hour before the beginning

RILEY TOLD ANYONE WHO WOULD LISTEN. "FOUND
lying next to a caulking gun and a broken oyster shell.
The cops call me, they say, Dude, we understand you
were among the last people to see him alive. I say, Yo man
that guy was *crazy.*"

Tragicomic, he also said. Something to do with the
structural symbolism of caulking and oyster shells, a point
made so often that finally Deirdre couldn't speak to him.
She built a white cube modern for her final assignment.

A *Vielzweckraum*, an all-purpose structure in which function evolved house, school, library, museum. Perhaps it would even be abandoned for periods, like a field is left fallow. She wrote a long essay, got a middling mark.

"The difficulty with tribute to innovation," came the professorial feedback, "is the failure of tribute to innovate."

Cleo told her later: "You have stress always. Like your mother."

Deirdre sat in a Postum booth. Her aunt's fleshy hands enclosed her own pale fingers, nails bitten to bloody half-moons. Behind Cleo, a man slid onto a counter stool and began to swing back and forth, impatient or nervous. Deirdre fixed on this motion, a relentless swinging powered by internal energies that were all about forward motion. She said, "I should go."

"You should eat," Cleo said and didn't wait for an order either. She swept the menu into her hand, glided to her feet and across the linoleum, disappearing into the kitchen.

Deirdre blew her nose, exhausted. A cold coming on. She tried to guess which menu item Cleo would deem restorative, then she noticed the man had twitched around on his stool, checking her out.

He said hello and she didn't try to hide her decision: talk/no talk. He had a jumpy voice that inspired caution. Kind lips but scheming eyes, dark brown. Sharp cheekbones, big hands, dark hair, a little greasy, spiking this way and that. His leather jacket had buttons shaped like skulls. Felt-pen handwriting on his wrist read, *Kirov — 2:00 p.m.*

Maybe that's what got her. Such personal scheduling chaos that he had to write on himself. That and the shoe-box. She sighed, nodding at the box. "Your pet ferret?"

He liked that, and she judged the laughter to be good. Not too much of it. It came out short and sharp, then trailed off into an embarrassed smile, the best thing he'd done since sitting down and commencing to swing back and forth like a verbal command that everybody stay in motion. Forward. Forward.

Now he raised his eyebrows, asking permission to join her in the booth. She shrugged.

He slid in opposite just as Cleo arrived with a cheese omelette. She returned with a coffee for him and he thanked her with a closed-lipped smile, high eyebrows and that wink of a blush. Self-consciousness that won him back the ground he'd lost by appearing too sharp by half.

He watched Deirdre eat. She kept one eye on him but relaxed completely. Architecture, she told him. A student or, technically, a former student. Not sure when she was going back.

"Maybe you're not going back," he said. And who could blame her, since there was only one architect in the last hundred years worth any consideration at all and that was the anti-architect Gordon Matta-Clark who opened the inside to the outside, who revealed what was hidden, who subverted negative space by making it positive.

She stopped eating, impressed. A young architect who'd made a career out of cutting open old buildings in unusual ways, Matta-Clark died tragically early of cancer in 1978. Inside architecture schools he was a god. Outside, virtually unknown. "How'd you hear about *him?*"

Well, he'd seen a monograph at a gallery once, but the real connection was deeper. He and Gordon Matta-Clark were linked. GMC, he called him. GMC was the greatest. He liked the office building with the boat-shaped cavity carved down through the middle. He liked the Parisian apartment building through which Matta-Clark had drilled a hole.

"Conical Intersect," Deirdre told him. "Of course, he only did that in the middle of rue Beaubourg because they were tearing everything down to make way for the Pompidou Centre."

But before she could explore the topic, turn it into a discussion about him, the questions were coming back at her. His eyes having no scheme in them either, at that moment. A fundamental sharpness simply snuffed out when the topic turned to her. After the shoebox had been opened, the contents explained. A Rolex. A Bulls jersey. A pair of sunglasses. Like somebody just out of prison, forced to leave with the pathetic evidence of all they had going in.

"No, no," he said, amused, then impatient to set the matter straight. "Fakes. Not worthless. But crap."

The watch was weighted to heft like the real thing, but made in Mongolia. A couple dollars a unit to smuggle into the country. Twenty-five a pop to street dealers who used to sell them from Winnipeg to Houston. The Chicago Bulls gear could have been the real thing.

"This is what you do?" she asked.

"Sort of. Not any more. To explain would be to bore you."

"Not at all. I get it," she said. "The link. You're Matta-Clarking commerce."

He stared at her. "You really think so?" he said.

Well, maybe. "Only too bad what you're doing is also completely illegal," she said, chewing a mouthful of omelette. Pointing into the box with her fork.

"Maybe, maybe not," he said, closing the box firmly. And here his plans for other product lines, things beyond fake, all those calculations vanished as he asked, such sincerity in the question, what brought a drop-out architecture student from Kits down to the Postum Diner on a crappy Saturday afternoon three days on the cheap side of Welfare Wednesday.

"You really want to know about me?" she said.

"I really want to know," he said. "About you."

the beginning

44   SO, WHEN HER OMELETTE WAS FINISHED, SHE told him about her. The story as she knew it. A building. A school assignment. Strange events. And while she spoke, he circled and recircled her words, with his attention, with his eyes. With his body, which shifted in the seat. With his expression, which migrated furtively north and south, crossing a border between what looked like faded curiosity and then, more surprisingly, something in the order of proprietary interest.

"One year ago?" he said of these events, as if somebody should have told him.

About a year, she said. Certain, all at once, that they were going to go for that drink later, talk about other things. Childhood, the things they had wanted and how those things had changed. She was going to touch one of those skull buttons, maybe even steal one while he slept.

But for the duration of the telling, she watched only his facial expressions. Particularly the one that came after the close of it all. Because at that point—after bouncing and jiggling and lighting smoke after smoke—he'd frozen, staring as if to be sure that he had understood.

"The brothers?" he said, intensely interested that this detail not be misplaced or misrepresented or misunderstood in even the subtlest way. "He actually said *the brothers.*"

And when she nodded, he had leaned sharply away, head against the back of the booth, eyes pinched closed so hard that he sprouted spiderwebs of white out into the tan of his complexion, his hands spread open on the seat to either side.

Then he relaxed, eyes still closed. Motionless for the first time since she'd met him. As if something he could not have anticipated had arrived suddenly, hard within him. And now he was steadying himself, waiting for a long passing dizziness to sweep on under him and through him and finally go away.

STONE CANYON

One

IN HEAVY TURBULENCE, COMING DOWN ON THE
City of Angels. Terrified, a new feeling. A new entry in
Graham Gordon's catalogue of mild psychiatric irregu-
larity. Compulsive restaurant napkin origami, check.
Diagramming obsession, sure. Hypnagogic startle, most
assuredly, six or ten of these jolting him awake before any
non-medicated sleep. Leaving him always with the sense
of something having exploded, very close by. Shards
drifting outward.

But here was a fresh one: heart palpitations on final approach. Maybe Esther's sudden desertion had brought it on. They were rattling and banging, shimmying from side to side. Graham had things to do on the ground, things for which he should be planning. Esther Gordon neé Lee, were she still around, would have told him: frame objectives, outline strategy, sketch tactics. But without her, his thoughts were chaos as they hit hard air and slid, bouncing down a layer, his organs suspended.

His father had taken him to Hawaii once, just the two of them. Left his fuming brother at home with the maid. They came in over Honolulu on a washboard road of air currents, the TWA 707 rattling so violently that an overhead bin popped opened and disgorged a red Samsonite jewellery case that hit the deck with a beady rattle. His father was laughing, looking across Graham and out the window, down to the curving bay, to swaying palms. He said to his younger son, *just like tobogganing.*

Sledding the broken clouds into LAX. Eyes closed as a slick ramp of cloud hammered by under his seat, the plane skating and jogging in grooves of air. Down and down. And then: *down.* With a bang and a screech, a puff of smoke. Graham blinked and coughed. Then he was staggering up the ramp, into the terminal. He was leaning into the counter at the car-rental kiosk trying to talk his way out of a Cadillac Escalade.

"It was booked by . . ." the woman said, finger to her screen.

"Fila Sarafi," Graham said. "My business partner. She does this sometimes as a joke."

"We have a PT Cruiser," the woman said, face frozen in a smile, video camera poised overhead to catch customer service in any way lacking. "It's smaller."

—

Last-minute trip, this one. Graham didn't much like the last-minute trip, although Esther used to chide him for complaining. Sudden requests that you be in another place were a function of market power, his wife would say. The greater you were in demand, the wider spread this demand, the more your delivery systems would have to accommodate. In addition to which—no argument of Esther's had ever consisted of a one-bullet list—you could think of failure as the complete collapse of the world's expectation that you do anything for anybody, anywhere.

Yale law and Ph.D. work in decision theory at MIT would do this kind of thing to you. Esther was more than practical. She was a structure built with the thick planks of rationalism. Keeper of ranked lists. Winnower of relevant detail from ambient noise. Graham and Esther managed 9.3 years. Why not 10? Graham could only wonder now if the decade mark might have imposed rational structure of its own.

They met by accident, something he enjoyed remembering. It couldn't have been planned, not even by Esther. Met at the end of a nine-hundred-kilometre pilgrimage north of the city to the Queen Charlotte Islands, where Graham—twenty years old, in the black heart of the period following his father's death—had gone not to meet people at all but to visit longhouses at the townsite of Kiusta, retracing footsteps Packer Gordon had apparently laid down himself at the same age. And getting nothing for those efforts either. The longhouses rebuffed him entirely. Surrendered not a single lesson, only posed a web of further questions.

But there she had been. The only child of an angling-mad father. A first-generation Korean immigrant who might have liked a son, the founder of a place called with quiet, unassailable exclusivity The Private Fishing Society, where Graham's charter flight had first come alongside. He stepped out of the Beaver onto an unstable dock and there had been Esther, right at the base of things. But no more.

Not even Fila would have found a PT Cruiser funny. So it was that Graham found himself Escalading the I-405 northbound from a height that did not leave him feeling in command, thinking of Packer Gordon again. How the great man would have enjoyed the Hummer, the Expedition, the Exfoliator. Of course he hadn't survived to see the SUV phenomenon precisely because of his own excesses. You could be an architect or a designer until you were ninety—a "viewed-object jockey," as his father's biographer, Cameron Lark, had quoted Packer Gordon saying near the end—you could direct the building of things, still be considered quote-worthy, still be judged to have a divine gift of the eye even if you were navigating the site with a walker. But you couldn't do any of these things if you had bad habits that would kill you first.

Packer Gordon had many such habits. They had brand names Graham had collapsed down to Chesterfield, Black & White and Ruth's Chris. Having a taste himself for single malt and a Dutch cigarillo called Panter, Graham was lenient on the point. But facts were facts. His father's set of habits vectored out to seventy-eight years of age and stopped there. Esther's cold formulation: lifestyle as vector calculation. Every chosen activity worked on you. What you ate and drank. The pick-up basketball, the recreational blow, psychoanalysis and poorly considered college sex. The sum of these decisions netted out to a distance and a direction. It was where your life took you, the final point you'd reach without changing constituent forces. And his father's inability to change those forces, to change himself, resulted in a constellation of still-beautiful buildings scattered across the planet— libraries, museums, airport extensions, one university dormitory and about two dozen houses—and a vector end-point during the unusually snowy winter of 1983.

Graham's phone was ringing. He was looking for his exit, feeling his father as if in his own skin, feeling how his father would have enjoyed this part too. Fila Sarafi. Her name. The fact she was calling from a hotel in Santa Monica. Her silk gown, black hair, pale skin. Her startled eyes, tiny whippet frame, lovely calves.

He opened the phone. He said, "Why do you book me these ridiculous vehicles?"

"Where are you?" Fila demanded.

"Coming up on Sunset. When's our meeting tomorrow?"

She was at Hotel La Molta, Santa Monica. A property done ten years back, at great expense, in the style of romantic ruin. Mahogany panelling, chocolate brown hardwood floors. Striped upholstery. Candlesticks everywhere. There were unhung paintings and prints stacked in the hallways. A convex regency mirror in the corner of the penthouse library bloated the shelves, the books surging self-importantly in place while endless tape loops of the Three Tenors whispered through hidden speakers. All this the desired effect, in its day. And all of it crap as of six months ago. Destined for the garbage bin with Graham and Fila riding to the rescue with their new eyes, new ideas. Which was crap itself, he knew. Bamboo, glass, reed mats, cube chairs, stainless-steel bars. Simultaneous tribute paid to Mies and Le Corbusier, Louis Kahn, Gerrit Rietveld and Truus Schröder and a whole range of guys who weren't even dead yet. Good and useful ideas, fine. Just not new.

"We meet tomorrow morning," Fila told him. "When do you see Zweigler?"

Graham said he was on his way. That he'd come up to the hotel after dinner.

"And the mystery, please explain this. I don't much like intrigue."

"You much love intrigue."

She had just walked into her suite from the deck. Graham felt her atmosphere change. The tamp-down of air, of sound. Bare feet on knockoff prayer rug. Heels hitting dark hardwood. A ceiling opening high above her. She was in the kitchenette. Sliding onto a stool.

"He invited me to his house for dinner," Graham told her. "We're eating hake."

"I do not like intrigue," Fila said. Running water now. "What is *hake?*"

"It's a fish. His brother is a fisherman. He brings Zweigler fish."

"And why is Avi Zweigler interested in you? Are you making a house out of egg cartons and car headlights

somewhere I don't know about?"

"Television producer. Fisherman. You don't find that funny?"

Fila took a long drink of water. Not that Graham could hear her drink—an ambulance had just passed, heading north, siren puncturing the air around it, then bleeding off to nothing. But he heard her surface from the refreshment. The break of her lips into a tiny breath of readiness.

"You okay?" she asked him.

"Where do I start?"

"Avi Zweigler, please."

Graham tried. A halfway answer for his impatient partner, the exotic, less recognizable syllables in Gordon Sarafi Design. Together three years now, working out of an office on the top floor of an old tower opposite Victory Square in a strip of the city hung between uptown and the grit of the downtown eastside. A neighbourhood Graham and Fila called the Middle East for an irresolvable contest of gentrification and decay animating its streets.

No, Graham told Fila, he was not secretly working on something appropriate for Zweigler's television show. His latest one, that was, the twelve-time Emmy-winning producer of sitcoms and reality cop dramas having scored another long-ball hit on cable television for the past two seasons with *Unexpected Architecture*, which wasn't really about architecture so much as it was about *dementia concretia*, a clinical impulse, frequently late-life, to paste stuff together. To build. Beer bottle towers, enormous roadside religious monuments, houses made of garbage. Sometimes a historical segment was thrown in to give the phenomenon the sense of long life and lineage. The Palais Idéal by Facteur Cheval. Those crazy Wagnerian mountaintop castle fantasies of King Ludwig of Bavaria. But *UE*'s contribution to the area lay in finding people mid-project and throwing them up into the prime-time air. So the slinger of structural cow patties in an Iowa field had his day. The mumbling manipulator of Popsicle sticks, eighty years, eight hundred thousand sticks and counting. People ate this up, Graham thought, because it enshrined an architectural impulse (which many people fancy they share), but openly mocked it too.

"Zweigler lives up Stone Canyon Road behind the country club," he told her, finally. "He described it to me by saying, 'You probably know this house better than I do.'"

"Who did it?" Fila asked.

"No idea. Not the point."

"What then?"

"Later. Two hours. Three, tops. I'll phone when I'm in."

"I don't want to hear later."

"You won't hear later. You'll *see* later, which is much better."

"Now," she said, sharp. Real anger milled there in the time Graham took to change lanes.

Iranian on her father's side, Irish on her mother's. Graham asked her once if this had been some kind of genetic experiment and if so which kind: cultural, artistic or political? She liked this sort of teasing, the wink at complicated ancestry that included individuals blown up in explosions as far apart as Tehran and Armagh. A rare honour.

"Uncle Finney died in a bus accident," Fila would say.

"Faulty fuel line," he'd prompt.

"Exactly. An accident." Although a short spasm ran the length of her mouth saying so.

Great Uncle Reza, meanwhile — not a blood uncle, but the brother-in-law of an aunt — had been shredded and entombed in a tunnel under the Shah's palace. 1965. Tracks of aluminium and a cart that could be moved by remote control. Blasting caps in a peasant loaf of Semtex purchased from an Egyptian called The Baker. It was a matter of public record, that one. Graham read the details Fila wouldn't provide in the *New York Times* web archive.

Climbing into the hills now. Up into the very rare Bel-Air.

He said to her, finally, "Zweigler has something that belonged to my father."

Fila Sarafi—daughter of Hajji (Henry) Sarafi and Fiona MacCullen—was silent. Graham knew his explanation was less than she'd hoped for. Like Esther had previously, his business partner preferred him on-project where roles were well defined. Graham front-loaded. He sold. He crafted large ideas at early lunches, made fiddly models out of napkins and business cards, drew pictures that didn't look like buildings at all, that were mere suggestions of buildings, suggestions of shapes of buildings or of feelings that might be inspired by the shapes of buildings, the tectonics, the materiality. And even if it could never have been predicted when he was in architecture school—with a tendency to plod, to brood, to seek enormous truths—clients would now listen to Graham talk about these ideas, even clients with very low bullshit thresholds, all because of his father.

And Fila would too, which said more. Fila who managed, who vetted for feasibility, who came from an engineering background and dealt well with subtrades. Fila who, in a previous job, had developed a minor speciality in moving entire structures. An old mansion. A conservatory. The thing was made of *glass*, for crying out loud. Fila plucked it from its eroded foundation, trucked it down to a dock somewhere, craned the thing onto a barge and across to the exclusive waterfront property in a rich suburb where she had envisioned it spending the rest of its days. She got a coveted write-up in *Architexture Magazine*. He carried away a deep impression of her power. And that Fila, Graham knew well, didn't like him floating around, following pure whim outside the scope of any understood project. That Fila needed to know what came next.

So, she asked warily, what did Zweigler have that used to belong to Graham's father?

A camera. Bolex Paillard 16mm film. Lenses. Batteries. Cables. Two film magazines. "Late 1960s. Early 1970s. I don't know exactly when Zweigler bought it."

Fila calibrated the transaction silently. Feeling for pressure points. Emotional tells.

Graham said, "A camera I haven't seen in many years. A camera my father used to film his projects."

"Oh, I've heard about that," she said, relief in her breath. Relief to have some kind of answer. "I saw that doc on PBS. They had footage he shot doing a house in Connecticut."

"Westport. The Haney House."

"And now . . . " Fila said, getting it all at once, "now you're going to buy it back."

Which, of course, because it was Fila speaking and because this discussion concerned his own conflicted and unhealthy desires, was quite close to the heart of the matter.

"*Try*," he told her. "I'm going to *try* to buy it back."

Two

HE LIVED ALONE. AVI ZWEIGLER TOLD GRAHAM
so in their first phone conversation. The words were
framed like a cautionary road sign, although it wasn't
clear winding up through the hillside mansions what
Graham should make of the warning. Then he was at the
long gate in the white stone wall, buzzed in without a
word, coming up around the enormous bank of flannel
bush, and Avi Zweigler's quite remarkable, quite unexpected house came into view.

Familiar lines. More length than height. More inter-locking planes and surfaces than anything quite so straightforward as a roofline linking vertical walls. Canti-levered roof beams. Stacked stone details. Fondness for the luminous expanse of glass.

Graham climbed out of the Escalade, sixty yards short of the structure. He stood looking up a set of steps carved into a slope. Long grassy treads and stone risers. He could see Zweigler watching him from behind the long curtain-wall of glass, deep roof beams above his silhouette, trac-ing the horizontal lines of the property.

Graham climbed the stairs, rising to a flagstone walk, then to more stairs and an expanse of deck. No railings. Away on either side, the house lay low against the hill, dwindling, it seemed, at the edges, disappearing into the banks of palm there, disappearing back into the hillside. Behind the house, the hills continued their climb and roll. From side to side and front to back, the landscape penetrated the building, moved through it. Graham thought, Not a bad idea, that.

Zweigler moved behind the glass, a light shift of weight on his feet. Graham thought of the warning about living alone. Not always alone, surely. Not even the Avi Zweiglers of this world had Packer Gordon build their bachelor pads. The largest ego would be made self-conscious by the echo, by the sounding out of interiors into open spaces. So this house spoke of former occupants. Those departed to places beyond. To other countries, other beds.

Flagstone from Montana. Helena slate. Graham admired the green marble used in a low exterior wall run-ning up to a sheet of glass, punching through and disap-pearing into the house. Late 1960s, he thought. Zweigler a young man then. Younger than I am now.

Avi Zweigler was on the walk, coming toward Graham. Tall, thin, unsmiling. A cream silk shirt untucked and billowing. Steel grey hair loose at the collar. On his wrist a silver band, black onyx discs embedded. Linen pants with a drawstring. Bare feet. At sixty-plus, Zweigler was a hard business presence, a man of powerful will and comfortable in his clothes. But another part of him was a memory of the younger self. Not a nostalgic memory, Graham thought, taking the firm shake. More a matter of good health, preserved evidence of past accomplishment.

"1966," he said, by way of greeting.

Graham looked past him, nodding. It held the eye. "Could have been built last year."

"I commissioned it. I pay attention to it."

"Stylistically," Graham said.

Zweigler nodded, no doubt aware that his house was again contemporary. That pendulums formerly hot with romanticism now swung high into the cool air of modernism.

They walked the interior lines of the building. Footsteps the only sound as they sighted down corridors that opened wide to decks, then shallow stairs and out into the grass. Glanced at angles into the high corners, seeing how the light had been allowed to reflect and refract. Running hands along surfaces, feeling angles and planes with their fingers, as if their eyes could not be trusted.

Sky blue ceilings in the kitchen. Fitted cedar plank wall. Deep green tile floor. Graham inhaled through a sieve of fingers. "You know the story here?" he asked Zweigler.

"After Lubetkin," the producer said. "I've done my reading. The profiles, the essays. I own galleys of the biography your mother sued about."

"Cameron Lark," Graham told him.

"The aluminium counters came later, of course. Cedar never really worked. Are you a purist?"

Graham shook his head, turned. He walked out into the central hall, touched a green marble wall that ran, uninterrupted, through the glass doors and down the outside pathway over to the pool hut.

"Neither was he," Graham said. "This is nice. Tinian?"

"Verde Issorie."

"Right." He was drifting, fingers tracing the deep sea-green swirls. "From Aosta."

"I like talking to professionals," Zweigler said.

They drank B+B on ice in a room that was not clearly indoors or out. The brick-red plaster ceiling rolled high, in a bubble above. The glass rising from the floor had a twenty-foot-square opening. No doors visible, just the absence of glass, which was itself only subtly present.

Zweigler was pleased to have surprised Graham. Pleased to have made the son's position uncertain by knowing far more, holding far more of the father than just that camera. Now Graham sensed that he owed an ear while Zweigler told the story. It was clear in the way Zweigler motioned him to sit. In the way the drink was placed in his hand, Zweigler's left folding over his right as if to lock the glass in place.

"I hired him because I admired the whole landscape approach." Zweigler sat on the edge of a long leather bench. One hand on a sharp knee, elbow up. He was poised to move. Poised to lose patience with his own need to run over the details yet again.

Graham had heard these opening remarks in various cases mounted in defence of his father over the years.

Cases that tended to overlook how Packer Gordon Incorporated was also a wholly peripatetic enterprise, born of a mind incapable of stillness.

"Although you could say that for him any landscape would do," Graham suggested. "Somebody asked him, Lark probably, if he'd ever put a building up next to another one he'd previously built. He said, *The day I start city planning, remind me and I'll hang myself.*"

"So he was old-fashioned," Zweigler said. "A monument builder. Contextuality was bullshit. I sympathize. It's a great preoccupation of our day, this tinkering with cities. He only thought about buildings: the office tower, the public library, the museum."

"The airport," Graham said.

"That's ego, sure. But there's no paradox in an obsession with landscape and projects all over the world. He got to know things quickly, then moved on. He was faster than the rest of us."

"So fast we don't know half of what he did," Graham told Zweigler. "He was beyond private, paranoid at times. My mother didn't know if he was in Toronto, New York, the Emirates. I doubt she knew about this house. I certainly didn't."

Zweigler's expression suggested he'd heard this kind of thing before. "Impatient and secretive," he said to Graham. "But considered too. Your father's ideas were the stuff of intense calculation. I could see it in his face when he first looked over this site. The thinking through of every beam and pillar, every sheet of glass."

Zweigler got up, moving off again through the kitchen in a long, restless figure eight. Outside, the air was still. Graham's eyes kept flicking to the invisible wall, the perforated perimeter of this building, and finding treetops so uncannily lacking in motion against the sky behind that they tested the eye with the question: Am I real? He saw a bird, finally, high in the blue. Far out over Will Rogers State Beach.

"The first time he came here," Zweigler continued, "we walked together from the road all the way to the top of the forest, then down the property line. I talked the whole time. I thought we needed to grade a central plateau, somewhere to target the sightlines. A focal point. I was pretty young.

"But he never disrespected me. He never took an attitude, which might have been reasonable given who he was, a man celebrated already at that age, as you know."

Graham was a toddler at the time. But yes, he told Zweigler, he knew.

"He just wasn't a believer in fooling around with a given topography. There was reverence in him, in that way. I remember he said to me, 'Try to listen to what the shape of the land is telling you. It's more about listening than talking.'"

"He said that dozens of times. Contradicted it just as many times."

"Just as I'm sure you have your own favourite rules to break. Or maybe, like some of us, you just have one long

path of deed from which you will one day spectacularly depart."

"Is that your plan?" Graham asked, smiling. He wanted to like Zweigler. Maybe he did already and was resisting the impulse, knowing how Packer Gordon would have liked this man. His B+B, his availability for a hand of cards, for an up-to-the-minute bullshit-free assessment of matters relevant to the here and now: politics, business, buildings, restaurants and crime rates.

But Zweigler wasn't interested in answering that question anyway.

"Don't let me make him out to be one of those incomprehensible architect-philosophers either," Zweigler said. "One of those guys who writes up an ice-fishing shack in some fancy magazine and calls it the point of departure for an exploration of nomadic dwelling and the transformation of site. Transformation of site, I like that. It means the ice melts in the spring. Your old man's ice-fishing shack wouldn't have been reinforcing themes about human isolation or challenging assumptions about the notions of waterfront or any of that crap."

Graham laughed. He read seven or eight of the fancy magazines monthly, but judged it inappropriate to take offence just then.

"I got very few great words out of him," Zweigler went on. "Most of the time he just paced the site. He was alone up here a week before the camera crew arrived."

Graham couldn't help sitting a little straighter as the point was finally reached. Zweigler was looking down the length of the room, head cocked. He could have been reconsidering the location of the fireplace, the enormous rising stacked-stone chimney.

"Who was the camera crew?" Graham asked. "Do you remember?"

Zweigler turned and squinted into the lowering light. He walked over and sat again.

"Nobody. A local kid to shoot. A guy with a boom mike. Your father found them in Santa Monica filming surfers with an 8mm Kodak. He gave them some basic shots, then he left them alone. Same as I left him alone with the property. I entrusted it to him. That's how I felt about it.

"But I was also busy. Critical point. I was working in feature films at that point, shooting in Venice. Very difficult. We were on our third director. We had a lead with something in the way of a small heroin problem. I'd just been handed a large sum of money by a group of investors advised by an attorney who was, no accident, the father of my young wife. May she rest in peace and never hear me complaining. We had good years and bad years, but I don't believe we ever set out to hurt one another." Zweigler paused.

"And how did you instruct him?" Graham asked. "All that listening and not talking he was reported to have done. What did he listen to you saying?"

"He knew my requirements, but what else was I going to say? Would I tell him how to position the guest house or the pool? Maybe I'd give Packer Gordon ideas about how to fuse his interest in the modern with the deep pessimism I read in him."

Graham wasn't aware of his face moving, but he must have shown interest in this comment with the tic of an eyebrow because Zweigler swivelled in.

"You don't see that he was a pessimist?" Zweigler asked, looking, scanning.

Graham thought it was time he refused to answer a question or risk never making it back to Santa Monica that night. Such hunger to know about his father. Where did it come from without dried blood and resentment to make sense of the connection? These houses were, what? Frozen music my ass, Graham thought. They were petrified fashion, style entombed in a glacier. Nothing more. Nothing less. And this was true despite the fact that he had built nothing himself, nothing that mattered. For all the drawing and modelling and big talk,

Fila and he had become fixers, not makers. Architectural plastic surgeons. Redesigning hotel lobbies, rebranding physical structures. However much they were paid for it, Graham understood that these projects were less architecture than a means to an architecture that never seemed to materialize.

"This is uncomfortable for you," Zweigler said. "I have ideas about the man based on my experience. I'm not so old I can't see you might have better ones based on yours."

"So you left him alone, you said. You trusted him."

Zweigler returned to his story, his chin pressed to a bent knuckle, balanced on the long length of a forearm. He was looking past Graham, into the heart of the structure. "I didn't think about him much, to be honest. Four months I was gone. We flew in on a Friday before the Independence Day weekend. My wife joined me for the final weeks of Venice and we were now returning, neither of us having seen the property since our last walkabout before the foundations were poured."

"Where was your wife all the time the house was being built?"

Zweigler's expression darkened. "At her sister's. Point being your father sent us keys in the mail. He had dramatic flair.

"We left the car on the road and walked up through the new gate, up past the trees and into the bottom of the ravine. Much as you did earlier. We stood there on the rise, holding hands. Christ, it was like he'd choreographed our reaction shot too. I was half-expecting to see a camera out of the corner of my eye."

"I know the feeling," Graham said.

Zweigler stopped. He thought for several seconds.

"The surprise for me was how much less of a building it was than I had expected. The walls didn't end so much as pattern off into nothing. Glass verticals, stone walls, terraces and decks. Your eye slid off the house and into the hills. It was as if he had gathered it together. A brief coalescence of structure. As if the land rolled along to this point, bundled up into a house briefly, then tumbled on. I suppose that effect is very hard to achieve."

Graham's turn to rise. He walked to the opening. Walked through and out to the edge of the first deck. Cedar, of course. He walked back in. "Did you like it?"

Zweigler breathed out. Made a face. "Not exactly. I felt, primarily, that I'd been betrayed."

He laughed, looking at his hands. "By the trees," he said, shrugging at his own lingering delusion. "By that cliff of stones up there. By the shoulder of the hill and the hip-line of the valley. By my view. I left him here, with them. And they told all."

"And did you ever see how this betrayal was captured on film?" Graham asked, finally.

Three

GRAHAM MADE HIS WAY NORTH ALONG THE FREEWAY
toward Santa Monica. Outside, California was body temperature and midnight blue.

Or it seemed to be. In fact, the Escalade dashboard
reported that it was ten o'clock in the evening and
seventy-nine degrees outside. If your body temperature
dropped that low you'd begin shutting down. Like maybe
Zweigler was, crushed under the weight of his suspicions.
The producer knew his betrayal at the hands of Packer

Gordon was a more complete and complex thing than he dared to admit. He knew the trees hadn't been in on it, or the ridge line.

"Part of what impresses me, Mr. Zweigler, is that I'm under the impression my father only did houses as favours."

Zweigler didn't shrug it off. The detail troubled him too.

Maybe a favour for your wife?

Graham didn't ask the question. He felt sorry for the man. You hear enough stories, you read Cameron Lark's catalogue of Packer Gordon's infidelities, and no mention of topographical betrayal goes unaccompanied by the more practical explanation. Did she hold your hand that first time you saw the house? Or do you only remember it that way?

All Graham managed was: "And where did your wife's sister live?"

Zweigler regarded Graham for a long time after that question. A time that could be marked by a slow ticking from the heart of the house. One of those ambient structural sounds that white out into nothing after twenty-four hours of exposure but that are still heard by the visitor.

Always more about listening than talking, the famous man had said.

Graham listened to his father's house. Listened to a failing irregular click that he associated with air-conditioning ducts, with electrical cables twisting in their humid grooves, interior foundation walls microscopically sloughing dust, dissolving molecule by molecule.

"My wife left me," Zweigler said. "Not right away, but eventually. Eight months, seven days later, although the timing doesn't matter much. What's true is that there was a period of time during which she wanted to be here with me. Then the period was over, more quickly than I could have imagined. After which, she didn't want anything to do with this place."

The full sad tale of the House of Zweigler. Graham listened without another word, then they had dinner. The camera could wait, Zweigler insisted. The hake could not. And so it was wheeled out by a house manager on a stainless-steel trolley covered with a linen cloth. A diverting story was told about the fish and the brother. And as he told it, the details of his brother's life seemed to give the producer great pleasure to reveal. Once in awhile they still got together at Chez Jay's. Drank Rolling Rock, ate peanuts and then the catch of the day. Such fondness. Such nostalgia. The brother had three boats and twelve full-time employees, Zweigler boasted.

Where did he fish? Graham asked, nodding and chewing without pleasure. Where off this smoggy city did fish still come out of the water suitable for the table?

Zweigler told him north. Then, "You had a brother."

Graham coughed, swallowed. "Have. Elliot."

They ate another mouthful in silence, forks touching porcelain.

"Why did you say *had*?" Graham asked.

Zweigler's expression was bemused. "You had, you have. What's he do?"

Graham said the word: *counterfeiter.* Zweigler, of course, instantly riveted. "Of what? You mean currency? Your brother is actually a criminal?"

"Half-brother. Yes, in fact. Once, while my father and I were away on a trip, he ran off a garbage bag full of twenties on the colour photocopier in my father's office. Suckered some guy into selling him a junker Plymouth

Fury. Got caught, of course. Now I hear he does fake watches. You want a Rolex? For fifty dollars I can get you a Rolex with a quartz movement made in Indonesia. It's weighted so it feels real."

"You don't approve."

"I don't care either way," Graham said.

"Different mother or father?"

"Mother," Graham said, thinking, Would Packer Gordon raise another man's son?

"What about your own mother?"

"Remarried after my father died. Moved to France. That's a long time ago. Twenty years."

"Married who?" Zweigler asked.

"A conductor. Of orchestras, that is. We're friendly. We talk by phone. They live near Apt, near a freshwater spring that promises health into old age. My mother was always . . ." Here Graham had to search around for words. What exactly had his mother always been?

"She was a vegetarian," Zweigler offered.

Graham nodded. "And then some."

They ate in silence for awhile. Zweigler finished a mouthful, wiped his lips and laughed again. "I like that. Your father's son, a counterfeiter."

"One of my father's sons. Mr. Zweigler . . ." The fish

was gone. The little dish of lemon sorbet. Zweigler didn't drink wine and Graham had sipped a quart of soapy Apollinaires.

"Avi," he said. "Call me Avi."

They went to his room under the hill. Graham finally saw what Zweigler had accomplished. A long room with display cases, Gordon material housed reverently under halogen. Models of his father's buildings. Plans. Perspectives. Photographs.

"Do you pay attention to this sort of thing? The collectibles?"

Graham shook his head.

"He's valuable. Less than Corbu. Less than Charles and Ray Eames. But more than some of the moderns that came just before him. More than Golosov. More than Thomas Tait."

He lifted a black leather box from a pedestal, opened it. Inside were rows of stainless-steel drafting tools laid out on red satin. Spring leg dividers, pencil lead compasses, protractors and stencils. Five thousand at auction, Zweigler said. "That's now, of course. I bought early."

Zweigler showed him a series of models. Cube moderns on difficult cliffside sites.

"Case-study houses," Graham said.

Zweigler touched a finger to his lower lip. "Ever built?"

Graham nodded. "I grew up in one."

Sold when his mother left the country. Then torn down almost immediately.

"I'm sorry to hear that," Zweigler said.

Graham didn't answer. The occasional thought of it hurt more each time than he expected. Although: who could blame the new owners? The house was too small for contemporary tastes, it leaked, and it happened to be on one of the finest waterfront lots on the North Shore. Three strikes. Yes, it was the only structure his father left in the city where they'd lived. But his father hadn't made it to the status of national treasure, someone whose surviving footprints would forever be preserved. So it was that a pink palazzo with a replica Parthenon grew out of the rocks, thousands of square feet, obliterating the simple lines Packer Gordon had left there.

Graham wanted to move on from these thoughts, and so he authenticated more of Zweigler's collection. Layering value onto it. Items he recognized and, if he were honest with himself, some that he did not. They were from Gordon's den, or from his office. Graham remembered his father using a brass T-square at a drafting table set up outside under a beach umbrella.

"Bahrain International," he said truthfully, pointing at the model of an airport, the sight of it propelling a flood of memories over him. Elliot and he had sat opposite their father's desk while he lectured them on the topic of filial harmony. Was it that precise lecture from which the infamous boxing match grew? Graham couldn't remember, eyes locked on the model then as they were now. The minaret control tower, a finger pointed at the sky. The tiny planes in the taxi queue, glued in place. Frozen in permanent readiness for flight. "He died before it was started. They took the designs somewhere else. Everything changed, of course."

Zweigler gestured. Graham felt the moment arrive. In a storage room off the west side of the display area, he showed Graham the Bolex Paillard. Familiar aluminium boxes and dark canvas sacks. Ever the careful collector, Zweigler had itemized the lot. The camera, the lenses, the cables and four-hundred-foot film magazines. Graham was conscious of his own raspy breathing, standing there with some unidentified part in his hands. A box with a battery pack, a loop of cord.

"I'm curious," Zweigler said. "Everyone knew what this gear meant to him. How he filmed every project. Kept archives."

Graham nodded. "My mother still has some film. And video from later, although he destroyed a lot near the end."

"Why did he ever sell the camera, then?"

Graham shook his head.

"Money trouble?" Zweigler said. "Plenty of geniuses get into money trouble."

"I don't think he sold that camera."

"I heard he was a gambler. No shame in that. I like the ponies."

"He went to the sports book, the track. Played cards. A big fight fan in his day. But he never lost or won much. He was controlled."

"More or less, Lark says."

"Cameron Lark takes fairly large amounts of coke, did you know that? He's a small man. A bitter man. Failed as an architect. Not much success with women or men, and he's tried both. The hard-on he's maintained for my father over the years is doubtless the most significant thing he has ever erected. What else can I tell you?"

Zweigler, surprised at last, laughed a long time. "That's good," he said finally. "I'm getting to know you."

"Losing the camera didn't have anything to do with gambling," Graham said.

"So what then? This confuses me."

He was the embodiment of what Esther called "deal strength." A very desirable kind of strength in her world. Strength that came from the nose, from the odour emanating from persons opposite in situations of negotiation. Were she observing and advising, Esther would say, *Three things you should understand about Zweigler* . . . Graham on his own couldn't come up with one.

"I always heard that the camera went missing," Graham told him. A long time ago. Late 1970s. "Last time I saw it myself, I was in my teens."

Zweigler considered things for a moment. "Twenty-five thousand," he said finally.

Graham coughed. So that was it. "I want to thank you for dinner," he said.

"At market," Zweigler said. "For you, Junior, we can do a little better."

"Oh, listen . . ."

"You have the bread, I'm sure," Zweigler said. "I'm well aware you've had your own successes. That chair. You made millions with the chair. Sort of a Barcelona by way of Gehry, which is no criticism. Millions are millions."

"Please. Not even close. It's the kind of thing we only ever sold to architects. The MOMA was lucky."

"Lucky. A kid in school."

"I was a year out of school."

"And this hotel business too. I know about that. New York. London. Santa Monica. La Molta, is that right?"

Graham nodded.

"And everybody writes about it. It's not architecture in the old-school sense, but it's profitable and not everybody can do that. You've done well at what you chose."

Graham winced internally. They didn't mean to do it, these older men whose view of the individual was a calculation of relative accomplishment. They shifted words, moved a mass of implication, all without knowledge. *What you chose.* The so-clearly different path.

"I went to the same architectural school as my father," Graham told him, restraining a lick of anger. "Only I graduated top of my class, not on probation."

Zweigler cracked a glance at Graham, amused by this attempt to measure up. He said, "If I have this room of models, drawings, all of it. If I think it'd be some kind of lasting success, something meaningful in life, to see it all in a museum one day . . . you don't think I know how valuable these things must be to you?"

Graham looked away. He could hear Zweigler breathing.

"I'm not a bad man entirely," the producer said. "I used to work with more than sensationalism."

"You've given me a nice dinner, a nice evening," Graham said. "I appreciate it."

"I worked with artists. People who cared about ideas. People who made a gift out of their own gifts."

Graham turned to be sure he understood these words correctly. "Oh, listen. I can't take this as a gift."

To which Zweigler merely shook his head and answered, "Of course not." Words that told Graham, in their simple authority, that now the real price would be named.

Back at the hotel he ran hot water, washed his face. He dialled Fila.

"Remind me why club chairs are so embarrassing," he asked her. "And mahogany panelling. I can practically see the meeting where it was selected. Why rip it all out?"

Fila said, "Because we can?"

"Correct answer, Fila Sarafi. For one thousand: are we going to store these romantic materials somewhere in order to save money when we change it all back?"

"Of course not," Fila said. "Because we'll never return to precisely this palate. Now. Am I coming up there or are you telling me the whole story right now?"

Graham was looking out the sliding door. Nothing to see beyond abstract city light and a slightly warped reflection of himself: a tall, pale man in a dark suit and an open shirt. He used to think he looked untrustworthy and was unable to explain why. Then a glance at an old photograph of his father delivered the answer. He was no longer the stocky teen. He'd grown into a familiar face that wasn't entirely his own. The same dark circles under the eyes. The same chin stubble. Handsome? He had no idea what that word meant. He only knew that he could not fail in striking up conversations with attractive strangers.

"Esther and I," he told Fila. "We appear to be taking a break of some kind."

Fila was smoking. Now a cloud escaped her lips, enveloping her words: "From each other, I take it."

"Mainly her from me."

Fila's cigarette crackled as she inhaled. As she waited.

"Late last year," he told her, "we had some terrible news. Funny thing is I didn't find it terrible at the time, only bad. Now it's curing somehow. It's strengthening. Getting worse."

Fila asked, "What happened?"

Well, many years of trying had happened first. Sex clocked against a calendar, two key days out of the thirty, enthusiasm dwindling. Then a bank of testing, his and hers, which eliminated one by one the possible explanations. Sperm count good. Motility normal. Ovulation, check. No endometriosis. No ovarian cysts.

"This condition is what we refer to as . . . Unexplained Infertility." And here the young doctor cleared his throat and reddened, seeing (maybe for the first time, an education in process) how the advance of understanding would on occasion fail to comfort. And sure, they declared war on the problem. A campaign was mounted. Hormone therapy. Ovulation stimulation. Egg extraction. Jacking off into a bottle over a dog-eared spread of Anna Nicole Smith (not Graham's taste at all, but preferred to a magazine full of models closer to his own age called *Fab Forty*).

And once, finally, in a Petri dish hovered over by a stupendously expensive rank of technicians at something called the Alpha Clinic, where they kept photo albums of successful outcomes on the coffee table in the waiting room, fertilization had even occurred. Life begun and transferred into Esther. Uploaded, she joked. Then, almost immediately, she had her period.

Graham only said to Fila, "What happened is she didn't get pregnant."

Long silence now.

"What?" Graham asked.

"What nothing. I'm sorry. I didn't know you were trying."

"You're angry," he said.

"I'm nothing. How many times did you try?"

"Years, Fila. Years. Then a final time."

Fila lit a fresh one. She took a drag, then blew it out past the mouth of the receiver. "Talk to me about Zweigler."

"It went fine. More than fine. He wouldn't let me pay."

Fila forgot everything else they'd been talking about and Graham was grateful just then for this otherwise maddening quality. Right that instant, she had no idea how attractive it was, ideas flying like electrons. You couldn't measure their location and velocity simultaneously. And that's where he wanted to be. Lost in that cloud of uncertain energy.

"You're joking!" she said. "You've got it? You have it there? I'm coming up right now."

Fila in motion. Fila bringing about action. She was knocking at his door minutes later, fingernails to the dated panelling that tomorrow they would make a case for tearing out. A case they'd win, he knew. They'd get the job, make the money, earn the write-ups, then go take the Tokyo assignment, which was how Fila had plotted their next move. Unless, that is, he were to come up with something indisputably more important. Some *place*, as he thought of it, because events of the past months encouraged him to believe that things lead on to other things in an angling line, pointing somewhere.

"And do I have a deadline?" Graham had asked Zweigler when he finally named that price. "Because to tell you the truth, I don't think you want a film made about La Molta. Or the next thing, for that matter. In Tokyo."

Zweigler said, "There will always be projects for you. One of them, the right one. That one I'd like on film. Shot with this camera. Do we have an agreement?"

In she came, brushing past Graham, setting a bottle of wine on the desk with a thump. And by the time he looked back in her direction she was kneeling in front of the aluminium cases, laughing lightly. "What amazing things must the great Packer Gordon have filmed?"

Graham opened the wine. There was a wash of slate and grass up to his nostrils. He was waiting for her to ask the next question. She was just thinking it, now, one thin hand on the chrome clasp of the camera case. Her other hand pulled back, resting on her hip. There it came, her hand rising to touch her jaw. She turned toward him, lips parting to let go the words. She asked. "Zweigler had film, no?"

Graham turned back to the wine, taking two glasses by their stems in one hand, the bottle in the other. He shook his head, eyes on the pour.

Four

HE PHONED FILA THE FOLLOWING WEEK, FROM Ike's Oyster Bar across the street from their office. There had been a tacit agreement, after their presentation together, to take Friday and the weekend off. Take a breather. She picked up. He said, "Me. How are you?"

She hadn't heard anything from L.A.

"How're you, as in *you?*"

Still tired, she said. Could you get jet lag going north and south in the same time zone?

He pressed. He broke new rules that were already forming between them.

"We're partners," she said. "We work together. We travel together. You're going through something. So we drank some wine in your hotel room."

"What I mean is . . ."

"What *I* mean is that in your confusion and what remains of your grief about life's disappointments you didn't take the opportunity to fuck me. So relax," Fila said.

Relax. He had a hangover from several too many at home the night before. *Hi, I'm Graham and I'm an alcoholic.* That hadn't lasted. He thought the truth was: *Hi, I'm Graham and my father was an alcoholic.* As a result, he now veered back and forth from wet to dry in long waves, always in transition from one to the other, unchanged either direction. And so this morning: swinging down. Harbouring a headache that would not be dulled with Tylenol or Advil, both of which he tried, a dull pain that hovered like his sense of things gone strange.

Ike stuck his head out of the kitchen, scowling at a staff member out of sight. Graham waved a hand, got his friend's attention. He held up two fingers and pointed at the phone, which caused Ike's expression to moderate

from pissed off to peevish. He nodded, went back to work.

"Well okay then," Graham told Fila. "I'm relaxed."

He thought, And why not relax? In his hotel room, where everything had seemed possible between them, they'd mostly talked about boxing. Camera gear arrayed around them, Graham told Fila he'd fought his brother in a match arranged by their father to settle things between them.

"You didn't get along?" she asked, innocent.

"You could say that."

"And what happened?"

Graham winced and shook his head. "I knocked him down and he didn't get up for three days is what happened. I knocked him into a coma. Three days with neurologists and ICU docs shaking their heads and saying, you know, maybe this idea of putting two fifteen-year-olds who hate each other in a ring together wasn't such a great idea."

She was staring at him, lost in details he knew couldn't jibe with the image of him sitting opposite. She said, "You hit your brother in the head?"

"Half-brother," Graham said. "I hit him in the ribs and he fell down and hit his head, in fact. But boxing is about hitting people. Head, ribs. It's what you do. Only I did it and he fell badly and it almost killed him. I *thought* I had killed him. Everybody thought I had for awhile."

He told her his father had shot film of that too.

Fila nodded slowly. "Which you were hoping to find."

Graham nodded.

She laced fingers between painted toenails. Stared again. "Why?" she said finally.

"Why fight, or why want the record of it?"

"Why either. Why fight?"

So many reasons. Because their dislike for one another was irrational and this might make them bond. Because they were boys and this might make them men. Because their father was at war with his own life and this was a proxy battle he might somehow win.

"Why the other part? Why want the film?"

Graham made a face. "To see me again. To see him again maybe. To see me thinking that I'd killed him. Terrified that I had, because, partly, I really wanted to."

Minutes passed. Fila not saying a word. And then the sequence of things got mixed up in Graham's memory. She reached up and pulled him in. Or he knelt beside her and looked at her and then she sighed and pulled him in. Or she said, *Are you okay?* And then he reached to touch her shoulder. She did say, "You sure about this?" And he nodded yes. Then they were holding on to each other. He was kissing her. Flavour-residue of lunch at the Ivy in her mouth, a trace of strawberry as her eyes closed. Eyebrows sloped in a way that was almost sorrowful, a black plastic sandal decorated with a yellow daisy falling off her painted toes. Then she pressed his head down to her chest, her thin arm cradling his head, his cheek against one of her small breasts. He remembered the gesture, the physical holding. Heat between their bodies spiking, long-dormant chemistry suddenly volatile. His hand was on her hip.

A pilgrimage may, on occasion, deliver returns unrelated to the pilgrim's investment. Those 560 miles north of the city in 1984 had introduced Graham Gordon to his future wife. Also, to a resort cook named Ike with big plans for the city.

Now a waiter arrived with Ike's soup of the day. Or, more accurately, he arrived with what Ike was *calling* soup that day: a firm light-green ovoid that could be cut with the side of a fork whereupon something soft and earthy-red flowed from the centre. This runny stuff tasted like poitrine fumé, the firm exterior quite a bit like split peas. So it was the essence of a soup influenced by the structure of a soft-boiled egg. Served on a large, white soup plate.

Oyster Bar was not the best description, really. Ike had them flown in from P.E.I. and Washington State, but the only one Graham had ever been served on the taster menus for which Ike was known had appeared as the cherry-infused centre of a handmade chocolate. Not revolting, but like a lot else happening at the intersection of the culinary and chemical arts these days not conventionally enjoyable either.

"It's comfort food," Ike would say, "for people used to a fair amount of discomfort."

Hence the airport executive lounge decorating idea, which Graham and Fila devised for Ike as the perfect mix of temporary at-homeness and the pure artificiality found in those borderless zones. Walls plastic white. Hidden lighting. No cutlery on the tables. Astroturf runners. Ike loved it. Graham and Fila got written up.

Now Graham's phone was ringing again, and he found himself short of breath by the time he'd fumbled it open. *Unknown number.* "Hello?"

"You sound completely freaked out." Esther. "Where are you?"

"I'm eating lunch."

"What *city* are you in?"

"Vancouver. Just back."

"How'd L.A. go? How's Fila?"

Graham set his soup spoon down, pressed fingers to the bridge of his nose. "Good. We bid on a hotel repositioning job—"

"As in you're moving the building, or is this the other kind?"

Graham breathed deeply a couple times. The other kind, of course. "They no longer wish the La Molta name to be associated with an exclusively artistic community of guests," he said, answering the question deliberately, "but desire a broader, sexier brand."

Broader but sexier, Esther mused aloud.

"Please tell me where you are," he said. "I understood you were taking a break, not that you were leaving for parts unknown. Are you all right? Please tell me where you are."

"I'm up at PFS," Esther said.

Quietly exclusive, that Private Fishing Society. Graham opened his eyes and watched Ike welcome some regulars. When he'd told Ike about the camera gear a few days prior, his friend had looked at him with complete confusion. He tried to explain, got halfway through and found himself losing the will to finish. He changed the subject. He said to Ike, "I remember when we first met, you hated fish."

Ike said, "When we first met, you were the only thing I didn't hate. And Esther."

And here they were again, the three of them. Changed of course. Or in the process of changing. How would the triangle look in six or twelve months' time? Old friends, stable? Two corners hating one another connected by a neutral third? Some other configuration?

Graham said to Esther, "You've gone *fishing*."

Salmon biting, it seemed. A hundred yards out at twenty, twenty-five pulls. You couldn't get a line in and out of the water without hitting chinook.

"I need to tell you something," he said to her, interrupting.

She listened, at least. Graham heard her sit back in what sounded like a soft chair, probably in the club lounge. He pictured her: skin darkened by the sun, now added colour rising in her cheeks as she focused on his next words. Korean features prettier in concentration.

"When I was in L.A.," Graham told her, "I met a man

who had a house built by my father. He's a producer. Avi Zweigler."

Esther registered the receipt of data. "Okay," she said.

"Zweigler collects Packer Gordon. Models, tools, blueprints. Amazing."

Still listening. No premature move toward a conclusion. "Okay," she repeated.

"Zweigler bought my father's camera," Graham told her. "The movie camera he used to film his projects. The camera he also used . . ."

"I remember," Esther said, growing impatient. She was expert at remaining calm in the face of an uncertain future, but always less successful hiding her feelings about the dead weight of the particular past. And discussion of this part of Graham's past, Esther had long thought, only revealed Packer Gordon to be (in addition to famous, a philanderer and bad with money) capable of cruelty. And that was a sunk cost, the valuation of which was irrational.

Graham heard her thinking as clearly as he heard gulls in the background at her end, the roar of an outboard. He said, "Zweigler found the camera in Vancouver. He told me he bought it from a woman named Cleo Angelopolous."

Esther was silent on the phone, patient while the numbers ran. Waiting for her solution, just as Graham had waited, blank in the moments after Zweigler told him the name.

"Cleo Angelopolous," Graham told Esther, giving up the last piece of information she needed, "told Zweigler she was the sole beneficiary of the estate of Pogey Nealon."

"Nealon," Esther said, voice flat, "the sadly misguided boxing coach."

Which wasn't wrong. But Graham still found exasperation growing inside his anxiety, which had itself been nested in something more conventional like grief and anger at things lost. He tried to explain, fighting words out his tightening throat. He tried to describe the sense of important pieces having found their place in a destined sequence. One: his father had built Zweigler's house. Two: his father had filmed them fighting, cruelly or otherwise. Three: a long-lost camera had made its way back through Zweigler's house to Graham. Four: something in the way of a commission from Zweigler. "This is leading someplace," he said. "Someplace good."

He said more, aware he was rambling by that point. But when he was off the phone—leaning hard into his hands, eyes pinched shut—he realized that she hadn't directly responded to any of it anyway. She'd only listened until he was done. Three, four, five minutes. Then she'd spoken her own words, unconnected to anything he'd said. She left him with nothing. She left him gasping for breath as if he'd been dropped into cold salt water far from shore. And now Esther was pulling away from him, disappearing. Upward, over the waves.

Five

SHE KNEW WELL ENOUGH TO GET OUT ON THE grounds afterwards. Better to get a line in the water than to sit and brood. It was midday slack tide. There was a nice wind, a high sky and stable barometric pressure. Every member boat in the club, every available guide was long out. Fish in their millions were wheeling around McPherson, Andrews Point. Heading south toward the rivers, the tributaries where they were born, swimming off toward death and eating all the way. Ideal conditions. But when Esther clicked shut her phone she sat paralyzed. She did not feel, physically, that she could stand, walk, leave the lounge.

When she'd asked for a leave of absence from work, her senior partner had agreed immediately. Such was her understood value, so presumed was her own inheritance of seniority one day. He only said, *If this is the best way for you to move forward, I support you.*

If. He wasn't sure, but he trusted her. Which instinct was the wiser?

Juanita, the club bartender, was polishing member mugs at the other end of the empty lounge. She watched Esther for a few seconds, then said, "You okay?"

Esther nodded and waited for the feeling to pass.

Juanita brought over a glass of water.

Esther said, "Sorry, not sure what's happening here."

"You're having a little crisis," Juanita informed. "You're deciding whether to cry."

Esther drank water. "Am I?"

"Sure you are. So cry."

"The truth is I don't really like to cry."

"Oh, hello. Is that so? I never knew that about you."

Esther motioned for Juanita to sit. She asked, "You don't have kids, do you?"

Not yet. Juanita was the youngest of six. Aunt to five nieces and nine nephews. And she loved kids too, but not having a boyfriend, much less a husband, was a minor complication in the plan to have her own. "Not really into the sperm banks, I don't think," she said.

"No, you wouldn't be just yet," Esther agreed. "For how long no guy?"

"Six months," Juanita said. "Last one had serious issues."

Esther smiled and nodded. "Like what?"

"Like he was a cheating son of a bitch," Juanita said.

They both laughed.

"Excellent. Better than excellent," Esther said. "Here's to cheating sons of bitches."

"Cheaters so rule," Juanita said.

"But no tears," Esther added.

"Oh, I cried," Juanita said. "Let's stay reasonable here."

Of course Esther had cried too, only much earlier. She cried when blackness first descended, before things had even turned between Graham and her.

Four words from a nurse, by phone. *I am so sorry.* And Esther stood up from her desk. She closed her office door quietly, bobbing in the wake of passing event, changed. She sat on the leather sofa under her print of the Vitruvian Man. She held her hands up in front of herself, examined the skin of her palms, waited for the moment. Then it came: the big weep. Mouth open, no sound. Five minutes and an unimaginable volume of tears. Her vision blurred with them. Her body sinking into them. They filled her throat and her nasal passages. And when she was finished—her hands inside her shirt holding her stomach, the front of her blouse wet, the hair around her face too, soaked—she emerged from her own past. Up to the surface, a swimmer taking new breath in an atmosphere that was itself suddenly new.

The past would not haunt her, she decided in the silent moment that followed. That particular past or any other. She went home early. She prepared an elaborate ban-sang, a table of dishes, favourites and several she'd never tried before. Dduk chim stew, oyster paeju, smoked duck, ginseng tea. Graham came home, blotchy with his own hidden tears. And to his abiding credit, he said not another word about it. They sat and ate and talked about the food, not much else.

He asked her, "When did you start cooking Korean food?" And they remembered together that it had been the new place that had inspired her. A townhouse steps from the water in a fashionable part of False Creek several times out of their price league. A zone of architect's buildings soaring glassy into the sky or lying low and steely along the shoreline, all anchored aesthetically around a once decaying, now handsomely restored piece of vernacular railway architecture: a roundhouse. The tribute buildings were all wrenched slightly out of shape, to Esther's eye. All pulled through the filter of modernism, elongated and smoothed out. But in concentric rings around the bricked-in circle at the heart of the roundhouse, the materials of old industry echoed outward. Brick and beams, steel roof members and triangular arches of timber.

Their own unit was on the waterview side of a building Graham's old firm had designed. A three-bedroom with long rooms and high windows, dark steel beams in the ceiling and a kitchen that opened onto a balcony that opened onto sea air, gull screams, the sound of wind in passing sails. It smelled new and was expensive enough to make them notice their own signatures going down on the mortgage. But they were in. They'd *bought* in. And on the granite kitchen counters, looking out over a quintet of cherry trees, brilliant pink blossom clouding the branches that first spring, Esther found something unexpected happening.

Bibimbap. Japchae. Bulgogi skewers done on the Weber. After a few weeks she was up to speed on green onion cakes, kimchee, gyuasang dumplings, a dozen of which took an hour to pinch into the sea cucumber shape desired and five minutes for Graham to eat. Even her own ideas eventually, hybrid ideas. Mid-Pacific imaginings from ingredients she was encouraged to try by the woman who ran the specialty import store she favoured, a place where Esther would even drop the odd word of Korean still lodged back there in her memory somewhere.

Graham enjoyed the development without saying much further. And so it was a matter of private reflection to imagine it as a nod to her parents, to their life work of self-improvement, one that had taken them from Seoul to Osaka, then via the fish-brokering business in Masset, on the Queen Charlotte Islands, and finally to Vancouver. Whereupon, by the fortuitous collection and sale of halibut and black cod quotas, her father was reborn as an international citizen, selling fish back into the Japanese market and into the high-end restaurant trade of the North American western seaboard. And she carried trace elements of this past, undeniably: family language, restless intellect, culinary interest. But the matter of the future, she decided, would be unencumbered by any of it. Old-school Korean male chauvinism wouldn't impede her any more than a proud Korean empiric history would assist her. Esther felt wholly of the moment in which each life decision was made—including her decision to pay tribute with food once or twice a month—and she refused, through reasoning, to accept a more burdened approach to life.

All of which, unpredictably, led to the biggest argument of their marriage. Three years in, before the stressor of children had even been raised. And for a moment, so critical was the disagreement that Esther wondered if they could continue. Late in the evening, in the tail hours of a dinner party for the ingrate partners of the firm Graham had joined out of school. A firm using him, Esther knew, for the licensing of that god-awful chair (Had anyone actually tried to sit in the thing? It was made out of riveted stainless steel, for crying out loud) and, of course, for his willingness to work sixty-hour weeks even if credit was oblique and remuneration an insult. They promised partnership. Esther kept to herself the view that the firm got the better deal in that exchange: Graham enslaved to them for life and the famous Gordon name on the letterhead.

Still, she'd spent the afternoon and produced a traditional five-dish ban-sang, which involved preparing a dozen different dishes if you included the rice and sauces and the traditional three kimchees (radish, cabbage and the watery one). A kaleidoscope of colourful food that she spread around on the table and that was sampled and passed from hand to hand, family style. It was a big hit— the meatball soup with mugwort and the wild garlic soybean stew, particularly—and a great quantity of Prosecco was quaffed in accompaniment. But at some point (Esther recalled that it seemed abrupt) it was after eleven and the partners were tipsy and pleased with themselves and the conversation got turned around to the topic of marital infidelity.

No personal stories, thank God. Esther looked around the room, wondering at that time who besides Graham could possibly entertain the topic without covering their mouths in shame. Architects were an impermanent lot, she had decided, their life interest in lasting structure notwithstanding. Slogging through the salt mines to about the age of forty-five, they bloomed late by professional standards and were thus, she theorized, coursing through with pent-up sexual frustration when they finally started hitting into the power alleys. The first wife might well get dumped at that point, a nurturer, someone who'd brought them through school. The second wife came aboard, a career move, not infrequently an architect herself. And then, sometime in their late fifties or sixties, you'd see the much-younger-woman-of-no-discernible-accomplishment appear on the arm at charity balls. Around the chaos and destruction of her ban-sang table—dishes still being picked over and commented upon, groans of delight for the spicy rapini—she could find only one first wife. And it was herself.

Still, out with the tired theories, the exhausted contemporary truths about why men did it and how they were inevitably busted.

"Women's intuition," said one, a man who did not so much sit at the table as spill around it. Lean, but of undisciplined limbs. He had long grey hair that flowed over the collar of his pink shirt, dark suit. He wore a topaz the size of a testicle on his little finger and was on wife number two. A woman Esther liked quite a lot, as it happened, number twos in general being sharp-witted if a bit frigid. Wife number two, in this instance, rolled her eyes. But off the boys went.

Yes, it was agreed, there was something about a woman's physiological makeup that gave her the ability to sense untruth. They seemed to be talking about some sort of smell or secretion, literally. It was medieval.

"The Bartholin's glands, perhaps," said Esther, who had being doing strategic planning with the Regional Health Board and chumming around with a lot of docs, from cellular biologists to gynos. And here, in response to her quip, the heavy-set letterhead partner of Egyptian descent—whose pregnant twenty-five-year-old wife sat in glowing, composed and gorgeous silence beside him— uttered a soft and undisguisedly sexual grunt of approval.

Graham, hearing her tone, started clearing dishes.

But why did men do it? (They went on.) Oh, agony that we could not know the answer. The idea that it could be for the pleasure of unfamiliar sex, for the smell of unfamiliar shampoo in unfamiliar hair, didn't even get fleeting consideration. No, it had to be the evolutionary imperative. *You see, it's in our genetic disposition to spread the seed, ensure survival.*

And here—Graham's pleading glances from the kitchen island ignored—Esther had to loosen the rules of engagement. "Now there is something I've never understood," she said.

They all clamoured at once to explain. The rationale, they assured her, was sound even if the behaviour could not be condoned. Oh no.

"But see, I don't, like, get the whole reasoning of it," Esther said, sliding to lower diction.

"Evolutionary psychology," said the Egyptian, very slowly, his hand finding the stem of his sparkling wineglass and beginning to twist it in place, "seeks an explanation for human activity by casting it in terms of genetic success. And the success of our genes, naturally, is a matter of producing copies."

And here the man removed his hand from the wineglass and patted his wife's midsection: third wife, three gentle pats, one per trimester.

Esther had been taking down irrationality as a professional for five years by this point. She knew how to do it in the middle of a room full of hardened competitive positions without losing a smile or communicating impatience. "The thing I don't get," she said now, "is that studies have repeatedly shown education and stable marital status as two of the social factors most strongly indicating wealth. So you'd think, at least among those who like finer things, that unfaithfulness would be contraindicated."

The Egyptian was prepared to play. He smiled and said, "Perhaps we are but vehicles for our genes."

Esther waited a beat, during which time the table focus was brought to bear on the statement. No escaping now.

"That would only make sense if genes were making the decisions," she said. "If brains were thought to be accountable, you'd think they'd look out for their own survival. And having made brainy choices like going to university for seven years and apprenticing for another five, you'd think the average architect's brain would be . . . *cautious* . . . about infidelity if only to avoid the crippling alimony payments."

At which point the Egyptian's expression drifted somewhere just south of pleasant, and the laughter around the table splintered at the edges.

"I suppose it's a matter of learning from experience," he said.

Graham could see it. Nobody else could. Esther's killing zone.

"If a billion years of evolution have proven that procreation means success," the Egyptian continued, "well then, perhaps alimony is the sort of sacrifice we must be prepared to make on behalf of our genes."

"Ah, experience," Esther said. "Such a dear school and yet fools will learn at no other."

The conversation continued after that, in a fashion. Esther finishing her opponent with a variety of shots from a range of angles. Graham saw it all at once as a boxing match that should be stopped. The opponent bleeding and staggering but fighting on.

And so the evening unravelled. It was midnight. Work in the morning. Of course, between Graham and Esther, the door closing on the last air kiss didn't end it precisely.

"You know," Graham said, in the bathroom upstairs. "I'm trying not to start a fight here, but what can you be thinking when you tell a group of people whose life work is architecture and based on ancient principles that they shouldn't learn from experience? I guess the Roman arch doesn't mean anything. The lintel. The cantilever."

She tried to explain, reasonably at first but irritation rising. Sure the arch meant something, but not because it was *old*, because it still worked *now*. "Anyway," Esther said, "your gang was talking about personal experience, which is where I was trying to make my point."

"Tell me this," Graham said, his voice cracking. "Tell me how you can say we shouldn't learn from personal experience."

TIMOTHY

TAYLOR

"Do you want the list of reasons?"

"My personal experience is that my father was successful because he started in a good firm before branching out on his own. Which I'm also trying to do here. Which

98

you're not exactly helping when you send my partners away feeling like they've been mugged at the high-school debating club."

"Graham, listen—"

"My experience is also that my father fucked a lot of women other than my mother, which may explain why I have a criminal for a brother. Or why my mother, instead of living nearby and badgering us about grandchildren, is hiding in France up to her neck in mineral water, tended to by the conductor of the Avignon Chamber Orchestra. Which part of this experience would you recommend I not learn from, Esther? Tell me."

It was an argument with unusual structure. They were agreeing, after all. Infidelity, bad. But just that instant, Esther couldn't live with the idea that they would agree for the wrong reasons.

"How can you not get this?" she asked him, her voice harshly raised. "It doesn't matter what your father did. His sociopathologies are a sunk cost. The present is your only guide. What you know today is not only enough, it is all you know."

Nine reasons why you should ignore experience (she lectured). One: availability to memory. Your great reservoir of "experience" comprises only incidents you remember. What of all you forget? Two: inherent bias. Your life delivers up a certain quality of experience, your reality being a subset of possibility, not the reverse. What of all you miss? Three: superannuation. Things *change*. The lessons of one's experience, such that they exist at all, have a stale-date. And she went on, although she couldn't remember later if she made it to nine.

Graham fumed for a week. Then they made up elaborately and suddenly, in the kitchen. Not a room with which, or in which, they had been previously intimate. "It's not a good time," Esther had said, under him, holding him very tightly. "Of the month, that is."

"Do we care?" he asked her, ushering in an era with a whisper. Hypothetical babies now peopling their subconscious. Not that they acknowledged trying, of course. Eighteen months, two full years might have passed without anybody watching the calendar or noting her periods.

And then they were suddenly watching very closely,

she remembered, catching her own reflection in the door as she left the lounge and emerged outside. Four years passing. The dinner party, the fight, the makeup sex disappearing into memory as everything significant in their life appeared to change. Esther became a partner. Graham left the old firm and started an independent career as she'd so long encouraged him to do. And with someone Esther had found for him, no less. Fila Sarafi. Met at a businesswomen's networking breakfast that neither of them had the time to attend, but had out of deference to enthusiastic bosses. Fila Sarafi, who had the whiff of something serious about her: accomplishment, focus, no bullshit. Fila Sarafi, who was beginning her own design practice, thinking about strategic partnerships.

Esther practically pushed them together. She more or less begged her husband to work late hours wrapped up in stresses with which only this new woman in his life could sympathize. To sleep with her as soon as possible, essentially, since by now their own sex life had fallen to zero. And this reasoning through, this self-recrimination, was unshakable in Esther's mind even if, technically, Graham and Fila hadn't had sex. Or hadn't by now, as they were clearly just about to. Which was bad enough whoever's fault it was.

All complete conjecture. Irrational. Esther was staring down on the jetty angrily, scanning the free boats. I hate myself like this. But what data points were there? Fertilized embryos planted inside her and failing to root. Life flaring out of them, bleeding out of her. Graham going quietly mad. Demons waking somewhere within if they'd ever been asleep. Los Angeles was wrong, somehow. Zweigler and the camera and the idea that he would now do something important. Something that he could film. Something that would put them back at the beginning and repair the damage. That whole way of thinking, that whole line of story unsettled her. It nauseated.

Leading someplace good, he'd said. Making this statement over and over in various ways. Someplace good as opposed to someplace bad. Those men destined to have three wives who nevertheless clung to their fundamentalist morality.

And here was the point. (She was making a presentation to herself, internal PowerPoint slides flickering on the inside of her skull right behind the eyes.) Here was the change that troubled her most. Because the good and the bad had never before been Graham's compass points. He was like her in at least this one respect, or had been. Getting off that floatplane, first time she'd ever laid eyes on him: sketchbook clutched to his chest, pens arranged in a neat row in his shirt pocket and evidence of such searching in his eyes, such commitment. Not to the finding of what was good but of what was true. Key distinction. This young man was here to find the answers to questions. Esther had watched hundreds of men get out of float planes on that very stretch of dock. Every one of them shouldering off the burden of having to answer questions about anything. The moment their feet hit the unsteady surface their eyes glazed over like they'd taken a hit of something strong (which many of them also did fairly shortly thereafter). But this young man—a little chunky, a little un-exercised, but with a nice face, a face that could host intelligence and kindness simultaneously—here he was stalking up the gangway like his future depended on finding something right there in the close and knowable future. He was completely atypical and she loved him for it. She wondered about him personally, not an impulse to which she had ever been prone. She enjoyed wondering about him personally.

Now she wondered about him personally again, but she didn't enjoy it. "I've taken a leave of absence," she told him on the phone. "I'm staying up here awhile."

His voice went very tight, rose a register. Leave of absence for how long?

"As long as it takes."

"As long as it takes to what?"

She could have said virtually anything and it would have been more reasonable than what she chose. A thought flashed in and it was selected. She told him: As long as it took to catch something really, really big.

Six

GS DESIGN GOT LA MOLTA. GRAHAM'S BID-SAVING speech was getting quoted in gossip that made its way back from a firm in the east to Graham's old firm where, despite the lawsuit required to get the Gordon name off the letterhead after his departure, there were still partners friendly enough to call from time to time.

"Structural frottage?" someone asked him. "What the hell is that?"

No *hello*. No *how're things?*

"Aesthetic," Graham said. "Aesthetic frottage."

Same day, after work, Ike already knew.

"Aesthetic," Graham said again, accepting what appeared to be a Windex martini. But he didn't really need to ask. The bar crowd talked. Ike wasn't above listening. And judging from the lengthy bang-path the gossip had followed from Los Angeles across the continent twice and back to the sidebar of Ike's, it must have been in motion fairly shortly after Fila and he had left the boardroom that morning.

Context problems, the board members had told them. They liked the spirit of the design but were running into problems with community groups. These were people whose approval they didn't need exactly, but with whom they had to live. (People for whom Disney was heritage, Graham thought.) And those folks thought the redesign would make La Molta stand out too starkly from the existing architectural tone of the area.

Graham walked them through it again. GS Design was, yes, committed to recladding the exterior entirely. Covering the brick and masonry with galvanized corrugated steel, Cor-Ten and Parklex for each of the building's three facing walls. Stripping the exterior down to frame and using opaque glass on the side street. This was the bold, industrial, frankly designed and neo-modern look that was envisioned, that was demanded.

"Is that modern?" someone asked.

Well, now it was.

"But isn't there a softer modern face? The buildings on either side are so close." The speaker was around fifty, a woman Graham understood to be a big-time area developer and collector of Lichtenstein. She paused to sort through options in search of the right word. "Isn't there an intimacy between adjacent buildings that must be respected?"

Graham hurried to agree without having a clue about what he would say after that. Of course, *intimacy* was the right word and that was precisely why the design worked.

Curious glances while he sipped water and waited for the idea to come. Fila looking on with an expression halfway between serenity and the kind of morbid anticipatory delight that Graham associated with the ringside at boxing matches. Blood was a distinct possibility, and she was quite happy to let him take this moment as his own.

But, he continued, respect for surroundings was not what had won this hotel group their various design awards for projects in London and Copenhagen. They weren't building family housing. What sold their locations to the young, moneyed international travellers they were attracting was a distinct sense of being away from home, away from safety, even a degree removed from what was wholesome. There was a reason why in the bedside table lower drawers you would find, instead of a Gideon, a long, smooth, neon pink vibrator. Tongue-in-cheek, whatever. The core brand quality was sex and quite possibly with someone you'd only just met.

"In the same fashion," he said, speaking slowly, "strange civic juxtapositions that leave stark architectural differences at a point of intimate contact may be thought of as a sort of aesthetic frottage. The sense of excitement is created by the unconsummated proximity, even friction, between strangers."

In the cab to dinner, Fila said, "Was tongue-in-cheek tongue-in-cheek?"

He didn't know. These things came to him. So, two trips a week back and forth, three weeks straight. Quiet

agony for Graham made feasible only by a Xanax pre-
scription, then one for Tranxene, and then a smoothing
layer of Zaleplon to help him through the nights before
and after each flight. And the effect of all these chemical
interventions was not so much to dispel his various pho-
bias but to blend them. Now he was falling asleep without jolting awake a dozen times, but plunging through
and dreaming of flight, of being terrified in flight, of
exploding in flight. Sometimes he even saw the vision
of shattering as if it were happening to him, as if his own
body was blown into a cloud of bits. His body and others.
Esther, naturally enough. He felt guilty about Esther.
But other shady shapes he strained to make out. Elliot
possibly.

Never Fila, who filled his waking hours instead. The
chemistry between them not so much neutralized by work
as redirected. A kind of frottage happening here too as
they hunched together over drawings. As they reclad the
building in enormous faceplates of silver, gun-metal grey
and yellow. The insides stripped and reassembled. The
lobby zinc and teak, chrome furniture, black leather.
The restaurant dominated by one red wall. The rooms
blue and white, with cubic stone tubs and aluminium
fixtures. The spa—of course, Graham wanted to say, for
whom the internal logic of these GS schemes gradually
solidified over the duration of a project—the subtlest,
foamiest, most organic and natural fusion of forest, sea
and lime green.

All of which left him back home, one last, worst flight,
brutal downdrafts on the approach, the plane struck as if
by the flat palm of God just as they crossed the beach line,
plummeting toward the stinking delta mud exposed by
low tide. Then soaring up again and over the chain-link

fence in a long parabola ending as they slammed home on the tarmac, so hard that beads of sweat broke loose from his forehead and exploded on the declaration card.

Business or pleasure. Somebody was really rubbing his face in it.

But he was back, and back for awhile. This being the understood distribution of labour between them. When it came to finishing things, Fila was their man. *Our in-house Imagineer*, she had once called him, with a small smile colouring her dark-painted lips.

Now the front-load was entirely finished, the client was inspired. The project well and truly underway. So it was her turn. She stayed. She moved into a house on Hollister Avenue owned by a friend Graham hadn't heard about previously. She'd keep things on track. She'd deal with trades. Happy to do so, liking this part. Liking the solving of problems in environments where these problems were the shank of a working day. When a counter was so sleekly envisioned by Graham, with such a long, pristine cantilever that it sagged three inches when the check-in desk computer was installed, Fila happily went about sourcing reinforcement materials, calling in guys she knew from garages that specialized in chopping down trucks into low-riders. She'd stand at the centre of the knot of tattooed burlies in the hotel lobby as they worked through various solutions. A guy holding out a rod of titanium stripping to show how it would work, a tapestry of skulls and flames down his forearms. Fila e-mailed in the odd question but stayed off the phone. Back in a month, stay out of trouble.

Last night before he left, she'd asked carefully, "And you're clear on what comes next?"

Graham said, "You mean Tokyo?"

Yes, Tokyo.

"Well, I was hoping also to spend some time thinking about the future too," he said.

She frowned. She rhymed off a list of names, people to whom they owed calls, projects on which they had already agreed either to bid or to discuss or to submit early-concept drawings. But she also said, Fine, fine. As if she knew that without both of them around there was only a limited distance they could travel with these assignments. As if she knew that Graham thinking about the future—theirs, his own, all of theirs—was now becoming inevitable and necessary.

"But we have plenty of work," she said. "So all I ask is that if you're planning to up and quit and become a cobbler or something, you tell me now."

He wasn't quitting, he said, kissing her. He was purifying. He was readying himself.

She kissed him back. Three hours later he was on the ground and safe. Home and alone, but hemmed in by ideas. He could feel them in the wires, coming into view, vying for a spot. Must track down this Cleo Angelopolous whose e-mail had bounced. Must think about a camera that demanded use. He sipped Glenfarclas that first night back, sitting cross-legged in front of a three-foot-square sheet of ivory vellum with charcoal and paper, drawing shapes and forms, clouds and lines. Listening to Tom Waits. (What was a Rain Dog, anyway?) Then shutting down the stereo to realize he'd been home an hour without turning on a single light. A realization that came to him in large part because he could no longer see his hieroglyphs, no longer make out the names in the phone book that was open on the floor in front of him.

Many pages of Ang. Just three listings for Angelopolous. No Cleo. No C.

No answer at the first one. Voice mail at the second: Helen and David. When someone picked up at the third, he barked, "Cleo?" Aware that he sounded manic. But he only provoked a long answer in Greek. Neutral in tone, hard to interpret as positive or negative. The voice belonged, he concluded, to an enthusiastic insomniac senior citizen of Greek extraction who had mistaken him for someone else. He tried to interrupt. He was looking for a film, a boxing film. But he was speaking into silence by that point. The person on the other end had hung up.

He went sheepishly to bed. Woke with the obvious idea. Pogey Nealon. Cleo Angelopolous. Death and inheritance.

He drove into Mary Street slowly. He remembered that the area had been rundown. Now it appeared to have advanced as far beyond that point as possible without actually crumbling from view. The corner convenience store looked like a military installation. Wire mesh reinforced with steel bars, sometime later reinforced again with welded lengths of rebar and angle iron. Each of the next three buildings on the south side of the street was boarded up, For Sale or Lease signs prominent. And at the lot where he was sure the gym had been—it had been an old modern, hadn't it?—he found only a wall. A stained plywood hoarding rising some fifteen feet and layered with graffiti. *Eat the rich. Malorum contra unum.*

He knocked at the door in this wall loudly. He pushed a buzzer button, then banged with a fist. He tried the knob, but it was locked. He called out, then stood for a long time just listening.

Nothing. It was empty, obviously. And slated for tear-down, judging from the hoarding. Which was disappointing on the one hand, surprising on the other. Who would actually build down here? But in the end—he thought this climbing back into the car, resisting a final backward glance—not surprising either. A long-gone place, long empty. A place no longer needed. It was a shell, a cracked shell. He felt guilty for being there and as he drove uptown with overblown caution, he imagined himself a suspicious sight on those streets, somebody the cops would pick for a john or a white-collar dope buyer.

Graham imposed order. Every morning, into the office no later than eighty-thirty, no matter how late he'd been up the night before. No leaving before five-thirty. In between, while answering phone calls and buying them time as necessary with other clients, he brainstormed without any specific objective. He opened up a valve in himself. Said, Bring on the ideas. He was solving an IQ test question that looked roughly like this: Avi Zweigler, famous camera, Cleo Angelopolous, link to a dark episode of the specific, personal past. What comes next in the sequence?

He leafed through back issues of the fancy magazines. He drew pictures. Little dense sketches. Very large whiteboard line drawings. Charts and graphs of various things that came to him begging to be plotted, pie-charted, blown up into representative squiggles across requisite axes. He phoned the one unanswered Angelopolous number, letting it ring a polite seven times. He went to Ike's for lunch every day at one.

"She's back in four weeks. Three weeks. I'm working on this thing. This kind of commission, although I don't know what it is yet."

Ike looked at him with sudden focus. "You're wearing the same clothes as yesterday. Did you sleep at the office last night?"

Okay, yes. He did sleep on the couch at the office the night before. Getting in at eight-thirty in the morning was the commitment and Graham was prepared to do what he had to do.

Ike brought lunch. It started with a cup of pear soup that came with a little wooden paddle. "Hickory stick," Ike said. "Dip and lick."

Graham dipped and licked. It was good.

Ike said, "Sleeping at the office. So you miss Esther. This is normal."

"I do, but that's not it," Graham said. "No, no, no."

"Three no's for Ike," his friend said. "You definitely miss Esther."

Graham took a break after lunch and drove out to West Vancouver, trying to ignore a new thump in the car's front end, a troubling sound, metal on metal. It came in loud. It made him grind his teeth to hear it. Then it faded, and he tried to push it out of his mind entirely. He was prepared to acknowledge the lunacy of the designer-car obsession. Everybody he knew professionally was driving an electric hybrid or sports cars they couldn't afford. Graham's choice was a 1973 Porsche, tangerine with a chocolate-milk interior. Not obscenely expensive to buy, but now he bled monthly mechanics bills. Miserable, not individually ruinous amounts of money for obscure parts that would opt on a given afternoon to thump, then wheeze, then die. And always afraid these sounds might signal some kind of total system failure, something that would leave him carless (Esther the rationalist had always bussed, of course), he'd accepted a relationship closer than he would have liked with a mechanic named Rudolph who charged $175 an hour but for that price would actually do house calls.

"Do not move the car," Rudolph would say in response to Graham's description of a given wonk or warble. Then he'd come around a few hours later sipping a take-away espresso and interpret the pattern of stains on the garage floor before lifting the hood or touching a wrench.

The thumping was now gone. And Graham wheeled down off Marine Drive into the tangled, overgrown streets above the water, through to one cul-de-sac, to the very end, where he parked on the verge, ratcheting the handbrake home and allowing himself a few minutes to indulge a very guilty, very secret compulsion. He stared down the steep driveway to what had been, unimaginable years before, the family plot. He blanked out the monstrosity built on top of what his father had made for them—the new house was no longer Corfu pink, he noted, now something like Miami sunset orange. He tried to see through this structure to the rock beneath. The roll and shape of it. The sense it would have given the eye when exposed. He imagined himself behind his father's eyes, looking down for the first time.

Five minutes, ten minutes. It never came to anything. And nothing this time either except for a black Hummer that idled into the cul-de-sac and honked, because he was in the way. So Graham threw the car into reverse and pressed it yet farther into a roadside hedge. The Hummer squeezed past and into that driveway, ass end rising to entirely block Graham's view of anything, fumes kicking back at him, swirling in the open driver's window.

Graham retreated. Out of those neighbourhood streets, then back into the city, past the beaches, back across the bridge. He climbed twelve flights of stairs to the GS offices at a determined trot, ready to grapple again with his invisible challenger.

Ideally situated to do so too, he thought. The Gordon Sarafi Design offices had an inspiring view: North Shore suburbs, inner harbour, container terminal and their own neighbourhood, the Middle East. Climbing out onto the creaking fire escape that spidered down the north side of the building, you could even get a glimpse back up the ridge line to the west, where the core of the city bristled glass spires, glinting in the rain, sparkling in the sun, throwing rainbows back and forth. Fila was known to perch out here while on the phone, weather permitting. Crow-black hair rippling in the harbour breeze.

He set up the Bolex, lens pointing out the window. Future projects, Zweigler had said. One of them, the right one.

So, he thought, the Middle East. Architecturally, a pre-war mess. Their own building was a pastiche of rococo, classical and the kind of overly Imperial flourishes Graham associated with the nervous fringes of the Commonwealth at the beginning of the twentieth century. The surrounding neighbourhood, meanwhile, was what you might get if you airlifted the seedier part of Amsterdam into a suburb of Prague and sprinkled in peek-a-boo views of Aspen. But here, nevertheless, was the place where it had all begun during those years when the city could still be all future ideas of a city. No matter that commerce had fled uptown, that the good families moved west into Point Grey and east to Burnaby and the Chinese herbalists had all fled to Richmond. No matter that the Middle East had become a grid of crack corners and heroin parks, pawnshops and welfare hotels, forgotten parking lots where limousine drivers and cops spent their off hours parked nose to tail, driver's window to driver's window, and the alleys branched out in every direction pasted thick with garbage. Here was still the point of origin. The civic stem cell.

Graham sketched. Charts. Visual interpretations of the tangle of fortune and poverty, beauty and disaster below. Smoking Panters, dialling the Angelopolous number. He was up to twenty rings now, able to key the number without looking at the phone. Twenty-five rings even while he drew plans of the city drug-traffic zones, closed commercial space, hooker strolls and mental-health housing units. Neighbourhoods, green spaces and then, inspired, greengrocers.

He let the phone ring thirty-five times. Once, fifty.

Age of buildings. Now here was a diorama that gripped him. Plotting the surface of the city by the age of structure, averaging zones and assigning a height to each, the topography of the city could be represented as a sweeping wave that rose up from the eastern suburbs and broke in an enormous crest at the shore. It kept him awake, that one, sitting on the fire escape, dangling his legs, looking out over the silver surface of the water to the freighters moored there, setting down the bottle gently so that it wouldn't tip on the metal grate, fall away into the night under his feet. He felt that congratulations were in order that he'd spent three weeks in diffuse brainstorming and come up with the single idea that from the city's burnt-out heartland, a great tsunami was rushing westward, hurrying back to the sea.

He slept that night. Only three jolts back from the near beyond. Only three explosions with the drifting shards. Only three times wondering what lay at the heart of that forming cloud. Then under. He woke up on the couch with a dry throat and a light headache to find a half-empty Glenfarclas bottle and a coffee cup full of Panter butts. A pad of paper lying open next to the phone with a number scribbled down next to *PFS*. Esther. In a flash panic that prickled his forehead with sweat, he punched through the outgoing call log on the phone's display: directory assistance at 1:00 a.m., no record of drunken dialling after that.

He drove home, metal on metal in the front end again. Was Ike right? Did he miss her? Maybe, but that wasn't the whole story. That didn't capture the significance of where she'd gone to hide. A place that had once before refused to give up its secrets to him.

The island where the Private Fishing Society had been built was steep-sided, black-rocked. Once rat-infested, the story went, the forests had been cleared of rodents in favour of the murrelet, a rock-dwelling seabird deemed to have been there first. And now, while it was misty, silent with the project of resurrecting something nearly extinct, the surrounding seas teemed. Humpback whales and sea lions, chinook and coho salmon, halibut and rockfish. An angler's paradise nine hundred air kilometres north of the city, an ordeal of cramped Beechcrafts and lumbering bush planes. Remote like nothing Graham had ever seen, then or since. Last landfall before Alaska northbound, and to the west, next stop Japan. An exercise in the whole idea of being removed, as far from anything as this res-olutely urban kid had ever been, but worth it, he rea-soned a little desperately, if he could find The Truth.

Nothing less than that. Graham's quest had been for proof that truth in structure, in materials, the very soul of his schooling as intoned by professors with near-Presbyterian resolve, was a matter dictated by landscape. And if that were true, well then Aboriginal architecture would reveal the truth more purely than any other form. Insulated as they had been from outside influence, these builders would have had only a landscape from which to draw. His father must have believed so — Graham reasoned, forced always to remember that his father had actually told him nothing of what he believed — or he must have believed so enough, in any case, to make a similar trek of his own.

Of course, when he was honest, Graham had to admit a motive beyond the architectural in the pilgrimage. Something hovered in his early twenties, a sense that he was *slipping*. That his high-school friends had all fallen away. That new friendships in architecture school had not lasted. That he was spending increasing amounts of time alone, at school, working late, sleeping little and that somewhere along the way he'd become a man without any family. Since his mother's remarriage, he hardly heard from her, consumed as she was with the isolating details of her macrobiotic diet and devotion to healing waters.

His brother, of course, was either slipping himself or entirely gone by that point. Graham had precisely two tortured moments of contact from which to judge. Elliot had moved out at nineteen, about a year before their father died. Nobody knew where he'd gone, only that he wouldn't say a word to anyone at the funeral, was quite possibly drunk. Graham refused to avoid him, although that would have been easy. In fact, he went to find him in the chapel. Offered an open hand. Elliot shook, but he shrugged afterwards. Not angry exactly. Graham only sensed in his brother a sad commitment to failure between them.

Then the second and last time, much worse. Graham in a taxi. He couldn't remember where he'd been heading, only that it was early in the morning. The airport? Possibly. The ride was twinned with memories of the Queen Charlottes and all that he'd found up there. He was, in any case, mentally absorbed already in that quest, in the idea of it. Not the best place he'd ever been, or thankfully would be. But glancing up to look at the cabbie for the first time when he turned his head to ask for a destination, there behind the Plexiglas, Graham found his long-lost brother. Shaved head, leather jacket, dirt in the creases of his neck.

Graham didn't remember much of what was said, only that after an awkward silence they'd somehow ended up talking about that prank architect from the mid-1970s, Matta-Clark, with whom Elliot was oddly familiar and about whom Graham didn't have much to say. Deconstruction, what was that? He'd never understood Derrida either. Graham was interested in building things, not disassembling them. But it was an obscure and unstable topic, in any case. Badly chosen. And it spilled them down through a quick series of less and less friendly exchanges, the pattern of which was only broken when Graham registered how fast Elliot was driving. In some inexplicable fit of fury, his brother's foot was slowly burying the gas pedal and they were flying through the morning streets. Tires singing on slick pavement. The smell of motor oil filling the cab. And not going the route Graham had requested either, but spinning off down Broadway in the wrong direction entirely. What the fuck? He yelled. He pounded on the driver's seat back as they slid into a new street, trees and parked cars blurring past. Did he scream? He might have, much to his shame now. But finally the cab stopped with one tire up on the curb and Graham was out, shelling money through the window. Elliot screaming at him: *Maybe it's best we just keep the fuck away from each other.*

Words Graham couldn't erase from his memory. Yes, they'd both been slipping. Slipping toward utter solitude with blackness hovering. A loosening frame of mind that allowed Graham to believe there was some lesson floating, ghostlike, above what remained of those very first Aboriginal foundations.

All that imprecise calculation going on within. Graham wondered how he could not have seen the precarious thing he'd been building, a dangerous hope. A hope that he could inherit a vision that had apparently not been willed to him. But he'd been too young to see it. Too blind and breathless from the effort of climbing in and out of float planes and dinghies.

"Damn!" he said, loud now. No denying what was happening to the mechanical world around him. Intensified thumping below, steering wheel vibrating too. Air was rushing past the open window, full of salt and sea. And Graham had to fight the car over to the curb. Steering wheel jogging dangerously in his hands. Something falling apart under there.

He limped to Rudolph's. Back across town. Honked at three times, given the finger once. Everybody in the world in a hurry now, no time left for busted-down tangerine nostalgia.

Rudolph's shop was tucked into a pristine glass and cinder-block building near Granville Island, in between boutiques that sold single-orchard olive oil and hand-raked fleur de sel. Graham waited nervously in a reception area that was strikingly like what they had planned for La Molta, with long black leather-and-chrome benches, hanging aluminium light fixtures, avocado walls, teak highlights and a Jasper Johns print. He took in his surroundings stoically, twenty minutes ticking by on the clock, feeling the expensive bad news coming out of the rear of the shop even before Rudolph himself appeared and Graham leaned into the counter to receive his lesson on the topic of *bushings*.

"Shot," Rudolph said, holding one in his hand for inspection, about the size of a greased-over Fabergé egg. Parts and labour worth about 50 per cent of the car's resale value.

"But she's an old-timer, yeah?" Rudolph said.

Graham knew where this was going. A place it had gone before with Rudolph's sly guidance. A man with access to an impressive range of second-hand exotics and wise to the cost-image dichotomy of the architect's car obsession.

"Maybe we talk about an upgrade, yeah?" Rudolph said.

Which is how Graham came to be driving a late-model Porsche Boxster S, the palest shade of blue. A colour he'd never actually seen on a car before. Not cue chalk, not robin's egg or sky blue. Lighter. *Lubetkin* blue. He was instantly proud of that one, the idea pleasing him enormously. Surely it was right where the communist hero of his libertarian father had belonged all along: on the skin of a vehicle worth about seven times what his old Porsche had been worth. And borrowed too, because he hadn't paid for it. He'd asked Rudolph for a week-long loan to decide which way to go and the mechanic had traded keys with him, simple as that.

"You won't get into trouble, yeah?" Rudolph had asked him. "This car is for trouble."

It was, Graham acknowledged. First thing he did at the wheel was not go home to shower as planned, but hit the highway. What were cars like this for, anyway? He pointed the Porsche at the mountains and hit the gas, flying, roaring like a plane. Up, up and away. Over the bridge again, the forest dropping away around him as he soared in an arc across the inlet.

It brought back that Beaver float plane, coming in low over the yellow brush of the west island. White-tail feeding in the marshy grasses below. Eagles wheeling in the updrafts off Pillar Rock (here an architecture student writes notes in a pad describing stacked sedimentary discs that wobble upward out of the sea). Putting down in Parry Passage, the old bush plane lowering itself arthritically to the water, Graham was riveted by the forests on either side. Impenetrable, a single mass unlike any monolithic structure he'd seen before.

He had been entranced, much to the amusement of the bush pilot, who asked him once, and then twice, if it was his first time up in the Charlottes. "Where?" Graham said, responding finally to the voice in his headphones, turning sharply from the window, pad of paper wedged between his knees. "Oh, here? Yeah, no."

Which made the bush pilot laugh out loud.

They were alongside at the Private Fishing Society. Here, his construction fundamentals professor had arranged for Graham to meet Dr. Lee, the club founder who also happened to be the inhabitant and namesake of The Lee House, a many-times photographed and published Arthur Erickson hidden behind cedars at the end of one of West Vancouver's most exclusive crescents. The good doctor (honourary) had been a friend of Packer Gordon, he was a patron, a contributor to the architecture school and a man who, through friends in Masset, was able to arrange a tour of the Haida village of Kiusta.

"Dr. Lee is an excellent contact for you." Graham's professor didn't realize the half of it.

Lee wasn't even at the club when Graham arrived, but he was put square by the club manager, brush cut, high-shouldered, whose first and last words to Graham were: "I understand you don't like fishing."

Which wasn't exactly true. He just didn't understand the impulse or have any experience with the sport. But the man wasn't posing questions, he was making statements about the world as he saw it. And with a single glance at Graham—his floppy hat and Bermuda shorts, his Topsiders and chamois shirt from L.L. Bean—the manager knew he didn't belong. He handed Graham off to one of the dock hands, announcing, "Graham is here to see Kiusta." Overly loud.

"What are you—like an archaeologist?" The dock hand asked.

"I'm like an architect," Graham said, awarding himself graduation and certificates.

"And you came all this way not to fish?"

They were walking along the dock now. Graham was about to answer, to ridicule even, to remind this kid with a sarcastic word about the enormous world free of recreational anglers just out of sight over the horizon in all directions, but in the style of a bad television show, he saw *her* just at that moment and felt his train of thought shudder free of the rails.

Hard to say just what quality he first perceived. Graham would later observe that she had a strong, square face, a full mouth and a compact, athletic build, that she was oddly beautiful. But all he observed from that first encounter was how she had lifted her eyes from what she was doing—topping up the fuel/oil mix in an outboard, as it happened—and locked on him a set of deep brown eyes alive with curiosity, humour and the suggestion that she recognized him. Either him personally (impossible) or some quality in him she hadn't seen in a long time. He felt *scoped out*, read through to his cells. And he liked it.

Japanese, he guessed. A sign of his own ignorance in these matters and a point with which a young Esther would have taken issue. He was drawing close to the boat where she was hunched over the motor, one muscular leg thrown up on the gunwale for balance, a Band-Aid prominent on her knee by being many shades lighter than her own skin tone. And realizing that he was staring, from quite close, and that his attention was provoking amusement, Graham pulled his eyes away from her, breathing hard, nervous all at once, and walked on by pretending to be arrested by a scuffle of seagulls at the bait table.

"Watch your step, man," the dock hand said. Too late, of course. Graham slammed a foot into the lip of the gangway up into the crew quarters, staggered a precarious step or two, then prevented himself from pitching into the sea only by snaring the handrail in his armpit.

It would have been the right moment to stand, to walk on with quiet dignity. But of course he turned back. He rehoisted his canvas bag, retrieved his sketch portfolio from where it was teetering on the edge of the dock. Then he stole a glance back at her.

She was staring after him, laughing silently. And then she held both palms at about shoulder height on either side of her, indicating all that was around them: the vaulting sky, the forests across the water, the fish in the deep, all of it. It was a gesture he worked to interpret later, lying in his bunk waiting for the announcement that the boat to Kiusta was ready. She seemed to have been saying, *Well, what did you expect?*

A light rain was picking up again, stippling the Boxster windshield. Their beginning, Graham remembered, had pointed him onward. As if she knew that a discovery lay in store for both of them. And he wondered now what was left in that original truth. How strong was the remaining link from him to that moment? From where he was now, up over the glaciers and the Garibaldi Highlands, over the treed slopes to the broken continental shore, across the Hecate Straight and up over the broom-splashed marshlands of Graham Island. All the way over, diving down to that seam of white foam where she had been waiting, where the longhouses still were waiting, disappearing under the moss that lived on that last threshold of the continent before it disappeared into the depths of the Pacific forever. From there to here. From her to him. From what he was the last time he set out on a quest to what he was now, a blur of Lubetkin blue across a ridge line hunkered over by darker sky.

Seven

GRAHAM'S PHONE RANG EARLY. INSPIRED BY A certainty that he must have carried with him out of sleep, he popped it open. Said, "Cleo. Do not hang up. I've been trying to reach you."

A man's voice: "Have you borrowed another car from someone named Cleo?"

Graham rolled back on the bed. Rudolph. His own car was long ready. The shop had been leaving messages at work, at home, on his cell. Did Graham have any idea when it might be convenient to come down and either swap the loaner or buy it as agreed?

Graham said, "Right. I've been meaning to call."

"You enjoy it?"

"I'm enjoying it," Graham said. "Only she's still out of town."

"Ah," Rudolph said. "The finance committee. Well, you just keep it then."

In fact, the finance committee that mattered was back in town. Fila took a few days off, then got busy trying to restore office order. There were phone calls to return. Mail that hadn't been opened. Some ruffled feathers among clients Graham had been gently avoiding. Fila said to these people: "Admin changes, this end. Nothing major. We're a little behind but catching up."

To Graham she said only, "Well? You've had your month."

"I'm close."

"I like the wave."

"I think the wave is my best one," Graham told her.

It was late afternoon. She was folded onto the couch with the phone in her lap, slender legs up beneath her. She was looking around the room at the evidence of his teeming, directionless imaginings. Looking in a way that he judged was not cool but was rather committed to something happening, now, with his co-operation or otherwise.

She said, "Esther's not coming back."

He looked at her a long time. He didn't disagree. He didn't wonder if she had new information. It only struck him that if one of them were to see the future, all at once, the pattern of it revealed, it was unfair that after all his efforts over the past few weeks it would now be her.

"Who lives on Hollister Avenue?" he asked her.

"He's useless to me," Fila said. "He's married. Are you hungry?" Dinner then. That night. The two of them. Things to be decided. She said, "Your house is difficult, I understand. But my kitchen is pretty good."

Graham took charge of food. He walked over to the T&T fish market, up over the hump of Victory Square. The cherry trees had dropped enough of their petals that the police were arresting Honduran crack dealers on a blanket of pink, their feet scuffing up petals as they were escorted to the paddy wagon.

He thought, Fish. Salmon. Salmon is perfect.

Ike walked him through an idea by phone as Graham stood in front of the T&T fish tanks, a hundred coho swimming sulky loops in the opaque water. Three dishes made from the same fish. You boiled the head for a broth. You used one filet on the grill and the other in a mousse. You used the skin for crisping. Graham didn't have a pen but had the basic idea.

He asked Ike, "Did you hate salmon back then too?"

All trophy fish. You kill a hundred-pound halibut and you get eighty pounds of wormy white meat. You kill a fifty-five-pound chinook and you're killing the village elders. Ike as a twenty-year-old thought these were not nice things to do.

That was the person they'd bunked him with up there. Graham lay in his rack thinking, *Well, what did you expect?* And in walked Ike, a storm cloud of black insight.

"So you don't like fishing, leave," Graham said to him.

Not so easy, said young Ike. They were out in the wilderness preparing themselves. Readying themselves for the big things they would do in the city on their return.

Graham didn't have time to argue, hearing an announcement come over the camp PA just then. He rolled to his feet, grabbed his knapsack. Only in the boat, moments later, bouncing across the sound, arcing wide around the reef, he thought, Maybe that cook has a point.

"Kiusta," the guy in the back of the Zodiac said, waving with his arm to indicate a swath of shore ahead. They were crashing through the swells, a sense of space collapsing physically onto Graham, pressure on his body as the Private Fishing Society disappeared astern. With his eyes fixed ahead, locked on the forest, he could conjure the sense of punching right out of one existence and into another. A sensation that should have accompanied his first arrival in those parts, all the hours crossing all the distance from home, but hadn't. Now, sixteen hundred metres of choppy water, and he felt true movement, as if plates and slabs of the earth were adjusting their position.

On the beach—the Zodiac whining away back across the water, the promise to return in two hours dissipating in the sea air—Graham waited for his guide to appear. He felt exposed, watched, foolish even. His feet slipping and sinking in the stones, his sketch pad gripped under one arm, knapsack heavy with gear: camera, bottle of water, extra sweater, Band-Aids. I must look desperate, he thought, but then his self-consciousness vanished, he was lifted perfectly out of himself by noticing that totems stood among the trees. Not visible at first, they seemed to emerge, to fade in. Bleached trunks against the black. The weather-worn faces forming a pattern only, a texture, like that of words picked up in the background of a radio broadcast. Voices from a shadow frequency, seemingly of critical importance but indecipherable.

"Boo," said a man standing next to him.

Graham was jolted through to his guts. He yelled. He staggered with the flash pulse of adrenalin to his brain, took a step sideways, slipped on a wet stone, went down in a tangle of limbs and canvas and rolled around in the sand.

The man helped him up, extending a hand and gripping hard, pulling him to his feet. He suppressed a smile doing so. He said, "Watch your step."

This man was Charles, a Haida Watchman. Fifty yards down the beach Graham could see his boat pulled up on the sand. He was mid-twenties, short, broad-chested, shoulders round with muscle, wrists thick with sinew. Good-humoured, but with a trace of personal hardness. This quality was visible in his physical frame, but there in his words too. In the delayed and shortened answers Graham was getting to his many questions.

Where did his family come from and where did they live now? Had his family ever lived here in Kiusta? Were they builders?

Charles measured every query, deciding how much detail to provide, if any. Sometimes he didn't answer at all, in which case Graham would hear about something important but unrelated. *Archaeologists say the Haida people have been here more than ten thousand years.*

Was he a builder himself, a carver?

They used to bring the logs over from Lucy Island.

They reached the top of the beach. Having read up on his subject in the library before leaving, Graham expected to find what was left of the longhouses right here. Twelve of them in a line facing the sea, housing some three hundred people at Kiusta's peak around 1850. But there was nothing, just the face of the forest.

Charles gestured him forward and Graham passed through a curtain of trees and into an antechamber of the deeper forest, the trees here spaced out, moss lying in a thick carpet underfoot, spreading relentlessly, gripping the footfalls and extinguishing the outside world. Wave sound was gone. Birdsong, human voice, even wind. All that was left was the sound of the forest's own organism, alive and breathing. Microscopic creeping. Hidden shoots unfurling. The invisible sifting of pine needles and cedar fronds above. The billion clicks and whirrs of botany.

Charles stood a few yards off, winding a dry blade of beach grass around his finger, waiting for Graham to figure out what he was looking at. It was a scent that finally reached him, a fragrance at the end of a series that ran through red cedar, groundwater, bark and fern. Then something else, under the fern. The funky rot of timber. And with that sense, shapes rose to view. The contour of the ground finally intelligible. Here were the rounded lines of fallen houses in a long row parallel to the shore. The square depressions where the firepits had been, squared around by the outline of fallen rafters and sunken corner posts. And glancing back toward the sea to get his bearings, to snatch a glimpse of the world he had left behind, Graham realized how the forest had grown around the village, completing its burial after the villagers had gone.

His pad was out. He had more questions, a lot more. And through Dr. Lee, Charles appeared to have been forewarned. So Graham learned how the longhouses on that strip of shore would have been built. Four stout, round corner posts dropped into holes two metres deep, marking out a square of nine to fifteen metres. Middle supports erected next, two on both the front and back wall line. Enormous gable beams then swung into place, fitting into keyhole notches in the corner posts and lap joints on the middle support. When in place, they completed the frame of the front and back walls of the house. Next: sill plates, top plates and purlins. Finally, the common rafters used to support the roofing material.

"What about the front pole?" asked Graham, who understood that this completed the house. A sixty-foot totem through which the front door was often carved.

Yes, Charles said. It did complete the house. And yes, that's where the door often was. But, in fact, that pole was usually the first thing erected.

Charles stood to one side while Graham sketched the pit nearest them, stroking down the shapes of fallen beams and cross members under the moss, imaging the structure as it would have been new. The smell of the hewn timbers. Of dirt from the freshly dug pit inside the house. Such simple ideas these were. And yet, like much of what was good in architecture, so much more complicated in the details. Quite aside from the monumental task of felling and hauling thousand-pound tree trunks by canoe from Lucy Island in the eighteenth and early nineteenth centuries, aside even from the job of turning such trees into planks on-site using hammers and wedges, steel adzes and dogfish skin sandpaper, there was the whole matter of how the house became so much more than a usefully walled enclosure capped with a roof at some comfortable distance above the head. How, in fact, the structure spoke directly to the greater world around it.

There were the carvings, most obviously. In this way, Haida architecture was a kind of text. If you knew the pictographic language, you could read the front pole for stories significant to the families housed inside. But the house worked as symbol on other levels too. The shoreline was a boundary between the forests on one side and the ocean on the other. These houses, standing in their long line, stood between. A physical reminder of man's position between what lies above and below. The village lay along a seam where two other worlds met.

They walked a mossy trail that traced the village site. Charles pointed down into the pit of a house near the centre of the row. Graham stared down into the sunken field of moss while Charles described the last great long-house to have been built on that spot. Built by a line of the wealthiest and most powerful chiefs in Haida history.

"Story House," Charles said.

Across the water, Graham heard the sound of horns. Now a bell. A brief clamour rising and tapering. And here the young architecture student, having travelled many hundreds of miles and having passed in and out of various moods since departure, now felt his journey take on something like a coherent *direction*. Story House. He wanted to know about this Story House. What had been the carvings on its poles? What did the carvings mean?

Charles stood off twenty feet or so and didn't answer. Graham scraping the soft lead pencil against the paper. Trying to let his hand find the things that should be remembered. The arc of the beach, the line of houses. The pit and the purlins in their final repose. If architecture was the unavoidable art, he asked himself, an irrepressible dialogue with past and future, well then, what sentence did the village form? The forest climbing above them and inland. The lip of sand disappearing into the water. The houses were like words spoken into the space between.

He'd finished his sketch before noticing that Charles was gone. He found him back down the beach at his boat. Gathering up the painter. Preparing to cast off. Aware their time together was coming to a close, Graham tried again. "I'm a student." As if this were the most important passport one could carry. "Architecture."

Charles nodded.

"How the thing is built, but also why. I'm not trying to copy anything, or steal ideas."

Then: "I respect your people and the way you did things. All I'm trying to do here is understand a little bit of the . . . of the . . . *thought process* . . ."

Finally, recognizing that Charles would stand and listen to him staggering around without intervening for as long as it took Graham to realize what he was doing, Graham said, "Was it about the landscape? Did they learn how to build these forms from looking at the trees and the hillside, the sea? Was that how Story House came to be?"

Charles scratched his chin. He said, "Your feet are getting wet."

Graham was ankle-deep in water. Charles drifting out now.

Graham stepped back onto the beach. Charles continued to think, checking the treeline, the breeze, judging the look of the water. A three-point fix that then appeared to free up his remaining words on the topic. "The great Chief Albert Edward Edenshaw built Story House in the early nineteenth century after the details of the carvings were revealed to him in a dream," he said. "The rafters, front poles and corner pieces. The carvings. He dreamt it. Then he built it."

His speech now accelerating with resolve. Three front poles, the centre one the tallest with a door carved through it. On it had been depicted a black whale, the *su s an*, a woman, a bird, a man wearing a skin and two children above him.

Graham scribbled frantically. Gulls screaming overhead as his pencil scratched the page.

And the story too, the words now coming so fast that Graham couldn't keep up, the watchman's boat drifting slowly off the beach, a foot every few seconds, the tide slack. Graham stood there, feet wet, and listened. Or tried to listen, tried to commit these words to memory, their shape and structure, their architecture as it was revealed. But the effort of it only having the reverse effect. He was lost in the stream of the story. The words slipping through him. Wet seeds pinched between the fingers. A son and a mother. An advice-giving bird. Some kind of whale-hunting monster captured in a trap baited with two children. These details were all that he retained. And that wasn't just true years later, not just true of Graham as he hung up the phone and stood in front of a tank of sockeye salmon in a Chinatown fish market, a man in a white coat with a dip net hovering above, waiting for him to select the one for the plate, the one for their bellies, the one that would go inside Fila and which he would then touch through her skin, his hand finding the taut rim of her navel. It was true immediately after Charles had finished. Because all Graham could find to ask at that point—a question that obliterated everything else he'd been told—was: "I'm trying to understand what the house was built to *tell* us."

Charles was about to pull out to sea. Graham could see his departure in the seconds before it actually happened. Charles said, "Maybe Story House isn't telling you anything."

Graham was now off the beach himself, clambering awkwardly into the Zodiac that had skidded up in the shallows. Late. And in which he embarrassed himself by being irritable, rude.

"Have a good visit?" Esther, of course. She sat manning the outboard with a big smile, happy with her world, wearing mirrored sunglasses in which Graham was troubled to see his own reflection. Sunburned, eyes bleary, hair plastering this way and that. He was a mess and his heart went hollow when he saw her strong face, beautiful black hair pulled back tight into a ponytail. Legs planted firmly on the plywood deck. Her knee Band-Aid speaking to him directly on the topic of readiness, thresholds of discomfort, delicacy. When had he become so fragile?

Maybe Story House is asking you a question.

"Don't worry about it," Esther was saying, swinging the Zodiac out around the reef and into calmer water. He was perplexed to find himself in the middle of a conversation that he did not remember beginning.

"I'm just saying . . ." Esther resolutely calm, smiling into the breeze, into the strengthening sunshine. "Sometimes you throw a lot of questions at these guys and you don't get answers."

He was alarmed to hear his voice crack responding. Some spluttered protest.

Esther looked at him, then away sharply. She tried again. "Most people come up here . . ."

"Who are these most people?" Graham said, a swirling panic rising in his chest. An awareness that he was growing hysterical. His eyes were streaming. He looked forward into the wind and it became worse. Where were they going? Not back to the club at all, he realized, as she leaned the boat over, carving a long arc south of Lucy Island.

Bruin Bay, it turned out. Although Esther didn't say a word the entire way. She just opened it up and he found himself gripping the seat with one hand, a side rope with the other. Feeling gravity wax and wane under his ass in a hundred cycles. Lifting and settling him with the waves.

When she powered down they were in a calmer, quieter part of the coast than he had seen previously. No other boats or people in sight. The water was deep blue, wind-rippled. The shoreline smooth. They were gliding along the water, the land slipping past, and all was unexpectedly silent.

"Sorry about that," he said.

"Just do this," Esther told him, baiting hooks and stripping off line. She handed him a rod and showed him the simple operation. Raise the tip when you get a strike. Let him run, then reel him back. "It's not rocket science, which is part of the reason people enjoy it. Just relax."

Not much else said beyond that. He let the line trail astern, its action invisible. He considered that he didn't understand what he was doing there, what this girl thought of him, why she would take the time, but that he didn't much care to know the answers either. He just looked out across the water, felt the line trailing beneath him, the weight of impossibly cold water, the heat of the sun above, and tried to imagine himself gliding along an infinite seam that divided everything above from everything beneath. And he achieved such surprising and immediate serenity in this fashion that he was unprepared for the enormous tug from below, his rod bending double, the line beginning to strip off the reel with a mechanical whine. He stood up sharply, alarmed. He raised the rod inexplicably above his head, as if he could sling the fish out of the deep and into the boat in a single heroic motion.

It broke the surface. A coho, she would tell him later, not badly sized either. Revealed in an explosion of water, of fish flesh, out of a geyser ten feet off the boat launching the invisible world into the visible. A silver flash of scales and the matte reflection off a single ovoid eye.

He fell backward, hard. He almost landed on her. Close enough anyway to see her expression of disbelief, concern, amusement, all wrapped up in one glance. The rod leaving his hands and making a splash of its own as the fish took it away from the boat, the length of it skittering across the surface, dancing in the waves, the cork handle bobbing down and shooting up, clear of the water, then disappearing behind the crest, down and away for good.

Ike found him under the covers, lights out, clothes still on.

"What you need is soup," Ike said. "I made some killer split-pea. Come on down to the galley. I'll set you up with a little table in the kitchen, all to yourself. You can cry little tears and no one will see you but the cooks."

"What I need," Graham told Ike, "is for you to help me get out of here."

"So you lost your fishing rod," Ike said. "These things happen."

"It was her father's rod. And it never happens."

"I never said I'd heard of it happening. But it must. Somewhere."

"When's the last flight?"

"All right, it never happens anywhere. You're having an anxiety attack. I have pills."

"I wouldn't have it on my conscience to deplete your pharmacy," Graham said, voice grating through his throat as if it were unfamiliar with this particular route from thought out into the open air. "I want you to arrange a flight for me. I need you to find Dr. Lee . . ."

"The rather unfortunately named 'Beaver' leaves at ten tomorrow morning," Ike said, sitting on the edge of Graham's mattress. "Sleeping as you are in a staff bed, you may be sure they will not bring in the helicopter. You are in overnight, dear. So as they say in these parts, Chill, dude."

Ike went to the galley and returned with sandwiches, soup and a six-pack.

"I don't drink," Graham told him.

Ike winced. "Think of me as a doctor," he said.

"I could do, and you still wouldn't be."

"Think of me as trained in the matter of what people should eat and drink in response to certain situations."

"I've never had a drink in my life," Graham told him.

Ike was incredulous. "Are you allergic?"

"It's a kind of allergy," Graham answered. "A contrary inherited aversion."

"Oh. I had one of those too," Ike answered, twisting free a can of beer and popping the top. "There is a cure."

Not Ike's last trip to the galley either, as they rambled across the topics at hand. On fathers, Graham remembered trying for a comparison. "Imagine you were descended from—"

"Escoffier?" Ike offered.

"Like that," Graham said.

Ike rolled them a joint. He said, "It's possible you take your work just a little too seriously. And Esther. Maybe she goes in for the uncoordinated dweeb. One must be positive."

Something Graham did not feel on waking the next day. Shuffling foot to foot, he waited on the jetty for the

Beaver to taxi over. The plane advanced with painful slowness across the steel-blue water, seabirds scattering from the kelp beds. An Asian man approached wearing a checkered jacket, old-fashioned Ray-Bans and a straw hat. He smiled broadly, leathery cheeks crinkling. He said, "So? Did you have a good time?"

Graham started. Then shook his hand. "Dr. Lee," he said.

Across the small marina, Esther emerged from the dock shack and shaded her eyes, which made Graham's forehead grow cool with moisture. Dr. Lee was asking about Kiusta. He wondered what Graham had learned, and he listened, nodding, while Graham stumbled through a few words of explanation. Something about beauty, decay, the inspiration of dreams.

Dr. Lee had a look on his face suggesting this was just the report he had expected. Then, in the manner of older men the world over, he revealed to Graham that he had a single thing to say—a very particular, premeditated thing—that would not have been affected by any reply Graham could have given to the original question. He waved to the pilot, who cut the engine with that small motion, bobbing in toward the bumpers, the dock kids scrambling.

Dr. Lee said, "Like a lot of people, I admired your father."

Graham opened his mouth to answer.

"But he didn't know what he was doing in the beginning either."

Graham closed his mouth, red-faced. He felt his sunburn, intensely. His headache. The taste of dope and the light fur on his teeth.

"Architects swirl around in a cloud consisting of one another," Dr. Lee said. "Part of a thing called style. Whatever they're telling you at school, that's the truth. Which isn't exactly a bad thing either. You've seen my house? Of course it's beautiful. Real art. But it's one-of-a-kind only if you've never seen the Barcelona pavilion. Or maybe if you've never seen the Villa Savoye or the Farnsworth House or the one Eames built in Los Angeles."

"Case-Study House number 8," Graham managed. "Pacific Palisades."

Dr. Lee nodded across the water in the direction of Kiusta.

"Your longhouses are from before that. From dreams. Sure, why not? I like that. Not too common nowadays. If you have one, a dream that is, I suggest you build it."

He nodded again, his smile now of a different sort. Friendly still, but knowing too. The presence of other information evident. He turned and looked back across the marina. She was still by the dock shack, working on something Graham couldn't make out. But she caught the glance and looked over, waved at Dr. Lee, who blew her a kiss.

"My daughter says you've met," Dr. Lee said.

Graham turned his eyes away from her, looked to the trees on the shore opposite. His bags were in the back of the Beaver. Dr. Lee's hand was on his shoulder, guiding him to the ladder. He climbed aboard and they wheeled out into the bay. He didn't see Esther again for eight years.

"You made a gesture like *this* . . ." he reminded her, holding his hands up. It was a Christmas party, her compact athleticism wrapped now in a midnight blue satin gown, black hair pulled back, lips painted rose. She had been leaned into conversation with the founding partner of a real-estate development company that turned out to be a mutual client. She broke into her own conversation, interrupted herself mid-sentence to beckon him over.

"Esther and I met years ago," Graham explained to the developer. "I'm with Beekman Shiller. I worked on the Palladia Towers."

"Yes," said the developer politely. Graham had never spoken to him before. Never met him, his role on Palladia having been models, 1:120 scale cardboard structures he assembled in a dingy basement underneath the vaulted room where the real architects at Beekman Shiller worked. Fantastically detailed mini-towers that were then surgically altered, portions cut away by X-Acto knife and rebuilt as required by the client or the lead architect or the engineer, Graham meticulously grafting on the new ideas and modifications as they were dreamed up by others.

The developer slipped away to the cigar room and Esther turned her full attention to him. She didn't remember the gesture precisely. She remembered the fishing rod, of course.

Graham shrugged, embarrassed but suddenly determined not to let go of another chance. He told her of a recently broken engagement, a pure fiction, the origins of which he could not place and which he heard coming out of his mouth before it was even something as particular as a constructed lie. There he was bullshitting this pretty girl who he wanted nothing more than to kiss. Her lips, her face. He wanted to kiss each eyelid. Her earlobes. And this face was now upturned as she listened to him intently, expression quizzical.

"I'm sorry to hear that," she said.

He made the perfect face. Stoic but not hard. A man drawing on reservoirs of internal strength that he did not know he had, but for which he was just then grateful. "It's been a year," he said. "Sometimes I think of her, but it's time to move on."

They danced. Twice, and a third time.

"I'm sort of on a date," she said. A journalist. He'd interviewed her for a story. Their first three dates had been related to the article. But pleasant, she reported. He ate well, knew wine.

"We've met," Graham said, smiling widely when they finally went over. Forgetting entirely, just in that moment, that he'd been dancing with the man's date for half an hour.

"Cameron Lark," the man said, his smile thin. "I had the honour to interview your father quite extensively in the year before he passed away. I'm working on a book."

Graham should have followed up on that, but didn't. He merely nodded, sipped his drink and watched Esther make her way across the hall to the ladies room. Lark took a silver box from his vest pocket and used the contents with a discreet sniff and a click of fingernail on pewter. He turned back, the box extended and eyebrows politely raised above what were, on close inspection, revealed to be storm-grey eyes, rimmed by bruised eyelids. Broken veins in the cheeks. He wore a tie with tiny, repeated Ganesh figures.

Graham shook his head and Lark pocketed the box. He said, "Do you suppose I'm at a disadvantage because I don't fish?"

"No?" Graham winced just slightly as if in sympathy. Then, calculating that the evening's break point had arrived, cordiality just that second exhausted between them, he offered to drive Esther home when she returned. She kissed Lark once on each cheek, saying good night and sorry. She was trying not to laugh. It was too ridiculous, this thing that erupted between people, that couldn't be stopped.

Graham had to guess Lark went home to begin his book immediately. It came out in the spring, bound up with many plates of his father's work. Photographically faithful, recording Packer Gordon's passage from early modernism through the glass years and into the concrete 1960s, the brutal 1970s. The return to houses, late. Many of them cedar, untreated, rough to the touch, slung close to the granite landscapes he favoured. Graham stared long and hard at these structures imagined and built by a man of twenty-eight, twenty-nine, then forty, fifty, then sixty. He'd had an entire career of artistry, no labouring in the basement building models for partners who might not remember he existed were it not for his surname. He'd spent his life building a distributed city of structures that by the end—while growing oddly elegant in recent years, holding and releasing shadow in brutal but poetic ways— looked as if they had been conceived in fury, drawn with a pencil held in a clenched fist.

In the text, Lark was famously less restrained, both positively and negatively. No structure touched by Packer Gordon did not tap directly into the very core of what was good and noble and forceful in architecture. No open interior space was not unified, was not powerful. No vaulted ceiling was anything other than a challenge to the limitations of material. No intersection of walls stood merely as the support for a roof beam, but was, without exception, unambiguous, unequivocal and unashamed.

The person himself, hoisted so high on wire-thin ideas, twisted in the wind. The architect in the year before his death had been bloated from a cascade of internal flare-ups and failures, confined to a wheelchair, a black satin dressing gown his more or less constant uniform, a nurse ever-ready to dab his chin and disappear into the next room. No third wife to hover protectively, however, because Gordon had by then no wife at all. Graham's mother having fled, seeking her own survival, and who could blame her? Lark fed on the aging, isolated great. He ate his liver and vomited the result onto his own pages.

Graham read a fair amount of this material. He heard more from others. But it was Esther who actually read the book closely enough to report back that Packer Gordon met Elliot's mother in Korea. "Your brother was conceived in Seoul. Lark doesn't bother saying whether his mother was local or ex-pat. Do you find that odd?"

That Lark didn't mention it? That the summit achievement of his father's infidelity was known so widely? Or was the detail odd by being revealed in only the third week of his own marriage to a young woman of Korean descent?

Esther said it first, kissing him. Holding him firmly and pushing him back onto the bed, putting her hands up under his shirt. She said, "Like father, like son?" Graham remembered the laugh that followed, although not his own response. He might have tried: which son?

Eight

EVERYTHING COLLAPSED DOWNWARD TO A SINGLE
point, to an event, a threshold. The weather shifted, barometric pressure doubled back on itself. Thin grey clouds
shot in from the west, high at first, a vault that mounted
up on the pendentives of North, South, East and West.
Then fell onto the city, after which there was nothing but
fog, like the dust clouds roiling after the collapse of something large and poorly designed.

Graham drove unsafely fast through early-morning

streets. Away from Fila, sleeping. Away from dinner remains, cold in her stainless-steel sinks. Away from everything before, toward everything that followed. Toward the obvious and right thing, finally delivered. Someplace good. It was 5:00 a.m.

The phone call had finally come the previous afternoon. Graham at the top of Victory Square with a salmon in a bag. Her voice was beautifully accented. Cleo Angelopolous.

Fifty times is very much a lot to ring. I think this person must have a lot to say.

Graham stood rooted, struck silent.

Hello. Is Cleo Angelopolous here. Now I phone you and you have no speak?

But he did have speak. He found it all at once. Standing and staring out over the pink square. Speak came out of him in a hurried, anguished torment.

Of course she remembered the camera. She sold it to the television producer. Yes, she had other things too.

What sorts of things?

I have drawings and books.

Film, did she have film?

I have movies of the boxing.

Yes. Those. Hold those. Do not sell those. "I'm just going to dinner now, but I'll come over first thing tomorrow. Name a time."

Fila was sure what it all meant. "Zweigler sent you to find the film. He knew she had it."

Her eyebrows arched high as she ploughed through an enormous plateful of overcooked salmon teriyaki, Graham's fallback position after he'd ruined the mousse by using soy milk instead of cream. She didn't mind. She didn't recognize the flavour from an old bottle of sauce at the back of her fridge. She was sitting at the kitchen island under her own high metal roof—the wind moving, sighing at the sheet-metal joints, breathing down through the tar paper—and she was voracious. Her eyes shone with appetite and certainty.

Now, diving down toward the Middle East, Graham punched the gas and the Boxster exploded from behind a slow-moving delivery van into oncoming traffic, then back again. It was a matter of seconds, only after which he realized that one of the approaching cars had been a police cruiser. Graham gripped the wheel and imagined Rudolph was somehow responsible for what he'd just done. That this car with its silver dials measuring speed and the number of times the crankshaft rotated in one minute—five thousand three hundred just then, unimaginable—was actually in control of events unfolding.

"Why would Zweigler care if I had that film?" Graham had asked Fila.

"Maybe he knows this Cleo person. Maybe they're in on something together."

TIMOTHY
TAYLOR

Far behind him, Graham watched the police car wheel around and speed after him, lights coming closer. Finally blinking right in his rear-view mirror. Red and

blue. Red and blue.

"And now, I've officially had too much excitement and too much to drink," Fila had said, off the stool and coming around the counter. "Ushering in the moment when I go to the fridge for a glass of water, lean over to kiss you and end up putting my tongue in your mouth."

She was so much shorter than he was. He'd never noticed that before. He kissed her, both of them breathing hard. And when her head rolled away to his chest, the heat of her breath hit him at the shirt pocket, right over the nipple.

Working as a couple, working well, Graham and Esther made the sound of industry. They talked in Gant charts. Issues, decisions, timetables. Did Fila make sense, at the moment she did, because in addition to volumes of dark hair and the kind of overt femininity that manifested itself in a bathroom full of moisturizers and scents and oils, she had a tendency to let swing the wrecking ball, to introduce chaos with a quizzical smirk, confident always in her ultimate advantage?

They introduced chaos. They tumbled with it down three stairs to her bedroom, to the cream cotton of her sheets. They were falling. On the bed, this was Graham's sense of things: the swan dive down toward water. Hands inside clothes, his across her stomach and upward, hers onto his hips and pushing down. But both of them plunging.

Not a word was said until afterwards, and then not many. Fila kissing his chest: "Uh-oh. Now we've done it." Her hair wet from sex. She released sweat, it would seem, only under these circumstances, then copiously. Her belly moist, flattened down, slick to her glistening black pubic hair. A neat, wet pelt. Graham's finger traced the clean top edge of it, a waxed and fragrant line.

"That we have," he said.

Then she slept. Quickly and deeply, light snores purring in and out of half-open lips. Graham couldn't. He wasn't drunk. He'd done what he'd done sober. And so he stared at the ceiling for an hour. Paced for another. Watched television with the sound off. Then, just as real fatigue seemed to take him, as he'd drifted down into hypnagogia, an epic explosion. He was thrown awake with such intensity that he thrashed in bed, scraped the knuckles of his right hand raw on the concrete wall above her bed.

"Jesus," he said to the ghosted particles of light that now hung at the apex of the lofted room, something visible at the centre of it. Something that had come apart in pieces and was still there too. The exploded object visible now as something that simultaneously occupied its before and after states. It had clean, square, white lines. It was a big house.

Where should we meet? he had asked Cleo.

Mary Street. Where he lived. Where he keeps these many things. I show you tomorrow.

I went. It looked abandoned. Empty.

Oh no, she had assured him. Nobody living there, but it wasn't empty.

Red and blue. Red and blue. They coasted behind Graham. They drifted around another corner together, the Middle East now opening in front of them. Then they hit the siren. A welp, then a wail. Sounds that articulated an idea quite clearly: *Think it over. You know how this works. I flash, you stop. Failure to do so, on the other hand, will change your life.*

A warning too late. At the crest of a rise, open curb to the right. He could have pulled over. But an impulse came to Graham that could not be resisted. He hit the gas again. Throttled up, red-lined the tach and exploded into Pender Street. Eastbound. Down into the heart of it. Of course they all knew how this worked and understood that their lives must now be changed, forever. The police car falling back a block in just those seconds, the Boxster slewing into Abbot Street, losing its grip on the pavement, fishtailing to the far curb and back, kicking up gravel that whined angrily off a mailbox. And then he was hard on the wheel and the gas again, aiming the car at an alley mouth that loomed out of the fog, a wormhole opening directly into the heart of the Middle East, where a white cube waited for him, floating pristinely above the rubble.

But this image was swept aside, at least temporarily, because here at the lip of the alley, asphalt gave way to old flagstone, period pavers that were slick as oiled ice. And Graham was again struggling to correct a skid. Seven thousand RPMs now as the red needle on the silver dial bounced over to the right and he clipped a utility pole, neatly removing his driver's side mirror. Then found himself addressing a bin and a garbage truck, and avoided both less by skill than by some pure variety of geometric luck. He threaded a needle of space between them leaving only the garbage man himself between Graham and freedom.

And here the eldest son of a famously bad driver had to be credited with remembering a little of the crash-avoidance portion of a high-speed driving course he'd once taken. Because he did not stand on the brakes. Faced with the almost-certain prospect that he was going to hit this man, kill him, Graham went for power and turned the wheel. Not hard over, just a crack. And so he passed the garbage man who was carrying a blue plastic bucket marked for medical waste. Left him standing there in the alley, bowlegged and dark-browed, plucked only the bucket from his gloved hand, thumping it off the left front fender and pinwheeling it up and over the roof in a starburst of hypodermics from the needle exchange. And out of this glittering halo, a streak of Lubetkin blue, heading for the end of the alley.

Gone. Into a new street he didn't know. The police lost behind him. And the fog now lying close, at street level, his view choked. He drove east, the street numbers ticking down to zero, then beginning to count up the other way. He turned north, guided by instinct. Guided by faint memory. He saw the sign: *Mary Street.* He turned down, half a block. He coasted to the curb.

Graham was on the sidewalk, up the steps. No time for caution, he thought. No time for considered action, only the clean impulse. A hand to the doorknob a final time, as if to give the house one last chance to open voluntarily. Then a quick step back and a boot to the thin plywood door in the outer wall. A shuddering crash and splintering door frame.

He was inside the wall. He was staring up the building's sides, even in this poor light a sight that stopped him, froze him with his head back, mouth open. Straight lines, clean corners. White, of course. He could not sort out, in the spilling sense of the moment, how much of what he was seeing he remembered from those years before, and how much of it was striking him as familiar just now. Someplace good. What followed in the sequence.

One more boot required. This one to the frame of the front door, which was also locked, but old. And with that easy movement—the door folded aside, it resigned— Graham was inside. He was moving to the stairs, then spiralling down. It was cold, wet, dark. Dogs barked in the distance, somewhere high above his head and behind him. And there were ghosts here. He could feel them. Ghosts at the bottom of the city.

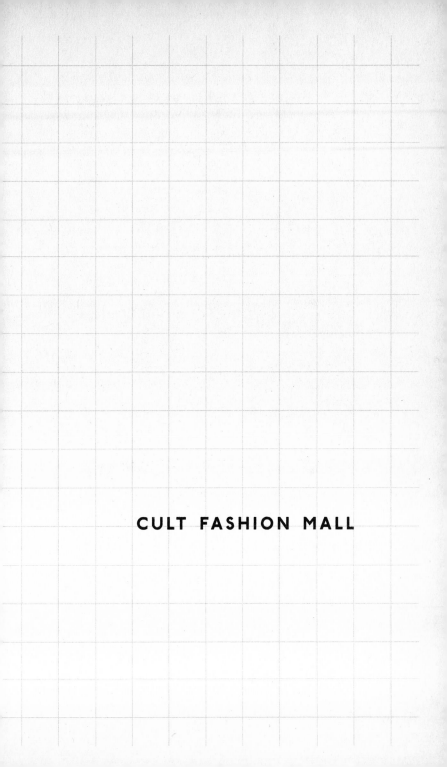

CULT FASHION MALL

One

FIRST THING THAT MORNING, IN CAME KIROV AT
a jog.

Elliot was sipping coffee in Apartment A of the Orwell
Hotel, paging through the ESPN web site. He caught
Kirov in the bank of video monitors his late-boss Rico had
installed back when this had been his work lair. An angu-
lar movement in the uppermost monitor, and there he was.
Transferring himself jaggedly from screen to screen as he
climbed first into the hotel loading bay, moved past the

big packing crate there, then up through hotel's defunct kitchen and into the lobby. Here Kirov disappeared for several seconds as he moved toward the lobby-side bar. Elliot could only hear him breathing heavily. Then his voice, not stating whatever business had driven him out of bed that early, but distracted by the crate instead.

"That box out back is for the Uncles?" Kirov's voice floated into Apartment A from a single crackling speaker.

Elliot shifted his gaze to yet another monitor, anticipating where his friend would appear, watching the man behind the Orwell bar register the question with an ambivalent shrug, a shake of the head. His expression communicated clearly what a crazy goddamn world the box in the loading bay represented. Carpets, as it happened. Ten by sixteen feet, two hundred sinneh-style knots per inch, four silk and four wool. Each in classic Azerbaijani patterns although, of course, not made in the ancient province at all but in a warehouse somewhere outside Seoul. But quite indistinguishable from the real thing, with the sale documents stamped in Iran, the authentic vegetable dyes, the years of artificial wear laid down by some kind of threshing machine, which had taken just twelve hours to beat these carpets back into the late nineteenth century. A very profitable point of origin for a carpet: $2,000 a piece FOB Inchon would reach somewhere near fifty grand once a duped *Antiques Roadshow* appraiser whispered the magic word: *Tabriz*. And that was just what would happen, everybody knew, Elliot and Kirov and the bartender better than most. After which point, nobody would think to ask where the lie began. Nobody would think to shrug and shake their heads and wonder why the hell the Uncles wanted carpets in the first place.

Rico had partners, "investors," as he used to call them. These men owned the Orwell with him and stayed on the scene after Rico left the country, even after news of his massive coronary failure on the beach of Cayman Kai had filtered back through whatever mysterious conduits had carried it. The man making coffee behind the Orwell bar was one of them. There were others who hung out in the lobby on any given afternoon. They helped set up the deal with the crate. They took Elliot's monthly rent cheque. The called him "the kid" and gave him enormous leeway because of how much Rico had trusted him.

On that grainy small screen, the bartender was just now saying, "You rolled out of bed just to come down and ask about the box?"

Elliot sat forward, curious himself. Kirov shouldered into view, blocking the camera.

"Is he awake?" Kirov asked.

"He's been up for coffee," the bartender said.

"Watching?" Kirov turned around, finding the camera in the corner of the lobby.

"Doubtful," said the bartender.

Kirov thought that over. Then his gaze tightened as he engaged Elliot through the cables, the floorboards that separated them. He said, "Mary Street. Someone's broke in."

And here he started in on the story, head still craning upward, but Elliot didn't catch any of it. He was on his feet, in one motion. Out the door with an image of Kirov shifting foot to foot, holding his straw cowboy hat in his hands. A man not known for nerves, now looking distinctly jazzed. A former boxer, Kirov was known more for the strange calm of his sport, a seemingly unwise lack of adrenal response to danger. His reputation built on a tough-guy lineage reported to include three dozen amateur fights, a stint in the Russian navy, then on a fishing boat and finally a shore leave in Vancouver that Kirov decided to make permanent. And if Rico's crew had tended to doubt this story at first, the bartender included, they didn't after Kirov took out a much larger man in the Orwell bar very late, piss drunk. Kirov staggering, outsized. But, when the violence was certain, changing like a blurry television picture set crisp with a twist of the rabbit ears. He came into focus, turned a quarter-turn. Then threw what was simply the hardest, fastest punch anybody had ever seen. A straight right that hit square and disappeared in a pink mist of nasal blood.

Elliot emerged into the lobby. He stood for a second, hidden from the bar.

". . . sky blue Boxster," the bartender was saying, "never seen one of those before."

Kirov: "Left side mirror broken off. You think I make this up?"

"Well, wasn't the place locked? What'd he use to get in?"

"It just occurs to me," Kirov said, "maybe you think people when they break into a place they use a key. Beer please."

The bartender turned to pour Kirov a draft as Elliot stepped into the lobby, catching himself in the bar mirror. He looked a little jazzed himself now. Hair spiking this way and that. Black suit crumpled, an old blue tuxedo shirt half-untucked. A thought invaded: forty years old plus thirteen days. Such precision possible because each of them in the room had been present two weeks prior, right in that lobby, at the surprise birthday party where ten kegs of beer and a guest list of aging punk bands had provided entertainment for a crowd police later estimated at three times the Orwell's capacity. Elliot thought, Forty plus thirteen days and my luck is turning.

He slid onto a bar stool next to Kirov. He said, "Coffee please."

Kirov spinning immediately to face. "Visitors. Mary Street."

"I heard. Junkies? What?"

Kirov scratched his head and thought about next words. Kirov who owed Elliot a great deal, everybody knew. His freedom, his wife, his job (which Rico famously did not want to give him and a point on which he'd only relented when Elliot insisted). Kirov who, twenty years before, ashore without leave on the edge of what the Chinese still called Gold Mountain, could not have known what strange life would follow. Kirov said, "El. It was your brother."

Elliot spilled coffee. Physical shakes fountaining up through him from the pit of his stomach, through his shoulders, down his arms. He struggled the cup back into its saucer, pulled the handkerchief from his breast pocket, wiped his face. And then his hands seemed unable to stop moving, as if performing tasks that his brain had not yet organized itself to assign. Handkerchief to the counter, but not to wipe up his mess. Fingers to the hairline, but not sweeping it back. Then to the inner pocket of his suit, not to extract a cigarette, only to stop there and drum insistently, Morse-coding something directly into his heart.

Finally, out came the smokes. Elliot fumbled one into his lips, cracked his Zippo and proceeded to light the filter, which blackened and flared and spit molten bits of itself onto his shirt front and was finally stabbed out angrily and replaced. All of this in ratchety motions he still didn't quite control. He took a deep drag of the correctly lit smoke, held it for several seconds, exhaled it in a geyser toward the ceiling. His mind exhaling too, a plume of thought escaping.

Then, to the bartender, "Anybody call about those rugs?"

The bartender shook his head, sombre.

"They blowing us off?" Elliot asked, dragging in more smoke. "After all that?"

"They're just late, Elliot."

"No phone call?"

No phone call. But they were just late.

Elliot nodded seven or eight times, vigorously. Hair flopping back and forth. A motion then punctuated by a sudden outburst. "Fuckity, fuckity, fuck," he said, standing. "Bad timing."

Elliot pacing now, thinking, thinking. Lighting another smoke, then stabbing that out too. Standing by the front doors, hands on hips. Staring out into the street through the etched O in the glass. His brain pumping and repumping the same information, coming up with little new.

Kirov tried first. He said, "I'll go back over."

"No no," Elliot said.

"I'll get someone to go," the bartender tried.

"No," Elliot said again, still bouncing from idea to idea. Before arriving, all at once and unexpectedly, at what seemed sure to be the worst one of all. "We call the cops," he said.

The bartender, immediately: "Yeah? You sure?"

"Why not?"

"Because maybe you don't want them going inside."

"Why not?"

"Because maybe they go snooping around."

"And I care about this why?"

"Well, Elliot. Ever since I heard of the place, you've never let anyone else inside."

"Okay. But this is different. They're cops. They're here to serve and to protect."

"Hey, hey." Kirov was smiling, shaking his head, hands up, palms out. "The cops are there already. Canine unit. They put a dog on him."

Elliot turning from the door with this news. Eyes on Kirov. Assessing the reaction and seeing nothing much. Images flashing instead: Graham on a sidewalk, an Alsatian with its jaws clamped around one of his French cuffs.

He came back across the lobby and sat down next to Kirov. He said, "Well. That's really fucking great." Words that introduced a long silence in the lobby of the Orwell Hotel. The bartender now turning away to wipe down the counter, mind no doubt already wandering to other matters: weekend football lines, the pickup on that crate out back which was late now and worth a phone call pretty soon. Business didn't stop for little problems like these, after all. Break-ins. Hopped-up yuppies in fancy rides cruising the eastside looking for pussy or smack or crack, whoever's brother they might be.

And all around the three men, out in the streets around the hotel and stretching away into the parts of the city none of them had the time to visit, a great many sirens could be heard. Cops and robbers. Good guys chasing bad guys. Serving and protecting. So many occasions where the intervention of the police was required, every day, all day. Never once had any of them actively sought help from this source. So they all just listened now, contemplating that large presence just outside those doors.

Kirov broke the silence with an apologetic shrug, seeming to regret the requirement that he make the point that followed. He said, "El, you remember that time we were in Seoul?"

Elliot already shaking his head: "Seven years ago, Kirov. Over half a decade. Long time, old time. Everything has changed."

"Still," Kirov said. "Prophecy is prophecy."

The bartender frowned at that. Everybody around the Orwell knew about the Korea trip; it changed everything. But the prophecy was news.

Elliot didn't offer to explain. He just sat with his head down between his shoulders trying to shake out a flaring pain at the base of his neck. A pain that would fizz upward were he to leave it unattended. Spiral into dizziness, migraine. Force him to lie down.

"Let me find someone to go over," the bartender said quietly. "We'll straighten it out."

No no no.

"I'm telling you, man," Kirov was saying. "That's what this is. The prophecy."

No no no.

"Come on," the bartender said. "Let me."

No no no.

"You might as well face it," Kirov continued.

"Face what?" the bartender finally asked Kirov.

"Face *Seoul*."

Elliot still with his head down. Thinking, I have my measure of what the world can offer. My portion of success, of happiness. I have a wife, kids. Twins even—will I ever be old enough to understand that kind of fortune?

And no particular trouble to speak of at the moment. Getting out of trouble, if anything. Changing things. Right in the middle of goddamn *changing* things for the better and here I can't shake the feeling that I was supposed to see this particular badness coming. Supposed to prepare for it.

Kirov was still looking over at him, but not pressing. It was good, Elliot supposed, that patience was one of Kirov's many underrated skills. Rico may always have bridled at his slow-burn energy, but Kirov could wait for the call. And so—in silence but for the deep inhalation and exhalation of smoke, and the ongoing swirl of sirens in the world beyond the Orwell doors—that's what they all did for awhile.

Two

SEOUL.

Where everything turned out to be either centuries old or invented, crafted and polished to a high commercial gloss sometime within the preceding seven days. It was a city of very long, very wide tensions in this way.

Elliot had looked around a place he'd only previously imagined. He had mused. He'd thought, Something's gonna change.

Here was an invisible river, misty mountains in the

central city. Towers disappeared into the bowl of grey over the old city, the low city. There were soldiers eyeball to eyeball just forty minutes from Taepyungyang, the city's western gate, a place where he stood for a long time feeling North and South, heat and shade, home and away. And another tension Elliot thought he would make something of a speciality: frenzy and calm. For every secret garden, a neon cowboy tipping his hat over an alley doorway in Itaewon. For every fallen gingko nut harvested and roasted by old men who wore gloves against the stench and ate them with melancholic shots of soju, a night market: a galvanized clatter of Mega Commerce, unstoppable midnight sessions of screaming teenaged rappers, vendors and shoppers in their thousands, a seething Migliore fashion tower, fourteen million bowls of dokpukki rice cake served out of a street cart.

1995. The turn. And it was Kirov who brought him there. Kirov of the red cowboy boots and the John Wayne posters. The Russian Marlboro Man of the Vancouver punk scene. He had a lambswool jacket and another one with a powder blue yoke and lemon yellow stitching.

"Beware the Russian who owes you his life," Rico had told Elliot when he learned the two of them were off to Korea. "Especially one wearing a ten-gallon hat made in Cheng Cheng fucking City."

This warning necessary, in Rico's opinion, because there were other parties who might take such a debt as threatening.

Kirov said, "Don't listen to him. In Korea we make good business. And maybe you find something else. Something about yourself you look for a long time."

"I wish you luck and something better," Rico said. And he — a man fundamentally oriented to the vacillations of the thing called luck and therefore disinclined to imagine anything better—was betraying a sliver of emotion saying so.

Elliot found a city of magpies. He hired a tour guide. Min Ju, twenty-five years old. They spent a few days doing the sites while Kirov rustled up meetings with suppliers in Dongdaemun and Namdaemun, keeping in touch by phone calls from the north end of the city where he was staying in a B & B he knew from a previous trip. Elliot was downtown at the Westin Chosun, encamped with all the global business travellers on the Gold Floor. Medical equipment salesmen. A deal team from JP Morgan. Two software geniuses peddling on-line banking and trading systems.

One counterfeiter, mid-reformation.

"What's your business?"

"Clothing. Accessories," Elliot would say over breakfast, eyes dancing away from the speaker always, out over their shoulder and into the thirty-eighth-floor aerial murk. "Import side."

And downstairs, out in those streets, where the breakfast room with its beige linen wall panels and Danish furniture seemed an impossibly distant memory of tidiness hovering somewhere in the clouds up above and behind

him, Elliot saw magpies everywhere, peering at him from tiled rooftops.

"Where?" Min Ju said, swivelling her neck. She never saw one the entire week.

"Right on the corner of the temple roof. Right. Okay. Now he's gone."

Min Ju returned to her tea. The magpie was a lucky bird, she said. If you saw one it meant you'd soon be meeting a person you'd missed a long time.

"Had a fortune cookie say that once," Elliot drawled, having learned that the verbal manglings of the American Midwestern tourist amused her. *"You gonna see an old friend . . ."*

Min Ju did the frown smile, which was (as far as Elliot knew to that point) the only one of her smile repertoire that she would not cover instinctively with her right hand.

"Maybe not old friend," she said, lips touching down on the rim of her cup again for a sip of Double Harmony Chrysanthemum. Eyes drifting shut with the touch of her lips to hot tea, a fragment moment during which Elliot regarded her candidly, the city humming around them.

Under the glass tabletop in their booth at the tea house, a turtle was making microscopic progress across a field of green pebbles. There were snails also, shells iridescent grey, although these creatures did not appear to make much progress in any direction at all.

"What now?" he asked her.

She consulted her list. "You want to see Deoksugung? You should look at this palace."

"I thought we saw the palace already." His own tea smelled of pears. He kept his eyes open while sipping so he might spy the magpie returning to the temple roof, just visible if he lifted his chin toward the high window above their table.

"That was Changdeokgung," Min Ju scolded. "We have more than one palace."

"What do you mean *maybe not old friend*?" He nodded his head toward the glass, toward the unseen magpie.

"I say maybe not old *friend*. Maybe you see someone who is not a friend."

He nodded, sipped. And now it was her turn to regard him without concealing her interest. "You are not a student," she stated.

He put down his cup and began reading the brocade of traveller's graffiti on the plank walls of the booth. One read, I am from Greenland! Nachachip Tea House Rock!

"Rocks," he said to her, pointing out the missing letter.

"You say you come to study Korean ceramics," she said. "Now I wonder."

"What's to wonder?"

"The only ceramics I see you touch is the piece you brought with you," she answered. "The pot you showed me. What is it?"

"The *urn*," he corrected. "I said I was coming over here to study Korean ceramics, yes. You are right. You are also right that I lied."

He wasn't hurting her feelings exactly, Elliot knew that much about her. She had projects, ambitions. She lived with her mother, father, grandmother and grandfather, her brother and his wife and their two children, all of

them in five ondol-heated rooms around a tiny courtyard where a one-eyed mongrel collie-chow cross gnawed on pork bones. She brought in more money in a good week than her entire family could manage in a month, maybe more (Elliot wondered) than all her recorded peasant ancestry combined. Such was the eclipsing power of the new languages she spoke: English, HTML and e-mail. She updated her Welcome to Korean Culture webpage through a PDA that was decorated with a Hello Kitty pendant made of jade. She'd toured around groups of soldiers, business people, the American national karate team, a Baptist youth group. She showed them the palaces and the markets and the Blue House. She brought them all through the family home in a long, stooped, apologetic parade, had them make kimchee with her grandmother, had them pull on traditional dress and sit through a tea ceremony. Min Ju knew the life where work was all. And sensing the same in him just then—this was after a day of the Jogyesa Temple, the Secret Garden, Insadong to look at celadon, during all of which Elliot nodded and processed what he was being shown in a way she didn't associate with the tourist at all—she found herself halfway down a cup of tea with this solitary man from a world many time zones away from her in all directions, the first intimacy between them just then taking hold. And she said to him, "Why are you coming to Korea?"

Of course, Elliot was still sorting out the answer to that question.

"It's expensive," she said. "Elliot hanging at the Westin Chosun. He has money."

"Call it luck," he told her.

She smiled one of the smiles that was entirely covered. Luck? Did he think so? Did he know about luck?

He thought he did.

"I have good luck now," she told him. "I am lucky since I am twenty-five years old. But I have bad luck later, maybe for ten years."

He leaned into the table, feeling the old boards bite his chest in a band across his heart. This was interesting. "Your luck changes?" he asked.

"Everyone's luck changes. My boyfriend," she said. "He has bad luck now and better luck later."

"So you're a good match," Elliot said.

She took him to the fortune tellers by Tapgol Park. Wouldn't take no for an answer, then held his hand crossing Samilron like he might make a run for it. Ahead of them, across eight busy lanes, he could see the tents, canvas flapping in the evening breeze, lanterns glowing on each door post. She made him pick a tent. And he did that using a technique he'd used so often since boyhood that it was now entirely subconscious. He imagined which his brother would choose—the largest one here, with padded chairs inside—then he chose the opposite.

"Ouch, small," she said.

They squeezed their knees in under a kid's play table with moulded plastic chairs. Perhaps this tent was for preschoolers, she never said. The table was, in any case, covered over by the voluminous support documentation of Korean soothsaying, spiral-bound notebooks of some three hundred pages each, a dozen stacked here and another dozen in a bookshelf behind the old man with tar-stained fingers who presided, black eyes nearly invisible behind a neutral squint.

Elliot handed over four items—twenty-five thousand wan, plus the date, time and place of his birth—and, receiving each of these in expressionless silence, the old man commenced to pore over his assembled texts, thumbing through pages gridded with numbers and characters, lists, charts, tables. He slid his finger down one column to find a particular row, which led him to a different page of a different notebook, to another list of numbers, to a single one of these. From there to a third notebook, several pages of which were fanned and refanned, characters plucked and sorted on a separate pad, a new chart growing on the paper beside him, a chart in which numbers were lined up and squared and chewed over considerably before a single word was spoken.

But when the words came, they came in a river. Min Ju listened a long time while Elliot grew anxious beside her. Then, finally: "He says you have worked hard. You have worked harder than others are willing to work."

The old man made new rapids with his words, warm flows and sharp, cold reversals. Min Ju rocked beside Elliot, taking her own notes. Scribbled reminders, questions to be asked later.

"He says you are successful because you work hard, but you are not too happy."

And here the old man paused with a black finger pressed down on some very particular character on some very particular yellow page of a volume he'd plucked out of the apple-box bookcase behind him. He breathed in and out, then—something climbing up off the paper and into his bloodstream, shivering up through platelets and into his brain—he began again at pace, Min Ju now jotting furiously. Falling behind. Finally waving a hand for a break. *Wait. Wait.*

"He says your luck now is good."

The old man didn't look at him, didn't register his relief, even his presence there. He only stared down at his pages, then up at the young girl opposite, focused intently, but with neither enthusiasm nor emotion. He looked, Elliot thought, as if he were computing an especially complicated and arcane variety of tax return.

The old man gestured. He flipped a page. He consulted a star chart. He punctuated his findings with a short movement of his brow and a bronchial dredge action that produced an oyster of phlegm, gusted up and out of the esophagus and deposited daintily into a spent sardine can.

Min Ju: "He says although you are a success, although you work hard and your luck is good, he says you have enemies."

Elliot: "It's true. I do."

"Sssss," the old man said.

"He says perhaps this luck has been for you maybe seven years."

"Maybe ten," Elliot said.

"But he says this is not always the way for you. You were unlucky before, maybe when you were young. Even a boy."

The old man paused during this translation to smoke, rolling a joint of black tobacco, pinching his face down around the first inhale, then disappearing in the grey plumage that resulted. Sweet, swirling inside the tent, gathering in a halo around the lantern.

"He also thinks maybe you were very sick once. Perhaps from your fourteenth or fifteenth year."

"Sick like how?" Elliot asked.

"He just say sick. You went to the hospital and there were doctors. He says you still have effects in your head from this sickness. Effects that return maybe once each year."

Elliot raised his eyebrows. *Not bad.*

"Dizzy spells," he said to her. "Headaches."

"Oh," she said. "Bad?"

He nodded. Fairly bad. Twice a year seemed to be the pattern.

Outside, the wind swept garbage and auto fumes off the elevated road, down across Samilron and into the park, where the trees were bent over with the effort of remaining green. Elliot imagined the tent as a microscopic thing, floating in a great cosmic soup. They made up a fundamental molecule, the three of them. Seer, supplicant and translator atoms held together by glowing gravity, one of the perfect triangles of need around which the human universe was built.

Now the old man was talking again, gesturing, holding a blackened finger in the heart of his dense page of calculations. Min Ju had to stop him to clarify a point, cheeks glowing red in the low light as she bore down hard over her notes. Writing again. The old man continuing, information rolling over them both, Min Ju now waving for another time-out. More questions, a seam knit down between her dark eyes.

"What?" Elliot said, finally.

They ignored him. Min Ju listened and the old man waved his arms wide, shaking his head, smiling for the first time, then sat back with apparently finality, whereupon he reached beneath his chair for the tobacco tin and occupied himself with that separate business, leaving Min Ju to do what she now evidently did not want to do.

"Well, come on," Elliot said. "You have to tell me."

She breathed out. She said, "He thinks your luck is so good this last seven or ten years . . ."

"That it's running out," Elliot said, grinning to relieve her of imagined pressure.

"He worries that you have too much luck now and that it must balance. He thinks that the balance will come. He thinks maybe in less than five years."

Here she scanned her notes, ran a finger to the margin. "He says you are married."

Elliot didn't nod. He didn't shake.

"He says that bad luck may involve your spouser."

"My what?"

"Spouser."

Elliot scratched his chin. "My spouse. My wife, you mean?"

Min Ju nodded.

"Like what?"

"I don't know. He only say problems."

Elliot said to her: "Don't you think maybe he's saying that because we're sitting together here, you and I? If he thinks you're my girlfriend, and that I'm also married, no doubt he figures some kind of bad luck is coming my way."

Min Ju stared at him. "Are you?"

"Am I what?"

"Married."

"No."

"Why don't you marry?"

"Because I don't have a girlfriend."

"He says you're married."

"Does he bat one thousand? Is he right every time?"

Min Ju consulted her notes again, staring down at them for a long time. Then, finally: "He says also that your unluckiness may start because you won't have children."

Elliot began to laugh. The old man leaned forward in his chair, barking several words at Min Ju, who only covered her mouth and didn't bother translating. Elliot shrugged at the old man, who waved a hand at him. Inverted to what you would think he meant, it looked like he was beckoning Elliot to approach, to speak. But the reverse intention was plain.

"This next part is not clear," Min Ju continued. "Strange numbers he does not see often."

Elliot made the same gesture the old man had made, waving in the pitch.

"He wants me to tell you that this is not like fortune telling at an American circus. Korean numerology is statistics. He has collected numbers all his life, gathered them slowly and observed to see that these are the right ones."

Elliot mouthed the words: *Okey-dokey*.

"He is not listening to spirits. He is making predictions based on information about people who have come before us."

The old man was a shadowed face at the back of the tent, obscured in smoke. No animosity in the neutral gaze that now finally rested on him. Old men, Elliot had learned walking many hours with Min Ju through the day markets of Namdaemun and around Hongik, were the least likely to cast disapproving glances at the westerner with the Korean girl they assumed to be his somehow ill-gotten girlfriend. Young men looked at Elliot with open hostility, while young women appeared to busy themselves with other thoughts. Old women assessed Min Ju with frank contempt, but old men merely swept their eyes over the two of them, glanced away and smiled.

But the old man wasn't smiling now either.

"He says that you must be very careful in maybe five years time. Maybe a little more."

Elliot raised his eyebrows and held his hands out in an elaborate shrug.

"Careful because there may be a death near to you."

Elliot faked amusement he did not feel. "My spouser?"

"He says if you are not careful, you may cause this death."

She was nervous, saying it, but the old man continued to smoke, looking at Elliot without judgment or rancour. Not the face, Elliot judged, of someone who messed with you because they could. It was, instead, the face of someone who, if they saw a difficult future, would state the surrounding facts in language of abiding simplicity.

Elliot looked back to Min Ju. "I'm going to kill someone?"

"And now," Min Ju said, her voice wavering a little. "He would like to know if you have any other questions."

Elliot inhaled deeply. He took the old man's smoke into his own lungs, the fumes of the city itself moving deep inside him. Then he let it all out in a string of anxious words. After which Min Ju, thankfully, did not smile, did not cover her mouth even though it must have been entirely obvious that he'd carried these words for years, had crossed an ocean with them, been through customs without their declaration. Waiting, waiting for this precise moment of release. She just repeated them faithfully, giving Korean breath to the longstanding query.

The old man took Elliot's hands in his, twisting them palm up, pressing them to the table. A tar-stained finger tickled the pattern of his creases and sworls, his knowing fissures and epidermal tells. He bent over these tracings for several moments, finishing with a slow circular rub of his thumbs over each of Elliot's fingers, ending with the thumbs, eyes up now and examining Elliot's face without malice before speaking. Min Ju translated in the tone Elliot by now knew well, the Korean words skipping a little ahead, her own repetition in English breathless, scampering to keep up.

He thought that Elliot had a good heart. He thought that Elliot's soul was connected to family and to history. But no, he did not think Elliot's mother was Korean.

"Well, look at you, we know this." Later, Kirov was unimpressed by the old man's ethnographic insight, although he was greatly impressed by the death Elliot was predicted to cause. Kirov breathed out through his teeth. He said, "Now this is interesting. Speaking as your business partner, this is very interesting."

Much later. Two hours. Elliot lost track of time on the way to their meeting. He looped the downtown core in a hard, fast arc. He took a subway, the city sweeping past in flashes, the stops announced with different birdsongs, Elliot watching a young Korean man reading a book in English and thinking for the first time, I don't want to go home.

More of this trip on foot. Down through Cheongjin-dong alleys where they cooked brill over grated barrels and old men sat on upturned plastic buckets drinking bowls of milky maakoli, dishes of dried smelt laid out between them. Down into the Myung dong shopping district and the lights of International Everywhere. U2 pumping out of the bibimbap houses and the Seattle's Best Coffee and the A&W. Shopping tribes in mid-splurge trance out front of the Lotte store, staring up its illuminated sides. Down, past this, into the streets where they did nothing but repair scooters, or fix chairs, or sell pets. Acres of parakeets. Cage towers of dogs. And all the way out and downward through the city, into Dongdaemun in a stunned and expressionless march, Elliot's heavy boots pounding out the cadence of a song from a previous and foggily remembered life. The title forgotten until he was across the street from the stadium, standing under the millions and millions of market lights. And then it came to him: *Thirsty and Miserable.* Here was the night market, just now winding up into its glittering night-long pitch, 10 p.m. and a long night of Mega Commerce ahead, and Henry Rollins was yelling in his ear.

"But perhaps . . ." Kirov was thinking this thing through. "Perhaps is not murder."

Elliot said, "Ah. Manslaughter."

They were up in some old-style boozery near the university where Kirov knew the waiter and the table of ESL teachers across the way. Where he ordered them round after round of berry wine from one of the mountain provinces, a sweet flavour edge coming just over the farmy, botanical underbody of the wine and making it slide down hard.

But that was much later. After important business was done.

Elliot found Kirov down one of the food alleys past a highway of kimchee stalls, a quarter-mile of stainless-steel barrels full of brilliant-coloured, aromatically fermenting cabbage and chillies. Bachelor kimchee. Kimchee with crab, with squid, with roe. Out through the open stalls cramming the Hung-immuno. Chambboug noodles, Chapchae and pajan pancakes. There was an entire city's worth of people eating right there on that corner, standing, squatting, crouching. Somebody selling silkworms. Somebody else with energy drinks: Bacchus-F, Wondi-D.

Kirov said he'd be in the one decorated for Christmas. "All the time, yes? Not just Christmas."

Elliot saw the Santas. He saw the candy canes and the reindeer that had been stencilled on the long clear plastic tent that covered the eatery, the strings of harsh white and blue Christmas lights. Long tables full of drunk businessmen stoking furnaces before a final blast through the poisons of late evening, drunk in clubs, fawned over by girls who would light their cigarettes and stroke their inner thighs just above the knee, or farther upward, in response to gifts, a detail Kirov had learned from his local contacts: DVD players, Palm computers. Electronics were best. But now the Russian just sat and ate contentedly at the heart of all this action, the fringed elbow of his suede jacket nestled against a tinfoil Christmas tree, not conscious of anything other than his food. Shoulders hunched over his plate of dokpukki, con-style. Arm thrown around his beer glass.

"You find out what you want?" Kirov asked him when he sat down, eyes glinting, some inner flame now well lit by afternoon beers and the anticipation of success in the market.

Elliot took soju. Then another. He pressed his partner. Yes, Kirov said impatiently, it had been arranged. He was scraping red chili sauce from the plate into his mouth.

"What do we have?" Elliot asked.

Kirov wiped his mouth. "Name it."

"The shit."

"The shit, my friend. The real thing." Kirov drained his beer and belched gently. "Come."

They entered Dongdaemun. What was this place? It was twelve airports stacked vertically. It was Disney World and St. Peter's Square co-morphed. Forty shopping malls grafted into one another at odd angles. Twenty-five thousand vendors and the entire world of what was available. Everything, everywhere, all the time. Clothing, jewellery, house and hardware. Toy, tool, weapon. Media and the means to play them. Code, of course: games, other, pirated and original. There was a two-storey building devoted to army surplus, another to linens, another to dried fish. And one to buttons. Elliot swirling through this one, impossibly cheered.

"How much for these?" Elliot plunged his hand into a four-foot-deep cardboard box of black coat buttons, each one the shape of a skull.

Kirov lead the way up to a mezzanine devoted to the output of an invisible industry manufacturing the small, gaudy and useless: baubles and beads, doodads and gee-gaws. Boxcar loads of two-penny items that could not be known to exist but to those who squatted here and sold them to wholesalers, perhaps even to them. They worked their way through this plastic glitter and across a catwalk, then down a far set of stairs that emerged outside the building, in an alley. Kirov held up his hand indicating their arrival at a designated spot. Then gestured to the structure opposite: a gleaming white building, cathedric sides slick with new rain. Cellular antennae stretching like spires up from the roofline and into the cloud.

"What is it?" Elliot asked, at last.

And here, Kirov was able to make the announcement that he had been waiting to make. He said, "Cult Fashion Mall."

Four floors of sunglasses and watches, mobile phones and cameras, handbags and designer T-shirts. Everything fake or fake-able. Everything for sale. Everything vibrating with the tension, the excited blood cells, the nervous synapse firings of monied desire. In Cult Fashion Mall, Kirov was telling him, you could bring any item of clothing or accessory the fashion world (anybody in the world) had ever seen, and they would make a copy for you in seven days. And Elliot stood transfixed, listening, looking up. Aware of a rain ballet going on in the streets to his left and right. A dance of flashing bamboo poles that lifted high the blue tarp awnings and scared up a magpie from a hidden perch, winging in so tight over their heads that Kirov flinched and cursed without even seeing it.

Elliot loved Korea, Seoul, Dongdaemun, more that moment than he had loved any place on earth. It converged on him, collecting on the surface of his skin, the air around him blurring with activity. It eliminated any possibility that he could conceive of himself elsewhere. This was the centre, his own if nobody else's. A centre of such intense gravity that it was possible to come out of his isolated self, even if only for a moment, and fully into some new connected version of that same self. Connected to history, sure. To family, why not?

"You know what this means?" he asked Kirov. "We're making our own stuff now. Real stuff. We're not just selling fakes any more, hey, partner?"

Where were they? Right, Hasarang. Mountain-berry wine from the provinces. Sweet and hard. The waiter kept bringing them food, trying to maintain sobriety at the table by the front window overlooking the flowing street. Some kind of salty radish soup. The crispy fish. Carrot pancakes. Elliot was insisting on the old-fashioned Korean drinking protocol Min Ju had shown him. Sleeve touch. Receiving with two hands. Turning the head away while drinking.

"You fall in love," Kirov said, smirking.

It was a heavy-beamed place with lofts where kids were sitting cross-legged, hunched in clouds of smoke and conversation. Kirov knew his way around. He pointed in the direction of the bathroom. Elliot climbed out of the building on some external stairs, into another hallway, this one utterly dark. Through a broken door was a room with a cracked urinal. Overhead, half the ceiling was missing, the side wall angling away and downward as if a corner of the building had been surgically removed. *Matta-Clarked*, he was elated to think, standing, spinning, looking upward. It seemed to Elliot at that moment like the only structure anyone could ever want to build. One turned inside out, one telling the story of having been manipulated like clay before firming into the thing that it was. All other structure, he was certain just then, was false.

Which made him laugh, standing there in the middle of an open room at a urinal. He laughed to hear the place speak in this way. Here he'd come across half a world to his father's mistress-country hoping to hear some kind of statement made and it had only, just then—standing in that negative space full of positive falling water, both his own and that coming down onto him, Korean rain soaking him through to the skin—it had only asked him a question.

"Your fortune teller," Kirov was trying to explain, pouring Scotch from the bottle that had arrived at the table. "He only say maybe you are responsible for this death. But perhaps this is not murder."

"Right, right. Manslaughter." Elliot had sufficiently regained his wits since visiting the bathroom, half indoor, half out, to register that they had changed bars. Now down in a cellar somewhere, falling downward it seemed. Descending through a series of rooms, the walls lined with shelves of old vinyl that a DJ was spinning on a lo-fi portable turntable. Boston at the moment. It would be KISS pretty soon, Kirov having shouted the request. *Destroyer! Destroyer! Flaming Youth!* The place was seamed out, overflowing.

"A person you have not known a long time," Kirov said. "Someone you miss, you look for."

Elliot nodded sagely.

"And you cause this death. But is not murder. What is that?"

Elliot took a drink, staring at Kirov over the rim of the glass.

He didn't remember when they finally arrived at the answer to Kirov's question. Not in the cellar bar, that much he knew. Not in the techno dance cube up in

Hongik, where Kirov insisted they go next, where Elliot sat in a stupor at the mirrored bar and watched the dancers in reflection, green glow ropes making circles and figure eights. He hated techno. Not in the little six-seat home-kitchen restaurant up in Jongno-gu either, where they ate a plate of barbecued pork with a dipping sauce and drank a litre bottle of Tsingtao between them to rehydrate, to sober up. Where the proprietor reminded Elliot of Min Ju, hard on the job at three in the morning. Hard on the job whenever it was required.

Kirov was in love with his wife and very drunk, so he talked to this woman like she were a cellular link through which he could speak directly to the one far away.

Someone you have missed a long time.

Kirov didn't need magpies. He spoke directly into the woman's eyes, not looking at her face or her bare arms or her hair or waist. A sobering Elliot saw amusement in those eyes, but no unkindness. Her lips even lifted at the corners in a silent laugh at the nonsensical bit of Korean love doggerel Kirov produced just before it was the obvious time of morning for a final bill, for hotels and bed. When Elliot tried to remember later where the riddle had been answered, he thought of Kirov at that kitchen table, tapped into love and oblivion simultaneously. And he didn't think Kirov would have uttered the answering word right there.

Later then. Somewhere. On the sidewalk, maybe. Through the years, Elliot could still hear it distinctly, Kirov rasping through the last of their cigarettes, Kirov saying, "Who did you come looking for? Not your mother. Not Vuitton, Gucci. Pah. You look for yourself."

Kirov trapped Elliot heavily to his chest with arms muscled from years on the fish boats, then in waterfront warehouses, then in the alleys at the thrown-open doors of truck-mounted containers with arduously deceitful manifests. Wherever there was heavy lifting, muscle, wherever there had been necessary lying or force, there had been Kirov. This man who owed Elliot his life. This man who now gave Elliot a kiss on both cheeks and said the words, which came out sounding like the very least that could be offered.

"Then, if you cause this death and it is not murder," Kirov sobbed into Elliot's ear. "Perhaps is suicide. Sorry. I'm Russian. You know this."

Running down through the early-morning streets in a cab, the light just rising. Kirov long in his B & B bed. The owner treated him well, he said, let him come in late. Although Elliot could imagine different motives. What if one had a lover in a faraway city? What if one had lives that opened onto other lives? Kirov could be such a man. His father was, of course. Long-lost Graham, he had reasons to suspect, was part of the same club. Perhaps only Elliot himself—who intensely loved each of the women who had rejected him over the years, wrote their names on his skin, carried lockets of hair— perhaps only fools of his kind had lives returning always to the solitary centre.

He let his hand fall on the urn, riding now on the seat beside him. It was a smaller thing than many people would have expected for the purpose, only about twelve inches high and six or eight inches in diameter, inlaid all over with the intricate pattern of black on grey on white that he associated with the finest of the form. The thing itself very real too, not fake although it would have been easy to copy. Elliot could picture the factory in Guangdong where such a thing would be crafted, then buried for a week or two in soil adding a century of artificial age. Harder with the contents, naturally. That texture, that very specific weight would be difficult to counterfeit even if it did seem to shrink and lighten in his hands in the elevator down from the Gold Floor.

"Yongjugol," he said to the taxi driver, and they were off, his thoughts streaming forward and back. Kirov. Take the Russian, another great lover. Perhaps he'd come here and found it a suitable place for the keeping of secrets. Perhaps he felt, after all, that one wife at home was not enough. Perhaps he felt that his wife—her name was Lucille Ball, no joke, and she'd been critical in the project of keeping Kirov in the country—was not important enough to hold him in a single life. Because when they had one woman, one life, these lovers, were any of them ever satisfied?

The taxi was speeding through the thin traffic at that in-between hour, not early or late, out the elevated road, past the night market, the city spread darkly around them. Then down an exit and around a bend and immediately slowing to a crawl as they came into the red-light district. A long corridor of sheet-glass windows. Girls parading, preening, advertising. Cars trolling this line, windows down. Elliot found himself short of breath, breathing deeply to make up a deficit. Impossible not to think of Min Ju and Kirov, his own father and brother, even of the man at Dongdaemun who smiled and said repeatedly, *Yes, yes. The real thing. We make you the real, real thing. You like Gucci loafer?*

They flooded his head. They spurred him on. They said, You want to be connected to family and history, then you'd best take a good look at yourself. The urn just now jostling at his elbow as if it too wanted to get off, get out.

"Pull over," Elliot said. Once and then again, louder. Finally gesturing with his hands to the driver who, although cordial and attentive, could not be faulted for failing to understand Elliot's phrase-book Korean at that dwindling hour.

They were stopped. They were here. It was his hand on the door handle vibrating with the awareness that something was going to change.

Elliot thought, Well, better get on with it then.

Three

THEY WERE LATE BY AN HOUR, BUT THE UNCLES did show up for that crate eventually. Elliot and Kirov went back when they heard the truck and found a black Durango pulling a twelve-foot U-Haul trailer parked at the loading bay. Two men in the front were eyeing the crate with cool detachment. "These the goodies?" one said to Elliot, out the driver's window.

"Those are your rugs," Elliot said. "Maybe you want grandfather clocks next. Rare English porcelain. Whatever your man says."

The driver smiled. "That's the idea."

Not their official name: Uncles. That was just what you called them if they were on your side for the moment. Otherwise, they were a motorcycle club involved in various commercial activities. And they didn't wear colours either, like those high-profile outfits the media love to cover. Never the denim vests with skulls and snakes except at weddings and funerals, that was the rule apparently. And no big gang runs into the hills either. No small-town takeovers. None of that movieland crap. Most of these guys didn't go for Harleys at all, but custom handmade quarter-million-dollar jobs that they wouldn't take around the block without an insurance rider. For actually getting from one place to another they drove SUVs like everybody else in the burbs where they lived. Their kids played soccer. Their wives were in book clubs. These two in the Durango arrived in matching golf shirts from some private fishing club they were always talking about.

"I don't get that part of it," Elliot once said to Kirov. "Fishing is fine. Rico used to fish. But the clothes. What are they, accountants?"

To which Kirov responded with a facial expression Elliot knew so well he could see it with his eyes closed. A head shake, a shrug, arched eyebrows, then a collapse of the features to the precise position they'd been in before. This quintessentially Russian facial dance meant, Who knew anything anyway?

Kirov helped lift the crate into the U-Haul. Nobody paid anybody. Nobody opened the box. Nobody noticed the sirens, still swirling. Coming close, then filtering away into the noise of the city. There was a quick handshake at the end of it, between Elliot and a man previously hidden behind smoked glass in the back seat of the Durango. He popped open the door when they were ready to go, stuck out his arm. Silk shirt. Slim neck-chain with a box wrench charm.

"Thanks," he said.

"Don't mention it," Elliot said.

And they were gone. Kirov and Elliot wandering back up to the Orwell bar. The lobby settling back to its regular formerly famous self. Dust hanging, smelling of cleaning products. All of it, undeniably, releasing pressure with the successful completion of the transaction.

Such changes, Elliot thought. When Rico had been in charge, in what Elliot still thought of as the glory years, the customer base had been strippers and their boyfriends. Gangbangers of no particular renown. A cash-rich slice of the economy with a simple consumer mindset, really. They wanted the biggest, gaudiest, fakest-looking monstrosities available. Ten bucks for an enormous pair of Gautier sunglasses with rhinestones that popped out if you looked at something too hard. Or that blue-faced Rolex Presidential, like someone was going to glance down at the wrist of this skinny chick in tiger tights and figure her for a thirty-thousand-dollar wristwatch. The thong-line and thigh-highs would have tipped them off to the basic scam.

"Consider," Rico had said at their very first meeting, long ago: 1984. "Consider the luxury retail rule of eights. Consider specifically *this* shit."

Rico was holding up a pair of expensive sunglasses that had been in one movie, then a half-dozen movie star tabloid shots, then more recently wrapped around every second glistening face going up Oscar's red carpet that year. A few months after *that*, the streets were lousy with a not-bad Taiwanese copy of the same thing. In Elliot's memory these were Ray-Bans, but they could have been any brand at all.

"The luxury retail rule of eights," he repeated.

"One-eighth is the cost of goods sold. You know COGS?" Rico winced from some unspecified pain as he poured them each a choker of Jack Daniel's. "Salut. No? You don't know accounting at all? Business? Banking?"

Elliot banked his money in three ammo boxes that somebody had left behind when moving out of the room he now rented in a house on Jackson Street. Green aluminum canisters precisely the dimensions of paper currency, with latching lids and waterproof seals. They were hidden in a crawl space at the back of his bedroom closet. The right-hand one was savings. The middle one was for immediate use. The left one was full to the brim of not-bad counterfeit twenties he'd made as a thirteen-year-old kid on the colour copier in his father's home office. Having measured the depth of those boxes and done the numbers, Elliot knew that one would hold about $50,000 in twenties and a quarter-million in hundreds. Excluding the fake stuff, he was therefore able to eyeball his holdings at about a thousand in cash. Such was the rudimentary nature of his accounting system.

"I studied history," Elliot said, answering Rico. "Is Cost of Goods Sold the sale price?"

What it costs to buy the stuff, Rico explained. Key distinction. "So one-eighth is what you pay for some moulded plastic, a couple of screws, a bit of polarized whatever. One-eighth is shipping costs. One-eighth is marketing. Meaning?"

Elliot sensed that no answer was better than a brash wrong one. "Check," he said.

"Okay, hustler, I'll tell you. The five-eighths remaining are retail markup and every last dollar of that is captured here . . ." Rico pointed a trembling index finger at the logo of the sunglasses. He looked about equal parts pissed and pleased doing so. "And anything where over half the value is captured in a nickel-alloy-stamped thingamajig the size of a booger isn't *illegal* to copy, it's a moral fucking *imperative* to copy. This thing is insulting you. It's check raising. It's doping the off-pace horse. It's leading right. And I just have a hunch that you understand this better than . . ."

Here Rico lost the rest of his sentence in a misty explosion of coughs only covered with a handkerchief after a great struggle with the pocket of his bathrobe. But the point was made.

Elliot considered it a long time, back home in his room, ammo boxes out. Piles of counterfeit twenties arrayed around him, $1,200 worth. He knew this exactly because he remembered that of the $1,500 he'd printed off in his father's office that afternoon, the garage in Horseshoe Bay had agreed to only $300 for the black Plymouth Fury.

"You drive a hard bargain—'59 is a good year," the mechanic said. Then, money safely in hand, he added very seriously, "Although this vehicle may not be suitable for longer trips."

Elliot didn't care how long the car ran, provided it got him home. Provided he could get it into position at the top of the driveway and have it leak a few quarts of oil onto the concrete by the time his father and brother arrived back from Hawaii. He had only their arrival in mind the entire time those bills flicked out the end of the printer and he shaved off the excess paper in the big flatbed cutter. The entire time the bills tossed in the clothes dryer with a bucket of garden gravel like he'd read the pros did it.

But he never got the reaction he was after. Graham took a tanned, smug expression on into the house. And it was a momentary reversal to think that he couldn't have given his brother a better homecoming present: a dumb-ass act of rebellion for which he was, judging from his father's expression, about to suffer at length.

Not immediately, however. Packer Gordon didn't do anything without getting his shirts out of a suitcase and onto hangers first, having a drink. Two hours, three hours later, he came down looking for Elliot. They drove the car back over to the garage after all was known of the escapade, the fake bills, the fake driver's licence. His father seemed remarkably unaffected by the proceedings as he led Elliot into that dusty front room of the gas station with the Ridgid Tool Girl calendar and the humming Coke machine. He seemed entirely calm asking for his son's money back, pointing out that Elliot was a minor. And then, his father suddenly seemed to Elliot quite a bit more than just calm and unaffected when the mechanic's grease-stained fingers went sheepishly into the till and Packer Gordon asked for the money back in fifties.

They never discussed it a word further. The bills went into his father's pocket and when Elliot opened his mouth to say something in the taxi back to the house, his father cut him off with an unrelated question: *You like Chinese?* Leaning forward, redirecting the driver with a few words. They turned around. They crossed town. The entered a part of the city Elliot had never seen before.

Low neon canyons with pink and green and red Chinese letters. One sign with an enormous rice bowl, steam swirling upward in a neon plume. One fantastic streetscape after another, then another, then they were in an alley, at a bright green door. Through that was a steamy, cramped interior of smells, staggeringly new. Elliot stood gaping, breathing it in, watching his father greet the owner, joke with a cook, hand the menu back to the waiter with a broad smile. *Bring us whatever you have tonight.* All of it, precisely because it was alien, unconnected, distant from anything he knew about them as a family, about himself as his father's son, about his father himself, all of it a huge and surprising source of relief.

Kirov had something on his mind. Elliot could tell from the way his foot danced on the bar rail, from the way he swivelled back and forth.

"Go," Elliot said eventually.

"We just forgetting all about Mary Street?" Kirov asked.

"I'm not forgetting."

"Your brother inside. Cops on the scene. With a dog. Did I mention the dog?"

"What am I supposed to do?"

"Go over. Make sure he doesn't get into trouble."

Kirov knew this much about Graham: what he looked like. And that much from a possibly out-of-date photo Elliot had shown him once, saying, "If for any weird, strange, impossible-to-explain reason, you ever hear about this guy being down in the neighbourhood . . ."

So now he pressed, like his conscience wouldn't allow him to sit still while the blood relation of his best friend might possibly be in trouble.

"Forget about it," Elliot said. Because protecting Graham was pointless anyway. If trouble were in store for either of them, it was already on the way. Already imminent.

"Huh," Kirov said. "I always wanted a brother."

Elliot made an impatient motion with his head and hand. Back off. And Kirov did.

Then Elliot went home. Not downstairs to Apartment A, but back to his real home where, he was painfully aware, he hadn't been spending enough time lately. This was the unpredictable effect of Graham veering close again. Graham downtown, Graham in Mary Street, Graham down in the basement, looking through the wreckage that remained there. These images collapsed down into a pointed imperative. Elliot wanted out the other direction.

He powered back across the bridge toward Deep Cove. Out the winding cliffside road under the lower reaches of Seymour Mountain thinking, as he often did on this particular stretch of pavement, how close he was to the wilderness right there. A long, rolling shoulder of green and ice and snow he'd only ever seen once, on a float-plane trip Rico had taken him on near the very end of their acquaintance. Right before Rico left the country. They'd gone up the coast, set the plane down on a glacial lake an hour by air to the closest concentration of people larger than a gas station. Six hours by foot to a highway if you didn't die of hypothermia or bears. Rico had thrown a line in the freezing water, produced a joint, then a bottle of wine they passed back and forth. The ocean stirring somewhere down to the west, a sense of the edge of the continent falling away.

"I'm going to miss trout fishing," Rico said when they talked about his departure. They were standing on that perfect miniature beach, a half-moon of sand and pebble from which a turquoise and emerald bowl spread in all directions away from the water, all the way up to a ridge line that seemed to crumble at the rim.

Elliot remembered asking, "This an old volcano?"

And Rico wiped his mouth on his sleeve and said, "I love this place. I've always loved this place. But I haven't the faintest fucking idea."

RIP Rico. Elliot sent the thought out the truck window and up over the ridge to where, even if it were thousands of miles from where he actually died, Rico's soul must surely have wended its way back by now.

"I ever tell you about the time Rico took me up the coast in the plane . . ." Elliot said to Deirdre, climbing down from the truck and standing in the driveway.

She was standing in the middle of the front lawn, eyes shaded with one hand, staring up at the facade of the house. "You're home," she said, without turning around.

"I ever tell you about that lake we went to?" he said. Then, watching her: "What's up?"

"In the Coast Range. You've told me several times," she said, still looking up. "I think I'm going to paint the house."

"Wow," he said, coming up behind her, sliding his hands onto her hips. Leaning forward to bury his face in the wave of her red hair.

"Seriously," she said. "You. Home."

"A little break in the action. Just wanted to see you all. How're they doing?"

She turned in his arms. "We're fine. They're upstairs with Malaya. Tell me you're okay."

Elliot took her by the shoulders, pushed her away just to the right distance, then kissed her on the mouth. "I'm okay," he said finally.

"You're not having a thing?" she said, hand to his forehead.

No. No dizzy spell to report. No clamping sensation around his skull as the headache took hold. And he knew better than to try to hide such an attack. Once had been enough, driving together into town. (Before the kids at least, just the two of them.) But Deirdre let him know very clearly what she thought of having to wrestle the steering wheel out of his hands and guide them onto the shoulder of the highway, her leg stretched down between his and hard on the brakes.

"You have never been to the doctor about this," she said. "You must be joking."

Of course he wasn't joking. So she made him go that same day. Which meant waiting an hour. And by the time he got into the examining room he really only wanted to know one thing. "Maybe twice a year," he said, answering one of the many, many questions incoming. "But what I really need to know . . . sorry, I gotta ask it this way . . . can these things kill me?"

These things. Well, the doctor said, sudden onset dizzy spells or migraines were fairly typical sequelae of head trauma such as you might sustain getting knocked out in a boxing ring. And no, you wouldn't expect such an episode to represent any kind of fatality risk. "Unless," the doctor said dryly, "you happen to be piloting an airplane when it happens. Scuba diving. Then you might have a problem."

Elliot went upstairs to look at the babies. They were fine, just as she had assured him. Sleeping. He hovered over them in the dim light of the nursery Deirdre had created in the wide room under the south-facing eaves. Huey, Dewey or Louie had been Elliot's name choices.

"Donald Duck's nephews, very nice," Deirdre had said. "We're not nicknaming band members. Besides, what if one of them is a girl?"

"Dewey. Or Louie. Louie could be a girl."

"Louie could not be a girl."

Which was academic anyway. Boys they were. Hugh and Louis. Born at 2:10 a.m. and 2:12 a.m. After thirteen hours of labour, they just filed out. Why no Caesarean? Because Deirdre was the woman he had fallen in love with and married. The one who sussed the strength of her twins to be extraordinarily high and requested medical dispensation that they see first light the conventional way. Elliot—who had never wanted kids until the moment she became pregnant, then had intensely—had to be helped through the resulting experience by a rather more patient nurse than he deserved. He who stalked up and down outside the nursing station and demanded action on every conceivable front.

"I am," he announced around midnight, voice quavering, "freaking out here."

"Try not to," the nurse suggested, steering him by the elbow back into the delivery suite.

Deirdre did her own job virtually solo. No epidural, which kept being offered at the moment she thought the end was in sight. No massage either, because Elliot had missed all but the last ten minutes of the first prenatal class. He rubbed her and she kept saying, Uh, honey, you're hurting me. But never getting mad.

"Just talk to m—" Deirdre began, then disappearing into a wind tunnel of pain, her cries blowing around them both and driving Elliot's head onto the sweat-soaked pillow next to his wife of two years, dredging out of him the answer: "I am so lucky you said yes . . ."

Deirdre responded sixty full seconds later as if there had been no interruption. When that utterly strange calm that lay between contractions had been restored, she looked up off the pillow, smiled weakly. Said: "Really, where the luck came in was meeting me in the Postum Diner that time because it was touch-and-go whether I'd let you sit down . . ."

Well, yes, he thought then, lucky indeed. Just as the pain returned, his forehead went back into the pillow next to her ear.

And yes now still. Standing over the miraculous twins. Aware again how the real beginning of luck in his life—defying the Tapgol Park prophecy, returning to him the right to expect good things of his life—was standing right in the doorway behind him. Watching him kiss a finger and touch each of their foreheads in turn. Watching him not at work on a weekday for the first time in their eight-year love affair. Wondering, just maybe, in what new direction Elliot's attention had been distracted.

He had never told her about the magpies, the prophecy, any of it.

Of course, when they first met he'd been back from Korea six months already. So much had changed by then, that part of the experience sank away beneath the surface and out of sight. There was the whole business with Rico, not what he'd been expecting. They'd been working together since 1984, eleven years at that point. And even though Elliot understood that setting up on one's own involved a certain disruption of the pecking order, since Rico was leaving the country anyway, Elliot reasoned it didn't matter much. It did, apparently.

Learning this, he didn't go to see his boss on returning. He waited until he had some product to show that his decision had been the right one. That waiting period, involving as it did the unstoppable engines of commerce that rumbled beneath the decks at the Dongdaemun Cult Fashion Mall, was precisely seven days plus shipping.

Kirov phoned on day seven. He said, "We are FOB Inchon."

Free on board. At sea. Two thousand units safely tucked into a container otherwise manifested for plumbing supplies. Elliot said, "Bon voyage." All was in order then.

He packed a joke gift for Rico. He had cases of old product in the basement of the Deep Cove house he'd just bought, across the Burrard Inlet from the city. He browsed and selected an original fake Rolex Oyster Perpetual, a pair of ersatz Oakley sunglasses, a DOA T-shirt (*Something Better Change*), a "signed" Scotty Pippen Chicago Bulls jersey authenticated by something called the Sports Memorabilia Merchandising Association of North America. Finally, a knockoff Swatch from the very early days that had sold rather poorly, having come in from the supplier misspelled *Swach*. He filled a shoebox with these items, one from each generation of a long partnership, then carried this upstairs and out into the misty afternoon.

For all the years Elliot had known him, Rico had worked out of Apartment A at the once-famous Orwell Hotel. Once famous, that is, in the early 1960s, when it became briefly the slum joint of choice for a certain class of visiting lounge act. There had been Vic Damone and

Robert Goulet sightings. Buddy Greco once. And most celebrated of all, an evening when Sammy Davis Jr. had shuffled through a three-song set on the brown marble surface of the lobby-side bar. Of course, as happened widely on the downtown eastside over those years, the Orwell slid from baroque to decadent to shabby and kept going. By the time Rico bought it, along with his cadre of "investors," it had descended to derelict, the walls alive at all hours with the sounds of the sex trade. Wall banging, anguish, violent climaxes.

Rico bought the hotel and put an end to all that. He evicted every tenant and leased the suites to a non-profit organization housing mental patients on independent living stipends, the rents paid directly to Rico by the government. There was still plenty of screaming coming out of the walls, still enough stormy tenant encounters in the ill-lit hallways, but none of this activity came close to what had been worst about the business of sex for pay: a simmering, endemic, predictable anger. Madness better suited Rico's taste. It was random. He lived quietly at the centre of a swirling storm of mood and temperament, unmoving, unchanging.

And invisible too, if he liked, which was the signal feature of Apartment A. The hotel itself, naturally, wasn't hiding. To find the Orwell you merely had to paddle the floating wreckage of Hastings Street to the very lowest number, 1 East. (There was no 0 and the street numbers started at 3 going west, for some reason lost in the dust of civic planning history.) Entrance to the hotel, likewise, not a problem. But if Rico wasn't at the bar, finding him became a challenge. Certainly none of Rico's hangers-on would help you. Elliot remembered this from his own first visit, a meeting Rico had requested, no less. Whoever was working the bar that day conceded only in pointing a thick finger at the blank door of the elevator.

This elevator, as it happened, had been condemned years before. Inside, it was festooned with officially stamped, sealed and multiply-signed documents enthusing along a single, easily teased-out theme. Great ruin (the papers promised in aggregate) to any person who used this device for the purpose of travelling from floor to floor in the Orwell, and possibly more so to any who encouraged or facilitated or even failed to physically prevent its usage by others.

Still, Elliot didn't have much of a choice.

Which is how he learned his first lesson about the very important man named Rico and his position at the invisible hub of the city's import fake trade in those years. Because if you took the creaking elevator from the lobby down a floor (Apartment A, Elliot reasoned, would lie near the foundation of things) you found only the unused basement. Here were boxes, cobwebs, a broken soft drink machine, exposed beams and cables originally laid in the 1920s, rodent spoor.

But if you tried going up one level, carefully inspecting the plunger-style floor buttons to make sure you weren't missing one, then riding up with eyes pinched shut as the elevator shuddered and banged up the shaft, you found yourself on the first floor, where the tenant apartments began. Here the numbers began counting at 101, 102, 103 and did not look back. Search as you might from here on up to the rafters—six distant floors above, each echoing with disembodied voices—and you would find no Apartment A. No Rico. Knock on doors, pose the question to as many blankly staring or animated or fearful or threatening faces as you would encounter. Nothing.

But if you took the elevator down to the basement a second time—Elliot's plan, in fact, had been to find a rear exit and avoid going back out through the lobby entirely—if, when you got there, you noticed and followed a faint but distinctive odour (dog, tobacco, takeout Chinese and urinal cakes) you would find at the rear of the basement, past the drink machine, a narrow steel door that opened out onto the bottom of a steep flight of stairs.

Originally intended to serve as a fire escape, these ran up and down the rear of the building inside a shaft of heavy wire mesh that had been welded in place sometime later. The mesh made the stairs useless to anyone escaping a blaze. And the fire department didn't bother about it much any more after the first time they came nosing around and discovered Rico's Rottweilers sleeping on the landing. Dogs no longer in their fighting prime, but who remained very convincing growlers. Anybody in any kind of uniform—policeman, fireman, mailman or pizza delivery guy—caused their sleepy features to disappear into a rictus of jowl and yellow teeth and glistening saliva.

Elliot nearly stepped on these dogs the first time he visited Rico. He was on top of them before seeing them, rounding the stairs, a grin spreading across his face

because here was a doorway. And it came to him in a fully three-dimensional flash: a plan and a section of the building showing, as it would from only this particular angle, what could be described in a generous frame of mind as a mezzanine. A dark, low-ceilinged slice of the building, suspended between the basement and the lobby floors, with no access but for this single hidden door and an adjacent window almost entirely obscured behind satellite dishes and pirated inbound cables.

The dogs rose to their feet in unison, fixing Elliot with the bloodshot eyes he would very shortly learn they shared precisely, uncannily, with their master. They began to drool, lips pulled back, and produce a sound that—appealing to some prehistoric code in a previously unknown part of Elliot's cerebral cortex—caused his entire body to flood with manic energy. Cornered, with no escape route, he felt himself swell. He was engorged with blood. His fingers thickened, his arms bulged, he took a step not backward but toward the dogs, aware only when he heard Rico's door burst open that he himself had been snarling.

"Jesus," the man said, looking at Elliot, impressed, which was rare. And then, as the dogs shrank off back behind him to circle and yawn and paw the landing in preparation for further sleep, Rico added, "But Kirov said you was a killer. Said you took a two-by-four across the head for him, although I can't imagine why anyone would do that."

It wasn't voluntary, Elliot tried to explain. But some impression had been made and could not now be diluted. Rico beckoned him into the front room of Apartment A. Elliot having at that time only a dim appreciation of who this character in the black jeans and the paisley bathrobe might actually be. He knew Rico was a bookie. A man with some local power to summon and to change lives. He knew also from Kirov that Rico was an importer of some profitable good, vaguely concerned that this could be heroin, but trusting an internal voice that said even Kirov in a desperate frame of mind would know enough not to get them involved with smack.

"We need work," Kirov had said to Elliot. "Here is a man who can give us work."

"Why don't you go ask?" Elliot wondered aloud.

"Because he doesn't like me. There is this problem. But he doesn't know *you*!"

"Great. Good thinking, Kirov. Do you even know what this man does?"

"Business!" Kirov said. "You always say you want to get into business!"

The fact that Elliot relented, went down to the Orwell that day, had nothing to do with any expectation that Rico would change his life. He only hoped for something better than another false start, which by 1984 he was in danger of assuming by default. Life had the shape of a thing you tried hard to modify, for its own good, and which would only spring back immediately and sulkily to its original shape. Take university, which he'd quietly gone about entering after leaving home. Having landed on Jackson Avenue, in a house rented out by a band who practised and argued and drank in the basement or the backyard, Elliot chose Simon Fraser University. It was closer than the University of British Columbia, where Graham also happened to be studying architecture and trying to become their father. But Elliot went that direction—due east over the working-class stretches of the city instead of west into its most exclusive enclaves—because, as a matter of happy coincidence, his roommates played SFU gigs from time to time. Elliot could make $10 an appearance as roadie, close to a week's rent. Which was not bad.

The plan simply hadn't worked out. Not the house, leaning, mouldy, rat-friendly as it was. Not the roommates either, who actually went on to accomplish fair-sized things in the then-burgeoning Vancouver punk scene. Forced to recall the band's name, Elliot would tell you. But otherwise he stayed mute on their association. But the university, the study, simply hadn't taken. No matter that he was plenty smart enough. No matter that in the shortened year he lasted he impressed one history professor enough to ask him if he would consider graduate work. (The paper that provoked the comment had been on Armand de Richelieu, 1602 to 1622. A twenty-year passage of the great man's story that stretched back from his appointment as cardinal to his first entrance into the priesthood, a decision Elliot posited as having been made at the behest of his mother and only because Armand's brother Alphonse, originally intended for the role, had rendered himself useless by going mad. "The brother angle is interesting," the professor told him. "I'm not sure I've heard it put quite that way before.")

But university failed him, drove him away, because that's where he was when he learned of his father's death. Sitting in the back row of an economics course he was auditing, about seventeenth-century mercantilism. Someone passed a note in. His mother was in the hospital, asking for him, it read. A choice of wording that caused a kaleidoscope of possibilities to fan through. His real mother? No. His stepmother? Possibly, although why would she want him?

His father.

Elliot remembered his departure from university as a series of steps. Up out of the chair, letting the writing desk slap angrily home. Out into the hallway. From there to the street, where it was a brilliant, brilliant day. High sky and sun and cloud. Views. Gulls. From there to the funeral (these steps, separated by days, lived as a sequence in memory). There Elliot kissed his stepmother and retreated into the back of the church, looking around for the body, finding that it was burnt to powder already, sifted into a grey ceramic urn the pattern of which rippled under the tips of his fingers in the cool room off the side of the chapel.

Graham found him there. Elliot looked up to see him storm into the room. He thought only: the fat kid is losing weight. He's growing into what is his, the ridiculous inheritance of good looks. There was a string of women, he was improbably sure. Blondes all, who wore blue dresses with polka-dot collars, who came from known families, who would grow fatter, although not just yet. Who were, for the time being, let's say from about age nineteen to twenty-four, wearing red underwear with black lace and screwing around with selected studs like Graham.

His brother crushed his hand in a shake, hissing, "What the hell is wrong with you?"

A question not worth answering because everything was clearly wrong with Elliot. Everything from his dress and state of intoxication to the sense that he had any family place there at all now that his father was gone, even his useless attempt at education out of some sense of what was expected of them as children. Education, jobs, marriage, kids. Did he seriously think that's where he was heading? Even if he wanted to, would anybody seriously let him?

He turned away. He left the chapel and university and Graham behind him.

Which left only roadie-ing for a time, a manifestly unhealthy rhythm settling. Elliot and the boys were either dead broke or drinking beer all afternoon in preparation for gigs that frequently did not pay as promised and left them dead broke. Everybody had a fuck job. Packing groceries or bussing tables or, in the case of their bass player, a job throwing fresh-killed poultry into the plucking sluice at the local chicken abattoir. Elliot himself drove a taxi part-time, renting from an old-timer and flashing a badly forged cab licence when called on to do so.

His year of fog, 1984. The city's music scene was at its pinnacle or at the beginning of the end depending on who you talked to, and maybe those two interpretations amounted to the same thing anyway. But it was unarguably a year of phase change for Elliot, whether he knew it or not, because this was the year that he acquired a life-long debt, payable by the very loyal personage of Kirov.

This came about unexpectedly, as such debts do. Elliot didn't even know Kirov, only having seen him around at the Smiling Buddha and the Commodore shows, conspicuous in his cowboy gear and for the rumour that he was AWOL crew from a Russian fishing trawler. A defector, celebrated for the fact. But they did meet, eventually and emphatically. Because sometime in the early months of that year, the Jackson Street house band had been asked to play in a group show at a warehouse in Japantown. It was their biggest gig to date, involving famous acts with recording contracts and continental tours. But it was also their last performance, because midway through a cover of "Nervous Breakdown," the lead singer—an overweight former ska trombonist they called Hemi—dropped unconscious to the stage. Dead drunk, of course. But Elliot only remembered that it had hardly interrupted the pacing of the song. One verse it was a Buster Bloodvessel look-alike staggering around the stage, the next it was Kirov up there with a red cowboy hat and green tooled-leather boots and, at that time, an almost impenetrable Vladivostokian accent scatting the final verse up to a screaming climax: *Crazy! Crazy! Sick and tired of . . . everything! Sick and tired . . . you better give me a place I can go you better not fuck with me just leave me alone otherwise I'm going to blow . . . up . . . I'm going to . . . I just want to fucking die-ie-ie-ie!!*

The crowd went bananas. He had a magnificent screeching voice. An angry, amplified macaw. Even Elliot—whose world view had evolved into a deadly, deliberate project of hating everything to do with the quest for accomplishment—had to acknowledge something satisfying had been created there. A new seam through the whole dense business of punk. Not the western gear. Not even the obvious way in which a Russian fisherman/defector in a red ten-gallon hat singing those particular lines communicated unequivocally his desire *not* to fucking die. It was the whole multi-dimensional ironic fakery of it. The sense that ideas, all ideas, any ideas, could be ripped off to humorous and modestly profitable effect.

Which would have been the end of it, had not the life-saving part of the evening immediately followed, descending on them like fast-moving weather. Mist, rain, confusion, a disturbance in the inner ear. The singer Hemi awoke. He reared to his feet, arms up. A drunken, enraged grizzly bear. Vengeance in a too-tight black suit. He tackled Kirov from behind, carrying them into the mosh pit at the front of the stage. From there out onto the street, much shouting and beer throwing going along with them.

Elliot had no interest in saving Kirov. He didn't know him. But on the sidewalk, where the utterly inebriated Hemi was taking winging, round-armed shots at the Russian, Elliot noticed Kirov was smiling. A detail that caused him to notice a second thing: that Kirov's feet were placed just so, one foot forward, open from his body. The other back and rooted below his rear shoulder. The sight flashed a web of memory through Elliot: the brute assault, calm skill waiting its chance. And he felt, however unlikely it might have been, a small connection forged.

Which is when the police arrived. One car, parked on the curb opposite, lights flashing. Then another, at which point beer bottles began lobbing across the street. Then a third, a fourth, and Elliot knew not to wait for them to throw open their doors. He stepped forward and grabbed Kirov by the shoulder. He said, "You feel like starting your deportation proceedings tonight?"

Then Hemi clocked him. A two-by-four across the back of the head for his trouble. Aimed at Kirov, no doubt, but nevertheless catching Elliot square. Down he went. Swamped with a terrible, familiar sensation. A sweeping dizziness, uncontrolled nausea. He puked some, but managed still to get up and grab Kirov, who was by now dodging swings of the timber by hiding behind a lamppost. He pulled Kirov into the open mouth of an alley, down to a broken door leading into a garage, a former taxi stand, long abandoned, the concrete floor a low lake of rainwater and piss, butts and needles, with a plank walkway laid on tires running over it all. Out a front door, busted open. Elliot staggering in the lead, head still swirling, Kirov following. Into another alley. Then a street. Then they were gone. Away and clear.

Kirov hung around Jackson Street after that, openly deferential to Elliot who, he'd tell anyone who'd listen, had taken a shot for him. The band drifted apart and reformed. There were new faces. The house became crowded. Kirov convinced Elliot to move in with him in a new place over in Japantown, just across the rails from the harbour, where the air hung with diesel fumes and was alive at all hours with harbour clatter. Crossing gates slamming open and closed. Train cars shifting. Ships sounding. Forklifts whining angrily along the docks. Kirov was trying to get into the stevedores union, it seemed. Not much luck here. A foreman had taken an instant dislike to him, which Kirov was pigheadedly ignoring. Going down week after week until angry words were finally spoken and Kirov tried to face off with the guy on the steps of the hall.

The guy laughed, shook his head, turned to a friend and said, *These fucking Russians.*

Kirov was prevented from doing anything more emphatic by an older, wiser man. Also Russian. He took Kirov aside, told him: "If you see one with a large belly and a beard, leather vest, tattoo here that says ITCOB? This means perhaps they do not always like the Russians."

"Who's a fucking Russian?" Kirov said. "I am American."

"Canadian," his friend told him. "Maybe you jump off the boat in the wrong place."

Kirov still refused to back down. "Who is *The Russians?* I am not *The Russians.* I'm Kirov, punk rocker."

"The Russians is business," the man said. "And with business, trust me, there is no punk rock."

Not yet aware how they were going to prove this man wrong, Kirov and Elliot laughed about it later. "ITCOB?" Kirov said. "It Cob?"

Elliot thought it was an acronym. Kirov thought the whole situation was something he should talk to his friend Rico about. "Right," Elliot said, who'd been hearing about Rico a lot lately. "Because he likes you so much."

Kirov was undaunted. That night he went to the Orwell for a drink, planning to lie in wait for Rico as long as it took. He came home less than an hour later, chastened.

"So what about those waterfront goons?" Elliot asked, laughing. "You get that all squared away?"

Turns out, Kirov said seriously, ITCOB meant *I Took Care Of Business*. As in, these guys had killed people. "But I tell Rico about you," Kirov said, brightening. "He said you should meet."

A suggestion Elliot chose to ignore, which was easy enough at the time, given that more important worries were hemming in. Kirov gave up on stevedoring just as Elliot was busted for his cab licence, slapped with a crippling fine and right when the ammo boxes were down to nothing too. Then, yet another month late on the rent, they were evicted. Elliot had paid rent on the cab until month-end but hadn't anticipated living in it. Much less with Kirov snoring in the back seat. Now he was dropping his friend off at some bar or other and trolling the nighttime streets for pirate fares. The clock ticking down to the end of the month where there was really, truly nothing waiting for him.

Nothing except Rico, that is. He sent one of his many associates around to find Elliot. A man with pounds of gold neck-work and homemade rings. Crosses, Stars of David, thorns, skulls and daggers. Elliot was sitting in his cab, curbside on Hastings, contemplating the true bottom of things in his life, monitoring dispatch, hoping to steal a call. This man rolled up to the driver's window on his low-slung chopper. He leaned into the window, chains rustling around his neck. He said, "God bless. Rico would like a word."

The next day. And this being Elliot's only experience with being offered a job interview, under the circumstances, he agreed.

He still went out driving that night, trying not to think about the following day. Trying not to dread or hope. He grimaced through a string of short runs, drunken flags, the food industry crowd shifting from their restaurants to their first bars and then their second. Then came the dispatch call for a run out to the airport. He could have let it go, but it was close. An easy steal.

"Flying out late?" Elliot tried, squinting as he looked in the mirror, the sun cracking up just over his fare's shoulder, concealing the man's face in a halo of white-blue. And yes, the question was born of boredom, Elliot thought now. But he'd also been curious about that whole universe of people who succeeded in being normal. The Straight. It's not like he had no exposure to these kinds of people growing up, only that they never really seemed to be *his* people. Or maybe he wasn't theirs. Those with jobs, salaries. Those that owned wardrobes, work clothes, casual clothes. Had bank accounts, year-end audits. Who voted. Who hadn't seen a rat or a roach in their entire lives. Who lived in pricey-looking glass towers on Alberni Street in the west end. Who were heading to the airport at six o'clock in the freaking morning.

"Late?" the fare said. "Early, I think you mean."

And here Elliot thought two things in a flash. One having to do with clocks. The difference between the Straight and the rest of them being that they lived in different halves of the dial, eternally opposed. I'm ready for bed here. This guy is out of his an hour early.

The second thing having to do with the fact that he was talking to his own brother. That the recognition was sudden and mutual. And that both of them, surprising one another in that fashion, had interrupted contemplation that could not be ruptured in any worse way than by the precise half-filial party opposite.

The brain occasionally wipes memory clean from these moments of peak emotion, of course. You lose details. Elliot thought it had to do with the brain shielding itself from further understanding than necessary. Take Huey and Louis. The miraculous twins. Right here, right now. The midmorning sun coming in under the wooden blinds, their skin going milky, translucent. His finger just now tracing a kiss onto each forehead in turn. Their mother standing behind him. He could feel her drawing closer to look over his shoulder. Wondering at him. Wondering if this was the beginning of something new.

Well. Elliot had memories of memories from those first moments of life. Hunched next to the gurney at Deirdre's head, shaking. She as calm as justice, holding his head in one arm. The physical ordeal passing out of her in those very moments and saying simply, whispering, "Tapgol Park? Where's Tapgol Park? What are you talking about?"

Him blubbering.

"Aren't you going to tell me what we have?"

"Brothers," he said. Not *two boys*. Not *twins*. And then he must have said something else, because all the medicos in the room were laughing. The nurse, the pediatrician. And for the life of him he could not remember what else had been said. Brothers.

In the cab, with his own brother, Elliot remembered silence from Alberni down the hill toward the bridges south. All the way up to the apex of the Granville Street Bridge, where the city spread around them, the water of False Creek rippling below. Everything was suspended. Night and day, north and south, water and sky, stranger brothers vaulting through the middle. Thresholded.

Did he ask about school? Did he ask who Graham's favourite architect was, only to have the question returned to him, edged in sarcasm? He thought that must have been it, because suddenly they were arguing about Gordon Matta-Clark. Or, at least, *he* was arguing. Graham was inclined to laugh, which angered him like nothing he could remember. He tried to make his points. Taking things apart. Anti-architecture.

"Why would I be anti-architecture?" Graham asked. "I'm an architect."

"You're in school."

"So, I'm becoming an architect."

"You're in school and you don't see Gordon Matta-Clark was revealing architecture by destroying it first?"

"Hey, listen. I don't know much about the guy. I always just thought of him as a bit of a joke. A punk."

"So you don't like punk."

"Oh, I'm sorry. Are you a punk?"

And on it went. Down off the bridge now toward the foot of Granville rise, driving faster than necessary.

"I'm in no hurry," Graham said.

Still faster. Elliot's foot mashing the pedal to the floor.

"As in, slow . . ." Graham slipped over against the door as Elliot wheeled into Broadway. Seventy kilome-
tres an hour, eighty, one hundred. Now he was cursing. Now he was pounding the Plexiglas, and Elliot kept his eyes in the rear-view mirror the whole time. Not watching the road much at all. That face. Bands of the earliest morning sunshine winking across the features. And out across the buildings of False Creek around them too (Elliot lifted his eyes into the world to swerve and miss a parked car). These buildings that tumbled down the slopes toward the water in a crazy pell-mell motion,

development gone mad, all soon to leak and leak badly and cost everybody untold millions. In those glass facades the rays of morning, animated by the motion of the cab, were ripping through the field of buildings in reflection. A wall of orange fire consuming everything in its path.

"Slow down!" Graham was yelling, hammering on the back of Elliot's seat.

And then they were stopped, pulled over. Graham was out of the car. He was forking bills through the passenger window. Twenty, forty, sixty, eighty.

"Forget it. Forget it. It's on me."

"I won't forget it . . ."

"I'll call you another cab . . ."

"Yes," Graham said, spit flying from his teeth. "Perhaps it'd be best if you did that."

And Elliot finding his fury, somehow, with just those words. Finding his response immediately: *Maybe it's best we just keep the fuck away from each other!*

Keep the fuck away at any necessary distance, he might have said. Keep our paths from crossing, our tracks from mingling. Keep on doing whatever it was we had been doing to effectively neutralize the blood connection, render them each an only child, reborn brotherless that one fucked-up summer of boxing, and brotherless through all of the years between, all of the consecutive minutes up to that very morning—Elliot watching Kirov stumble into the Orwell bar with his news, Graham cuffed on the Mary Street sidewalk—when they had unexpectedly veered toward one another again. Elliot struggling to hold it off, true enough. Trying to disengage. Going home. Arriving in the middle of the day, checking up on the kids, on Deirdre. But knowing all along that something had already been breached, some new unknown thing now taking shape in the very immediate future.

And Deirdre sensed it too, Elliot knew. Without fully understanding. Just drawing close to his shoulder now, she knew. As her touch grew near. Then a trace of scent. Finally, real warmth, coming in the instant before her arms went around his waist, encircling, enclosing him. There was a question alive in her hot breath, even if she did not shape it into words.

"Don't worry about it," he whispered to her. "Don't worry."

Those words just as her cheek hit the middle of his back between the shoulder blades.

Four

DEIRDRE WATCHED HIM PULL OUT THE DRIVEWAY, the truck tires squeaking on the pavement. The unasked question was: *Are we going through one of those times when you try to reinvent everything? Where everything changes?*

It couldn't be denied that he knew her well enough to hear the words, even unsaid. She'd lived a life not letting others know anything, then found herself being under- stood improbably well by Elliot after how much time? As long as it took to eat a Cheese Whiz omelette. To gather coats and disappear out of the Postum under the calm gaze of her Aunt Cleo, who didn't endorse her niece's choice so much as acknowledge with her eyes that objection was likely to be fruitless. *So much like your mother.* The time it took to walk the streets into the wee hours. Stand down in front of the hedge by her apartment in Kitsilano and work themselves up to a kiss, holding each other so tightly, with such sudden desperation. The time it took for her to think she'd never forget the smell of him—rain, leather, off-vanilla. It was a very short time, really.

"I want one," she said, touching a coat button shaped like a black skull.

He looked down. He said, "I travelled a long way to get these, you know."

She plucked at one near his throat. He smiled. "You need it for a spell, maybe."

Maybe, she thought. Maybe exactly that. A spell to hold him in place for a second, let her have a good look at him. Because he slipped from view somehow. He turned off a few degrees from centre and vanished. He was a master at trapping the incoming question, turning it around in flight, leaving it back in the hands of the sender who was, in Deirdre's brief experience to that point, revealed in the process.

By now he was on the highway, speeding away. Gripped by whatever furious sense of event was spawning within him. He'd gone downstairs to make a cup of tea, or that's what he said he was doing. Next thing she knew he was out the driveway, accelerating away.

Was she furious, angry, pissed off, anything? She leaned into the window, forehead to the pane. *Doesn't it worry you, really? Aren't you scared?* These were the housewife questions she would get from neighbourhood friends if she had any. But no. Possibilities dwindled quickly after they first moved in, as the neighbours took stock of their comings and goings, the late-night visits from Elliot's friends. Her own tendency to be aloof and suspicious couldn't help.

Leaving Deirdre to pose and answer the question herself. No, it didn't worry her. And no, she wasn't scared, despite the friends that some of his friends had. Yes, it made her angry. But it never lasted even when she tried to make it last. Elliot was helplessly tangled in his own projects, his own life, his own thoughts. But he was tangled up in her too. He worried about her, about them. He called constantly. He carried stress enough for both of them. Was he shaping up to be a bad father? Well, she couldn't deny that he wasn't shaping up to be a normal one. But she didn't have a lot of experience with that kind anyway, her own having flown away forever just before her sixth birthday to begin a second, presumably better family.

Flew away. The detail her mother never failed to mention, as if getting on an airplane made it somehow more understandable. To Denver, apparently. What did that mean? She'd never been. Had no idea. But always the stated destination, the means of transport, as if using an airport, checking baggage, crossing borders, doing all the things that Deirdre and her mother couldn't afford to do was somehow an explanation in itself. He was different from us. Deirdre once thought, still a little kid at the time: My father flew away because he was some kind of birdman. Not a human at all. He had to go back and live with other bird people. Here was the most reasonable explanation a six-year-old could come up with as to why the man was gone from the picture accompanied always by the images and sounds of some great shape taking to the sky.

"Hello." Two sweet syllables. Very quiet, so as not to wake the twins. Sometimes Malaya spoke and Deirdre could remember with absolute clarity the feeling of wanting to be picked up, held to her mom's chest, have her hair brushed. Sometimes Malaya spoke to the twins, getting them ready for bed, and if Deirdre was in the room she could feel herself getting sleepy.

Now Deirdre turned and smiled. Shook her head, meaning, Yes, that was Elliot, and yes, he's gone again. But there were no words out of place from Malaya, ever. She communicated with strong looks, pumped full of her own survivor's type of certainty. Now she gave Deirdre a smile, over which her eyes communicated a firmness of opinion that comforted. And that opinion was: We have held enough strength back, kept a reserve for these occasions. He'll leave a hundred more times, that's just the way it is, and still we won't be depleted. Malaya who had come from the Philippines ten years before, sending virtually ever dollar she had made in that time back to her parents and then, when they died, to her brother. Malaya who would, no doubt, continue sending her weekly envelopes back for as many generations as were gathered up under the umbrella of her own industrious lifespan.

Elliot had once decided that Malaya should immigrate to Canada and sponsor everybody over to live here. He exploded into activity when the idea struck, contacting lawyers, finding out the bad news that she didn't qualify and then proposing adoption. "Why not?" He became stubborn on the point. "There's no law against us adopting a fifty-year-old. Is there?"

Malaya found this all quite funny, shaking her head, saying little. Elliot would do anything to make her life better, he'd transform everything. It was his fundamental belief: that all could change with bursts of energy in sufficiently concentrated form. All could be reinvented.

"He's going to phone from the truck in five minutes," Deirdre told Malaya, who was humming as they went downstairs and into the kitchen. "Not to say sorry, just to say goodbye."

In the kitchen, they found tea things laid out for the two of them. The water just boiled. Their favourite tea bags in their favourite cups.

The house of the personal cultural revolution. Deirdre swept Malaya into this appraisal: each of us is willing to reinvent as necessary to achieve certain ends. Because, undeniably, it wasn't the first time that change had loomed. Their life together had been a series of regimes separated by shakedown, or attempts along those lines. Elliot got it in his head that something was structurally flawed in life and suddenly the faces changed, the surroundings were torn down or refurbished.

Or they moved.

"Would you believe me if I told you that I owned an old house in Deep Cove?"

This question was posed as if purely hypothetical, over breakfast at the Postum.

"How old?" she remembered asking, as if that mattered most.

1930s. A craftsman place. Rundown, but it had good bones.

They were living at that time in a leaning, slope-floored house near the railway tracks, quite close to the first place he'd ever lived after moving away from home back during his punk years. Nineteen years old then. Over thirty as they spoke. He shrugged and avoided analysis, but she knew he wanted them down there out of some allegiance to a choice made early in life.

Now he pressed her, pointedly. "Answer the question," he said.

"Of course I'd believe you," she said.

They'd been together a couple of years at that point. Married six months, which had been a revolutionary event in itself. He was gone on a buying trip somewhere. Came back a week earlier than scheduled. Found her down at the library where she was working part-time, just filing architecture books the moment he came jangling in across the open area by the librarians, eyes locked on her alone.

"Matta-Clark, please. Anything you got."

She smiled but made believe the request was routine. She turned to the shelves, ran a finger down the spines. Moved around the corner to the other side of the stack and found Matta-Clark in a volume on deconstruction.

"That house he cut in half," Elliot said.

She leafed the pages and located the project. "Splitting," she said. "1974."

"I know, I know," he said. "New Jersey."

"And?" She was staring up into his face. His eyes red from lack of sleep. His hair strawing this way and that. He wasn't even looking at the picture, which showed the brilliant effect Matta-Clark had achieved, light blowing through the building, revealing it.

He put his hand across the page with the photograph. He spread his fingers wide over the house ripped vertically into two. He said, "Marry me."

The imperative was not something that normally worked with her. But right that moment, she didn't even examine resistance as an option. She held back something that might have been the throat-knot preceding tears. She said, "I'm off at three."

Just them and a Justice of the Peace. She woke up with a boyfriend and went to sleep that night with a husband. Were they changed by it? Perhaps not as much as other people were, but she put that down to their capacity for revolution. He convinced her, without ever saying anything specific about it, to enjoy not knowing the future. Not knowing, for example, that he owned an old house out in a former working-class neighbourhood across the Burrard Inlet from the city, now a commuter suburb full of professionals and minivans and organic produce stores.

He paid the bill and drove her straight out to have a look. He brooded the whole way, alive to the strangeness of this particular revolutionary impulse. Were they really going to move out of the downtown eastside and take up the life of gardening and pool maintenance? Well, he argued (his own debate, she sat in silence on the ride out, smiling, listening), they could still be who they were. They didn't have to become people who wore Nikes and khakis, who ate arugula. He just wanted to get away from the crack and the dope. Didn't she want the same? Didn't she want to maybe see some grass occasionally?

"You like grass, El?" she asked him.

"I like grass," he said. "You think I don't like grass?"

"Well, we've never really talked about grass before, Elliot. I didn't assume you felt one way or the other about it."

If he had another weakness beyond being cagey and prone to unexplained absences, it was that he really never saw the humour in himself. And as if to make that point, an electric lawn mower was the first thing he bought after they moved in.

"Look," he said. "You plug it in so you don't need to fill it with gas."

The house had been built by the original owner, with huge front pillars supporting a sleeping porch on the upper floor. The exterior shakes were falling off, the upstairs windows had been painted shut, there was bright green wall-to-wall covering the floors, drop-ceiling acoustic tiles all through the main floor and unforgiving fluorescent light. Deirdre loved it immediately for being everything they would have condescended toward in architecture school: a structure that called for nothing but pure restoration. The reassertion of an old idea.

She unpacked boxes and looked around. She pointed out the things they could do to bring it back, something dawning on him while she sketched ideas. He was staring at her. She said, "So you forgot I went to architecture school?"

No, he hadn't forgotten. He just couldn't have anticipated how much he would like the idea of doing what she was suggesting. Say the words *renovation, home improvement,* and he would have been running back downtown. Describe gutting a room, tearing out everything added later to see what the original materials had been, and he was amazed you could actually do that kind of thing. He was in favour, as a matter of principle.

It took six months. The local paper wanted to do a write-up: *Packer Gordon's Daughter-in-law* . . . It was the only time Elliot's enthusiasm flagged. "Ah man, I don't know. You mean they'll take photographs?"

Then, of course, he changed his mind entirely about

keeping it low profile and decided they should have a housewarming party. "Invite the neighbours. Nice people. Do a nice thing."

"A nice thing?" she said.

"Like with dip and stuff."

"Dip?"

"There's one made with artichoke I heard about. You serve it in a bread bowl."

He was grooving on the idea of a party where people didn't drink directly from the spout on the keg. Where the bathroom wasn't plugged with your junkie friends gossiping over a fix.

She invited the neighbourhood. She rang doorbells, introduced herself. They said, *Oh yes we noticed all the construction.* Or: *How nice to meet you, have you sorted out the recycling program?* Everybody was delighted to come over. Everyone offered to bring something.

Elliot invited Rico, who came with his usual extended posse in half-a-dozen beat-up, mid-80s cars that they double-parked in the narrow street. One guy on a chopper painted up with a graphic crucifix, Christ bleeding to death. He idled the bike onto the strip of lawn down the side of the house and thumbed off the ignition.

Deirdre was sipping a drink, trying to chat with an Indian doctor and his wife who lived across the street. She was embarrassing herself by failing to retain anything that was said, repeatedly distracted by those arriving. These were people she'd seen dozens of times and yet who, walking down the flagstones and out into the first backyard she'd ever owned, were rendered unrecognizable. And she was thinking, Of course I'm the worst person alive to try to pull off something like this. I have no social skills, no grace. Only a stubborn, solo nature that means I don't have any of my own friends with whom this bad mix of people might be diluted.

The man on the chopper climbed off and stood. He peeled away a tiny helmet to reveal a crown of thorns tattooed around his bald head at the temples.

"I have a good friend who rides motorcycles," said the doctor. "He carries his wife along in a sidecar."

Elliot tried hard, as Deirdre knew he would. He worked the backyard as evening fell, a smoke hanging from his lips, Long Island iced tea on the go. "Hi, how are you? Welcome to our home. Hi. Good to see you. Mr. Pearson, from down the way? Judge Pearson, sorry, I'm Elliot. Elliot Gordon. Well yeah, in fact yes. Uh-huh. Yeah, that was my father. Try some dip."

Judge Pearson was at Packer Gordon's funeral, he told Deirdre later. Then, leaning a little close, he noted that he didn't remember seeing Elliot there. It was vaguely accusing. And something in the comment brought her very nearly to a sharp and anti-social place. She felt it well in her, the desire to put her drink down, square up on the guy. Say, "Different mother, all right? The mistress's kid. Good enough for you, bitch? Okay with you if we move in here?"

Kirov arrived with his wife, Lucille, who needed a bathroom immediately. "Hey, Red," Kirov said, locking Deirdre in a vodka-fume-y, seconds-long embrace. "So beautiful. Will you show Lucille the powder room?"

"You okay?" Deirdre asked, leading her to the quieter bathroom upstairs.

"I'm good, I'm good. I just need a smoke. You got a fan up here?"

Deirdre perplexed. "You can smoke outside, Luce," she said.

Lucille gave her look like *come on.* "Better not."

Downstairs Deirdre cracked off the stereo volume a notch or two and went to find Elliot.

"Is Lucille on the pipe?" Deirdre asked him. She could tell from his eyes—wider than normal, slightly rigid in the gaze—that he was struggling to keep this whole play moving forward. Part of him wanted somebody else to ruin it quickly. Start a fight. Or a fire.

He said: "I ah . . . I ah . . . I don't know." Then he kissed her on the top of the head and moved off into the crowd.

Deirdre extracted a cigarette from a holder Elliot had very proudly brought home from a downtown flea market the week before. It was a golden globe with a handle on top that, when you pulled it, caused the sphere to bisect itself, to yawn open and reveal some four dozen cigarettes, each in a slender tube that flowered out of the interior in a white blossom of nicotine.

"That's Christ crucified on one side of the gas tank . . ." The bald man with the crown of thorns tattoo was talking with the two heavy-set women with flat-tops who lived in the house next door. ". . . and the stone rolled away on the other. Right?"

They nodded and sipped their drinks as the sun disappeared over the ridge. Deirdre thought, watching, Well, at least the party succeeded on the score of people drinking. And given Elliot had made the punch, she imagined unfamiliar headaches up and down the street the next morning.

Now Rico stood in a corner of the lawn, next to the hedge, barking, "What? What?" He was wearing a wide-collared polyester shirt patterned over with photographs of the Taj Mahal at sunset. He had just been talking to the Indian doctor, who had moved a few paces away, standing awkwardly. Suspended between a conversation he didn't want to continue and a safer one that he apparently had not yet located.

"Should we maybe . . ." she said to Elliot at the two-hour mark, making a motion as if to sweep people toward the door.

"We're just getting started!" he said, smiling widely, falsely.

Kirov was drunk. Arguing with the judge about capital punishment, which he supported, but only if it were carried out by neighbourhood committees to make everybody take personal responsibility for the value of a human life.

Judge Pearson offered a pained chuckle. "Well, ah, you see, I'm in family court. This is really outside my area."

At which point Kirov put a finger to the middle of his chest. "Everybody this is inside their area. So, you think someone else pull this trigger. Is so easy?"

"Young man," said the judge, squinting. "Are we talking about firing squads?"

People trickled out as the light started to fail. "I have Tiki torches!" Elliot said. But it didn't stem the tide. "Jesus!" he said, when they were down to Rico and Kirov and crew. Lucille lying on the grass, arms spread, gazing

up at the stars.

"It's past nine o'clock," said Deirdre, who was tired herself.

"Nine? Fuck nine," Elliot said.

He didn't tell anyone to go. She didn't either, of course. What she couldn't know is how quickly, after someone started in on the electric guitar out back, the entire neighbourhood apparently reached for their phones at once.

"We've had complaints," the police officer said after ringing the doorbell a long time. Deirdre climbed out of bed eventually and answered in her housecoat. "Five or six, in fact."

"From people on this street?" Elliot was incensed when she went out back and told him. "Those hypocrites were all here four . . . five hours ago."

"Grow up!" she said to him, first harsh words of the evening. "Did you want to change your life or not?"

Yes, he did. No, he didn't. He didn't know exactly what he wanted, the worst part of the scattered energy that composed him, that made him so willing to try things, change things.

Malaya had tea ready. Deirdre took hers out back. So they kept to themselves after the housewarming. So they weren't hosting dinner parties. She didn't care. When the twins were born and Malaya moved in, Deirdre found a tight little community build itself right there, spilling out of the house and down the grass on sunny days, right down to the sea. Maybe Elliot still had questions about the choices they'd made. She didn't.

Once she said to him, right after the twins arrived, "All I ask is that you say the words, Elliot. Say, What I'm doing is not illegal. Say, There is no chance that one of these days I'll be leaving my family to spend some time in prison."

And he had said those words, very nearly. He only slipped in a small change. He said, "What I'm starting to do now is not illegal . . ."

Rico long gone. Elliot trying to evolve the business, she knew that much. He was trying to make *real* things, he said. And she could see the signs too: different cars parked in the street out front, different voices on phone calls for Elliot that came at different times of the day.

All of which was fine, to a point. All of which Deirdre had more or less seen before. And then, a difference that shook her. Malaya and Deirdre arriving home from grocery shopping just a few weeks before, grocery bags and strollers and Louie screaming and the whole parade of them piling inside to find a stranger, looking entirely relaxed, one arm up along the back of the sofa, reading a magazine. He was polite when confronted. But the adrenal spike, the moment of real fear, Deirdre knew in an instant, that was the point. And because he succeeded in scaring them so well, he precipitated in her the full anger that had only threatened before.

"Who the fuck are you?" Deirdre said.

He put the magazine down. He stood up. He held his empty hands out.

"No," she said, pointing a baguette across the room. "Just answer the fucking question."

Which he never did, in fact. Instead, he calmly suggested that Elliot should be called. Elliot who was at home that week, imagine the chances. Only out on some ridiculous errand. Buying aloe plants, she remembered. He was going to fill the house with natural remedies. *Cloves and rosemary for menstrual cramps. Stuff like that.*

Malaya phoned him, then hurried the twins upstairs. Deirdre sat with the bread across her knees like it were a serious threat to the man should he rise. She kept her eyes squarely on his face until she heard Elliot's truck, heard his feet on the walk. Then she swung around to see his first reaction on entering. Fear, surprise, no surprise. Give me something.

Nothing. Elliot's expression didn't waver. He nodded at the man. He looked evenly over at Deirdre. He said, "Sorry about that." Then he took the man down to the bottom of the garden to talk. Deirdre watched from a bedroom window upstairs. Then when the guy was gone (around the side of the house, he never came back inside), she had simmered long enough.

"You have children!" she screamed at him when he came in. He stood in the front hall. She stood on the stairs looking down at him.

"Yes, I have children."

"He was threatening us!"

"He wasn't threatening. He was inquiring about progress on—"

"That fucking cocksucker son of a bitch—"

"Honey. Honey. Please."

"Maybe you grew up in a goddamn war zone, but not my kids! Understand me?"

This was unfair. And she knew it hurt him. But the blow represented everything frustrated in her as a result of having told him all there was to know about her own childhood while he largely withheld his own. She'd pressed on occasion, dredging up detail on just the one story that he was willing to retell as often as she could stand it, but never explain. The story she had drifted into herself by journeying to Mary Street on another matter entirely. A fight with his brother. A boxing ring. A head injury. A four-week hospital stay, three days of which he was in a coma. He had pristine memories of waking up in a white room with white coats ringing the bed.

"Very much like everything you've heard about the afterlife," Elliot said of the experience. "Diffuse light. People in white. Then I noticed the clipboards."

It was the Intensive Care Unit neurologist with a group of interns, in fact. Elliot let his eyes drift closed, feigning sleep. He heard, "Bed two, Elliot Gordon . . ."

"The architect's kid."

"That's right. Fifteen years old. Got himself knocked out boxing three days ago. Apparently hit his head on the ropes going down, fell badly. But vital signs are now stable. So what else should I be looking for?"

"Intracranial pressure."

"Sure. We had a cranial impact, some bleeding, some buildup. But we see here that pressure is down since surgery."

"Neurologic signs?"

"He's not awake yet, but they are improving. He's now localizing to pain and opening his eyes when you shout at him. We're still feeding him, which is going well. No more meds at this point. It looks like he might wake up in the next day or so, so we're just going to support him now to give him the best chance. Okay? Questions?"

And only when the voices were gone, out in the hallway, down the hallway, did he let his eyes open again to assess what all of it meant.

"And what did all of it mean?" Deirdre asked him.

It meant there was a machine next to his bed, heart rate, temperature, blood pressure and breathing ticking across various displays. It meant there was a feeding tube taped into his mouth, just now causing him to gag. Causing a nurse to appear at the door, sliding smoothly into view.

"Okay, Okay," she said, trying to smile.

It meant that there was something hard, metal, clamped to the top of his head, so fixed to him that when he grabbed for it, he felt it tear his scalp. He felt it flex his own skull.

"Don't touch that, honey," the nurse said. Then, "Please!"

That was the intracranial pressure monitor, he would learn later. No, he didn't tear it out. But he wanted to. And Deirdre was left considering this detail just as she had each of the others. It wasn't that such an experience didn't teach you anything, a point of view Elliot advanced often. Deirdre only thought that his entire family history had been compacted down into an experience or, more correctly, into a moment. A moment when Elliot first touched his fingers to something metal embedded in his own body. A moment when he encountered the hard, cold, irrefutable evidence that he was struggling to recover. As a result, his family and the experience had fused over the years into something like antimatter to him.

Now he was looking up at her, begging her not to be angry. And she only turned on the stairs and stormed up, leaving him there to beg. Came back downstairs only after a very complete brushing of her teeth, flossing, brushing of her hair. Came back downstairs to find him still standing right where she'd left him.

"Remember what you asked me?" Elliot said.

"When?" But she thought she knew.

"The very first question you ever asked me."

"I wondered if you were carrying your pet ferret around in that box."

"After that."

Out front of her apartment in Kits. They'd just walked around the entire city, it seemed. All the way from the Postum up through the west end to the park, then down across the bridge and into Kitsilano and now they had strolled past boutiques selling mountain-climbing equipment and high-end baby gear. Down a hedged lane and around front of the townhouse she rented with friends. Cleanly painted. Grass trimmed. Flowers blooming in rows along the walkway and a peekaboo view of the ocean. Syringe-free gutters that she was about to throw over entirely to be near this dishevelled, overcharged stranger opposite.

"You said, *So are we, like, having some kind of personal cultural revolution here?*"

Deirdre allowed herself to be taken to his chest, with that. Something inaugurated—by a decision, a phone call, a moment's hesitation followed by first action—and an aperture into the future was opened, a pinhole through which the crazy bits and bytes of revolution would flow.

She embraced it, didn't she? Angry or otherwise. When Rico's tattooed biker friend pulled out of the front yard after the housewarming party he managed to tear a twelve-foot-long furrow down the middle of the neighbour's front lawn. Nobody ever complained. When Rico had to drag Kirov away from the judge and his wife, Lucille back up in the bathroom, Elliot walking around with the bread bowl and artichoke dip trying to look like he was having fun. Halfway down his second pack of cigarettes for the evening. Deirdre realized that sympathetic eyes were on her. Women from the area automatically thought to exempt her from blame. They weren't hypocrites at all. They, like everybody but Elliot, simply didn't know her.

She was supposed to be alarmed by the chaos he brought her, day after day. But she wasn't. She wasn't oblivious; she could *see* the chaos just fine. But she had to acknowledge something for the first time, tea in hand, the sea roiling at her feet: it didn't alarm her because she believed him. Believed for all his scattered frenzy and short attention span that he really was trying to build something. With every personal cultural revolution. Trying to build something really good.

Five

HE WAS SPEEDING BACK INTO THE CITY. SPEEDING, which was itself unlike him. A charged-up life needed habits of deliberate slowness. Elliot wolfed his food. He made more snap decisions than he could remember. He spoke so fast as a matter of course that he was used to a motion from Kirov that involved a single finger drawn downward in a line, as if adjusting the RPM of a turntable. He drove slowly to compensate. He drove a big truck very slowly and counted an angry honk from anybody in an imported vehicle to be a sign of something healthy in his life.

Nobody was honking at him now as he sped that winding mountainside road back downtown, phases complete and phases beginning. Popping open his cellphone to call Kirov.

So began the flow. Phone calls and more phone calls. A kind of weightening of the sky, as if before a heavy rain. He'd watched Rico do this countless times at the beginning of some new thing. Rico, who carried three cellphones and spoke a different code into each. Bookie code. Trade code. Marital infidelity code. Rico, who circled the same block endlessly, impossible to tail or tap. Who ran an empire, when he was not slung into the invisible space of Apartment A, in a cloud of incoming and outgoing cellular connections.

Elliot used one phone and no code. He said to Kirov, "Find out what happened to my brother."

And Kirov went off to do just that.

Then Deirdre.

"Ah, here we are," she said, answering.

"I had to go," he said. "I forgot to say goodbye."

"Yes, well."

"I'm going to have to stay downtown a few days."

"A few days or a few weeks, Elliot? I only want to know."

He'd never lied to Deirdre and didn't particularly want to start now. So he said nothing. They drove together, silent. Three, four minutes. Both of them breathing, thinking and deciding.

"Something's going on," he said, finally.

"That much I can see."

The phone vibrated in his hand. Kirov already back on two. "I love you," Elliot told her. "You believe me when I say that, don't you?"

She said, "You better hope I believe you. You better hope I keep believing you."

And more. Elliot got it in a rush, a single breath. He'd better hope she kept on believing that things were evolving in a good direction, that neckless heavies in golf shirts sitting in their living room without permission were worth whatever he was planning for them.

Then she hung up.

Elliot sighed. He wasn't stupid enough to have thought she'd forgotten that incident. And he was relieved that she saw in it his efforts to make things better. Because there was a good reason, a reason oriented to them, to her and the kids and Malaya too, why he'd taken the man down to the bottom of the garden, far enough that their low words were snatched at, nearly taken, by the sea.

"I told you the operation is yours," Elliot had said to the man down in the garden that day. "There's no need for pressure."

"This isn't pressure," the man said, then pulled out a pad of paper and a pen and did like Elliot had heard the Uncles did at their private clubhouse meetings. He wrote a name down, that squeaky felt-pen noise the only thing to be picked up by a tap. By a cop in a nearby tree with a directional microphone, if such a thing were even likely. The name was a big name. Not local, bigger than that.

"You're kidding," said Elliot, who tried not to know much about the Uncles' business, but couldn't help knowing this name.

"You don't think they like nice things?"

Sure, sure. Everybody liked nice things. Only nobody wanted to pay for them any more. He went through it one more time with the man. They had a turnkey system: suppliers, shippers, warehouses. All in place. Elliot was out, but Kirov would stay on.

"Kirov," the man said, wincing, turning.

"Stays on," Elliot said with a little more force than he truly commanded.

The man waggled his head, then nodded.

"And you're off to the Caymans maybe," the man said, smiling.

"Doubtful," Elliot said. "Very doubtful. I'm out for family reasons."

"So what's coming in?" the man asked, all business again. "He likes Tabriz. He's not so crazy about some of that other Azerbaijani stuff."

Elliot rolled his eyes. "You guys are killing me."

The man looked at him, sharp but friendly. "No, we're not," he said. Then, "Well, you'd better get on in. Your old lady's in the bedroom window. She doesn't look happy."

They ambled back up the grass like a couple of guys returning from lawn darts.

"You ever fish?" the man started in, like they all did. "Know a sweet place if you're interested. You have to be a member, but I can get you in. Nice house, by the way."

His phone was still vibrating its second-line reminder.

Elliot said, "Kirov. Go."

"Your brother. Arrested," Kirov said. "Fuckers took him in."

"Sure we have the right name?"

"Broke in at five. Arrested at eight. What's he doing down here at 5:00 a.m?"

"The name. The name."

"You recognize Graham?" Kirov said. "Graham P. Gordon."

"Shit," said Elliot. "He was in there for three *hours*."

"Graham P. What's *P*?"

But there was much more that Kirov still did not know. And so he was off this line and back on the phone at his end. There were lawyers he could call. Both Crown and criminal defence types, contacts quietly held on both sides of the ledger. Somebody would know where, on what charge and with what likelihood of conviction.

Elliot drove straight to 55 East Mary. Found a tow truck out front securing the car, a Porsche. Pretty nice. The driver emerged from under the sleek lines of the front fender and caught Elliot watching. He said, "This you?"

Elliot shook his head. "What's up? Meter out?"

"Nah," the towie said, heaving himself to his feet. "It's going back to the dealer who's apparently been missing it for the past month."

Elliot made a face. "As in stolen?"

But the towie was on to more important things, slamming home the hydraulic controls and jerking the front of the car off the ground. As the tires lurched free of the pavement, dangling, all that money, all that engineering became pathetic and helpless.

Elliot went inside. He was thinking: 5:00 a.m. A bad hour for entering long-abandoned spaces, much less those on the side of town far opposite your own. But here is where Graham had gone, most certainly. Step one, to the threshold. Step two, extinguishing the butt end of a slender cigarillo. (Elliot picked this item up. He sniffed it seriously, as if the fragrance would unlock answers.) Step three, and he was through, the lobby shaping darkly around and above him. The grey spiral of stairs rising airily above, and dropping with contrary heaviness below.

Elliot closed the door and stood for several minutes in the centre of that space, aware as he had been countless times before of two sensations. The building itself, inhaling and exhaling, a matter of beam creaks, the trickle of hidden water, wind ticking through cracks in exterior walls. Then, a feeling of being pinned in place where lines intersected, some driving through the room from scattered compass points, others dropping down from the smashed skylight high overhead, half-covered with plywood but still offering a glimpse of sky, down through the screw of the staircase into the darkness below.

Elliot descended to that dark place, stood on the bottom step. Did Graham throw this old light switch here? Pressing the ivory *on* plunger released a corresponding black ebony *off*, which sprung from the brass plate an inch below. Or did he see the other lights and wonder at those? The bank of portable halogens that Elliot had rented and set up on tripods in each corner. Lights that, when activated, threw the room and its contents into unforgiving white relief, almost free of shadow, like a nighttime archaeological dig.

A dig that had revealed nothing. Found objects, sure: drifts of newspaper, cans of film spilling out of themselves, journals of fight notes, magazines annotated with thousands of words scribbled vertically up the margins. An incomprehensible library, in total. A lifelong investigation of violence in the ring and no indication that conclusions had ever been reached.

Elliot sifted this material through his fingers. He read as much as he could stand. But nothing he found helped him answer even the most basic questions he might have about the place, like why? Why them? Why here? And the sense of a riddle unsolved left him physically unsteady. At the end of the first long Saturday he'd spent down there, he remembered standing up from a carton of ephemera—restaurant napkins, fight programs, old photos—and dizziness had swept down on him. A hard spell that had him reaching for something to hold, missing the railing with an outstretched hand and landing on his ass on the lower step. Where he sat with his head swirling, eyes closed, waiting for the headache to descend. Which it did, hard.

Elliot's brain was vibrating now, but not from dizziness or migraine. There was, instead, a vibration arriving in his head, transmitted through the tissue of his body. A distinct hum, warm and insistent, surprising him, leaving him stranded as he traced it back down through his body to where his cell was set to vibrate against his thigh in the side pocket of his pants.

Kirov. "Where are you?"

"At the O," Elliot answered.

Pause. "*I'm* at the O," Kirov said.

TIMOTHY

TAYLOR

Elliot took a breath in, long and deep. "Okay, I'm somewhere else then."

"What are you doing there?" Kirov asked. "Why go

there?"

"Go where?"

"There. There. Where you are standing."

"Kirov . . ."

"Yes, my friend."

"What do we have?"

Quite a lot. Break and enter, for one. Taking a motor vehicle or vessel without consent.

"Summary conviction offence that one," the booking

desk sergeant at the Main Street police station told Elliot. "But he can still do six months if the judge is in a bad mood."

Elliot went straight over. He identified himself as Graham's brother and watched the man's expression migrate from mild boredom to mild curiosity, mildness of revealed expression being a cop hallmark in Elliot's limited experience. They were struggling to understand what Graham was doing there, or here. And now they wondered if Elliot would help them to understand.

"Any history of mental illness?" the sergeant asked Elliot.

Elliot said no, not really. Then, "Him, you mean?"

The sergeant's eyebrows raised a millimetre. "Just him for now. He's the one in on resisting."

No, he hadn't taken a swing at anyone. But he'd been what you might call uncooperative. "Cursing. Carrying on. We had to call in a canine unit. Brother, you say?"

"Half-brother." Elliot nodded. "I'm thinking this is some kind of misunderstanding."

The cop's expression was again entirely neutral, although Elliot guessed they'd all be glad to have the matter cleared. Get the yuppie out of his cell and off his desk. The cop said finally, "You don't own the building, by chance?"

No, but he was the only person who used it. And he knew the owner.

"You rent it?"

Not that either, really. The owner was his wife's aunt. He looked after it for her. They could call her, but he really made the important decisions about the place.

The sergeant pursed his lips. Then said, "Got some ID, son?"

Last time he'd showed ID to a cop, he'd been in a room just down the hall. He didn't mention it.

"Gordon. Gordon," the sergeant said, sucking his teeth. "You famous? Somebody in your family famous?"

They sent him across the street to the remand centre, where a sheriff put him in a visitation room and told him to wait. He found himself staring at cinder block, listening to sounds he hadn't heard in a very long time. Distant doors slamming. The buzz of locks opening and recharging. The low-timbre voices of staff, who talked in the same flat style the cops had, designed to disclose nothing but the barest meaning of the words. Insinuation, inside, did not play.

Elliot had been inside for less than twenty-four hours, a long time before, but that was enough. He said to Rico after that experience, "How the hell did that happen?"

Rico said, "So we don't sell fake watches any more. Times change. Think of this business as a series of six-month exclusives. After that, somebody's doing it cheaper or it's illegal."

That man intervening on Elliot's behalf, helping clear things up, that had been Rico in his prime, 1984, 1985. He pulled a string from his lair under the Orwell floorboards

and a lawyer showed up in court, stinking from what was either a lot of booze the night before or a smaller measure the same morning, but who nevertheless made spectacularly short work of the matter. He rose to his feet before the Crown had a chance to open her mouth with a summary of the file. He addressed the judge in a manner that suggested they had a long, if slightly weary, association. And he then proceeded to explain something that nobody present had thought of before. Turned out that the private investigator who'd been dressed like a homeless person and climbed the fire escape of Elliot's apartment building to photograph him sorting Rolexes and Baume & Merciers and Patek Philippes into paper bags for distribution to the street tables, well, that individual had been doing something that the Criminal Code referred to as "trespassing at night."

Elliot's lawyer spoke to this detail: "Surely the administration of justice is cast into some disrepute if sleeping, possibly female, tenants of Mr. Gordon's building must endure private individuals climbing the fire escape at night in order that the legality of this trade be tested."

Elliot heard the Crown say, "You are shitting me," which precipitated a tirade from the bench and no doubt hastened the dismissal of charges.

"So no watches," Elliot asked Rico. "What's next then?"

They were back at Apartment A. Rico was watching college football on four different televisions, smoking a cigar. He was fielding a phone call approximately every thirty seconds. He said only, "The Glory Years."

Which was more enthusiastic than Rico normally was, but not inaccurate. A fair term to describe the remainder of the 1980s anyway. Watches had been only the beginning. Quartz blanks made for exactly twenty-five cents a unit out of a factory in Taiwan. Wrapped in a fake metal designer casing, they came in at $2.99 per watch at a thousand units out of Hong Kong. Every maker imaginable. Zenith. TAG Heuer. Omega. Piaget. $10 to $50 on the street. Elliot and Kirov worked the tables themselves for one season and then couldn't have afforded the time if they'd wanted to. They built Rico something like a franchise operation, signing up gangs of street vendors. Elliot learned never to let a facial piercing, a neck tattoo, conceal the born trader.

But the fact was that, hustlers aside, the product moved itself in those years. *Fake* was not even remotely a deterrent, a downside. It was the selling feature. These objects were exactly what they were: expressions of luxury that happened to tell the time. Symbols, emblems, in every other sense. Only unlike the originals, they were cheap enough to be disposable too, a very contemporary bonus. So the Swiss watch industry took issue with it and drove a bulldozer over a container load of fakes. Nobody in the trade took any notice, at least not at first. It was petulance, irritation, Elliot would have argued. Those old Swiss corporations knew the truth better than anyone. If you identified with your Baume & Mercier, if you were proud to be seen wearing one, then just how strange was the impulse to identify with a purely functional, mass-market object understood to signify the handcrafted original?

The truth was that in front of the television cameras that day, Rolex and Cartier, and whoever else was in on the media drama, crushed $50,000 worth of watches that would have been worth an inconceivable $50 million had they been real. The act only underscored what they were doing. All of them, the world over: the Taiwanese factory owners, the Air China flight attendants with their carry-ons full of merchandise, the greased-up customs agents, the truckers and wholesalers and dreadlocked street vendors. With the fake, Elliot thought, they were taking apart the symbols of luxury, democratizing, deconstructing them, monkey-wrenching the exclusivity of the real. Which made the fake more real than the original, more honest. Nothing was withheld.

Tell it to the cops. Tell it to the lawyers. What sold like legal drugs eventually began to sell like semi-legal drugs. Then, just like drug drugs. International agreements were struck between government trade mandarins who wore real watches. Rolex hired a legal team that scanned transactions all over the world looking for something that was now being called copyright infringement. There were rumours of undercover cops trolling the flea-market tables looking for fakes. They all should have taken notice. Elliot should have reasoned onward from Rico's righteous indignation at the five-eighths value caught up in the imaginary qualities of a logo, and arrived at the conclusion that such magic was probably controlled by people with a little defensive wizardry of their own. It was, but Elliot didn't. So he found himself looking at cinder blocks, listening to metal doors slamming open and closed. Locks buzzing the end of freedom.

The lawyer had walked calmly from the judge's bench to the table where Elliot was sitting. He said, "How about a drink?"

Later, Rico told Elliot, "Don't forget, you've promised never to sell these items again."

Elliot took the photocopy of the judge's order. "I have?"

He had. So they moved on to ripoff perfumes, home-silkscreened designer T-shirts, then sunglasses. The next really big thing. Oakley, Vuarnet, Ray-Ban, Gaultier, Revo, Bollé. When the 1980s turned into the 1990s, suddenly they couldn't bring the shades in fast enough. They dropped the street carts and began selling exclusively wholesale. Cases of designer clones that a Chinese contact with the unlikely name of Garfield Yum agreed to ship in from Hong Kong hidden in fifty-pound bags of rice. The misdeclaration of contents meant cheaper Canadian import duty, not to mention better ocean freight rates. A lesson in cost of goods sold, well learned. Elliot and Kirov were pulling in goods at about half the cost paid by competitors, increasing Rico's market share, winning what had started to seem like a game neither of them could believe they'd taken so long to discover. If once every couple of months another smaller package came in with the shades, marked *For Delivery to the Mandarin Orchestra Society*, Elliot passed it off to Yum or threw it in a UPS pouch sent to whatever address Rico left on what they called the black-phone voice mail. An unlisted mailbox where Rico had taught Elliot to check for instructions.

But Rico was pleased with them. More than pleased. Elliot's ammo boxes were filling steadily. The money was, in Rico's own words: "A tide that raised all fucking boats." And in answer to the question, when Elliot finally asked, Rico answered simply, "Passports."

Yes, passports. He'd seen one before, hadn't he? Well, he didn't need to see these.

But whose were they? Elliot was failing to get it quickly.

Rico sighed. "You are aware that people want to come to this country? More people than are legally allowed to do so? These people, if they want to succeed, need passports."

"From where?"

"Think about it. Canada. Not to stay here, of course. To use going south."

"But made where?"

"You need to know all this?"

"I'm curious."

"Israel and Indonesia. It's complicated."

Elliot judged he didn't need to know more. Kirov, the only immigration problem he'd ever known close up, had circumvented the law in a different way. His friend didn't need a passport because he'd fallen in love with the girl who worked in the Happy Planet Café, pulling iced chais and assembling breakfast bagels for the backpackers and pot tourists who stayed in the hostel next door. Too lovestruck to think of tactics, Kirov had to be advised by Elliot (who hadn't had a girlfriend for longer than three weeks in over three years) on the obvious angle.

Kirov blushed at the suggestion. To which Elliot said, "You like her?"

He did indeed like her, Elliot knew without understanding why. She was plump, monosyllabic, bored and seemingly not holding vast intelligence in reserve. Elliot found out her name was Lucille. Then later, in some completely unconnected conversation, that her last name was Ball. He wanted Kirov to be happy, so he offered advice.

"Say something about being Ricky. Should get you a date, anyway."

Next time they met, Kirov told him he'd tried the gambit. "She has heard about this television show before. She said her grandparents used to watch it."

But it worked. Elliot heard all about it from a yet more grateful Kirov. They were dating. They were moving in together. It all happened very fast. And now she actually smiled at Elliot, squeezing off his morning espresso, and he was forced to consider what Kirov saw. Understanding women to find his friend gorgeous, he wondered, Weren't there leggy Siberian girls with high cheekbones and *Danger* stamped in the drop light of their irises by whom Kirov might be more exotically diverted?

Apparently not. Kirov belonged to Lucille Ball. So Elliot looked and looked and waited to understand what specific physical thing it was. And a full month later, he got it. Watching her move heavily to the coffee machine, mother sun tattoo peeking out above her thong line. She turned sideways, cocking the white cup under the spigot, turned enough that Elliot could see the round push of her belly, the chubby roll of her from the silver studdery in her navel, down below her sagging waistband, and he knew what it was all in that very instant. Kirov loved the belly roll. It was deliberate, unapologetic, sexy. Very sexy. He was visualizing sex with Lucille just that moment. In dry grass on a ridge overlooking a cove and a field beyond where dirty-faced kids played kick the can and ate huckleberries. But the much greater surprise—standing there, thinking all these crazy thoughts, staring like a lech—was that he found the point of her sexuality so clear that his chest ached.

Although not for long. When he thought back on this period, he didn't remember suppressing his heart. He only remembered that somehow over the course of eight years working with Rico—the glorious last half of the 1980s and the first three years of the 1990s—he'd evolved into a different person without noticing an increment of change. He didn't like the sensation this provoked: a feeling that he could not vouch for himself. He couldn't swear that this Elliot, here and now, this very moment, was the real one.

Two events were pinned in memory to this emerging inner queasiness. The first was the publication of a book by a man named Cameron Lark. Elliot might have missed it entirely had he not ambled by an uptown bookstore and seen his father's face on the cover of a coffee-table book in the window. He squinted at it. He went to skim the pages, standing in the racks.

He didn't think he cared much what might be found on those pages, although his heart still beat hard as he riffled through the colour plates. His father in front of what looked like a chapel. His father standing with a man who wore perfectly round glasses with heavy black frames. His father looking ragged, in a wheelchair, an arrangement of what appeared to be children's blocks spread out on a card table in front of him. The early years (white cubes and things on stilts), the middle years (concrete high-rises), then late years (cedar houses perched on rock outcroppings). Elliot tried reading some, but found that the text chased him back to the pictures.

> Here the pleasure of the positive green space is an intentional, well-kept secret. A moment made physical by the obfuscation of surrounding structures. These allow a stolen glimpse of sky, intended for soulful. . .

That passage under a photograph of a simple garden.

Elliot flipped back to the beginning. Then forward a little more. And here he moistened a finger, dabbed it to the paper, then rolled over page 109. A photograph of a low city in poor light identified in the caption as Seoul, 1963. A few sentences later, he reached the crucial one:

> . . . It is perhaps part of the obscure and personal program of the man that so little is known of his time in the Hermit Kingdom capital, other than the fact

that Seoul was where Gordon fathered
his first son, and from where the baby
boy was brought home shortly after his
birth in 1963.

The page warped inward, the black ink appeared to darken under the words.

But no anguish. No chest beating. No epic drinking session followed. There was nothing in the discovery to distress, only to perplex. In 1963, the mother he'd only ever been told had died a month after his birth, was either *from* or merely *in* Korea. There was less knowing than unknowing in it, and double-edged unknowing too. Yes, he wondered about surrounding circumstance. About how going to Korea to study ceramics—the recorded reason for his father's trip—could possibly have motivated what ended up becoming his own life. What other forces had been at play? Love, lust. Something. But even more so, how much did the discovery retroactively change *him?* What had he become as a result of turning that page? How could he have survived previously, completely severed from the truth of who he was? The real Elliot.

He looked in the mirror a long time, found no evidence there of anything Korean. He had olive skin. He had dark hair. Fine. He also had dark circles under round, red eyes. He had a two-day growth of beard. His teeth, which had not been well cared for, were now darkening a little at the roots. He didn't know what any of it meant, only that his features were now backlit by some new thing loose inside him, some new foliage, growing wild.

Two weeks later a second event, complementary. Kirov's wedding. The ceremony had been at the O, of course. The bride wore black, a long socklike gown cut to reveal her wedding vow hennaed in Cyrillic script up her spine from lumbar to nape of the neck. Kirov—whose matching vows ringed each biceps—was delirious with joy. He wept openly when Rico and Elliot unveiled their gift to the newlyweds: a 1973 Cadillac Brougham, bright red, with a set of black Texas longhorns as hood ornament.

Elliot accepted Kirov's embrace, hoping a long toast would not follow, which it then immediately did. Kirov laid out his thanks in tightening concentric rings. From the larger community (there were 250 people crammed into the Orwell lobby, another few dozen drinking on the sidewalk out front), to friends, then to family, then to Lucille herself. Then, when there really shouldn't have been any more rings, to Elliot. And here something changed in Kirov's delivery. Because he was now crediting his friend with nothing less than a fundamental reordering of his own life. With helping him shape up and sharpen his focus and straighten his aim and understand what was truly important, even to believe in himself and all that he could accomplish. That last word rang on in the smoky air long after it was said.

Or at least it rang on for Elliot. Not entirely from embarrassment, although there was a measure of that. A brighter, less stoned Lucille would have reasonably hoped for a toast that ended with her. But what struck Elliot more was the unexpected assent in that low-lit room. Here were former punks and headbangers, a dozen people Elliot knew to have kicked heroin and several who hadn't, drinkers and those from every one of the twelve steps of recovery. Here were colleagues from the fake trade, the headshop crowd, guys who sold concert merchandise or pirated porn, ran indie record labels or managed bands or were tapped into clandestine pine-mushroom picking operations. And the sense Elliot had coasting out the far side of Kirov's toast—people were whooping and cheering and downing mugs of beer—was not of the underground, in any cultural sense, but of a free enterprise mosh pit. They were the post-punk entrepreneurial class, he thought. A kind of badly mannered, foul-mouthed, contrary-minded middle class.

"The hate bourgeoisie," he said aloud, but to himself.

"What're you skulking around down here for?" Rico stood in the doorway of Apartment A. Elliot, who by that point in their relationship would let himself into Rico's outer sitting room where the many televisions and video monitors were arrayed, was down near the bottom half of a bottle of Rico's house white, sipping from the neck of the bottle. He had his feet up. Feeding himself stale Nuts 'n Bolts from a couch-side bowl. He was watching a fight on some obscure Spanish-language satellite sports channel. Two Mexican fighters. Garcia and Jimenez, according to the punch stats at the bottom of the screen. Neither of whom were likely to become household names any time soon judging from their complete lack of defence, their wide-swinging offence.

"We got a wedding going on here," Rico said, lighting a usable cigar butt from the pedestal ashtray by the door.

"Watch this," Elliot said. "This Jimenez just got clocked and took a knee. But he's going to come right back."

Rico came over. The ref had just separated a clinch and was cautioning Jimenez about holding. The fighter was waggling his head back and forth, trying to shake off the punch he hadn't seen coming.

"You have money on this?" Rico asked.

"I just know," Elliot said. "Garcia's all pumped because he caught him. But he's overlooking the small detail that Jimenez's defence sucks so bad I could have hit him. Now watch Garcia wade in cocky and get spanked."

On-screen events unfolded as Elliot predicted. Garcia pushed Jimenez to the ropes, let his hands go, then walked straight into a right-hand counter. It caught him flush and down he went.

"Hey," Elliot said. "I'm good."

"You should get back up there," Rico said to him, eyes still on the screen. "Kirov is asking after you." He keyed off the sound and stood watching the silent television for a moment, the card girl just now circling. Round 11. The championship rounds.

Elliot said, "We're just businessmen."

Rico, whose interest in a sporting event had been piqued, did not immediately answer. Jimenez continued his counterattack in the new round, driving the stunned Garcia back across the ring and into the opposite ropes.

"I mean," Elliot went on, "I used to think we were tak-ing something apart and showing people how it worked. I thought what we were doing had importance beyond . . ."

Rico sighed, still looking at the screen. "Beyond mak-ing money?"

Jimenez was flagging.

"Rico? You really checking out? Heading south?"

There was a minor risk asking, since he'd never been plainly told. Still, there had been signs. More and more the coordination of new deals had fallen entirely to Elliot and Kirov. More and more the people who worked for Rico were calling Elliot with updates on trucking, on the port and customs. And when he'd ask about Rico, he'd hear about more property being sold. Something in Whistler. Or a B & B on one of the islands that Elliot would never have believed Rico to own.

Now Rico sat on the arm of the couch, eyes still on the television. The Jimenez comeback was over. Garcia was nailing him with every conceivable shot. There was blood running fiercely from a gash under Jimenez's left eye. Twenty seconds remaining in the eleventh. The ringside doctor, were there any justice and mercy remaining in the sport, would stop Jimenez on his stool before the twelfth. Or maybe he wouldn't.

"You could say I'm in the process of leaving," Rico said finally.

"And how's that going?" Elliot asked him.

Rico winced and coughed, got up to pour them Jack Daniel's. Seemed cops in the Caymans cost a fortune and negotiated long and hard. "We're getting there," Rico said, handing him the drink.

It would take another three years for Rico to get there. All the way up to 1995. Three years during which the feel of the trade eroded from anything you'd ever call Glory Years into what felt more like a bitter endgame. Everybody scrambling. Nothing lasting for long. It was sportswear for awhile. Chicago Bulls, L.A. Lakers, Nike, Fila. These were the big winners. Kirov learned about a company in Guangdong that made major league baseball caps indistinguishable from the real thing, which was no surprise really given the real thing was made just down the road. But while product life cycles had always been short—exclusivity followed by competition segueing to legal troubles—now it all happened impossibly fast and the downside was steep. Rumours swirled about private investigators on payroll with some of the major sports franchises. Anybody new—buyers, employees, warehousing or trucking companies—was a source of suspicion, fear, precaution. Busts were on the rise.

Rico didn't leave the building any more without circling the block three times, then driving a few blocks one direction and doubling back. He frequently left by the Orwell front door for no reason at all, then returned a couple minutes later by the back way, to sit in Apartment A with a baseball bat across his knees, waiting in vain for somebody to come through the window. His guys were now tailing shipments out of the port, redirecting the trucking company by cellphone to first one new delivery address and then another. They'd have the truck heading out to Abbotsford, then double back down the highway. Somebody hanging twenty car lengths back, watching for tails. They never caught one, which Elliot thought was a very good thing for all concerned.

Then one sunny Saturday morning Kirov came to find Elliot with the news that a Los Angeles wholesaler had discovered a private investigator on staff, undercover. A mole.

"So tell Rico," Elliot said to him.

Kirov shook his head. Elliot's first moment of understanding that some kind of succession plan was now in full swing.

"Well, what do you want me to do?" Elliot asked Kirov. "Go mole hunting?"

That wasn't the primary concern. The primary concern was that these wholesalers were looking for help with the cost of a hit man.

Elliot choked on a mouthful of omelette. Here he'd been having a quiet Postum breakfast. "Jesus," he said, wiping his mouth. "Fuckity fuck."

Kirov shook his head sadly.

"What did you tell them?"

Kirov sighed. He said, "I told them I think this plan would most definitely take the fun out of it."

Elliot's relief was enormous, immediate. Then later he wondered about that too. Was he relieved because he thought Kirov might have gone for it? He hoped he hadn't thought that, even subconsciously. He was in this business to make money, fine. He was on the borderline between what was legal and not, okay sure. He was an outcast and an outsider and a person nobody was going to write up in some fancy house and home magazine for keeping the Gordon name great. Guilty on all counts. But forget about hit men. When somebody started talking about whacking people, you needed new lines. You needed completely new ideas.

Kirov thought maybe a return to westernwear. "There are two-piece boots coming out of Thailand. Really nice."

Elliot passed on that idea without having a single better one. Then the moment came. All that was merely shifting and unmoored, now in motion. Personal revolution that dawned, appropriately enough, in a dollar store. Chinatown. Five hundred square feet of cheap plastic shit. He was just looking for a pen. And sifting through the offerings—deciding which animated Disney character he disliked the least: Mickey, Sylvester or Pooh—he came across what perhaps only he, in all the world, would know on sight to be a very rare object.

The misspelled Swach. It brought back a flood of memory, and he liked that. Vintage fakery. It turned out the man had a wagonload of them, all stashed away for the past eight years since the fake watch business had tanked. All purchased originally, of course, from Rico.

Elliot bought his remaining stock and returned triumphantly to the Orwell, the back of his truck stacked with boxes. He wasn't even sure if he got it right away. If he processed right through what the purchase represented. Maybe only when the first few wholesale buyers had gone bug-eyed looking them over. Maybe only after he was down to one box remaining. Only then did he realize what had happened. He'd aged one critical generation. He'd been around long enough to rip off ideas from earlier years and to have an advantage doing so.

Kirov contacted their hat maker in Guangdong, who put them on to a plastic jewellery maker. Elliot wrote up a spec sheet, describing the imperfections of the copied Swatch right down to the misspelling and the blurry paint under the numbers. Two months later, they were on top of a new six-month exclusive. A fake fake that, looked at in a certain rhetorical light, was the first *real* thing Elliot had trafficked since punk music and probably including that. Elliot was thinking about whole new directions.

"The thing I like about this is that we're making them ourselves," he said to Kirov. "These are our ideas. Real ideas."

Kirov was altogether less inclined to analyze, but he went along with the notion.

"And the stuff is excellent," Elliot continued. "Where did you find these guys?"

It was a bigger question than he could have imagined. Somewhere outside of Seoul, Kirov told him. "These guys can make anything. Literally, anything. New, old, whatever."

Seoul. Elliot breathed in. Deep, deep. Then out. *Yeah.*

———

Rico should have been proud. He should have seen the good new thing they were building. The glory years were over. He was leaving town. They were moving on. But in the black-phone voice mail he left the next day, Rico didn't sound like he saw it that way at all. He was wheezy, coughing long and hard at least twice during the message. Must talk. Meet me at the float plane. Such and such an hour.

Rico didn't say a word about where they were going and, as far as Elliot could tell, the pilot didn't even know. They pulled free of the steel blue water of the inlet, soared up over the ships at berth, the container terminal, the railyards. They climbed slowly through an altitude from which the downtown eastside could be seen as the old city it was. Hemmed by towers to the west and suburbs farther east. Here was a craggy grid of streets, evidence of brickwork and solid old buildings. No needles visible from this height. No bad johns.

Rico pointed north, an arm extended across the pilot's chest toward his side window. The pilot gave a thumbs-up and they hauled over, a wingtip pointing earthward, another to the sky. Elliot gripped the seat back and felt his stomach flip. His eyes were suddenly locked inside the cabin, seeing all the detail of the old bush plane wrapped so tightly around them. The fake wood panelling on the dash. The analogue dials, now spinning, heaving. The improbable cigarette lighter, a pilot's convenience from another era.

They flew a long time, nobody trying to talk over the engine's roar. Up the green valleys and into the bush. Here the mist hung in bands along the flanks of the mountains. The major and then the minor highways dropped behind them until the only evidence of traffic was the power lines and tendril logging roads linking the clear-cuts. They passed low over a ridge line seeming to break into true wilderness. Unlike anything Elliot had ever seen. For a moment just above the crest of this ridge, he could look down at the trees and see them singly, from directly above. See the rock and moss and rough grass on which they grew. He thought of their impossible distance from anything. The degree of their isolation should the plane go down. What a fine and rare quality their *lost* would be.

Rico brought fishing gear, so they fished. Then they drank a bottle of wine, carrying it away from the lake a short stroll. Rico pissed against a lichened boulder while Elliot looked away, shivering. The time had come, Rico finally told him. And with those words out, he was for several minutes uncharacteristically expansive. He spoke at greater length than Elliot had ever heard him speak before. Yes, he was leaving. Not today or tomorrow exactly, but soon and suddenly. And the big message, the reason they were there, is that Elliot had to get out.

"Get out?" Elliot said, shocked. "I'm just setting up this new thing."

Rico wasn't interested in the new thing. The time was here for total change. Don't be listening to Kirov. *Beware the Russian who owes you his life.*

"Well, it's easy for you to say," Elliot tried again. "You've got a plan B. What am I supposed to do?"

"Sell," Rico said. "That's what you're supposed to do."

Sell what? What did he have to sell?

"You have what I'm leaving you," Rico said. "I don't forget friends. I'm giving my share of the O back to the investors. For you, I'm leaving the team, the system. You have people. You have contacts. You have companies set up for freight forwarding and import."

Elliot spun away, frustrated and surprised. Not ready to really mount an objection either. Rico was, still, a man with whom you were best to choose your words carefully.

Rico said, "Why? That's what you want to know. Why get out?"

He pointed west. Elliot faced into an increasingly chilly breeze, wishing he had a heavier coat and trying hard to figure out what the hell Rico was talking about. "I need to get out because of the Canadian Shield," Elliot said.

"Shield. This ain't the Shield, moron. It's the Coast Range."

"Okay. The Coast Range."

"This is the side door into North America," Rico said to him. "This is the side door into the western world. You follow?"

"Rico, I'm freezing here," Elliot said.

"I know you're smart enough to get this," Rico said. "Side-door access to Gold Mountain. The real fake market, the real direction all this is going, is people."

"I thought Soylent Green was people."

"Don't be a wiseass. This is serious business."

"What it is," Elliot said, "is women and children doing three weeks in a twenty-foot box with a space heater and a bucket for a toilet."

"Or in the belly of some rust-bucket scow that ain't safe for tuna no more. I'm not pitching you on the idea," Rico said. "I'm telling you to get out."

"I had no idea the Caymans was a choice based on ethics."

"It's a choice based on fatigue, you punk. Fatigue I'm trying to spare you. Fatigue you might otherwise feel after twenty years or maybe after one of those scows goes up on the rocks and people drown."

Elliot stared. "Jesus," he breathed.

"That's probably what they were saying, only in Chinese," Rico said, then spat into the lake.

Elliot looked away and winced into the cutting wind. This sucked, he thought. But he couldn't afford to quit working just when he'd latched onto his first real idea. "Rico, man, I'm not into that. I'll never be into that. But I still have to think about my future. My own plans."

"Plans," Rico said. "Fakes. What is that?"

"I'm not in fakes any more. I'm in anti-fakes. I'm in reals."

"Shit. This Swach thing."

"I have other ideas."

"All that shit is beside the point. The market is moving in an ugly direction. I'm giving you a way to get your piece and get out."

Rico was right, of course, although not for the reasons he was giving now. Not because Elliot had a chance to sell an existing system to some party who might not like to get everything set up from scratch. Not because getting *stuff* across imaginary lines called borders was a thing from yesterday and getting *people* from across those same lines was the business of tomorrow. He was right because of how inexorable Elliot's move away from fakes (and what was faker about the Rolex than the misspelled Swach anyway?) would lead him in a five-year loop straight back to regular fakes again. Vintage fakes then fake fakes, then fake old things of a widening variety that were less and less ironic and removed and about themselves and more about being, well, fake.

Still, Rico didn't know any of this future. He only knew Elliot should be moving on. "You come from nice family.

Truth is, I never really understood what the hell you were doing down there with all the drug addicts and pimps."

"Listen to you."

"That's my people," Rico said. "That's not your people."

"What do you know about my people?"

"You don't think I know where you come from? Big-name famous people. People who build things."

"Okay, great. Now you're going to tell me about my family."

"Don't get your toga in a knot. I'm a friendly," Rico said, peeling the foil from the second bottle of wine and drilling home the corkscrew in a practised motion. "Just be a smart kid and sell. You keep your ears open and you'll learn soon enough to who."

Somewhere, a door crashed open and another one closed. Elliot rubbed his eyes and turned to the one mirrored wall of the remand centre visitation room. So Rico and he had their little chat. Then a decade passed and here he was just coming to his senses. Just now trying to sell what Rico left him and to precisely the same party that Rico had been suggesting. Pushing ten years, more than forty years old, and here he was listening to doors open and close in a prison, all movement carefully governed, staring into the wall from behind which he could have been observed the entire time.

Hearing a voice now too. Someone missing a long time.

This is crazy. You hear me? It's fucking crazy!

Elliot stared into the mirror. Thinking, Oh my God. His face stared back in reflection. It was no other. There was no face behind his own reflection. Nobody in the dark room beyond.

*I am sick and tired of the way . . . Listen. You better fuck-
ing listen to me!*

Last thing Rico said to him on their mountain was, "So
you're not going to take any of my advice, are you."
Shaking his hand in the way of last words. Although, as it
turned out, they weren't exactly last words. True last words
came after Elliot and Kirov were back from Korea. A week
back from a tent off Tapgol Park and a room half-cracked
open to the sky, filled with rain. Elliot took his shoebox of
ironic souvenirs over to Rico who, to his credit, received
them in the spirit intended. "That's a brief history of
marketing genius right there." Turning away to cough
into a handkerchief. "Can't shake this fucker cold."

Those were the last words. Elliot never saw his mentor
again. The Orwell continued to be a hub. And when
word came back that Rico was gone, on one level all that
Elliot could think of was what an enormous waste of time
and effort his move had been. Less than ninety days of
sunshine lying on a beach and sipping capirinhas, enjoying the spoils. Then he coughed a final time.

They cleaned out Apartment A. It seemed somehow
expected that Elliot would oversee this operation, and so
he tore up the carpet, repainted. He left in the video
monitors and the bank of televisions but replaced the sagging couches. All of this activity more out of respect for
Rico than out of any desire to erase him. But during this
process, he also found his shoebox. It was in a wall safe for
which one of the Orwell people had the combination.
Rico hadn't forgotten it, the man told Elliot. Only he
didn't want to get busted going through U.S. customs one
last time for a fake Chicago Bulls jersey.

Fair enough. Although Elliot still wandered the driz-
zling streets with the box under his arm, aware he was a

picture of nervous agitation. Aware, when that moment came, that the girl in the booth at the Postum had noticed. Aware that she was going to decide one way or the other about him, but that he could affect the outcome of that decision. Aware finally—a nice awareness this one—that the way that decision could be positively affected wouldn't be a matter of pretending anything, but of listening and being honest instead.

So Elliot listened. And what a good listen that turned out to be. He had a feeling he assumed was what people meant when they described *moments of moral clarity*. All was ordered and aligned in the words of her amazing story, a story that had him shutting his eyes, dizzy with the intensity of the connection between them at that table, strangers in a present moment, and the history of other moments that had brought them there.

Afterwards, they walked the town together. Their own city where they had lived their separate lives. And he told this stranger as much as he had told anyone about himself, ever. Not without interruption, naturally. She had plenty of questions.

"What do you mean you never want kids?" she asked early. "People are always saying that and changing their minds."

Or later, on Graham: "You've never seen him since the cab ride? Never spoke? You should stay in touch with family."

And, still later: "I guess all I'm saying is, You don't look Asian at all."

He stopped cold in the street. "I don't?" All those years since Lark, eye-flirting with himself in mirrors thinking, I could be. It could be. She could have been. My connection to history and to family. It might have been.

She laughed at him, then kissed him. Which, then as now, seemed to leave only one door remaining. Back then, the door had opened gently, soundlessly. A door at the end of a hallway that smelled of hardwood and laundry, bike tires. A heavy wooden door to her room at the rear of the apartment, soundless on old-fashioned hinges.

Now—staring into that mirrored glass, examining his own reflection, all that he had and might become—the last door was proving a noisier affair. Unlike the other remand centre doors, which were sprung and relocked somehow by electric charge, this last one required actual keys. And out there in the hall, a sheriff or a deputy was patiently applying himself to the task of finding and operating those keys, a matter of much jangling and rattling and false starts.

And cursing too. Cursing and carrying on just like the sergeant had described. His brother's voice. Right there at top volume on the far side of the steel.

You guys think you can fuck with me you gotta another think coming. I'm going to . . . you just watch . . . You fucking just watch. When I get out of here, I will take action!

Elliot had to smile. Because they were going to do just that. Take action. Somehow, he felt unreasonably sure, the two of them most certainly were.

STORY HOUSE

One

THE SUN CAME UP IN AN ANGRY HAZE, ILLUMINAT-
ing a building, a white rectangle of serene dimensions
that appeared to float above the ground, to be unconnected in any physical way with the earth beneath it. This
was an optical illusion. But it persisted until the sun was
high enough to cast shadows, to reveal that the blackness
below the building was in fact a pit, dug out deep beneath
the foundations, which had themselves then been par-
tially removed. And now, with the rising light slanting

onto the scene, each lattice of scaffolding, each steel support member anchored in the shoring, each four-by-four timber laid in the criss-cross support cribs that held the structure aloft by its compass-aligned corners, each of these surfaces threw a hard black shadow. A pattern that widened and spread through the excavation, twisting and coiling in place as the sun rose, bringing to mind a machine that was both enormous and minute in mechanism, that moved very slowly and yet, in small parts of it, seemed to hurry at the same time.

Like a big clock, Zweigler thought. Just like the counterfeiter's wife had said. Darcy. Deirdre.

At which point, as if in response to that very idea, the sun on-screen crept to a stop and seemed to quiver in place. Then it unsprung and began to drift back toward the east. The shadows beginning to whirl in place once again, though faster this time, rushing the whole scene back toward dawn, toward orange and then pink, red then bloody maroon. Finally to the blackness that had come before dawn. A blackness that now absorbed the white structure entirely.

Silence followed. Then, after a few seconds, the faintest ticking sound. Not a clock at all, he didn't think, but a drip of water. Or the creak of a floorboard. Rhythmic, ambient, not foleyed. Steady for several seconds, before his field of vision was suffused again in white as the building burst again to view, punching backward into the day before. Or *some* day before, Zweigler noted, because now the scaffolding, the support cribs, the pit were gone. And the building was back on its own foundation, plugged to the ground. Shining white and clean, 55 East Mary Street laid out in front of him at what was its pinnacle moment. Stripped and empty, camera ready and not yet revealed to be fragile with interconnected faults.

"Quite nice," Zweigler said. "That was really quite nice."

"Thanks," responded the editor from somewhere over his shoulder. "From there I thought we cut to our title sequence. Then out to whatever happens next."

Whatever happened next.

"And I was thinking maybe we use the animated plans at this point," said the editor.

"Let's have a look."

Zweigler stretched his legs out in the cool darkness of the editing suite, waiting while the clip was located and loaded for viewing off some whirring hard drive in the guts of the editing machinery. It was possible to enjoy himself for a few seconds just then, thinking of the sequence he'd just seen. It was a good opening for the final episode of a series that had gone better than expected until just recently.

"What do we have in the way of wall footage?" Zweigler asked. "What about we wind the whole sequence back farther, take us back to before the wall came down. You think?"

They could do that, the editor told him. "Here's the animated sequence."

Zweigler sat back and watched as a blueprint unfurled down the screen, first flattening, then leaping into 3-D, the lines springing out of the paper. Now the rectangular simplicity of the building spun into place, a line-drawn jewel. Three simple parallel planes connected by that filigree coil of stairway. The structure was really glorified in this rendering, he thought. Lifted not just out of the ground on stilts, but out of the world entirely, out of the paper on which it was conceived and right out of any human context at all. Perhaps that was where it was meant to be. There on-screen in animated form, where its proportions, its clean expression of ideal, its architectural rigour and lack of equivocation were made transparent, indisputable. Where even the strange decoupling of form and function evident in the building was somehow a stable notion, rendered in a white space out of reach to human hands.

Zweigler sighed, watching. The editor was now reading the voice-over text that had been prepared by an architectural consultant. Golden sections and DNA strands, equal debts to the moderns and the Haida Gwaii longhouse, subtle expressions of light and materiality. Zweigler listened, not listening. He thought of money, briefly and intensely, as was his practice. Up on anxious stilts himself, just at the moment. He added the numbers he'd have to pay out of pocket himself to get things moving again if, like the building, the brothers ended up hung over a pit. If nothing further could be agreed between them, if they broke their contract with him and the building ended up dying, frozen in a place of no compromise.

TIMOTHY
TAYLOR

It was a long series of numbers, in fact. One each for fixing problems with the roof, the walls, the windows, the foundation and the soil. Perhaps not the soil, he reflected.

Perhaps there was no dollar figure assignable to soil because it likely couldn't be fixed.

Could he then—thinking outside the box now, he encouraged himself—could he sell the idea of a building rotting in place on television? Decay in physical structures was inevitable, after all. Celebrated even by those builders who had so inspired the famous father, who let their villages rot in place (if they were no longer required for use) without flurrying to intervene.

Zweigler sighed. Fine in theory. But dull, no? Not the climax he'd been hoping for: an architectural gem, an architectural name revealed in some extraordinary way. Truth and authenticity. He thought of his reputation, calmly. Did anybody important care what he was doing up here? Yes, he decided, several did among his financiers, insurers and partners. And even people inclined to stroke off the money, forgive the wasted time, even those who were aware of the Gordon name and understood how it might be profitably publicized, even some of *those* people would be troubled, he estimated, that Avi Zweigler had failed where he advertised a personal interest. A sign of weakness that, surely.

About three-quarters of a million, he figured, the long series of numbers finally giving up a sum. And that would be only the beginning. Fixed, sealed and painted, somebody would then have to keep the place up. Real costs the avoidance of which would return the building along a straight line to precisely the ruin they'd found it in.

"Do we have all that recent 16mm transferred?" Zweigler asked. He interrupted an extended comment on the layered use of light in the structure. Here was another idea he remembered hearing first from Deirdre. She obliged him by coming on set just once. It was always good to suggest the family life interrupted outside the frame, but she'd ended up talking architecture with him. Surprised him, standing there with the babies in their twin stroller on the lip of the site. She was the smartest of the group, he found himself thinking. Smartest for being able to say what she knew calmly, not exploding with emotion or some violent denial thereof. The building was exceptional, she believed, because its proportions were unstrained, because its components had been minimized as far as materials would allow, because it harvested light in three distinct layers. And more too. But she was also the smartest in Zweigler's mind for knowing when to call it enough. Nobody else involved, himself very much included, had the brains to do the same.

Yes, the editor was telling him, all the 16mm footage shot so far on the Bolex Paillard was transferred. "Hours and freaking hours of it."

"Not good?" Zweigler asked.

"Everything was fine until a couple days ago," the editor said.

Zweigler looked away and winced. Nothing from the beginning could have suggested this unsatisfactory stasis. It had descended so quickly and unpredictably. Nothing from the first pitch he'd received from a visitation room at the remand centre in Vancouver. Graham Gordon. The one he sent away with the camera and a wish for . . . well, he didn't quite know for what. For a film to erase the one that looped endlessly in memory, the one showing the slow erection of his own prison? Perhaps that was it. Or payback. A possible explanation that was less flattering to what Zweigler still thought was a fundamentally good disposition toward humankind. *Take this camera and go destroy yourself.* Zweigler knew well enough that cameras in general, let alone Packer Gordon's, had that power.

Here Graham was borderline delirious. He'd found a spectacular thing, he told Zweigler. Hidden behind a wall in a block full of shooting galleries and Chinese restaurants. Dated by materials to such-and-such, inspired by so-and-so, ideologically capturing . . . Zweigler didn't

remember all that the building was supposed to have ideologically captured. Graham said a pure architectural
idea with all its merits and faults. He said modern yet
organic, something Zweigler had not understood then
and was still not sure he did now.

"Slow down," Zweigler said to him. "Why are you
telling me all this exactly?"

Because it was built by my father. Graham was yelling.

Then, another eruption at his end of the phone.
Somebody talking in the background. Somebody trying
to take the phone. The receiver dropped in the middle of
a dispute, voices raised. There was much crashing of
metal furniture. And then somebody else was in the
room, a third voice giving the order that they knock it off
right that instant.

Avi Zweigler listened remotely through a phone he
imagined was lying on the concrete floor of this echo-y
place. Listening with something like a descending mist
around his ears. Cold and salty. As if he were much
closer to a northern sea than his situation on Stone
Canyon allowed.

"Your brother is there with you?" Zweigler asked
Graham when he came back on.

Graham went straight home and e-mailed the pictures he'd taken the night before. They were ghosted by
the flash and framed like they'd been taken at the trot,
or drunk. Or both. But Zweigler could make out the
shape of it looming in the blue night. He could extrap-
olate the geometry of a wall stretching away to its corner. The flat roofline above. The admittedly familiar
arrangement of windows. In his own collection of
models and photographs there were several possible
matches. Possible.

Still he rejected the idea at first. It was ridiculous, off the schedule, unplanned. Who had the time? Here he had a guy in Vermont who was up to 110 feet on a spire of dried chicken bones mounted on his garage. He had a woman renovating a salvage U.S. Navy coastal frigate into a cruise ship somewhere in the Gulf of Mexico. A Unitarian chapel made of Pepto-Bismol bottles. A sixty-foot roadside crucifix of old dashboard cigarette lighters, burnt blue and winking evilly in the sun. The country was awash with unexpected architecture that, he increasingly suspected, was being built with *Unexpected Architecture* in mind. Nobody needed Avi Zweigler to turn on to a new show at this exact moment, especially not one about truth and authenticity, when the numbers weren't even tailing off on the old show yet.

But there he was, two o'clock in the morning, standing over the kitchen telephone. Pacing away and returning. It was something he hadn't done in forty years, not since he'd last been in love: waking at two in the morning to call someone, to make sure some communication was immediate and complete. He stood there, finger floating above the one button. Around him his utterly unused kitchen, pristine granite and aluminium surfaces, untarnished copper, three Matisse sketches his hard-won ownership of which had scarcely registered in his consciousness over the past ten years. And under the soles of his bare feet, the warmth of the day still bleeding out of the stones at that late hour.

"That's quite a building you've found up there . . ." Words that he knew would inaugurate great action. Graham's gratitude was volatile, combustible. He raged about the vision before his mind's eye already, of what they would create together.

With your brother, Zweigler said. Surprised and pleased to have agreement so early.

No no no. You and me, Graham said. Elliot didn't know anything about architecture. Elliot didn't care about their father's reputation. He didn't work well with people. He was difficult. He had moods. He hung out on skid row with violent people and drug addicts. This was an architectural idea. This was an important idea. This had nothing to do with Elliot at all.

Which was wrong from any angle you could think of, Zweigler knew, especially from the angle of what made good television. But there was no need to discuss it further with Graham. The truth of the situation, he knew, would find a way of imposing itself. And the truth here was that these boys canted inexorably toward one another—Zweigler saw two halves of a Gothic arch leaning in shakily toward a keystone—and nobody could avoid that structural reality.

Still he was surprised to receive that second call at six the very next morning. That first loop of dispute between them having taken just four hours to knit itself closed and already, Zweigler registered, this action calling on him to borrow against his own sleep. But there it was. The phone ringing. Elliot, who introduced himself in jumpy, staccato tones. Then informed him: "I was not totally in favour of you being involved. I mean, at first."

"Have we met?" Zweigler asked.

"Television, not you personally. See, my dad recorded his buildings on film."

Silver nitrate fan, Zweigler thought. "But more people will see this on television than they would on film."

"Could be," Elliot said. "But he didn't shoot film for publicity either. He shot for the record. Anyway. My mind was changed by the *Antiques Roadshow.*"

Zweigler was listening hard, trying to imagine where this one was calling from. But nothing. Dead silence but for the voice and nothing on the call display either. "How so?" he said.

Well, he'd been watching the *Antiques Roadshow* last night, Elliot explained, and it suddenly occurred to him that the money shot was the fake. Some guy with his collection of antique pistols, the Colt single-action long-barrel prize of which turns out to have been stamped in Guangdong. "Or Tijuana, more likely. If it came from Guangdong, they probably wouldn't catch it."

Point being that the fake made the show real. It made the other objects on the show real. And the people, who stood there next to the objects pretending they didn't care much about value, the fake made them real too. And all this got him thinking that the prevalence of fakery on television made the whole medium more real.

"Mary Street is real," he declared.

"You know it's by your father," Zweigler said.

Suspected for a long time, he told him. And with Graham's arrival on the scene, Zweigler's interest, Elliot thought they both should be aware that while he was in favour of telling people about it, even unveiling it on television, he had just signed a purchase agreement on the building. Bought contents and all from his wife's aunt, for a pittance. "The neighbourhood is bad. You can't give stuff away down here."

"And," Zweigler said calmly, "what should we be aware you intend to do with it now?"

The more complicated question. Elliot had thought about it for some time and still wasn't sure what his obligations as the new owner should be. It would involve restoration, that much he understood. But to what? "I'm

TIMOTHY
TAYLOR

278

not sure what the hell it was," he said. "Something good for the neighbourhood though. Something that won't be a crack house in ten years."

How readily the arch of tension took shape around that keystone. How obvious it was, just at that moment of leaning-in, that Zweigler himself was being locked in place by the force at work between them. It wasn't an uncomfortable sensation, this squeezing. It was exciting. It was a swirling view of the stars.

Zweigler put Elliot on hold and punched up Graham on the other line. He stood himself under a Gordon arch in his own house, one that blended his indoors with his outdoors, that absorbed the azure of Pacific dawn and pulled it right into his living quarters, that gave the room its lungs. He related the news to Graham, listening as he breathed heavily into the other end of the line, a ship's whistle sounding somewhere in the background.

"He knows it was built by my father," Graham said, "because I told him."

"He says he's known for several years. There are carvings—"

"Fine," Graham interrupted. "Put him on."

Elliot clicked into their phone space. "Top o' the morning," he said.

"I cannot believe you would do this, you bastard," Graham said.

First words.

"Don't hang up," Zweigler said, then reasserted calm by putting Elliot on hold for thirty seconds and saying a slow string of words to Graham that ended with: ". . . so you decide how important his co-operation is now."

Over to Elliot. He said only, "He's all right now. Are you all right?"

Elliot said, "Tell him he's lucky I don't hire another architect. There are others. Tell him I bailed his ass out of jail, which cost me more than I spent on the building."

"I won't tell him that. Neither will you," Zweigler said. "Graham, you there?"

To their credit, they both more or less managed nice for the few minutes Zweigler ran through his idea. Six episodes, he thought. The story of a discovered structure, a rediscovered name. The story of co-operation in service of a good cause: the bringing back of an important structure, built by an important man, and doing so in a neighbourhood that didn't have a lot of good news day to day.

"Bringing it back from what?" Elliot asked.

"From what it was originally," Zweigler said. "Back to its true self."

"Which was what?" he asked again, tone pointed, syllables jangling.

"Hello?" Graham said, speaking around a cigarillo he was now smoking into the phone. "A house, I'd say. Sorry, are we arguing about this point?"

"We're not arguing," Zweigler said.

". . . a house capturing the confluence of a man's ideas. Plenty of flaws too. But capturing them quite perfectly."

"Flaws?" asked Elliot.

But here Zweigler interrupted to keep things moving forward. The important point, he said, was that people were endlessly interested in three things at that moment in the history of non-fiction television: renovations, old things discovered to be beautiful and/or valuable . . .

"And real," Elliot said.

Beautiful and valuable and real. And third, Zweigler went on: "Struggles by pairs or teams of people to co-operate despite what might not be entire accord between them."

"*Survivor*," Graham said. "We played that game once already."

"Think *Eco-Challenge*," Zweigler advised. "My point here being that we have a show with strong elements. I see a real shot at weekday evening U.S. households."

Stubborn silence.

Well, Zweigler also knew how to turn negotiation into a more pointed affair. They didn't want to work together? They couldn't stand the sight of one another? Nothing could possibly concern him less. They were now locked in place. Graham wasn't going to let go of a chance to see the building made great again in front of a few million people and under his direct guidance. Graham the hotel designer, overshadowed, finally out from under. And Elliot. Here was the more interesting case. Elliot couldn't even explain to himself why he'd struck fast and secured the building. He wasn't trying to keep it from Graham at all. He was trying to hold a memory and understand his own connection to it. His own connection to a great and respected man.

"Mary Street is real," Elliot had said.

You bet it is, Zweigler thought. Only now it was time to quietly force the matter to its close. "You don't have my support unless you co-operate. Neither of you get what you're after without my support. So where does this leave you? It leaves you, if you'll allow me, twenty-four hours to decide. In the meantime, I'm going back to bed."

Zweigler listened to be sure they'd both signed off before hanging up himself. He sat utterly still for three minutes. He thought: Three minutes to sell myself on the idea. Three minutes to run through the complicated way in which I might finally take back power from the man who had removed so much of it so many years before. *May she rest in peace and never hear me complaining. We had good years and bad years, but I don't believe we ever set out to hurt one another.* Of course, whoever did set out to hurt? Sociopaths. People who were swept into the beds of strangers, exotically famous strangers or otherwise, were responding to different cues altogether.

Then he began phoning people.

"We're going to break schedule for this? What's the rush?" This was Raul, one of his partners at lunch the following week. Raul was an ambitious twenty-eight-year-old Mexican American somehow inhabited by the soul of a skeptical seventy-three-year-old Jewish grandfather. Zweigler and Raul got along uncommonly well.

The rush was to capitalize on an agreement that wouldn't last.

"Story House," Raul said. "Run it by me again."

They were at the Beverly Hills Four Seasons, sun knifing in between the palm fronds. Zweigler said, "Architect, client. Program, envelope. Vision and reality. These are basic tensions. We can repackage this concept around any number of projects. Architects and clients reliably fight, in one way or another, trust me."

"And in this particular case?"

"Legacy and warring sons," Zweigler said.

"Gordon left the building to them?"

"Not quite. You could say the building found its way back to them."

"And . . ." His friend was struggling to think of the right questions to ask. The project had an interesting aroma, but was an unusual shape. "What kind of building?"

"Call it some kind of a perfect structure, perfect architectural idea. In bad shape now, but you can still see what was extraordinary about it. Clean, transparent, thin lines. All of which is extremely popular now."

"What about these sons?"

Well, the architect was their brooding visionary, their obsessive dreamer. "Not that he has no reputation himself. He did La Molta."

"I know La Molta."

But Graham Gordon was also at that stage of his career when he was carrying around a head full of bigger ideas, waiting for bigger commissions, bigger stages. He hadn't had his Expo pavilion, his Olympic ski jump, his business school library or museum renovation. And he was getting to those middle years when the big ideas had to come off the page or be lost to the built world forever. Commissions had to flow. "Hyping the Gordon name makes a certain amount of professional sense from that perspective."

"And the other one."

"Half-brother. Difficult, but smart. Married to a former architect. Go nuts with that if you like. He has money from some kind of shady business past he doesn't talk about. One of those guys who tries again and again to go straight, to be respectable. It never takes. He's a good foil."

Raul wiped his mouth with a napkin. "Plus they hate each other."

Something in the neighbourhood of hate. "They don't trust each other. But the point is we don't discover Le Corbusier buildings very often. We pretty much know where all the Neutras are. What we have here is an architect's architect. Famous but not overbranded. And dead twenty years this year, so our timing is good."

His friend sucked his teeth. "This is going to be expensive, I take it."

"More than an *Extreme Makeover Home Edition*. Less than a Super Bowl half-time show. But we give them a budget and lock them up in a completion contract. They're on the hook for overruns. We're insulated unless they lose their minds and walk, in which case, I suppose, we could always sue them."

"Great," Raul said. "And with no plans, no records, a survey showing an empty lot . . . we're going to take their word that it's by the old man?"

Escape avenues yawned open to the left and the right; Zweigler sipped iced tea and powered on down the middle. Both brothers believed that it was by their father, for their different reasons. Zweigler thought that when two people of such difference agreed on something, there had to be merit in the idea. But this wasn't the reason he gave Raul. To his partner, he only said that he owned a model of this particular building. He'd taken it in to an architectural historian at UCLA. "That building isn't just by Packer Gordon, it's very probably his first."

Did he chastise himself later? Did he go down that long room and find the model and have a look with his own eyes, measure it against the photograph? Maybe take it out to have it authenticated in some fashion similar to the way he described? No, of course not. Some force had been loosed in the world, released from an undisclosed grave. And Avi Zweigler saw himself astride it. Riding it like a man would two horses. Reins in one hand, camera gripped in the other.

He moved up north. Eight weeks, he promised himself and others, and they were going to shoot the whole thing. Not like one of those surprise renovations done while somebody is away for a week. But the show needed an element of hustle. The twentieth anniversary of the man's death made a good marker, a good pressure point.

Zweigler sorted the partners, plugged in replacements on active productions, let his lawyer know. He took a room at the pointy end of a hotel someone had designed to stick like the prow of a ship out into the harbour, huge white sails in some hardened, weapons-grade fabric, shuddering stiffly overhead. Old man Gordon, he thought with a smile as he climbed out of the taxi, would have hated it.

But out there at the tip of that prow Zweigler felt immediately and unexpectedly close to the man. North across the water and over the mountains—at some distance he didn't know and couldn't imagine—would lie those structures that first inspired him. And all around Zweigler, the city Gordon had chosen to live in but hardly touch. (Once to build a house that ended up hidden behind a wall for decades. Once again to build a house that was sold after his death and destroyed by the new owner.) And to either side, the ocean, which lapped meaningfully at the barnacled piles under the hotel. Those waves working the shoreline and providing an early-day reminder—Zweigler took 7:00 a.m. walks around the hotel's promenade deck with a freshly squeezed blood-orange juice—of how each day, every day, the rhythms of the natural world were oriented to decay.

These were ideas that the brothers then did all in their power to make flesh. No immediate harsh words after those first ones, a kind of quirky half-smiling détente having settled, but in their oppositions, in their fragile co-operation, they were born for the flickering grain of the small screen. Zweigler lined up a nice editing suite at a post-production house in town where he spent his evenings with an editor and a director of photography he'd flown in from Toronto. They'd order in platters of sushi and review the day, cutting together tape, fast-tracking episodes just as the boys themselves were fast-tracking progress toward an as-yet unspecified objective. What exactly were they doing? Nobody felt compelled to immediately say. The Bolex, which Graham undertook to set up in the corner of whatever room was the locus of activity that day, never asked. The first unit that filmed them being filmed didn't ask either.

They spent a few days tearing out an interior wall that had been added on the main floor. Then they began removing decades' worth of personal papers that had belonged to the last tenant.

"Garbage really," Graham said. "Should have been cleaned out a long time ago." In this interview he was filmed in his spare concrete townhouse down by the water. Zweigler and the DOP liked the location because on a sunny morning—and the weather was hot, hot—Graham was bathed in harsh pink. Graham in his slim grey suit and white polo, unshaven with his hair growing out. He spoke out of that neon halo, looking like something designed by Koolhaas gone slightly to seed, the light seeming to authenticate his ideas. Or, if not that, it made him seem to believe very strongly his own ideas, which was visually persuasive.

To wit: paring down, stripping away. Removing the trash. Detoxifying the building. Cleaning out and coring to the original shell. Graham interrupted himself: "Can we maybe draw the blinds?" His eyes were tearing.

The editor smiled in-suite, pointing, "We'll snip here, obviously. But watch this."

The camera zoomed. Graham's eyes were red and glistening as he said the words: "With the toxin of later years removed, maybe we get some true look at the architectural idea. With all of its genius and its failing, the pure idea of the structure."

He looked quite mad, yet one was inclined to believe him.

Elliot, for his part, didn't agree. The first unit met with him in a diner down on skid row. Excellent visuals over his shoulder from the counter where he drank a cup of coffee. People drifted back and forth out of focus behind the dirty front glass. Elliot in his leather jacket and an old tuxedo shirt, hair shaved recently but coming back angry black against the untanned fringes of his scalp. Elliot almost cheerful, by comparison with his brother's controlled mania. They weren't trashing the contents of the building at all. They were storing them. He had the space somewhere, or friends did. A web of connectedness stretched away into the shadows around Elliot.

"I don't even know what he means by *detoxifying*," he said. "Architecture talk. As far as I know, the building could have been designed to house that library."

Was it a library?

"Yeah yeah. Of course it was. Books, papers, films. Maybe I can't understand half of it, but I can't read Chinese either, can I? Or not much of it."

Either way, a crew of movers came to dominate the building for a period of several days. Working against an inventory Elliot had compiled, no less, chicken scratch on crumpled foolscap but exhaustive. Everything the former owner had left: sheaves of drawings, shelves of books, file cabinets full of paper and ephemera. It was a library, really. One that had accumulated over the years, Zweigler guessed, from the fungal way it seemed to spill from room to room. From the way that the papers had to be peeled out of the corners in which they had been stacked, much of it spoiled from water damage. Some of it mouldy. But none of it discarded. Elliot made sure of that while the trucks carted it all away.

By the weekend, Zweigler thought he could hear new air moving through the building. It sang in the upper floors and sighed down the stairwell. Graham strode with new confidence from floor to floor, making sketches and notes in a leatherbound folio. And it was his estimate of toxicity that seemed, just at that moment, to be the right one. The building breathed again. It came alive in its own emptiness, cleanliness.

"This is superb," Zweigler told the DOP, looking at footage later that day. The empty building glowed. Cleaned out, scrubbed down, up from under decades of grime, it revealed itself in layers of light: spilling white into the upper floor, growing foresty and greenish on the main, then fading to twilight amber and blue down below where the frames of the windows made long shadows at virtually all hours of the day. And through these gilded spaces, the brothers could be seen to walk, first alone in their thoughts. Then spiralling toward one another, meeting at the main-floor landing where a work table had been set up. Cameras rolling on two sides of them. The great man's Bolex Paillard emitting a smug whirr. The main 35mm unit Steadi-camming up and down the staircase, in and out of rooms in response to their movement.

Elliot produced a bottle of white wine from the side pocket of the raincoat he was wearing. A couple of Dixie cups from the other.

"Hey," he said, pouring for them both. "Your health."

"I don't drink while I work," Graham answered, laying out papers.

Elliot held one cup in each hand. He cocked his head a few degrees over to one side, as if doubtful he had heard correctly. "We're not working. We're talking."

Graham was black-suited today, a silk shirt coming untucked around his middle and undone probably one button farther than he was aware. He considered his brother for several seconds, Elliot rocking on the heels of his boots and waiting. Then Graham finally took a cup. "So we're talking."

"You first," Elliot prompted. "I'm the client."

Graham nodded, a slightly pained expression directed downward at his sketches. The fundamental thing to understand, he began, was that they were standing in a structure that represented Packer Gordon's best ideas about the perfect house at a very early moment in his career. As such, and since they did agree that they were honouring the Gordon name with this restoration, then their job was to get the place back to a form that made clear those original ideas. "We're together so far?" Graham said. "You're nodding like you disagree."

"Nodding," Elliot said, "is for agree."

"Because there's no point in me moving too fast."

"Let me have it."

Some difficulty was presented, Graham went on, by the fact that evidently the house had never been finished. Or at least it hadn't been found decorated as originally intended.

"And we know this how?"

"Because boxing posters and wall charts of heavyweight championship lineage, a couple hundred thousand pages of manic scribbling in black bound journals, I guess I'm just thinking that wouldn't have been it."

Admittedly, there were no photos to guide them. He'd contacted his mother and discovered that she never knew about the place. "No surprise there," Graham said. "But a little more surprising that there was no film of the structure. No publication of it. No pictures. No plans. No drawings. No mention in his diaries. No mention in Lark. And, in no small part because of the Berlin Wall put up out there in the early 1960s, none of the local architectural historians even knew a Gordon existed here."

"Hmmm," Elliot said. "Maybe it isn't his."

Graham stopped cold. He looked away and winced. "Can you do me a favour?" he said. "Can you not be flip on this particular point? I'd like to be trusted here, if nowhere else: the structure came from our father's creativity, from his intellect, from his brain. There is a Haida motif carved into the base of the pillars in the basement and at the ceiling on the upper floor. That is, if you'll allow me, a clear architectural reference. There are also distinct debts paid to Lubetkin and Eileen Gray in the structure, by whom it is well known he was influenced. And I should think that those elements pretty much triangulate and give us our point of origin."

Elliot said, "I believe you. Don't worry. Plus you and I should have guessed he had some connection to this building based on our own."

"Fine, so. Knowing these things, I'm fairly confident I could bring back the envelope and the basic internal structures. Both are fairly simple, but beautiful in precisely that simplicity, in their lightness and prescience of design. The stairway is fabulous, spiralling like a coil of DNA down the centre of the structure, linking its layers. That's Gray right there and not Mendelsohn, by the way. Lubetkin you can find in the sky blue ceiling upstairs, the rather unusual vertical planking used to finish the main-floor verticals, much of it gone but some still there on the south wall. Also in the terra-cotta tiling, the limestone and a number of other areas. And of course you have the basic longhouse configuration of this high central area, the family zones lofted up to the left and right and the carved elements I mentioned earlier."

"But," Elliot said.

But there were a lot of problems with the building as well, Graham told them. Inherited flaws and failures that had come over the years, and here was where some hard thinking would be required. The roof, for example, was made of coal-tar pitch and paper that, aside from having failed at numerous points as evidenced by wall staining, was carcinogenic, associated with toxicity from reproductive to neural. "Pitch is a bitch. So we'll be reroofing at the very least. And on the topic of authenticity and truthfulness to the original vision, I think we have to be prepared to improve and change the house so that it lasts."

"Question," Elliot said.

Graham waited, sipping his wine.

"How common is it, in an architect's opinion, to design a house without a kitchen?"

Graham hadn't overlooked the point. He'd noticed that the former occupant appeared to eat only what could be boiled in a kettle or reheated on a hot plate. His theory here was that a kitchen hadn't been completed by the time the house changed hands. But he was only partway through this point and Elliot was already heading down the stairs to the basement.

Graham sighed and followed. And when he entered the room, his expression did not flicker much beyond annoyance to find his brother standing over by the ring posts, where they were still embedded in the concrete pad.

"And gyms," Elliot said. "How common were those?"

Graham shook his head. "The gym wasn't started until the 1950s. Dad would have produced the drawings fifteen years earlier than that."

"So maybe Nealon commissioned those drawings."

Graham said, "Can we be serious?"

"This is me being serious. Why not Nealon?"

"Because he was a *boxer*. He took head shots for pay, got messed up in the ring and took it out over the next several decades on kids. Who knows how he got this place, but he didn't commission it."

"Like he must have been a crook living down here to actually own a building?"

"It doesn't make any architectural sense as a commission," Graham said. "There is too much of Packer Gordon in these walls."

"But what did he want these walls to do?"

Graham was shaking his head.

"Office building? Police station? Morgue? He built churches on occasion. Is this some kind of church?"

Elliot began to shadow box between the four posts, dancing in circles that brought him closer and closer to his brother.

"It wasn't finished," Graham said. "But it also wasn't a commission. That's my real point. It was an inspired, personal structure."

Elliot bobbing, spinning, flicking out a left hand. "Like maybe he had an inspired, personal idea about how it was to be used."

"Don't," Graham said.

Elliot danced up close, weaving, dodging, speaking between half-punches that swirled the air between them. Speaking between breaths now. "Do you," he said. "Graham Gordon. Know with absolute certainty. What our old man was thinking. When he designed this structure?"

Graham watched his brother for several long seconds. He said, finally, "I'm very uncomfortable with you doing that."

Elliot straightened up.

"No," Graham said.

"Okay," Elliot said loudly, brightly. "Well then, how are we going to go about restoring it?"

Graham stared.

"Have more wine." Elliot joggled the bottle back and forth, holding it out.

Graham held his glass out for the pour. "I never used the word *restoration*."

"You're thinking we tear it down."

"I don't know about that. But it'll have to be fixed, regardless of how he thought the building would be used. And even if it's only a monument we're building, an exercise in pure form, we're going to have to be open to the possibility of a radical idea."

End episode one, Zweigler said to himself at the monitor. Pull to a wider shot of the room. Then an exterior: building at sunset, Graham emerging from the front looking to the horizon. Elliot following some minutes later, humming, locking the door behind him.

Locking the door, as it happened, on the last discussion anybody would be having about the theory of the building for awhile. Because, to Zweigler's great satisfaction, all the cleaning and stripping away, all the bringing back of light and returning to the beginning, and talking about exercises of pure form, all this did not fail to turn up far more pressing problems than what they were actually going to do with the place. Pressing immediate problems like leakage and mould, revealed in their full glory by a hot weekend rain.

They returned on Monday to a lake in the basement, standing water on the main floor. Wet walls up top.

It was bad, the project engineer told them, allowing of course that—as one strongly suspected was the case with calamity of every kind—he'd seen much worse. Zweigler had brought this man aboard the week following that first brainstorming session. It was agreed that a general structural inspection of the building was required, but also that—whenever they finally agreed on a program for the building—the boys would need someone to act as a general contractor. Fila had been asked and turned them down immediately. There was a contract she would have to complete in Tokyo even if Graham wasn't joining her, she told Zweigler.

"Is there any way I can convince you to delay it," Zweigler said to her, upon hearing this news and travelling across town to the GS offices. When they spoke, she was backdropped by a fantastic outlook over the old city, one that Zweigler very much wanted to use again, to have an excuse to use again.

TIMOTHY TAYLOR

The answer was emphatically no. Fila told Zweigler, "Graham and I have worked hard to be in demand. The only thing we can do to ruin what we have is to ignore our real work for projects like this one."

Zweigler waited. Then asked gingerly, If Tokyo was their real work, what kind of work was Mary Street?

Nostalgia, regret, a woeful attempt at personal healing, she said. You would have thought there were no three worse qualities in a man or mission, separately or jointly.

So they needed an on-site brain and it wouldn't be hers. They needed someone oriented to the feasible, to the indisputable reality of what they had in the here and now. An engineer, a project manager. Gimble was this man's name. A perpetually out-of-breath five-footer who could lift his own weight and who tore into the project of assessing that building like every undiscovered fault was a survivor buried in earthquake rubble.

Gimble said, "Okay. Look at this. Good job we got some rain. Now we know where the leaks are. Which is to say. Precisely everywhere."

They were up on the flat roof, the three of them and the ever-present cameras. Gimble was pointing out how the seal had long been lost around every scupper, every vent, every roof penetration. The skylight too, broken and now loosely boarded over.

Elliot was distracted. He was looking down at the roof gravel. He said, "What's this?"

Graham couldn't see it right away. He had to stand back a little, then move to one side so that the light was right and the furrows threw shadows. A geoglyph. Not the Nazca Lines exactly, but distinct. "A triangle," he said.

Elliot stared down, musing. "And letters."

Graham hadn't seen those. "Sorry?"

"At each corner. *B, P, S.* Letters."

Graham looked again and saw his brother was right, one letter at each corner of the triangle.

Gimble cleared his throat. He looked at his watch.

Graham could not take his eyes from the shape. An equilateral. Anchored around the shape of the skylight. A simple and complicated thing.

"Okay, Gimble, go," Elliot said.

Because the seals were lost, Gimble went on, water pooling on the roof over the decades had been flowing down virtually every vertical surface in the building. Inside and out. For God knows how many years. "You with me here?" he said to Graham.

"Yeah yeah."

"Because here comes the bad part."

They went down the scaffold stairs and into the top floor, west side, where Gimble's rot man had torn out core samples. The news was advanced decay. The news was also mould.

"And that's something we gotta deal with before we do anything else," Gimble told them grimly. "Fungal growth. Gets me real uptight."

Here Zweigler cut his demo tape from Graham standing with a cylindrical sample of the east wall in his gloved hand to a doctor they'd tracked down in a structural fungus lab out at the university. This doctor had been preparing wooden structures, soiling them in various ways, and watching them collapse under layers of blue and green fur over enough years to have become the undisputed area expert on the topic. He identified the hostile party in this case as Aspergillus. Spreading too. Out of the basement, into the back of the main floor, up the exterior walls and into the ceiling. Clinging and enclosing the building like a malignant and microscopic vine. Even so, the doctor explained, it wasn't the distribution of the fungus that most concerned him. It was the concentration of its spores in the airy rooms and inspired open spaces of 55 East Mary Street relative to that outside the structure.

"Several orders of magnitude higher inside than outside is what you'd call very unhealthy," the doctor said. Aspergillus attacked the nose, ears, eyes and throat, made them run, block up, redden and tighten like a sphincter respectively. That someone had managed to live there for fifty years suggested mucocutaneous membranes that were one in a million. "For the rest of the population, it's strongly advised to avoid entering the premises under any circumstances. And absolutely to wear a mask and breathing gear if that advice cannot be followed."

"Sorry, what?" Graham's face went tight, his eyes seeming to redden immediately on receipt of the news. He was in the east room upstairs at a second more private work table he'd built to spread out plans and drawings. He'd just then been explaining into the lens of the Bolex how they were going to have to rethink the whole arrangement of windows in the north wall. It wasn't so much a matter of light, he said, as it was an issue of transparency.

"One of the flaws, as I see it," he said, standing several inches too close to the camera, causing his nose to widen sharply with each slight movement he made toward it, "is that the longhouse drew the eye of the person passing into its interior through the power of the light within, which is to say the fire in the sunken firepit that would have been visible through the doorway in the front pole or by virtue of the smoke. But in this case the passerby is held out. Now, new materials would be one way . . ."

And in came his brother wearing a face mask and a white paper bodysuit.

Outside, by the time the cameras had tumbled down after them and out into the front yard, their discussion of events was already in full swing and tracking toward dispute. One of unusual structure, Zweigler thought later, in that it appeared to involve a third party, just slightly off camera, invisible to viewers. A third point on a triangle in which Graham and Elliot were bouncing around, trading rhetorical positions, opposing and supporting each other and occasionally talking about different things entirely.

Graham was incredulous at the severity of the mould lab verdict, yet oddly excited too. Structures from this era weren't even known for mould, he pointed out. In the architectural strata of the city, this could be the only Aspergillus in a structure older than the 1970s.

Elliot said, "So just our luck that in a building so drafty you can't light candles, the old man would manage to seal off parts well enough that they can cultivate an advanced civilization of water-based plant life."

Graham was pacing, hand to his chin. "Mould is bad."

"So we call a mould expert."

"Or consider more radical options."

"Options," Elliot said, hands wide. "Throw me options."

Graham walked in a circle. He gestured with his right hand, a circular motion that increased in speed until it cranked out enough energy for further words. "We know the roof is shot. We didn't know the curtain wall was rotting too. No fault. But what we have here is a set of ideas built in the materials of the time and those materials simply did not work."

"Okay. So, Graham, like—"

"We rebuild."

"You know, I hate to break it to you. But I knew that much already."

"Completely rebuild. Ground up. Same ideas. New materials. You said teardown before. You were right."

"*You* said teardown before."

"Okay. Then we agree."

"Come *on*."

"This wood frame?" Graham said. "Should be steel anyway. Better for the purpose. The curtain wall? I want to go Mylar. Absolutely thin, bulletproof, links nicely to a thin roofline."

"Ah, for chrissake, Graham, stop."

"I'm just trying to help you to understand . . ."

"So you want to make your mark on things. Fine. Do it somewhere else."

"This isn't about me. We tear it down to save the idea. The tribute is in revealing the old ideas. Exploding them. Evolving them. The tribute is in the improvement."

Elliot was wincing like some uncomfortable tone had just started up in his inner ear. And while Graham continued, the look resolved. Not to anger, Zweigler didn't think. More like the rise of something long suppressed, an old bloody-mindedness.

"Right, right," Elliot said, spinning and walking to the corner of the pit, where he found a sledge hammer leaning against Gimble's lunch cooler. He picked this up in a fluid motion, hefting it in his hands. "Might as well get going."

Elliot shouldered the hammer, coiling hard, then releasing. The steel head slammed home into the stucco, which shattered and sprayed, the shards skipping and bouncing off the dirt and pavement, sounding off the plastic wall of the Porta Potti.

Silence fell around them.

"It's just something built by the old man, hey, Gray?" Elliot said, shouldering the hammer again. "I mean who gives a shit about that, right?"

He hefted for another swing.

"Okay, stop," Graham said. Then he was in motion. "Stop. Can't I make a point?"

Graham reached Elliot with a hand outstretched to stop the hammer, to physically enforce a change of mind.

But his action came to no good result as Elliot swung and the hammer landed again in an explosion of stucco and splintering wall frame. And Graham was instantly on the ground, writhing. It took a moment for everyone, Elliot included, to realize that he hadn't lost an eye to a chip of plaster at all. It had nicked him well up the forehead. And the injury, while bleeding copiously, was treatable.

As was the fungus, calm experts would later say. Widespread, serious, a health hazard. But for a certain amount of money and with a chemical solution so caustic it arrived in a black tanker truck attended to by men in blue rubber suits, it could be cleansed away.

There followed a week in masks, uncomfortable days, surreal footage. The mould-removal contractor snaked silver aluminium tubing for an air circulation system through the building. The men working the chemical spray units clomped from room to room under the high-pitched wail of the compressors sitting curbside. The temperature hit 36°C in the building. It was a very particular vision of a very particular ring of hell, Zweigler thought. And when the images were in, the editor laid down a track of ambient dance and it worked.

Graham never did get to explain his point about the teardown idea. It was merely understood to mean that there was at least that much agreement between them. The building deserved some sort of preservation. Zweigler shook his head to think that this was how far they had come after three weeks, but at least it was motion. Graham was now wandering the site with his mask on and his head bandaged. Waiting for inspiration. It had to be said that the camera treated his head wound well. Nelson at Trafalgar came to mind. Cassius Clay between rounds against Liston in the first fight, when some evil substance had gone into his eyes off Sonny's gloves. Although very unlike Ali's painful squint, Graham's affliction didn't clear up quickly. It seemed to set in, to take root on his forehead. To cause more pain with each passing day, with each fresh update from the terrier Gimble.

"Faults have a way of connecting to other faults in complex idea-based systems," Graham said to the Bolex upstairs. Nobody else around. "Anybody can tell you that."

"Load-bearing foundation walls. Quite large cracks. That's the story." Elliot was in the Postum. He was applying hot sauce to a pale yellow shingle of eggs. "Leading us to conclude that either the soil is bad or a portion of the slab has heaved."

Elliot forked a piece of omelette into his mouth and chewed deliberately, looking to the front of the restaurant with its watery light. He swallowed and said, "I think it's the soil."

Graham rolled his eyes and scratched his head and shifted his chair in the burst of morning sun that came through the blinds and directly into his eyes. His hair was unwashed and grown out to his shoulders. "We have some hairline cracks in the north and south basement foundation walls. So, yeah, if there were pad sinkage then . . . Okay, then you'll see some of that."

From off camera he pulled a cigarillo into frame and took a long drag. When he finished his thought, he puffed out an uneven cloud of silvery smoke with his words: "But it's not the soil. That's Elliot talking through his ass. It's the foundations, which we can fix."

And he was right. Gimble brought in his foundation people who kicked stones and messed about in the basement for an afternoon. Then started some preliminary digging that resulted in the east wall of the foundations being excavated clear. Then the south. Then, when suitable shoring and support members had been installed, both the others. Only then did they emerge from the hole and report officially to Gimble (who'd seen it all coming, naturally) that the foundations were actually crumbling away in handfuls that a child could gouge out. Too much water in the original mix, it seemed.

"You don't see it often," Gimble panted. "But a crew'll screw up time to time. Shit happens."

"Fuckity fuck," Elliot said, staring down into the hole at the corner of the foundations where the tap of a boot had dislodged a shower of gravel and sand.

"Well, don't look at me," Graham said. "I didn't do the slump test."

"I'm talking to Gimble. Okay with you, genius?"

"Hey, go fuck yourself. Okay?"

"Are we sideways?" Raul asked Zweigler on the phone that evening. "Sounds like it's sideways. What's the score now: roof, walls, foundations, beams . . ."

"Not the beams," Zweigler said. "The wood's mostly good."

"What other parts are there on a building?"

"And I wouldn't say sideways," Zweigler said. "What's the worst that can happen?"

"Somebody wakes up and decides it isn't worth restoring?"

"That would be a bad outcome," Zweigler admitted. "But the owner did sign a contract. And why would he decide that anyway? We're paying."

"I'm paying," Raul said.

"They don't care as long as they're not paying."

"What about he fires his brother. Fires this Gimble. Burns the building down for insurance."

"Burning the building for insurance would be good. There's a final episode."

"Fair enough," Raul said. "But we're not getting that lucky."

"You worry too much. You should come visit. The weather here is spectacular. The sushi is unbelievable. We got some uni the other day? It was sublime."

They talked sushi for awhile. But Raul didn't think he should visit just for that.

The next day Graham apologized. To Gimble, who squirmed and went to find his builder's level. Then, asking that the camera be shut down, to Elliot. Zweigler watched the few words, the handshake, with a sinking heart. New filial harmony would not necessarily be a good development. Unfilmed new filial harmony would be useless whatever happened. Then, just as Elliot took his leave to go after Gimble, Zweigler noticed the Bolex still running in the corner and was again won over by the possibilities.

These were seemingly endless at 55 East Mary Street. Graham had been right about the foundations, yes. But, then, so too did Elliot end up being right about the soil. In connection with the bad concrete news, Gimble had hired building hoist contractors to prepare the structure for foundation replacement. But as the pit steadily deepened under the building, it seemed that bad news came out of the hole with every shovel of fill. In every barrow load of broken, decaying concrete that was pulled up from under the floor joists. With every ominous skeletal rattle as a member of the support crib slid into place, growing like a railway trestle under the corners of the building. The structure looked good in the morning light, as Zweigler saw on film. It made good television for them to have had such an unbroken run of good, visual problems. Still, all recent developments seemed to signal something running hard and fast in a bad direction and at a speed not quite anticipated.

"Basically what you have here," the foundation engineer told Gimble and the boys in a hasty sidebar halfway through the shoring, "is a dead load on the basement slab that exceeded the bearing properties of the soil beneath it over quite a few years. You design a thin pad for a normal basement then put the Library of Congress down there, well, it doesn't always work out. I think we probably also had a water-table shift and the soil properties changed. In any case, you've got basement pad heaved every way to Tuesday."

Graham looked a little ashen, explaining this latest to the camera after the foundation engineer disappeared off around a corner with Gimble to smoke and, no doubt, talk about how much his crew was getting paid for all this. For the past couple decades, Graham thought, the pad had been moving downward into the soil at something like a quarter inch a year, which was breakneck speed in structural terms. The effect had been to increase pressure on the foundation walls above the pad. And that force— Graham sketched it with a shaking hand in the air of the top-floor landing—had been transmitted up the walls, which were bowing inward as a result.

"You can't see it, but we're about three inches out of true here," he said, which would explain several other problems too. The roof seals would have been strained as a result of the pressure on the walls. The water in the basement would have come in through cracks in the foundations. The cracks in the foundation would have started the rust in the reinforcing material. And so on.

Elliot found Gimble and the foundation engineer working on third smokes with the foreman from the building hoist company.

"Okay," he said. "I need options."

The foundation engineer spoke first from behind brown Ray-Bans. Vintage Taiwanese fakes, Elliot was irritated to notice. "I hear you've been talking about a teardown and rebuild."

"Not an option," Elliot said.

The man expelled a breath through puffed cheeks. "Well," he said. "You need a new foundation. You know that already. But like I was just saying to Gimble here, if I were paying to hike up the building and pop in a new bottom, I wouldn't be putting it back down on the same kind of shallow slab that failed the first time. I'd definitely put down piles."

"Okay," Elliot said, nodding rapidly. "Piles?"

Long concrete support pillars drilled down through the weak soil to the more useful load-bearing kind below. "Or to bedrock. Either works."

Time for Gimble to shake his head. "You know I'm here. To do whatever. Only what're you in for already?" He looked directly at Elliot. "Mould removal. Plus we have to do the roof eventually. Walls."

Graham arrived around the corner. He'd finally lost the forehead bandage, but retained an angling welt and a wounded look in the eye. "What's happening?" he demanded. "What're we talking about?"

"Just telling your brother here," Gimble said. "You want to have a think about next steps. You're already looking at crap stucco, drywall shot, lathe in the walls rotted out. Now seems like your foundation is mostly not there any more. Plus, and I've been meaning to mention this . . ."

Gimble paused for breath.

"Half those windows have to be replaced and they're one-offs. I can tell you. Custom aluminium jobs. Extruded from custom dies. Might as well be a million to replace them now. If you could find the people."

"I could get those duplicated," Elliot said.

"Well then," Graham said to Gimble.

Elliot turned to his brother. "I think Gimble's trying to make a point about cost."

"Go. Cost," Graham said.

"As in, prohibitive cumulative cost. As in, we'll nuke the budget and be into our own pockets if the foundation needs piles."

"Piles?" Graham said to the foundation engineer.

"In my opinion," said the foundation engineer. "And you can't drive piles anyway with that building sitting in the hole."

Here the building hoist crew chief, silent up to that point, began to shift in his boots.

Graham looked blank. Elliot felt his face going numb, the onset of dizziness, the cold fingers of a headache closing grip on his brain stem. He sat heavily on an upturned bucket and pressed fingers to his eyes.

So they'd have to move the building, the hoist crew chief finally said. Jack it up, shoot skids under her. Crane it onto a truck. Move it to a holding site. Then, once the piles and foundations were in, truck it back and set it in place.

"Oh man," Elliot said.

"You okay?" Gimble asked him.

"Hey, hey," Graham said. "We can do that."

Well, sure, you *can* do it, the man said. It just wasn't a very good idea in this case.

Elliot kept his eyes closed, pinched the bridge of his nose with one hand. "Fine," he said to Gimble. He was fairly sure this one wasn't going to make him pass out. He stood, unsteadily, then said to the hoist crew chief, "Why not a good idea?"

Because here you had an old timber modern skinnied out at every joint to make it look like a wafer of air and light. "And," he said, "if I were to move such a thing, I gotta tell you I'd be worried about really breaking shit."

"Breaking shit?" Graham said. "Fila and I moved a heritage conservatory. The thing was made of *glass*."

"Yeah, but where is she, Graham?" Elliot said. "Oh, right. Tokyo."

"We picked that thing up off the lot in Southlands. Got it onto a barge. Out onto a truck at the far end. Up a 20-per-cent grade road to this ridge lot in the British Properties."

"Put it out of your mind," Elliot said, the dizziness finally passing, the headache settling in but manageable.

"Listen to me," Graham said.

"You're the guy who wanted to tear the thing down two weeks ago," Elliot said. And this was the first time Zweigler had heard him raise his voice. "You think I'm going to trust you to move it?"

"You never listen to me."

"Half the time I do," Elliot said. "It's all I can handle."

"You know, fuck you. This time really."

"Hey, you too. What about the money? Where's that coming from?"

"I'll sell my house," Graham said.

"Only trouble there being that when she finally divorces your ass you won't have a house," Elliot said.

And here they reached for each other, almost slow motion, Zweigler noted, who thought he would suggest they slow the film down anyway later. But right there, two cameras running, may God be praised, Graham reached out and grabbed his brother's shirt front, just as Elliot reached over and pulled in his own fistful of cloth. And they pirouetted there, in place, with everybody frozen around them. The camera crew. Gimble and the boys. Two guys walking down the sidewalk pushing shopping carts. The breeze disappeared. All was briefly silent.

Zweigler stepped forward, gingerly. He put one hand on Elliot's shoulder, one on Graham's. He said, "Deep breaths. Okay?"

The sun began to set. The building sank in shadow.

In the cool dark of the editing suite, forty-eight hours later, Zweigler watched again. He watched the building descend fully into that blackness, then burst through into the dawn of day. The clock unsprung and spiralling into the past. Zweigler watched all this footage twice, then the 16mm footage, then the mock-up animated plans. He watched and he thought about the arch and his keystone place within it. And then he sat for a long time without bothering to ask for lights and he didn't think about anything. He didn't sleep, drifting in the place between, untouched by either the euphoria or the vision that was said to crowd that space.

The editor said, "You all right, Avi?"

He jolted vertical. Fine, fine. More than fine. Awake and staring at his own wristwatch, only then seeing something. The spiral of those endless chronographically accurate seconds launching a tendril of inspiration that could not, Zweigler estimated, cause any more harm than had been caused already were he to act upon it.

He would go find her. The smart one. And why not? He gave the address to the taxi driver, then leaned back in his seat next to the gift basket he'd ordered at the hotel. Minutes invested to cross town and surprise her might yield a calm idea. He could use a calm idea.

Twenty minutes later they were crossing a bridge that looked like it ran straight right up into the mountains. He finally said, "Uh, where are we going exactly?"

"You say Deep Cove," the driver grunted. He was Russian. "So I take you Deep Cove."

Out front, looking up at this magnificent old house with its peaked shingled roof and dormers, Zweigler thought, *So this is how it really is.* He rang, he knocked. Nothing. Nothing but music playing around the back-yard. Music floating in over the laurel hedge that backed the cedar wood fence. Some kind of thrashing kids' stuff. Punk.

Zweigler pushed the gate open. "Hello, Deirdre? Avi Zweigler here."

He walked into the backyard, the gift basket held out in front of him, an advertisement of his good intentions. Beautiful flagstones bordered a kidney-shaped pool. Ivy grew in lush volumes over the pergola. There was a book open on a chaise longue and a playpen set up on the grass.

He did call hello several more times and got no answer. Enough information, Zweigler was saying to him-self with each step across the flagstones, past the pool, the low flower beds. Enough information to guess maybe that nobody was home and that he should leave. But if nobody were home—this was another insistent voice that kept repeating the question in his head, ignoring entirely the possibility that somebody was home, and had heard him, and was merely not responding—then why did it seem clear even from this distance that there was a baby in the crib?

Two, in fact. Zweigler drew close enough to see their shapes through the mesh. Close enough to look down on their utter perfection. Thin hair swept forward over soft foreheads. Arms creased round at the wrist and elbow. Both on their backs and fixing him now with startling attentiveness. He was, for a moment, entirely gone in the sensation of being observed by something (two some-things) for which every viewed object was still pretty much the first of its kind. Zweigler included.

Lost in the moment, that is, until she spoke from directly behind him: "Please move away from the crib."

An order he did not obey, strictly speaking. Because he spun around instead. Startled by her voice, startled again by her face, framed by a torrent of Deirdre's red hair, features gripped in something worse than anger, a very cool variety of fury instead. But then these impressions were swamped by a third startle, the worst one, this having to do with the long-handled dandelion weeder she was holding cocked in both hands like she were winding up to line drive his head into the ocean at the bottom of the garden.

"Move away from the crib!"

"Hold on. Please. Hey."

"Drop the basket and put your hands where I can see them. Now!"

L'Occitane and The Body Shop, persimmons and pesto collapsed to the flagstone walkway. He heard a jar smash and smelled caperberry tapenade.

"You guys just come in here like you own him, own us. But it's over. We're out. And I know perfectly well what it means to take a crack at one of you guys, but I swear . . ."

"For God's sake," he croaked, the flowers now out of the way, gesturing toward his face. "We met. I'm the producer, Avi Zweigler. I interviewed you!"

She never apologized. She only plunked him down on a lawn chair and brought him a glass of lemonade. Then she nursed the twins in turn and gave him what attention she could. No she did not know where Elliot was, but that was not entirely unusual either. He'd had occasion to disappear in the past for short periods. Sometimes long periods. Theirs had been a relationship where she had to get used to the unannounced separation.

"Two months is not unheard of. Am I telling you too much?"

"No no. Please." Sometime after the weeder had been put away, Zweigler's hands had started shaking uncontrollably. She would have cracked him one, and he knew it. Now, after one attempt to sip the lemonade and spilling it down his shirt, he abandoned the glass on a side table and folded his hands tight in his lap. Tried to make small talk. He hadn't seen her around.

"I kind of avoid the whole thing, as you may have noticed."

"We were grateful for the one time you came."

She nodded and laughed. A not-entirely warm laugh. "You're really hooped down there now, aren't you, Mr. Zweigler."

"Avi," he said. "I actually came to ask your thoughts on that."

"They exist to oppose one another, that's my big thought. And it's true whether they try to make amends or not."

"Pessimistic."

"Maybe. But you might also want to get comfortable with the idea that people trapped between opposing and roughly equal forces do quite frequently get themselves destroyed."

Zweigler nodded, squinting. He knew this to be true. Why then did he need to hear it from her?

Deirdre called inside and an Asian woman emerged through glass doors. She came down and wordlessly took the twins. Deirdre then disappeared into the house, returning moments later with something small, closed tight in her hand.

"What's that?"

She was already escorting him out to the car. She said, "This is me many years ago, asking some of the questions you're asking now."

He stopped at the corner of the house. He turned to look at her.

"Yes. I was there. Long story," she said. "Now you're going to know it."

She still held the object tightly as they walked the rest of the way down the driveway to where his cab was waiting. He stood by the door before climbing in. She held her hand out toward him, still closed. She told him, "For

your personal viewing pleasure. Not for quotation."

"All right," he said. "I promise."

"For you to destroy afterwards."

He squinted at her. No, she didn't have copies, she told him. That was partly the point. He was incredulous. She was insistent.

"All right," he said. "I promise that too. I'll destroy your only copy of whatever it is."

She opened her hand to reveal a black plastic ovoid

about the size of a key fob. A USB flash drive, in fact. Many megabytes of something enclosed.

He said, "From Mary Street?"

She nodded. "Exteriors. Interiors. Interview footage. I did a lot of work on it, you'll see."

He should have known she knew something. He should have known from the way she'd answered questions those weeks before. "And Elliot . . ."

Of course Elliot knew she'd been there. But he didn't know about this artifact. "There is something about the whole experience that I don't necessarily want him reliving."

"And what is that?"

She raised her eyebrows and extended her hand another inch. But when he reached for the data key, finally, she snatched her fingers closed one last time. She said, "Don't think for a minute I'm in favour of what they're doing down there."

"You're not?"

"I think it's a bad idea. Ill fated."

"Care to explain why?"

She opened her hand again.

Zweigler took the key. "That's it then."

"It's not much. But it's all I need to know."

"Okay." He nodded. "Well, thanks for not hitting me anyway."

"Thanks for not being one of the Uncles. Don't even ask."

"Fine," Zweigler said. "I won't even ask."

She looked at the sky, some final thing on her mind. She asked him, "You have kids?"

No, no. He didn't.

"But you wanted them?"

"I like you," Zweigler said. "I think you're the smart one in all this for staying away."

"You think I'm being personal."

"I don't mind, really. Yes, I did want kids. My wife left me before we'd had the chance."

"I'm sorry about that. I met Elliot in the diner where he tells me you've been interviewing him. I knew I was having kids with the guy before I kissed him. It was nuts."

"But you waited."

"No," she said. "He had himself tied before I got to him. Had sworn off children. Now I'm being personal again, sorry. I threaten someone with a garden tool, they become family."

"So he had himself untied?"

"Never did, no. It just stopped working at some point, I guess. But what I'm really trying to tell you is that it's an example of something good happening a long time after he'd given up on the idea." And she smiled with warmth this time, with none of the chill she'd shown earlier, white-knuckled behind the weeder.

He climbed into the taxi and rolled down the window.

"So after I watch this," he said to her, holding the key between two fingers at his ear. "What's supposed to happen after that?"

"You're the executive producer."

"Humour me."

"More. The man wants more."

"Only because you have more," Zweigler said.

She nodded slowly. Okay. A serious question deserved a serious answer. After that, she told Zweigler, looking over the cab and up into those impossible mountains, it wouldn't be such a bad idea to go talk to the other brother's wife.

Two

DIGITAL DISCONTINUITY. THE TENDENCY FOR information to be lost as the digital media for its storage changed format over time. Spool tapes went to floppy disks then to smaller floppy disks. Iomega Zip was replaced by burnable CD, flash drive, memory stick and iPod. And all of these were, in turn, rushing onward to other forms entirely. A lot of recorded conversation, a lot of historic image, a lot of history itself got tilled under in the process.

Zweigler looked at the popping, skidding fragments of video on his computer screen. He leaned back in the nylon-mesh chair he'd wheeled up to the writing desk at his harbourside window. He thought: This was recorded onto Betamax, transferred later onto VHS, retransferred to a hard drive, then a CD, then back to a hard drive and finally zapped out the USB port into this little key here. Every ancestor image had been destroyed, Deirdre had told him, leaning down into the taxi window.

Now he was squinting at what she'd given him in disbelief. Not because the structure looked that much different than it had on his own first sight. Here too the beauty of the line was clear. The chaos of the building's survival. Halls stacked with boxes, the shelves of the upper rooms lined with bookshelves, leaning, warped, overweighted.

He stared with disbelief because the occupant of the structure lived and moved in front of him. An old man, Pogey Nealon. A bit blurry, a bit grainy. Shot as if the cameraman had been more inspired by cinéma-vérité than was wise, the view roving shakily between his face and his hands, between the man and the building above and around him. But breathing and talking and taking apart the building around him with his words.

Off camera, her voice. She said, "Start anywhere."

They were in the basement. Nealon with one arm up on a corner post. Blinking into the light they had set up somewhere out of frame. He said, "Where were we?"

"*Kill the body . . .*"

"Right. See that's what I'm trying to show you down here. Around that time, I couldn't figure the place out. I figured I'd just leave it to rot. Not my business."

She waited. Zweigler thought he could hear her waiting.

Nealon began again: "Because I couldn't see any practical purpose in it."

The images cut away from the interview here, a montage of interior views carrying on over the conversation. Water lapped in the skylight, shadows rippling below. Stains crept down an exterior wall. Mushrooms grew along a baseboard.

Deirdre: "And you never wondered about an architect because you didn't think there had been one."

"I was sure there hadn't been one."

"Then you meet this lawyer."

Now exteriors. The blank facade, worn and sunbleached. Cracked windowpanes and weeds.

Nealon: "I was fairly unreasonable at that time, but I'd just had my one professional fight and got spanked. You could say I was in an adjusted frame of mind. Receptive to new ideas."

"And he said . . ."

"Well, he said what you said earlier. The advice."

"I just wondered if you could say it, though. I need you to say it on camera in order for people who see the film to see you saying it."

"You mean whoever watches this thing won't hear you asking all these questions?"

An unsteady handheld shot was bringing them back into the foyer now, down and around the stairs. Zweigler sat back with a smile. It was nice work. She had cut it together well.

Back on Deirdre, mid-pause.

"No," she said to Nealon. "When it's edited, probably not."

"So I'll just be talking up here, shooting off my mouth?" But he said it. He said it with a frown of bemusement, as if its meaning were becoming less plain with each mention.

He scratched the tip of an unshaven chin. He moved uneasily on his feet.

Kill the body . . . and the head will die.

"Which led you to a conclusion."

"Yeah," he said, the camera wavering, pushing in close. "I decided the place was supposed to be a school."

Jump-cut. A wide shot of the roof. It panned 360 degrees taking in the cityscape, then returning to Pogey. "I've been meaning to reseal that," he said, pointing down at the skylight. "Thing's been leaking . . . oh, fifteen years."

Back inside. Back downstairs. Nealon moving in the ring, hands up. "We had lots of kids. Twenty or thirty a week. There were more families down here, then."

"Kids learning to fight . . ."

"Box," he said. "Learning how to box."

"Are those different things?"

Nealon stopped circling. "Normally."

Nothing from Deirdre now. Just a long silence and the mounting pressure of the lens.

Nealon again. "So that's what was supposed to happen here, I decided. I'd take care of my body to preserve my head. Teaching happened here. Teaching, boxing. I ran my school."

Nealon walked away from the camera. A directionless loop.

A young man's voice came in close: "Let's get outta here. This is *nuts.*"

"Do not turn that camera off," she whispered, looking into the lens saying so. "You run that thing until we're out."

Nealon arrived back in front of the lens. "Then," he said to her, not speaking to camera at all, "it was over." And here he walked out of frame again, disappearing into a tangle of metal shelves next to the ring.

He re-emerged a moment later carrying a small film can. Maybe fifteen minutes of 16mm footage, Zweigler guessed, sitting forward with interest in his chair, elbows to his knees. Nealson said, "Just watch this one."

Her voice: "What is it?"

"My last students." Nealon came close to the camera, then crossed over to the other side of the room. He seemed buoyed somehow, as if a good idea had just saved his day. He swept aside a canvas sheet to reveal a 16mm projector. Opened the film can and removed a reel, which he mounted and threaded through the machine.

The tape popped through a number of transitions here. There were wheeling shots of the stairway again. Then a long take of Deirdre talking to the old man, shot from the far end of a hallway. Shot into falling darkness.

Zweigler chuckled. It appeared the cameraman had been having second thoughts. Like maybe he wanted to get the hell out of there. But here Zweigler sat straight again, because outside his own windows night was falling and they had jump-cut back into interview footage. Nealon at the ring post. Mid-sentence: ". . . brothers," he was saying. "They came down with their old man. I didn't get it at first at all. I just taught them what I could teach them and assumed they'd learn the lessons."

An exterior: the building glowing orange in the late light.

"And what happened?"

A new visual, again. Zweigler watched the fizzing surface flaws of film stock. A boxing ring. Clean and swept. Two boys dancing in their corners. Images like those that might be captured on a Bolex Paillard. Then trapped on video as it rolled on a screen.

Nealon: "Not that he was a bad man entirely. Only the three of them were somehow bound up in that thing together."

"What kind of lessons did you teach them?"

"You know rock, paper, scissors?"

Breathing deeply. You could hear the old man breathing.

Boys about to box, at the very instant before a bout begins. One heavy and pale, the other lean and dark. Snapping out hands. Bobbing in that impossibly hostile boxer's crouch. Eyes framed between gloves.

Deirdre: "Like the game you play with your hands."

Zweigler's breath now a solid thing moving in and out. Tidal.

Nealon: "It's a game where everything is locked in from the outset. Everybody knows how it works and still everybody loses, eventually."

Fighting on-screen now. Zweigler leaning in toward the screen for detail, for understanding. They were hitting each other. Hitting hard. They were hurting one another. And all the while their expressions ungodly calm.

I think I've had enough.

Keep shooting.

The fight mounting in intensity and violence. And in the back of the frame, Zweigler seeing, finally, the Pogey Nealon who was contemporary to the footage. A younger man, lean and hard. T-shirt and grey sweats. This younger version of Nealon watching carefully, studying the action through round bells and continued violence. Through his own shouted words to someone off camera who refused to be revealed. *Time time time!*

"Oh God," Zweigler said, standing sharply. Knocking his chair over. Knocking a lamp over. Not hearing the smash of ceramics or the sound of the radio in the next room or the long call of a ship moving astern out in the harbour. Eyes locked instead on the small space of that screen, on the smaller space of the ring behind it. The collapse of the end: the punch, the fall. The boy down and falling away from them. Zweigler breathing through his fingers now, conscious all at once of the larger, framing presence. The eyes on this side of the glass. His own, yes. But those original eyes too. The architect behind the camera.

There was a flash of white screen, then a swirl of oversaturated colour. They were outside again. Nealon front and centre. In an alley. Night falling hard. No time to light the shot. And so the man was illuminated only by the flames licking out of a garbage barrel. Nealon holding a film spool. Smiling. Dropping it in.

The camera now hustling away. The image slipping sideways. As if the cameraman had started running.

Riley! Come on.

Images flashing. Dirty grass. Sunset. A white exterior. Rising walls and a dome of darkening sky.

Then blackness.

Three

ONE OF THE PRIVATE FISHING SOCIETY DOCK KIDS came to find Esther when the *Story House* executive producer flew in. He was a day earlier than he said he'd be, but that didn't mean he surprised anybody arriving. It was hard to be stealthy approaching the very edge of the world. And when you hauled into view around Pillar Rock doing 130 knots in an MD600 charter helo just that particular shade of metallic black, people on the water also tended to call ahead with the news of your approach.

She heard the bird come whining in low over Lucy Island. She saw it vault over the trees, then bear down on the club. She watched its approach for a few seconds, then ducked back into the dark of her beach shack, where she'd taken up residence after her short stay turned into a medium stay, which was now promising to be a stay right through to the close of the season.

The kid came around half an hour after they touched down on the pad.

"What's the profile?" she asked, not looking up from the fly she was tying. Herring. A silvery pattern, long as your hand. Tied onto large barbed hooks and made of real polar bear fur. Such was her desperation, such was her complete inability to catch chinook since she'd arrived, Esther had resorted to fly casting. She was becoming an eccentric legend around camp, although nobody voiced a word on the topic. They'd see her out there in Bruin Bay, balancing in the whaler. Throwing out heavy-gauge fly line over the water. But if it was bad luck to know somebody not catching, it was welcoming bad luck into your own *soul* to talk about it.

"Well," the kid said, scratching where the sunburn was peeling off his brown shoulders. "Whoever this guy is he's got a lot of money."

She knew that much already. She retained enough of her former self to smell money on Zweigler over the phone. She hadn't lost it entirely over these . . . how many days had it been?

"Okay," she said to the dock kid. "Tell him I'll be out."

She watched him thump off down to the dock and back over to the helicopter pad.

One hundred and three days. Hard sun, salt air. Not a single chinook. Her own fault too. *As long as it takes me to catch something really big,* she'd told Graham, giving him the news about where she was. He'd been stunned with her decision for all the wrong reasons. He thought they might fire her at work. He really had no idea. *Something enormous. Over forty. No, over fifty pounds.*

Did she calculate the possibility that the earth—the soil, trees, water and subterranean populations—might hear her and turn away? Because it wasn't like she couldn't get members over fish. Investment advisers, cable television giants, pharmaceutical industry made-goods and, this week, the motorcycle club who took over the entire PFS for what dock staff cheerfully referred to as Bubbapalooza. Everybody was coming in off the water with plenty of fish, including the mighty chinook.

She put her rod out over water—which she now did only by herself, safely away from members—and the seas went silent beneath her. Up and down the shoreline of the remonstratively named Graham Island, cellphone in a Ziploc bag. She haunted the calm mornings, looking for ideas. She throttled back the four stroke to about half, shifted her weight forward in the swivel chair such that the bow would drop and the hull would plane. The wave slap quieted down to nothing and she traced the shore, staring into the forest as it passed. Acres and acres. Waiting to discover something.

Which she did, several times, only nothing relating to fish. There was a cove she'd never seen before with a crescent of black sand, space to beach and a strip of accessible forest. There was a particular tide-free rock with teeming bird life. There was—most notably, and the single discovery she knew she would keep to herself—a beached merchant ship, half submerged in a kelp bed twenty klicks out of camp along a lonely stretch of rocky shore. Washed up on the teeth of the North American continent. She returned to it weekly, mesmerized. Observed it in various tides, never seeing the entire vessel and never venturing too close. She wondered how it got there. What the ship had been called. She theorized about its crew. But not once in all that time did Esther's city-self assert that things had grown too strange. That her trance state and a three-month slump combined to imply a failure in the underlying structure of event, the actual probabilities that whirred at the heart of every human and material bit of business.

Her edge-of-the-world self was roughening. She swore. She drank a bit too much, blaming it on proximity to the deep, to places where the land could be felt tipping off into the unknown. She was louder and found different things funny, including this very thing: a slump of epic proportions. The PFS founder's daughter who had caught precisely one fish over twenty pounds since arriving and that was an octopus.

Off Klashwun Point, that one. A long ways from home and alone. She was trying strips of herring, lightly smoked, then left out until they were rancid. Threaded onto hooks, two filets side by side reconstituted as a single body with cotton thread around a cluster of bead shot, the bait could be made to flutter convincingly at a slow mooch. And it worked. Or she thought it had, when something very heavy hit and stayed on. Something that pulled down vertically, almost snapping the rod, seeming to sound hard. Although, of course, it turned out only to be something very heavy sinking.

Seventy pounds. Pulled up over forty minutes on the light line she'd gone to in an increasingly random attempt to mix up the variables, return the spin of things to a wobble-free plane.

All that time to pull up an octopus. All that time, hope fading, but not extinguishing entirely until the shape came murky, then clear at the side of the boat. And that sucked. Not because it was worse to catch an octopus than another coho. Not because the octopus went to waste either. The kitchen, headed by a new and experimentally minded chef with an outsized crush on Esther, turned it into a half-dozen different things over the next few days, including octopus satay, which she tried and quite liked, to octopus kimchee noodle bowl, which she could not finish.

No. It sucked because it sapped her belief that problems presented themselves with the primary purpose of being solved. She was unmoored here. She was getting drunk, quite quickly after fruitless days out on the grounds. She was lying on the sand at night, imagining the stars still drifting apart from that originating Big Bang. Imagining how the constellations would look in later, more diffuse arrangements. Trying to name constellations, something she'd always promised herself she would learn to do and for which, of course, she'd never had time.

And Graham was calling now too. Strange phone calls at odd hours. She'd taken to clicking the phone on without any *hello*. Just letting him rant into phone space. Garbled pleas for advice. His new fixation involved a building supposedly built by his father. His brother and he were co-operating in its . . . what exactly? Restoration. Demolition. Sometimes it sounded like they couldn't decide how to honour the old man. And of course, problems. Slumping foundations. Cracked footing walls. Leaking windows. Personal acrimony, like nobody could have seen that coming. And now the building was out of the ground, rotten roots exposed, a white cube suspended. And as night appeared to follow goddamn day with these two, they were locked, frozen, glaciered in dispute.

"Which is why the producer has suggested maybe you might talk with him."

She cracked silence. "Me. Are you out of your gourd?"

She had her feet up on a bucket. She was lying in the sand. Last night she'd done the same thing, fallen asleep, and the incoming tide had caught and soaked her.

"Yes. Yes. Yes," Graham was saying. "I am out of my gourd. So is he. So is Zweigler. We're all. Out of our. Gourds."

"Do you know the names of the constellations?" she asked Graham now. "We have five minutes left here, by the way. The tide's coming in."

He didn't. But he tried. Orion rode a horse, he thought. There were bears also.

She told him about the Big Bang. Or the part of it that had interested her lately. Perhaps, she said, the world continued to carry out the imperative of the Big Bang each day, each second and in each molecule of itself. Perhaps it remained a relevant physical phenomenon. Perhaps the bits of us—here she folded hands across the bare torso exposed by her bathing suit—perhaps they were floating farther and farther apart. Minutely but irrevocably disintegrating.

Long silence after that.

Which could be looked upon as the triumph of the fragment, Esther went on brightly. And the best they could all hope for is that when they had drifted entirely apart to become an infinity of particles, some new thing would be formed.

"Like what?" Graham asked.

She never answered. But she thought, Like a cloud. Which would then elude observation by happening on a level, in a perspective, that was unavailable to us.

She made Zweigler wait until late that afternoon, five full hours. He would have unpacked and explored his quarters by then, had a drink at the bar, tried and failed to relax. He would just now be starting to calculate, to glance at a wristwatch good to many more atmospheres of depth than would ever be required, good to a level of chronometric accuracy no boiled egg would ever justify, but which was not a piece of time-telling jewellery anyway but a meter for tracking the expense of being stationary anywhere for any given period of time.

Twenty-five thousand a day, she guessed. Plus the chopper. Make it fifty. Zweigler might have a lot of money but he would not pass the time without looking at his watch when it was costing him that much.

"Hello," he said, rising from the bar. "You're here. I'm glad."

"I'm here," Esther said. "You're here."

The lounge was filling up with guys back from the mid-afternoon slack tide out on the grounds. Bubbapalooza nicely in swing. The bikers and their various non-biker business and political associates were crowding the bar. Juanita earning five times the normal tip rate and selling ten times as much Molson Canadian and Jack Daniel's as she normally did, along with B-52s and something called a Swollen Nipple, which nobody ever ordered up here otherwise. But little else was different. The fishing, as everyone knew, was always good.

Zweigler was jostled slightly from behind as a heavy-set man in a leather vest worked his way in close to the bar. He'd just been saying something about Graham, Esther cupping her ear to catch it. The music was a bit louder than normal too: Little Feat, Alice Cooper, ZZ Top.

Esther said, voice raised, "How's he doing? How's it going down there?"

"You're in touch, I take it," Zweigler said, not answering either question.

"I get the odd phone call," Esther said. "I only worry that these are now coming in the middle of the night. You'll know by now that Graham has a manic streak."

"Manic isn't always bad," Zweigler said. "His father was intense on project too. Reportedly didn't sleep."

"I read somewhere that he slept quite enthusiastically," Esther said.

"To answer your question: fine. I think he's fine. A little stressed. What's he told you?"

"Not much directly."

"And indirectly?"

"Things are hung up. The client is AWOL. The architect doesn't have a brief. Elliot thinks he wants an art gallery one day and a needle exchange the next. Graham meanwhile awaits the radical idea without authorization to do anything with it when it arrives. How's that?"

"Not at all bad," Zweigler said, sighing and sitting back down on his bar stool, causing Esther to note for the first time how tired he looked. Perhaps he had not guessed how exhausting the conflicted Gordon family energy could be.

Juanita cracked a glance their direction. Esther said to Zweigler, "How about a drink?"

Zweigler took B+B and seemed to note his surroundings only with this transaction of glasses and ice cubes, bottles poured and recorked, and the chit that Esther swept away from him and signed herself. "Thanks," he said, looking around. "This is nice. Where are we exactly?"

Esther told him, describing the big picture as it would look from this point over the curve of the horizon to the last place for which Zweigler had a remembered mental fix. These islands, the strait, the mainland inlets, glaciers running south, the highlands and then the British Properties and down into the city. A quick nine hundred kilometres.

"Ah, yes," Zweigler said. "I have a friend in the Properties. And here? Is this a club?"

She ran through the story. Salmon, halibut, rockfish. It was angler heaven up here, something her father had recognized early. And while there was money in the charter and tour business, he'd envisioned something for members only. Hence the PFS.

"And you were a guide, no kidding." When she got to this part of the story, Zweigler did not separate himself from the rest of the male population by failing to be pleasantly impressed with her. "And you still come up. You like it here."

"It's a getaway," she answered.

"And is there . . ." Zweigler was curious about something, but choosing his words with great caution now. "Is there some kind of convention going on this week?"

She shrugged. Lots of different kinds of people enjoyed the isolation on offer.

Zweigler said, "And the fish, presumably."

Yes of course. That was important.

"So tell me about fishing."

"You're interested?"

"My brother's a fisherman. Commercial. How're they biting?"

"Same as they do for your brother. Reluctantly."

He frowned. "But I saw a lot of fish getting hoisted up on the scales down there earlier."

Esther looked to the window. Outside, the day was winding down for the dock crew, and they were celebrating with loud music of their own. Tupac. The soundtracks at cross purposes did not seem to bother anyone.

"Angling is a calculation in three dimensions," Esther told Zweigler. "Long, Lat, Depth. Do it for awhile and you learn how to pick coordinates that produce results. Not per try, maybe. But per dozen tries. Over time."

Zweigler nodded and sipped.

"But just when you begin to assume those skills will always serve you, the fish do something different and all your accumulated wisdom isn't worth squat."

Zweigler squinted up at her. He said, "I see your point."

"Mr. Zweigler," she went on. "I'm impressed that you're here. Impressed that you found me. That you thought to come here and ask for my help. Because that's what you're up here for really, isn't it? Nobody knows what to do next, and you thought I would have suggestions."

He didn't say yes or no. But he didn't change the arrangement of his squint either, from which Esther judged she was right.

"He's a bit nuts. You know this."

"What's nuts?" Zweigler asked her. "You mean irrational, brooding, a dreamer? Not like you?"

Zweigler made space at the bar for another leather vest, thirsty, shouldering in. And when the tray of Jägermeister had been poured and carried away, he got his elbow back on the rail and turned to Esther again. He understood things were off between her and Graham, he told her. And yes, he was aware from personal experience that pain seemed to clarify things. "But it blinds you too, for awhile. Blinds you to things under your own nose. Like the fact that your young man has a gift."

"Young man."

"Speaking about architects, he's young."

"Speaking about the world as I know it, he isn't young. He's not in training any more. No element of his story is understood more clearly by considering his age."

"You are so sure."

"My own gift, Mr. Zweigler. Certainty."

"But not so much lately," he said. "Lately, you find that all your accumulated wisdom isn't worth squat."

Esther looked away. He wasn't bad, this Zweigler.

"I've been thinking about your television show," she told him. "Shows."

"Oh, yes? And what have you decided?"

"You traffic primarily in the cringe-inducing conflict, the on-camera fight."

"That's harsh."

"Only here you've wrapped it around the topic of what kind of cork floors to install, how to frame a view of the mountains out the window of a toilet alcove. Business that's become incomprehensibly popular of late. But conflict remains the heart of it."

Zweigler held up his hands, as if his palms would make it plain. "Conflict remains the heart of everything," he said.

"And so you're here," Esther said. "Ask."

"Come back with me. We need someone to help them focus, help them decide."

"Hmm. That would be good television, wouldn't it?" she answered.

"Good for you too," Zweigler said.

And how did he figure that? she wondered.

"Because conflict is your game too," the producer told her. "And like me, you're not so much interested in eliminating a given dispute as you are in controlling it, mapping it."

"Oh, I think I have this one mapped already," Esther said.

Zweigler sipped his drink and did not believe. He looked around the room again, slowly. At the far end of the rail, a group were watching a satellite feed of the *Antiques Roadshow* while a Bubbapalooza senior told a story. "So the guy says it's probably made in China and Ricky tells him, Maybe you want to take another look, cocksucker. Doesn't look Chinese to me."

Which pleased Zweigler enormously. He smiled, looked back to Esther. She shrugged.

He cycled back to the matter at hand. "All right," he said. "Mapped. Try me."

"Graham losing his mind," Esther said.

"Doubtful."

"A couple of people who hate each other and cannot even remember why."

"Possible."

"A very bad outcome pending."

"Impossible. This is television."

"Irreconcilable ideas."

"Well, that's where you come in, isn't it?" Zweigler said.

She'd been wrong before, of course. Professionally, personally. What was unusual about her present situation—

she reflected, leading an at-first bewildered Avi Zweigler down to the dock—was the comprehensive and sweeping way she now appeared to be wrong about everything.

Did he know where the name of his own show had come from? *Story House*. Well, naturally, he knew that too. It was an old Indian building.

"Kiusta," she said to him as they bounced across the waves, ninety minutes of light remaining. Zweigler knew the name. He was a devotee after all, and a well-read one at that. He just wasn't tops in geography.

"You're telling me it's right here?" He sat up straight in the Zodiac, hand gripping the side rope, eyes now locked on the far shore.

"Where there is no building, you understand? No perfect structure. No inspiring timbers. There wasn't when Graham came here, and there wouldn't have been much more back when the old man visited. They didn't build these longhouses to be preserved, you understand? They built them to live in, to move on from, to let them return to soil. What you see up here is what's left after nature takes its course."

"Built to rot. Built to decay," Zweigler said. Marvelling at her, all at once. Certainty was a powerful thing in the hands of the right people.

She looked across the boat at him. "Sure," she said. "That's partly what I think. But our architects. Of course neither of them could accept that. They had to be inspired. By decay, by ghosts if necessary."

They were standing in the long room made by trees just inland from the beach. They had walked the moss path to what would have been the centre of that row of great houses, to where the greatest one would have stood. And here they stared down, working the enormous timbers with their imaginations, refelling them, smoothing them with dogfish sandpaper, adzing them to size. Splitting and hoisting them upright, pushing out the walls, raising the beams, and watching together as roof and wall planks floated in from the forest around them and fit snugly into their places.

Four

IT WASN'T HALF-BAD THERAPY, GIVEN THAT THE fishing had failed entirely. Like angling, Esther supposed, the heart was its own calculation in some particular number of dimensions. Maybe three, but possibly more. Three you could see, anyway, and she was supposed to be trained in the matter of ignoring those things you couldn't.

"Let's start with an understanding," Esther told Zweigler. "Those two aren't going out of pocket on this deal. Graham makes plenty of money but hasn't saved a penny. Elliot probably has, but we can't use his money without unsettling the balance between them. So that means we're talking about your money."

It would be difficult, Zweigler told her. They were in for more than his partners had been comfortable with at the outset.

"Well then, maybe we're talking about your personal money," she said. "In principle."

Zweigler surrendered his in-principle agreement with a frown and a nod, a turn of his head toward the window. Her first success, her first step back to herself having taken just fifteen minutes. A hundred dollars of billable time that had passed as they'd loaded the helicopter and Esther and Zweigler sat buckled into their seats waiting for liftoff.

So now there remained the small matter of finding what other money would make Zweigler comfortable. Foundation money for upkeep and for publicizing the place and for generally returning Packer Gordon to the place of prominence he'd once enjoyed. There were those sorts of dollars around. Esther just wasn't the person to go about raising them. Too brusque, too opinionated, too little experience asking for money at Daddy's knee in early life. But she knew such people, plenty of them. They were yacht club members, lawn tennis players. They sat on the board of the opera and the botanical gardens. They excelled at lining up benevolence in the gunsight of self-interest. It was in their marrow, in the enamel of their perfect teeth.

Her senior partner was such a person who, not incidentally, grew faintly emotional with the news of her return. "Oh, listen," he said on the phone, relief in his voice, "I'd love to help you with this if it'll help you decide you're ready. We've all really . . ."

Missed you. Was that it? Was she missed in her absence? She didn't have a solid sense of having been gone somewhere and come back. It wasn't that she returned home to precisely what she'd left either. Three, getting on to four months, and landscapes had not failed to change. Looking down on her city from temporary, borrowed digs in the west end not far from the park, she could squint a certain way, shift the twenty-first-storey view to a certain angle and see a place where she'd never lived. A place where she had never known anybody, much less developed grooves and patterns, favourite and least favourite things. All was unknown, and she liked that sense of things. She didn't push for it to clear or for it to steady into firmer notions. This is my home. Or possibly, this is no longer my home. Those resolutions could wait.

Three dimensions, then. Two parties and disputed ground. She went to the ground first. Story House, as they were all calling it now. It was Graham's single and critical position in this matter, she calculated: that all of his father's early ideas about structure were expressed here simultaneously. That all of his ideas about structure everywhere—all this built business that textured the lip between earth and sky, that was itself compressed between the accomplishment of its height and the certainty of its decay—could be found here. At 55 East Mary, specifically: long high windows, very thin layered floors, that spiderweb of staircase, the hidden Haida references. And others, she was sure.

In she went, overcoming irrational physical fears, climbing across the narrow gangway linking the building to the side of the pit over which it hovered. She walked each of the empty floors, recording the space in advance of considering opinions about its next use. It was shabby, she thought. It was plainly rundown and hard to admire. Still, the quadrants of the upper floor could have been serene. On the main floor, she could imagine the timbers would inspire a feeling of solidity. But down in the basement she had less luck visualizing anything positive. It was dank. A broad space with steely, unkind light. It was cruel space, and yes, of course she had a bias stemming from the specific cruelty she knew had taken place here. Cruelty that was connected to her inexorably through the people she loved. Or had loved. But in the end, she thought, all these feelings came down to a distinct physical queasiness. And that she attributed to the fact that there was no earth beneath the cracked concrete pad. It was set up, held up, impermanent.

"Only place you might not want to go is downstairs," the security guard told her. He made a wobbly motion with one hand and held his stomach with the other, aping motion sickness.

He was joking, but it had an effect on her. The floor didn't exactly move, not discernibly. Everything seemed to be pinned, clamped, wedged and vised well enough into place. Nothing was moving independently of the whole, a good structural feature surely. Still, the building communicated a light wind outside to the soles of her feet. An almost subliminal shiver that came and passed. It left her unsettled. There was a great offence to the architect being committed here—this opinion came to her unexpectedly, not a line of thinking she would have anticipated, but fully formed when it arrived—the structure hoisted in place, preserved, fluttering dryly as a butterfly might on a corkboard.

—

"Yes, precisely," Graham agreed when she spoke of the impression. "It belongs on the ground. In the ground. It is nothing without the ground." She found herself looking at him carefully. If she shifted her gaze, adopted a certain narrowness around the eyes, did he become a place she'd never been? What about her to him? She was tanned, darker than she'd been since they met. She'd been catching her reflection in plate glass since arriving back in the city and thinking, Who is that person?

He made a face of commitment, preparing to say something. He began: "I've . . ."

Missed you. Missed me. Esther wondered. "I've been thinking about what you said. That you thought the fragment had triumphed with us," he said. "Molecules drifting apart, forming some new thing."

The second dimension of matters. They didn't meet at their own place. It wasn't an issue of neutral ground, more of perspective. Something was unsatisfactorily hoisted between them too, preserved and possibly lifeless. Their sense of one another suspended. The effect of personal changes on the thing called *them*, still quivering, uncertain.

Graham, whose eyes were bloodshot and darkly rimmed, said, "You look amazing, by the way. God, you look healthy. How are you? How've you been feeling?"

Better to meet at this expensive grocery store around the corner from their place with its Kobe beef and tins of Beluga caviar, with its complete absence of anything Korean. The store had been at the centre of Graham's argument that they should buy here. The epicentre of the neighbourhood, he'd said. A good building and food had that power. And even though she had never shopped here, travelling east and under the light-rail tracks to various Asian markets instead, he hadn't been wrong about the neighbourhood. The artificiality of those new waterside streets had lifted. The condos had weathered into their places. The crowd at that hour in the coffee shop, midmorning, had the lingering quality of regulars regular enough to be listless, to show signs of wishing they were somewhere else. These were indicators of a neighbourhood pattern descending. The stifled yawns and idle arguments, their own meeting, the separated married couple over civil Americanos, one complimenting the other just now on how great they look, these were signs of a city planning success.

Esther answered his question, trying for the truth without any of the chill she felt toward it. "I'm not sure how I am, really," she said. "But I'm trying not to be anxious about not being sure."

Do we talk about this further? she wanted to ask him. You and I who never did terribly well dealing with ourselves as a discrete topic. Who did so only once, committing vocally, openly, enthusiastically to the idea of parenthood, and then failing. Esther thought at the time that it must have indicated some lack of resolve on their part. Maybe Graham had not wanted sufficiently. But it could just as easily have been that she wanted too much, too suddenly. That after years of not wanting much for them together that couldn't as well be wished for them separately—health, success, friends—that she had let herself slide into wanting a change in matters between them. And when that did not come, another change came hard in its wake. Foolishness to think so, perhaps. But she could not shake the feeling. And surely, in either case, they would do no better talking about themselves now. If she were to ask about Fila, for example. If she followed the line of inquiry that would lead them both to answers in that area.

She said, "I'll be honest, since you raise it. You don't look really well."

It was fairly safe personal territory. Discussing themselves separately had never been difficult. His and hers problems. They would engage reciprocally and she remembered Graham offering decent advice. So now: his problem. Child of alcoholism. Of course, under stress he was drinking too much. And not sleeping either, although Graham thought this was a symptom both of the problem and the possible solution. He was on to something. He was possessed by it. He'd been led to this place and he wouldn't rest now until it was realized.

Graham pulled a paper napkin from the box and began to fold it intensely. "I went looking for this film and brought home a camera. I went looking for something to film with the camera, something my own, and I found this building that could well have been the first thing my father did. Now you know quite well that I've had issues with my father over the years, including the fact that he never taught me shit about the field he inspired me to pursue. He taught me useless stuff. He taught me about a certain kind of bearing, a certain confidence, a certain social certainty. He modelled for me how to be the kind of man . . ."

Graham strangled on the words while Esther stared, thinking, Don't say it. Don't you dare . . . *the kind of man woman inexplicably go for.*

He didn't. He returned to his point. "And yet here, in Mary Street, we have nothing less than the sum total of all he knew. The real, lasting things that he believed. And

I cannot avoid the sense that it was given to me. That I'm supposed to do something with it."

He'd made a little paper house in just those few angry seconds. A box that folded at a forty-five-degree angle around what Esther imagined might be a garden.

"But what?" she asked.

"But what. But just at the moment when I think I know what has to come next, Elliot is stalled. He's stuck trying to protect what the building was in the first place. Which we don't know. Which neither of us know. Which neither of us can remember because neither of us were around at the time. Elliot's stuck trying to figure out something we were never told. Understand? And given that every major component of that original building has to be replaced anyway, I'm therefore inclined to work with those *ideas* that were original. The man's ideas. Blow those up, shatter them, explode them. Then reform them, rework them, forge them into something new. That's something which would be ours. That's a tribute. That's original. But what. But when Elliot and I enter the same room we end up hitting each other."

He sat back. Breathless. Not defeated, she could see, but casting about for new angles, ways forward to some vision that was forming. It was, she had to acknowledge, a more single-minded Graham than any she remembered from over the years. He had latched on to something, maybe thinking of it as an only chance. He wasn't letting go. He was looking to her for help.

Imagine my help, she thought. And out it slipped. "Fila. Yes, no, or what?"

She surprised them both with the question. His eyebrows came up. He had to refocus. But his answer didn't waver or turn back on itself, and Esther judged it to be truthful. Nothing had happened between them before Esther had left. After that, yes. There had been the L.A. trip. There had been the period of time when Graham had been unable to get a call through to Esther. And during that time, yes, they had fallen far enough down some axis together to have crossed over, to have rebalanced intimacy between them.

"Meaning you slept together." She didn't visualize the offence. She didn't imagine them rolling in white sheets together or covered in sand or grass from fucking outdoors. It wounded her in pure theory, a clarity of feeling with which she was able to feel significant pride. Or almost pride, but for the sudden wave of nausea that accompanied the insight. She set down her coffee cup, sharply, aware in an instant of membranes and tubing, sacs and pathways within her. A messy assemblage of stuff that worked and stuff that didn't, stuff that would fail or perforate or grow cancerous or merely wear out in future, all according to some unknowable schedule.

Graham, who had noticed none of this, was still answering the question in the new voice he seemed to have found. ". . . and so yes. At a point we did sleep together. But what I'm saying is that we're not still falling down that axis together and we're not by mutual agreement. Plus, you left. You've been away. But now you're back."

She answered, "I left. I've been away. But I'm not back."

Words that may have nauseated him in turn. She could not be sure. He only sat a fraction straighter in his chair, as if to rearrange the air inside him. He straightened a cuff, then a strand of sandy blond that had fallen across his eyebrow.

He said to her, "Fila is in Tokyo."

He was right to divert the discussion in this direction, and she let him. Tokyo was a project he was supposed to have been working on himself. A big deal for GS Design. For a pre-market retail concept company branding a line of ecologically minded smart toys for the North American eight- to twelve-year-old set. Climate-change sims. That sort of thing. They'd worked on getting the gig for over a year. Now she was over there designing everything from the toys to the packaging to the retail stores.

"The biggest thing we ever won together, and I'm back here because I don't want to be anywhere else. I'm here because I believe this is the someplace good to which I've been heading for a long time."

The third dimension himself, interestingly enough to Esther, didn't entirely disagree. They met at an old hotel on Hastings Street to which he had provided apologetic directions and parking advice. When she pushed open the door she saw a surprisingly young-looking man bounce to his feet off one of the stools at the lobby-side bar. He stood up straight, staring at her, looking like he might bolt. Then, apparently changing his mind, he let his shoulders down and came across the linoleum to pump her hand.

"I'm glad to meet you. I'm really glad to meet you."

"You said you lived here?"

"I know. I know. Bit rough. My *pied-à-terre*."

He led her into the lobby and sat her at the bar. He went to work preparing tea for them behind the counter. He was telling her about the Orwell. About how he knew the owners. He was opening tins and closing them, dropping spoons. He was clattering mugs off the countertop and generally making a mess. Then he stopped cold, remembering something he'd planned to say.

"You know, whatever you know about me, I just want to say that I've wanted to do something different for awhile. Something more . . . substantial. More concrete. More a thing people can see. I have kids now."

She nodded, watching. His intensity was entertaining. The high bounce he took between each successive idea. She found herself trying to suss the physical similarities. Trying to see the brother in the brother. And not succeeding, except perhaps for something similar going on in the eyes. An undeniable burn behind the brown.

"I saw it originally as a straight restoration project," he was saying, looking over at her sharply to see if she was listening. "Chrysanthemum?"

She nodded. Chrysanthemum tea was fine. "Mary Street, you mean?" she said.

"Yeah, well. Graham doesn't know what the hell it was in the first place. So restoration is a problem. I mean, restore to what? I just don't see how we can create a tribute to the man just making that shit up. Sorry."

He poured the tea and watched her take a sip.

"Nice," she said. "Where do you get it?"

Now here was something he'd been hoping she would ask. It seemed there was a Korean grocer around the corner who had a special stash of things for those who knew

to ask. Tea, yes. But he also had a cooler with twelve kinds of kimchee. He made his own songpyun. Elliot spoke a sentence in stumbling Korean for Esther, smiling broadly.

"I speak it so seldom I've lost a lot," she told him. "An endless source of humiliation to my father."

"I have tapes," he said, eyes bright. "For the truck. Borrow them. It'll come back."

"Thanks," she said. Then smiled, then laughed.

"Go ahead," he said. "Say it."

"You just don't look particularly . . ."

"It's fine, it's fine," he said. "I've dealt with it."

"Are you angry with him?"

"Graham? I feel like punching him in the head, but it's not anger."

"I meant your father."

Oh. He was reeling in a silver tea bulb out of his own cup and stopped with it halfway, the metal canister tinging against the rim of the cup. He said, "A lot less angry than Graham, believe it or not."

She let him talk kids for awhile. There seemed to be a point here that Elliot felt needed making. That he had them. That he'd felt the need for them. She watched the man opposite—sipping, smiling, speaking of how great it was to be a father—and found herself believing him entirely. There was an oddly, strikingly physical presence to him. He had muscled forearms and a lean waist and he was, all in the instant of this appraisal, quite obviously a man who would have children. Such men had to breed like certain kinds of horses had to breed, because some higher breeding power demanded it. Of course, not every evolutionarily selected and purportedly happy father is built the same way either. Elliot and Deirdre had separations, it seemed. Work-related, but longer than most people considered necessary for work. This past six weeks, for example, Elliot had been hanging at his *pied-à-terre*.

"How's Deirdre feel about that?" she asked. Then immediately, "I'm sorry. That's none of my business."

"Hey, you're family," he said. But he didn't answer.

"How old?" she said, covering quickly.

Seven, no, eight months old. Not even a half-beat of recognition as to why she would be asking. He only came back with: "How about you two? Ever think you might?"

It was the most destructive question in the world relative to the general comfort level people felt in asking. She looked at Elliot and forced herself to see a brother-in-law. And with that thought she was able to answer the question without feeling a wound tear open.

"We tried for a long time. At first I thought we weren't very lucky. Later, that we were quite unlucky. Still later, I guess I just realized that we didn't have any luck in this area at all."

Elliot stared at her for several seconds. He said, "Luck."

"None in that area," she repeated. "And now . . ."

He bounced off the edge of the counter. He swung back to the matter at hand. "So Graham and I don't agree on direction. But he's not paying. And I'm not totally ignorant either. I know what the whole thing means. I'm proud to be my father's son."

"I believe you."

"You asked if I was angry. But what you have to realize is that it's possible to be proud of being related to a guy who was . . . well . . . okay, he was a prick. But I have eyes. I've seen the result. I've been in the Haney House in Westport. I've been to other sites. I've probably visited more of his work than Graham has, although I'm not telling you this because I think it makes me better. For what it's worth, I've seen a thing or two that Graham's worked on and I'm capable of being impressed there too. They build things. My father and Graham both. That's good in itself, even if neither of them is my favourite architect."

Then he reddened, like he'd just said far more than he'd wanted to say thinking about the conversation in advance, looking in the mirror that morning perhaps, half shaven, considering a family of proud, unreasonable pricks, just seconds before he cut himself, right there on the point of his very proud chin.

"And who is your favourite architect, Elliot?"

He exhaled. He turned to her. It seemed he had a very specific and thorough answer for that one.

Her senior partner phoned again. He had the local Institute of Architecture, the city, the province and various private sources in for some. Her father had reportedly been generous. "So we have our yearly budget that'll run the place," he told Esther, "five years' worth, assuming your boys will agree to a museum and certain neighbourhood programs to be worked out later. And, naturally, assuming your guy is in for the capital improvements."

He wasn't quite yet, Esther said. But would be soon enough.

"Try to see my position," Zweigler said when she tracked him down. "I don't even live here."

Esther stared. She'd gone down to his hotel, met him in a bar hung out high over the water with the mountains opposite and the blue sky overhead and float planes taking off and landing while piano jazz and a fake waterfall tinkled in the background.

She said, "You're the world's leading collector of Packer Gordon drawings, models and writings, and you're telling me you don't want to see the Zweigler Collection housed in his very first building."

It was a rhetorical hammerlock working against his windpipe. The idea had been in the back of his mind, hadn't it? And the evidence was there for others to see, the artifacts of his obsession. If he strained hard against the offer now, he wondered if he might not disappear into unconsciousness. Zweigler agreed and Esther moved calmly on to gathering in the other two.

Graham was easy. Small museums were hot, plus she'd arranged already for a visit from *Architexture*.

"You are kidding me." He was impressed, he was excited. She'd been living in an endless coffee-table drift of these publications and never read a single word in any of them. And having no particular reverence, it was a one-phone-call job. She said to an editor, in effect: Packer Gordon, son Graham Gordon, famous chair, GS Design, La Molta, youth versus age, restoration of modern ideas, dead zone in a major city, discovered gem.

"They're sending Cameron Lark. He's their stringer out here."

Elliot, who had to agree to pass the building over to the new foundation for the same nominal price that he had paid, was only a degree more difficult. He asked to be on the board of directors.

Esther told him, "I think that could be arranged."

Of course they still had no agreed design. They still hadn't agreed on what would be preserved and what would be destroyed, Esther knew well. But pieces were falling slowly toward their places. In sets of three, she thought. Esther, who had been dreaming threes lately. Crystalline objects floating toward one another, large triangles growing smaller and smaller. Pyramids spinning in the black void of delta sleep. She awoke wondering if this REM fixation was a product of something she had been taught. Some rule about the tension of threes she could no longer remember, but which now appeared to explain everything.

———

In the meantime, what they needed was a practical plan for the structure, which now seemed to lean a little west on its scaffolding, cocking an ear to the wind as if it had overheard a rumour. There had been rain. Now a milky sun was drying the ground. The building seemed to shine. The local papers picked up the story and ran small blurbs. The first tiny traces of an event taking shape in the air of public awareness.

They met at Ike's, which Esther chose for being halfway between Graham's office and the hotel where Elliot was staying. It was in the neighbourhood. It was available to them for an entire Sunday afternoon, and Ike promised her a conflict-management taster menu with Korean highlights. "I call it my gangbang san."

She was looking over the list of things he had suggested serving. Not a menu, precisely. More like an agenda. Items were numbered, with sub-numbering and, in the case of the squid, sub-sub-numbering. Item 5.2.3 — Cuttlefish foam. Well, it turned out the squid could be puréed, then emulsified in light oil, then whipped with a bit of gelatin to stiff peaks. Voila foam. "Hot it up with a little Korean hot pepper sauce. Fluff it onto a little pillow of iced seaweed. It is, swear to God, very nice."

Zweigler set up cameras while Esther went around the corner to a coffee shop to clear her head. As always (and she'd long given up fighting it) emptying her mind involved steadily tightening circles around whatever was of immediate professional concern. So she didn't have a conventional mediation on her hands here because they weren't really in dispute, her two parties. Graham and Elliot's desire to honour different angles of view on precisely the same personal history were not competing. What then brought the oddly wistful Elliot and the spastically assertive Graham into the same building? One thing that seemed clear was that it wouldn't depend on any common view of their father. It would rely instead on their ability to shape an envelope—a building, a structure—that said something acceptable to both of them about themselves.

"I'm assuming we come to some agreement today, some buildable solution. And I'm assuming we do this without any particular acrimony." She addressed the assembly: Graham and Elliot, Gimble for feasibility, Zweigler for the purpose of telling the tale. She worked a seam of Astroturf, moving to make their eyes move, to provide herself with a gauge of focus. It was tight as she began. It became tighter. Now that they had fused form back to function, now that they were no longer disagreeing about how the building should be used, they were merely discussing means, specific solutions to specific problems.

So began their tumble toward ideas. They started over drinks. Some kind of margarita flavoured with multiple fruits on different layers as you progressed through it. Layers, she noticed, that resisted mixing while the discussion swirled. Gimble thought they had to start with solving the pile problem. Without foundations, they were nowhere. He wondered aloud about dropping them through the building, cutting holes then patching them. Elliot wanted to talk about lightness and transparency. He wanted to talk about preserving the original sense of the structure as a thing that had been thinned to the point of failure but not beyond. Graham was trying to synthesize these two discussions while introducing yet a third: the longhouse.

Food arrived and was whisked away. A caramel-crusted oyster. A sliver of black bean cheesecake. A soft-cooked quail's egg yolk in a miniature champagne flute. These creations disappeared in between sentences, as they worked the borders of what they knew.

The longhouse, Graham was saying, was a structural matter of thresholds, a matter of the intersections in a number of axes in a single physical place. He tore a sheet of paper into small squares and dealt these out in a shallow arch around his place at the table. There was the horizontal line of houses parallel to the beach. He cut shapes to denote topographical lines and laid these inland and seaward from the houses. There was another horizontal line that ran through each house front to back, from the hills behind through to the sea in front.

"The X and the Y axis," he said. "So we have our position on earth. We have our structure on the threshold of land and water, pinned on the spot between."

And here he paused, because the absence of a third plane floated above the table without being mentioned.

Elliot said, "Okay, so."

Okay, so. Graham modelled this dimension with a rough variety of origami. The central square of torn paper, the central most important house, was lifted from its place and poised on a tiny three-point prop made of folded paper. It left the house quivering above the tablecloth.

"Let's call that Story House," Graham said, balancing a strand, pinched to a thin wick with dampened fingers, coiling vertical out of a tiny hole in the torn square that Esther had not seen Graham make in the first place. "And that's your Z axis."

Running from the heat of the firepit at the centre of the longhouse and up out the smoke hole, up to the infinite cool of the stars. Running from the man who built Story House, to the son who would build the second and the grandson who would build the third. And so on. That was the chain of links joining those men in the doorway of their longhouse, to the particular threshold of beach, to the sea and mountains above and below, to the earth itself pinned onto some particular breakpoint between the measurable now and the infinite universe.

"That's the idea," Graham said.

They were at dish 2.4 by this point. Something Esther thought was caviar suspended in a spicy fruit jelly but could not be sure. It took a second to slurp out of the sliver spoon in which it was served and then the table was bare again but for the origami Indian village, a tendril of paper smoke drifting upward out of a longhouse of central importance.

Elliot sat thinking, tapping his chin. He rose sharply, began to pace.

"What?" Graham asked him.

"What you were saying. Z axis."

Graham tried again. The point was that people seeing the longhouse in use would have actually *seen* this other dimension. It wouldn't have been hidden in a theory, wrapped up in moss, an inspiration waiting to be sucked out of the cedar breeze through a cool but empty stretch of forest. "It was known to exist because you could *see* the fire, you could *see* into the structure."

Elliot scratched his chin. "Didn't they close the front door?"

They probably did, in fact. Slab doors normally covered the oval entryway through the front pole. "But you could see the smoke, see what was going on within, see that link rising from here up to . . . there."

Elliot was still considering this point. "So we're talking about seeing into the structure."

Yes, Graham thought. *Seeing in,* as in to make the structure understood. Just as the longhouses wrote about themselves on their own exteriors. They explained the dreams that brought them into being. They weren't hidden behind walls. Or in the deep past. Or in memory. They were exploded, they were open.

"I'm still confused," Elliot said. "Is this a physical opening we're discussing?"

Graham had his hands up, palms out. "I don't know. How do we expose the thing, make it understood? Not through preservation. Not through trying to touch the structure without appearing to have ever touched it."

Elliot stood absolutely still. Graham was saying ". . . as if we were trying to preserve a single statement made by the building when . . ." Hands now wide and fluttering. And Elliot did not jump in because he could no longer bear another second of suspense. He did so more from a sense that the idea had been passed to him.

"When maybe . . ." Elliot said. "The building isn't making any kind of statement at all."

"When maybe the building is actually asking a question," Esther said.

They both looked at her. They both waited for her. It seemed she had to push them over the edge with whatever she said next, and so she chose: "Graham, I want you to listen to what your brother has to say about an architect named Gordon Matta-Clark."

Gut call: Esther left the room. She didn't want to hover over every development. She also didn't want to pressure Graham by being there to witness how he might choose to use an idea he didn't introduce himself. She made room for his pride and went to find Ike, to compliment him on 3.3, an oblong ravioli the size of a lima bean that released an intense burst of flavour: some kind of fish, sesame, pepper, spinach. A mini japchae explosion at the taste buds.

Ike was working on dessert. Dish 4.0. Lemongrass, sliced whisker thin, tempura deep fried, then stuffed gently between the two sides of a thin-shelled chocolate egg. When the shell was cracked—Ike showed her, he made her try some—the lemongrass unsprung, surging from the cavity, climbing out onto the plate and forming a little puffy cloud. The chocolate was chocolate, but these filaments dissolved on the tongue. They left a trace of crisp and tart, a savoury grassy zing. A little, Esther thought, like the flash of longing Ike was trying to speak about without saying the words.

She'd only been back there five minutes, she guessed, when Zweigler came to find her. She didn't see him come in, only heard his voice from over by the door. He said, "You certainly won't want to miss this moment."

She looked up sharply. The producer's expression hovered at an ambiguous point from which any number of others could flow. He could reach anger from there, Esther thought. He could reach elation. He was within striking distance of a number of different peaks.

Zweigler found laughter instead. The kind you'd expect from someone who, after a long struggle, surrenders to a craving completely different from the one they'd been resisting. In this case, Zweigler surrendered to his own final episode right there in front of them as Ike put final touches on the final dish of the afternoon. Those eggs: impossible, delicious and fine. Not food at all, Esther decided. Mechanisms of ingredient and idea instead. And maybe more like food than real food for the loud statement made about its own creation, the strident way it executed a sensory program on the plate.

Zweigler had laughed himself down from a guffaw through a tubular throat rasp to a half-cough half-giggle that looked like it would shortly start to hurt, physically.

Ike lifted his head. He said to Zweigler: "Speak. Choose life."

Zweigler did. Recovering his composure, just, he said, "Okay. Here. This is good. Now they're talking about cutting the building in half."

Five

UNEXPECTED OPENINGS. NEGATIVE SPACE CREATED where it had been positive. A strange visual lightening of the structure and, not incidentally, an elegant solution to the problem of the piles. From the standpoint of brainstorming, they were on fire.

Gimble could be thanked for playing a larger role than expected. In fact, he was thanked, several times. Graham and Elliot both thanked him immediately. Later, Zweigler thanked him. Then Zweigler's partner

Raul thanked him when he flew into town. "I understand you helped crack this thing open, as it were."

Gimble stammered, "All's I said was let's go back over and climb around the building."

Esther swept back into the dining room and found them frantically drawing and redrawing a plan of the building, slashing lines through it at various angles, Gimble looking on with amusement and a small measure of concern.

He was saying: "See. That still leaves you a problem with the piles."

Elliot: "What about we move the building to one side first, drop piles . . ."

Gimble shaking his head. "Not enough lot."

Graham: "I still say we can lift it."

Gimble shook his head again, then forked in one of Ike's chocolate eggs, which he chewed very carefully, wincing a little as if it were (Esther judged) the most delicious or the most unpleasant thing he'd ever eaten. But when he spoke, he didn't reveal which. He only drank some water, cleared his throat and said, "Listen. Let's go back over there while it's still light. Go have ourselves a look-see. I'll show you."

Fifteen minutes later they were clambering around the side scaffolding. Elliot and Graham like kids, Esther thought. Running up and down, pointing at windows and corners, hallway through-lines and the central drop of the staircase.

Graham climbed onto the roof. It was five o'clock. Shadows were lengthening, the light going rose. He said, "So we drop piles on each corner . . ."

Gimble shook his head. "That still leaves you no piles in the middle. Which you need. In my humble opinion."

Graham began to pace the rooftop. All the way from the north side to the south and back, east and then west. Elliot watched him for some minutes before moving himself. And when he did, he didn't look over at his brother at all, but down to the gravel instead. He was following something marked there, Esther noticed. It was a line, or a furrow, dredged through the small stones. Messed up and walked over more recently, but still visible. Elliot followed one long straight line to the south eaves, then another almost as far as the east, then a third that brought him all the way back toward where the rest of them were standing. An equilateral triangle that bracketed the boarded-over skylight at the centre of the roof. A triangle opening toward the street.

Here he lifted his eyes and looked at his brother. Eye in the eye. His eye in his eye. First such moment of mutual regard in a very long time. And again, done so framed up all around by a four-sided structure encouraging them to pay very close attention to each another.

Graham put a finger to his lips. He traced the triangle again with his eyes. He said, "Now here's a thought."

Esther didn't stick around long to admire her handiwork, such as it was. She didn't feel deserving, she'd done so little. And then there was the outstanding matter of that big fish she was supposed to catch. Her deal with Zweigler was an accord such that he could move forward. She'd delivered. Her deal with herself had been to have a look at Graham close up. She'd done that too. Now, back to the fish.

She extended the leave of absence. "One month," she told her senior partner. "Thirty days. I'll be back or I'll be too embarrassed to come back."

"You are coming back," he said, clicking through his calendar. "In the office starting Monday the twentieth, then?"

Call it the twentieth, they agreed.

"Good," he said. "Twenty-six more days. I can handle that. Have you seen the drawings, by the way? Very nice work."

It was nice work. Graham had nice work in him. And these drawings were now being flashed around to the funders and partners and permit granters and contractors on the project, to the folks at *Architexture*, who were talking about a major publication on the structure, the images causing in aggregate something like a collective intake of breath. Esther was not so immediately distracted from goings-on that she didn't admire how much of that work, that idea, had arrived in one earth tremor of inspiration. There were a constellation of details still to consider, of course, and they were all up until the wee hours doing so. But much of what was splendid and striking and bold and simultaneously original source and downstream tributary about the plan came all in an instant.

Graham laid it out on a large sheet of paper in his looping hand. They would split the building in two, cutting down through three floors in a line from front to back. They would pivot these two halves away from one each other, opening the building like a book. The pie-shaped opening, an equilateral triangle overlapping that gravel-furrowed inspiration for the idea, would then be closed in with translucent flooring to rejoin the separated halves of the building, and a sweeping, rounded glass front piece, through which, from the street, a dramatic, immediate and honest view of the structural guts of the thing would be given, including the central staircase, which would remain precisely in its original position, tailing down through clear light, sheathed itself in some kind of invisible structural shaft.

A striking idea, Esther would allow, and one that seemed to immediately prove itself when Gimble saw in it the solution to their foundation piling problem. Following Graham's plan, they would be able to drop the outer piles first, then swivel each half of the building away to meet these marks. Centre piles could then be dropped into the exposed earth directly beneath the structure. Since the footing and slab could be poured with the building in place, the rest was almost straightforward. Nobody could find anything to disagree with. So they were talking about how to make the big cut. They were talking about materials. Graham thought the translucent flooring would work with a new fibreglass process he'd heard of. Glass for the verticals. The staircase could be fixed in place with a series of thin steel coils reinforcing a Plexiglas tube.

Esther left at midnight with the boys still going strong in one of the top-floor rooms at Mary Street under the portable halogens. She found all at once, seeing the time, that she wanted out of the structure. Having shocked it back to life, she wanted away from the frantic pumping of this enormous organ called agreement.

Graham resurfaced the next afternoon. He got her on her cellphone. "I want you to stay," he told her. "Please stay. At least until we make the cut." It was a big deal, this symbolic breaking of earth on the downtown eastside. A really new architectural thing happening over there. "Maybe for the first time since the building went up. Think of it. A lot of people are excited and proud that he built here first. And we're doing it again."

Esther told him, "Graham, truthfully. I'm about to land here."

"Where . . ." He let the question trail away.

He sat back in the bar chair at Ike's after he'd hung up. He was stunned that she'd left a second time. Stunned as he would have been catching the same punch twice. And he didn't immediately want to recover from the impact either. He wanted, just for a moment there between sips of mineral water, her words to put him under. To stiffen him, as they used to say.

Of course they didn't. And of course, there were now immediate, minute-by-minute issues that demanded his attention. Cameron Lark, for one, who had just arrived at his elbow.

"Hello again," he said.

"Oh, I see," Graham answered, still wobbling from Esther, now looking level into a face that threatened him once more. "So you're working for *Architexture* now?"

Lark said, "You might not realize how big a fan of your family I am. I adored your father. I was good friends with your mother while she lived here. We still e-mail from time to time, although not so much since the lawsuit."

Graham set down his soda. "My mother has e-mail?"

"I own one of your chairs."

Graham drove Lark to the site. Zweigler's camera operator swung the Bolex lens close as they climbed out of the car directly in line with the front doors. Another camera rig stood off by the lip of the site, panning and zooming and waiting for the action to begin.

Gimble's cut crew was set up and ready to go. Their tools—slung from belts and racked outside the engineer's shed—were an arsenal of saw types. Quick cuts, abrasive wheel cut-offs, masonry, chain and hand jobs that glinted blue in the chilly sun that had come up that morning. Inside the building, the air was alive with laser light coming from levels set at surveyed points in the foyer, basement and front and back upper rooms. These were mounted on brackets, their heads spinning silently on bearings, casting out a red beam that striped the walls, the ceiling and floor of each room, marking the cut in a razor-straight north–south line. Walking the interior, it seemed to Graham as if the building had already been sliced through in one great samurai stroke, and was now releasing a bead of blood along the incision.

"Just in time," Lark said with a thin smile, as if the halves of the structure might hive apart at any moment. He was taking notes in a Moleskine and framing up snapshots with a tiny brushed-aluminium digital.

The building was by now rebraced underneath and up the outside walls. The stair column had been closed off and reinforced with steel verticals dropped down three storeys around the spiral structure in a cage braced at the top and bottom. When the building was split and moved, this would hold the stairs in place as a single unit until the new flooring and beams could be installed. There had originally been plans to run additional support members through the building under each floor on either side of the cut line too, but Gimble had pored over his drawings of the building long enough to decide it was an unnecessary precaution. The skeleton of the thing—that invisible timber grid of verticals and north–south horizontals that was largely untouched by decay—seemed to lend itself precisely to the cut envisioned, columns and beams toward the centre of the building having been more closely spaced than toward either the east or west side. The building concentrated itself, bulked itself toward the centre as if anticipating division.

Gimble was in the engineer's shed with the cut-crew boss. They nodded at Graham and Lark, their question written in the wrinkling of foreheads, the angle of raised eyebrows. You ready now? Finally?

Everyone was ready, Graham thought. Elliot too, although his presence on the site could only be sensed. Graham smelled him in the room as he entered, as if he'd slipped out seconds before he entered. He heard footfalls in the rooms above them as he showed Lark around and it didn't bother or perplex him. The effect was, in fact, mildly calming. The two of them circling the same idea now, no closer to each other than before, and yet somehow properly aligned. Locked in some stable non-destructive orbit.

Graham told Lark the story of how they'd come up with the idea while the cutting tools roared to life. Now, as they watched, long rips were made through the walls and floors, through the ceiling plaster of the front hall, which was spraying away in a powdery shower. Graham and Lark stood just outside the front door and watched them cut across the floor to the stairwell and around it.

The critical idea, Graham explained, arose from the reconciliation of two positions by the addition of a third. So you had your modern ideal re-emergent, stripped of much of its original ideological freight and repackaged as aesthetic. And then you had your high-tech elaborations on those same ideas.

"Things built of titanium," Lark said.

"Don't get me wrong," Graham said, "I like titanium."

They were coring out the staircase now, carving it out of each floor until it stood fixed in its reinforced cage, standing tall in the flying dust. Under the braced floors, Graham could see light emerging from the basement. The building becoming porous, malleable in their hands.

"So we seal it. We make sure it doesn't leak," he shouted into Lark's ear from close. "But we leave a lot of it as found. In fact, we tear the structure open to show how it was found. Pocked stucco and broken paint layers, places where the wood was intended to be smooth and has now been splintered or roughened with age, these things stay. So we change it dramatically in order to show it precisely as it is, as it has become."

Outside, they walked in a wide perimeter around the structure, watching as the exterior cuts began. The team was using a spinning abrasive wheel saw mounted on rails. It climbed up the side of the building, wailing, opening a smooth incision.

So, Graham went on, the building may have incorporated the modern ideal, but it was in the end something formed not by space, but by the things drawn into that space. "And in this version of itself, it makes space by physically holding the objects that we connect with my father's work. His models, drawings, writings and tools. Even the people who come to the museum. They become part of a field of elements by which the dimensions of the space are defined."

Graham said these last words over relative quiet, as the saw climbing the north wall had reached the parapet and been shut down by the operator. Sounds that had filled the atmosphere all along were now sensible in the singing air: routine shouts coming from behind the building, horns honking in the not-distant streets, sirens, gulls and the white undercolour of industrial noise from the harbour. Lark was listening to these with a cocked ear. He was fleshing his portrait of the thing in front of him, pen poised above white pages. Hand trembling slightly.

Not so Graham, who had heard these sounds now for long enough not to register their cycles and peaks, but who was also distracted by something moving high at the roofline. Large, black and white. A bird, he wondered. But then, as he shaded his eyes and squinted, he saw immediately that it wasn't a magpie or a crow but a person's head, rising slowly as he walked from the back of the roof to the front, revealing shoulders, then arms, then legs. A person who had emerged from the temporary stairs scaffolded up the rear corner of the structure, emerged into the clear white light and now stood staring down. Not over the side of the building. Not down on all of them to meet their upward and quizzical stares. Because Graham was not the only one looking up now. Gimble too had noticed Elliot, and had stopped what he was doing, a wrinkle of disapproval sliding into place around his left eye.

"What's he looking at?" the engineer mumbled, as Elliot stared down at the roof, tracing the shape of something with his eyes.

Graham knew from his brother's position what he was looking at. A tracing in old gravel describing precisely the triangle they would open there in just a few days to enormous effect. And Graham was as confident about that—his brother considering the same future he was, just that moment—as he had been about anything he had tried in his life before.

"And now we wait, after all the buildup?" Raul was asking Zweigler, twiddling an uni toward his mouth with inexpert chopsticks. Then, "This is *ridiculously* good."

Zweigler had a mouthful of rice and urchin roe wrapped in seaweed too, only he'd overhit the wasabi. All at once—the sensation sweeping into his sinuses, his tear ducts, his frontal lobes—he was loaded up with horseradish heat greatly in excess of system tolerance.

"How can it be so good? You okay?"

Zweigler swallowed green tea until his eyes stopped running. "Because the sea where they get this fish is pristine. No pollution."

"That's it?"

"I'm telling you."

"And where is this unpolluted sea?"

Zweigler pointed his own chopsticks into the harbour. "Way north," he said. "Where I went to find Esther."

Raul nodded. "So when do we hoist and swing this baby? What's this?"

"That's toro, from the belly of the tuna. High in fat and flavour," Zweigler said.

Renewed rain made this unpressed discussion of next steps possible. After a sense of lifting, the clouds rising high, down everything came again. Deluge rains that greyed out the mountains opposite, that hung down low over the far shore. That whipped the inlet into foam when it was windy, or stippled it hard when the air was still. And at night, when the day's weather seemed always to abate by half, this piece of ocean merely heaved and shuffled, mumbling like something very large and slow growing impatient.

Since they'd managed to drop the outer piles in the week before the rain started, Zweigler said he thought they'd be able to move the building next week.

"Next week's weather is good?" Raul said.

"Next week earliest if it stops raining as of tomorrow,

since Gimble wants seven days for it to dry. I'm trying to be optimistic."

Of course, the rain didn't stop as of their tomorrow, nor would Gimble get his seven days. Ahead of Zweigler and his partner lay a schedule, a physical thing stapled onto a series of days across a wall calendar in Raul's Los Angeles office. Some compression of this physical thing was possible, but not much. Because there quickly came a point when the force applied to its opposite ends—the rain on the near side, agreed air dates on the other—began to buckle what lay between. There came a point, in short, where weather be damned.

But not just yet. Time still for another piece of uni, for a tiny rocketship of flavour called a spicy dynamite scallop roll. For more green tea than either of them thought it possible to hold. ·

"You ever worry?" Raul asked.

About what, Zweigler wanted to know.

"About these guys getting along too well now?"

Zweigler shook his head. He'd been watching footage and cutting. He'd been rebuilding a thing on which he'd come so close to losing hope. But he'd also been entertaining a thought or two about the future. About a place where all that material from his long room stretching into the Bel-Air hillside would finally come to rest. Where models would be lined up under glass cases. Where tools could be laid out on blue velvet cloths. Where drawings might be set by a curator to hang in precisely the right places.

"This is a good outcome," he said. "This is good TV."

It was, Raul agreed. The reality of which enabled Zweigler to make a couple of harder decisions, ones that he did not share with his friend. Were the show to do even half as well as Raul was now telling his own people that it would, then Zweigler would move. To where? Not sure. But sell Stone Canyon, donate the collection to the foundation, cut the ties forever. Get out of television entirely and wish everybody well doing so. That last item an important detail, because it was a wellness he felt within him. A wellness linked very much (but this was impossible, he repeated to himself lying awake at night, completely impossible) to the sensation he recalled of falling in love.

Impossible why? He might rise from bed, arguing with himself, and stand in the middle of his bathroom or in front of the sliding glass doors. Looking out over the softly textured waters of 2:00 a.m.

Well, impossible for one thing because there was no specific far-side party to the transaction. There was, instead, something like a consortium. The counterfeiter's wife made him weep in his bathroom eight hours after having seen her nursing those twins. Esther too, not tears precisely but something close. He'd travelled around a significant curve in the globe to find her, to bring her back, and in the helicopter, in all of their dealings, he had felt utterly pierced by her, seen through. And then—God, this one was perhaps the most compelling in the middle of the night standing, now naked, in front of the black glass—the third corner of this energized triangle. Fila. Remembered above a view of the derelict old city, slim hipped, fine jawed, steely blue eyed, like a goddess looking out over the sack of Rome. He thought of her and gave in immediately, enormously to his desire. Only then, in the moment of wrenching and gasping that followed, his knees buckling to the carpet, his surrender passing from her specifically to the composite. That equilateral through the heart of which he dreamed of flying. He wanted to find the dead heart of empty space between them and wormhole right out of this universe and into his next one.

A week later, Lark entered everybody's life again with renewed questions and yet another lens: a photographer from the magazine, who huffed at the rain but had a schedule of his own to meet. These were the before shots, he said, and there was only so much time available before there would be no more before. So off he went, snapping through his own visual dismantlement of the building.

Outside, the rain had changed shape and texture from something that slanted down in sharp strikes to something that sheeted over the city in billowing walls. A softer and wetter rain. Gimble didn't like it at all. "Now we'll need ten," he announced. "Days, that is. To dry."

And what if they didn't have ten days? Lark wanted to know.

Gimble shoed the scribbler out of his office. "I don't do interviews. I do the other things."

Graham answered Lark's glancing questions and wasn't bothered in the least, his thoughts being extraordinarily ordered of late. "I'm hardly noticing the delays since I'm busy with a million things. For instance? While our foundation drawings are in and permits are apparently inked and ready to go, we are now having some late discussions with the city about our glass choice."

Colour and opacity, it seemed. Planners in the City of Glass having a thing or two to say about the reflective quality of the built environment. Sea green and medium reflection was good. Chrome-y and mirrorlike were bad. Watery and hardly reflective at all—as Graham had proposed— well, this detail was the cause of much deliberation.

"So we argue about transparency," Graham told Lark. "Big deal? Small deal?"

"They're all big deals," Graham said. "But if you mean do I think we'll come to an agreement, then I'd say yes."

Such confidence. He didn't know where it came from. Not from Esther, who he'd given up phoning. The day before, she hadn't even picked up. That morning he got her out on the water. But not fishing, she said, which upset him somehow. He understood that to be the deal. They were apart in order that she would do that thing while he did this thing, and if they were both successful then some other things might next be considered. But she had to put a line in the water.

"Graham," she said. A warning before sharp words.

He listened hard through the phone and had a first-time thought: Was someone with her? But he refrained from asking, afraid of a positive answer. He liked the sense of capacity that he felt surging within, but it was also an imprecise, untested feeling.

"I'm just coming in to the beach," she said now. "I need both hands."

He let her go. He went to the site. He stormed to the site. Hauled up in a cloud of spray, the Porsche coughing with the moisture (and impossible to repair because he'd been cut off by Rudolph, sent a $575 bill for the Boxster side mirror and stroked off the client list). Now the little beast was wheezing on startup and backfiring on the downshift. It was showing rust spots at the trailing edge of the front wheel wells and was no doubt poised to blossom with many more. Graham didn't care. The building was safely wrapped, draped over entirely with waterproof sheeting by Gimble and within a few hours of the first raindrop too.

"Just our," Gimble had said, straining up the walkway and onto the east scaffolding with an enormous roll of blue plastic, "luck."

Up he went. A few hours later the building was wrapped. Walking the rooms and halls gave the sense of being inside a cloud. Aqua air on the upper floor. The rain strikes on plastic forming a beaded curtain of sound that didn't shape to the building walls, but ballooned instead, an aural sphere superimposed over what was visible and four-cornered. On the main floor this effect was muted, as it would be in a forest. And down in the basement, where the blue deepened sharply in the fallen light, it was a king salmon's midnight.

Here, almost a full week later, he found Elliot. Not the only day they'd crossed paths in the building. They'd both been cruising, sniffing dimensions and feeling spaces, saying their extended farewells to the original. Not ignoring each other—Graham had by this point developed a variety of warm feeling toward Elliot, one that he sensed in the wry return smile was reciprocated—but never stopping to speak long, either.

That day, he'd gone looking for his brother, one specific thing outstanding between them. It was the kind of thing Graham thought they'd better deal with before all the action of the final stage began. Much work remained after moving the building, of course. But Graham had a strong sense of that hoist, that lift and skid, that dramatic repositioning being the last thing that they would preside over together. A last joint act that would then be followed by an unknown future between them. Perhaps the present goodwill would continue. Perhaps it would blow back up the mountain the way it had come. Either outcome would be the one they had to live with.

In the meantime, this bit of next-to-last business, which took the shape of a cedar box. A ten-inch cube with plain sides and only a simple carving of a raven to decorate its lid. Contents uncommonly light for the otherworldly weight it held and represented.

You asked for these, his mother's note read. *Have them with my blessing. It's rare to find the perfect resting place.*

Graham carried the box up the scaffold stairway to the top floor and listened for his brother. He heard, inside, that the rain was lightening. That the sphere around the structure had grown thin. That it would soon burst and leave them all exposed to the demanding light of new sun. Beneath that sound, only one other: a scratching from far below. A tiny abrasion being worked and reworked.

He took the scaffolding down a flight to the main floor and re-entered the building, but the sound came from still farther below. This was interesting because there was no longer any access to the basement other than by the cordoned-off main stair. Graham considered matters. Then, realizing what his brother must have done, he squeezed through the steel reinforcing bars and endured a mild wobble as he took his twenty downward steps. Here he set the cedar box on the last thick plank and looked out into the deep sea light of that lower room.

Elliot was hunched in the northwest corner. He was holding a sheet of paper up to the wood planking along the foundation wall, scratching with a pencil across this surface.

He said, without turning: "Check this out."

Graham crossed the pad and looked down over his brother's shoulder. And as Elliot's pencil rubbed back and forth across the surface, a graffiti ghosted into view. *Gordon.*

Elliot rocked back on his heels. He stood in a smooth motion, the paper fluttering up in his hand.

"When did you do it?" Graham asked.

Elliot smiled and squinted. He looked at his brother. "I didn't," he said.

Graham raised his eyebrows. He took the paper and looked at it more closer. It said what it said. Somebody had taken the time to notch the word, to scrape the letters until they were clear. "Pogey Nealon," he said.

Elliot shrugged. "I have to ask. In your memory, is he really the bad guy?"

Graham made a face.

"Like, he was letting something out on kids?"

Graham waggled his head. He felt bad about saying it earlier. He told Elliot as much.

Elliot said, "I thought at the time you admired him."

That wasn't far from the truth. Graham had trained harder than his brother during those weeks for a reason: because the old man was a repository of all that was to be known about the business at hand. "He was an expert," Graham said. "I boxed in high school, you may recall."

"I remember. I didn't."

"I remember that too. You watch now though."

"I had a friend who was a bookie. We'd go see fights together. I have a level of fascination." Elliot looked up, caught his brother's eye.

"Can't watch it myself," Graham said. Crooked, brutal, exploitative. It was other things too. "But then I don't have much time for it. Sports. My life became work shortly after we last saw each other."

"The cab ride of the Valkyries," Elliot said. "Me too. Maybe we lit a fire under each other."

"And you've done well."

"Ah, no. Not that well."

"The place in Deep Cove is fantastic. I read the thing in the local paper about the renovation. Deirdre did that?"

Elliot nodded and scratched his chin.

"Why'd she quit?" Graham asked. "Architecture."

"Change of heart. What about yours?"

"Mine," Graham laughed. They had moments when something like common ground and something like a different mother tongue were simultaneously revealed. *Yours* as a synonym for *spouse* was diction Graham might have called Blue Collar Possessive.

Elliot waited patiently. If he sensed Graham's calculation flash through, he chose not to be offended. He only said, "I liked her."

"Well, you know," Graham answered. "I liked her too, but . . ." Then he laughed again. But he had a metallic taste in his mouth now, all at once. A residue of bad bacon at a diner around the corner. "Anyway she hasn't quit what she's doing, she's just taking a break."

Elliot was looking down at the paper again. "You want to know about Pogey?"

"What about him?" Graham asked.

"How he died."

Graham's focus came in a little tighter on his brother. For the first time in their long and turbulent acquaintance, he thought he saw something really new in the features. Always darker-skinned, always the other side of some kind of aesthetic wheel from Graham himself. Yet his brother had never seemed actively *foreign*. But there was that quality of blood issue between them now, Graham thought (wishing he hadn't thought any of these things at all, because they were spinning slightly, pulling other thoughts to themselves and increasing in mass).

And that blood issue had less to do with their father's infidelity than it did with the gulf between home and away. Somebody had been the original home. The other had come from away. And it didn't matter where either of their mothers was born. The point was that each of them was the mirror of the other in this regard, but only *to* each other. Nobody viewing them from any other angle could possibly see the reflection in this way.

Genius, Graham thought. Now you've missed whatever he's been trying to tell you for the past few minutes. "Sorry," he said.

Elliot repeated himself. A suitably fantastic story that remained fantastic in the second telling. Pogey. All the way from the top down to the bottom. Right through the shaft of the skylight down three flights to the concrete below. This concrete, right here. No, Deirdre had not seen it, but she'd been pulled in by the fall. Pulled down by it. And then, in a way that no fortune teller could have predicted (because, Graham learned, there were fortune tellers in this story too), Deirdre and Elliot had been pulled together by the event. The fall had bonded them. The building, somehow—and here Elliot acknowledged with a shake of the head that this was a weird and atypical thought for him—the building had allowed him to have his children, releasing him from a prophecy to the contrary.

Elliot watched his brother now. He didn't appear to have been affected much by the story of Pogey's death. The fall itself, the brutal end. A broken back, a multiply fractured skull, long lacerations that had opened the man's chest and back as he plunged through the glass above. Even the detail about not dying on impact, but five full hours later, seemed not to overly upset him.

Yet Graham grew oddly angry with Elliot's mention of Tapgol Park, the prophecy. His face darkened. His eyebrows came down just as they had in the moment before they'd grappled at the lip of the site a month before, embarrassed contractors and subtrades arrayed around them, voracious cameras just beyond that. Only now, Elliot didn't feel any reciprocal fury rising. He even took a step back, to communicate this fact. He turned a degree to one side, a defenceless position. He stared down and away at that carving low on the wall. He thought, Maybe his own sympathy for Pogey had only been forged through Deirdre, the vague guilt she felt. Through Cleo, who had been protective of the man during his life. And then through his own involvement with the madness of the old man's later years. Having tried to decipher the code of his scribblings, his charts, his impossible journals, his boxes of ephemera, and having failed entirely, maybe Elliot had artificially ramped up his own sense of what that fall must have meant.

Graham hadn't quite recovered from whatever was flushing through him. Elliot glanced back at him cautiously and judged this to be the case from the half smile, half grimace. From the way his brother's attention had been deflected downward to the graffiti. But he was trying. This much was plain. He was trying for an improved tone when he gestured at the rubbing that Elliot still held. As he suggested that they might frame it. Mount it in the foyer. Make it part of the permanent Zweigler collection.

Elliot laughed. Sure, why not? Then he did something he'd never done in his life before. Elliot reached out and put his hand on Graham's arm. He said: "What's in the box?"

This motion, this touch, had a startling effect. Graham came up out from under the feeling that had taken him. He emerged on the surface, excited, hard-edged and renewed. Whatever Elliot thought was in the box (photographs or nothing at all would have been his guess), this reaction was unexpected.

Graham picked it up in both hands, one on the lid, one securing it from underneath. He held it as if he intended to make a flourish of its opening. And then he stalled, somehow. His eyes wide and quivering, his lips working in advance of something very exciting, very important that he had to say.

At the O later, Elliot worked through the possible scenarios. In the first, the simplest, he'd stolen the wrong urn. But what, in that case, were the ashes of somebody else doing stored in a goddamn celadon container in the waiting room of a white-bread funeral home like the one Graham's mother had chosen?

He cursed himself. You prick. Like nobody knew of celadon in 1983? Like there were no Koreans around maybe?

Steal was the wrong word anyway. What was the better one? Take stewardship of. That was it. Where were they headed otherwise? To a vault in the side of a memorial to be sealed off and never looked at again. And after toting that urn around for almost ten years, after having looked at it each time he'd gone in to make a deposit or withdraw against those ammo boxes, Elliot no longer felt guilty. The contents of that urn had absolved him years ago. And when he lied it through customs into Korea, the contents said to him: I'm proud of you, my son.

Of course there were other options. He briefly favoured the one where Graham's mother had split the ashes into two. One for Korea, one for west coast of North America. Celadon for the lover of the slut that produced her husband's first-born. A wooden box with Haida carvings to house the mighty chief that impregnated her unexpectedly to father a second. And real Haida work too, Graham had insisted, describing the box with such reverence that you'd have to believe he was sure of its provenance.

But then a lot of people were convinced they owned the real thing, in defiance of evidence to the contrary.

From where? Elliot had asked his brother. His entire insides felt dry.

Graham actually laughed. "Um. My mother. Did I misunderstand the question? From where else?"

But he understood they rarely spoke. The colonic irrigation enthusiast musician wacko urine drinker she lived with was reportedly anti-social to elements from his prize wife's past. Had he talked to her directly or just signed for the package?

Graham said, "Hey, listen. This is important to me . . ."

Option three: he was being fucked with by a third and unconnected party. Somebody had sent Graham the box by courier. Well, who couldn't fake a return address in France? Child's play. If Elliot were to do such a thing, he'd hire his own runner to dress up FedEx and put down a fake return phone number that led to a voice mail: *This mailbox is full.* That'd buy you a week at least. If he'd had his wits about him, he would have demanded that Graham show him that phone number.

He'd gone to the Orwell to find answers. A long shot. "What's up with the Uncles these days?" he asked the man behind the bar.

Up how?

"Up up. Mood. Disposition," Elliot said. "I know you know."

But the man didn't think he knew much about that.

"Come on," Elliot said. "It's me."

Which was enough for the bartender to say: "I hear the man down east asks about you. He liked the carpets. He liked the eighteen others he bought for the clubhouse. He's doing Louis the twenty-ninth furniture now or some goddamn thing."

"Louis the sixteenth," Elliot said. "Maybe. But there was no twenty-ninth."

"Sixteen, then."

"But it's working. They're getting the shit they want?"

The man shrugged. He'd said enough.

Elliot looked around the lobby, craning his neck this way and that. Empty. A bit dirty too. As if someone's attention were distracted by other things. "Where's Kirov?"

"You don't hear from him?"

"Not lately. If I did I wouldn't ask."

Another shrug. "Outta town I heard."

Out of town. Stranger and stranger. Where out of town did Kirov have to go, now that he was working for the Uncles? Elliot swung by the Happy Planet and talked to Lucille. He was overseas, she said. Smiling widely. "Haven't seen you around, El."

Overseas where? he wanted to know.

Lucille thought Taiwan. "Where you been hiding?"

"You didn't ask him where he was going before he left?"

She looked down into the espresso cup. Two shots and it was full. She said, "No point asking every time and him not telling. Came a point I stopped asking."

She leaned into the counter, gently swollen tummy wrinkling up her tank and pushing down her waistband. "Right," he said, taking the cup and going into his pocket for change.

"Don't worry about that, El," Lucille told him. "Just hang out a bit. Tell me what're you doing with yourself these days."

Option four. Calm right down. Someone was playing Graham.

This possibility was intriguing but hard to explain. Who all would that arrogant son of a bitch have pissed off over the years? Elliot thought about this as he made his way back out to Deep Cove, first time in several weeks, though he'd phoned every day. Who might want to roll Graham Gordon? Well, there was Esther, obviously enough. Fila too, maybe. It hadn't taken Elliot long to suss that the partner was a playmate as well. That day the producer brought her around she went so feline in Graham's presence, Elliot thought she might spray. Then she split of course, in a hurry and a cloud of piss. Graham could have leaned forward and pecked her hello on the cheek and made her feel like she belonged in the room, but he didn't and off she went to Tokyo. Dumb bastard. Which was another thought. Maybe his own mother wanted to crank him up.

Crazy talk. Elliot pulled up in front of his house and heaved an enormous breath in and out. He would let this weight go, he decided. He would not try to figure option one from option two or three. What he'd done was done. Whatever Graham wanted to do, he could go ahead and do. He could set up his pipe from the roof down through the opening and pour down the old man's ashes if that's what he wanted to do. If that's what he believed he would actually be doing.

"Let me see those again," Elliot had demanded.

Graham wary. "What the hell is wrong with you all of a sudden?"

"I'm concerned that they might not be real."

"I am confused by this response." Graham's anger now layered over with real distress. "I ask you a simple and I think understandable favour . . ."

"Open the box!"

"I will not."

They struggled. Graham hugging the cube under his right arm, throwing out a long-inexpert left hand, again and again. Elliot dodging this and flapping his own hands uselessly. He thought he cuffed the top of his brother's head once. Maybe smacked him in the ribs. Nobody was hurting anybody, just stirring up the air to a boil and going white-lipped furious in the meantime.

He could have said something, right then. *Go ahead and put whatever's in that box into the new foundations, just don't be thinking it's the old man. He's already part of the soil someplace very far from here.*

But he didn't say that or anything else like it. He couldn't. The memory was his own, and something stuck in his esophagus even with the thought of its release. Those girls staring and the cab driver shaking his head and the two drunk university kids who stopped their puking into the gutter to look up and see what the hell Elliot was doing.

There had been no wind. He anticipated no scattering. Of the portion of his father that he had been allotted (subconsciously, he was back on option two, they each got half), he was able to account in memory for 100 per cent of it descending into the sewers directly beneath hooker row in Yongjugol. The glass windows with the girls lounging behind. The limousines with visiting American businessmen glowing red next to their drunk hosts. The cars crammed full of other guys. Guys everywhere. Spilling out of doorways and jamming the sidewalks. Smearing the glass with their breath. Looking in on these women whose faces were cracked open in smiles so purely inauthentic that it was breathtaking. Some of them no doubt mothers.

He poured gently. The ashes sifted out of the urn in a long steady stream. And then—as planned out in the cab ride over—he had stood tall right there in the middle of that blinking neon alley and dropped the celadon to the pavement. Let it shatter. Let the pieces find their way to the slots in the grate, encouraged by the edge of his boot.

Now he started in his truck. New sun in his eyes. He thought for a moment that he had slept the night out front of his own house, after all that time away. But looking at the dashboard clock, he realized this was not the case. He'd only dozed, and briefly. Or maybe he had not even dozed. He'd just reached that state between, then been interrupted by fingernails on the glass near his ear. Startled back to the surface.

He sat up straight, sharply. He rolled down the window. He said, "Malaya. Sorry. Dreaming here. What's up?"

Malaya nodded sadly. Then she shook her head.

He found the note on the polished wood counter she had so carefully selected and finished herself. He read it from top to bottom, turning the paper over, finding nothing on the back, then reading it top to bottom again. Seven full repetitions of this cycle until it was memorized. Or until, at least, he understood it well enough to know that the words wouldn't change on the page. Not physically, not in meaning or intent either.

Deirdre and the twins had gone away. Not any one place in particular that she was prepared to tell him. Just away. And not forever either, or for a week or for six weeks, but for an indeterminate time. Away. Which left him at home, he supposed. He was home. She was away. Or did she think, maybe, that where she was, where she and Hugh and Louis—ah, here came the tears, a warm salty gaspy on-your-knees-gonna-choke-myself flow of them—that maybe *that* was home? In which case it was pretty hard to deny that what he'd thought all along was home, these boards and timbers, plus of course the dirty dishes and toys, the infant Philly Flyers jerseys tossed over there in the pile outside the laundry room, that all this was, in fact, in Deirdre's mind now, *away*.

And that hurt. A feeling brought about directly by thievery and lying and conceit and arrogance and all of the forces that had arisen in his life since his renewed association with his brother. That hurt more than anything.

They gave Gimble six days in the end. It was all they had, they argued. Graham sat back and didn't press his own view, which was mixed anyway. The producers paced and gesticulated and said it had to be Saturday. Gimble said no earlier than Tuesday. Then, he said, very unwise to proceed any time before Monday. Then he said Sunday and was informed that his building hoist company was union and couldn't get the guys out Sunday for less than triple time. Then he gave up. He said, "What day would be best? For television. You tell me."

Saturday, Raul said. Or wait. Here he interrupted himself and looked over at Zweigler. In fact, Friday would be better. That's right, Friday. In the morning. Early morning. First light if possible. Raul said, "If you wanted to think of it in terms of an event that will be filmed and watched by millions and make you look like a hero, that really would be the best."

Graham sat half smiling in the corner of the engineer's shed during all of this discussion. He thought through several long loops of reason that didn't have much to do with the task at hand. Gimble, for example, had handled the negotiation poorly. Graham channelled Esther, beautiful powerful Esther, to arrive at this conclusion. He'd played his cards as if he had many, as if the flexibility lay with him. When in fact, anybody could have told him, flexibility always lay with those who had lots of money. American cable television might be crass and packaged and designed at its root to sell you a branded universe, but it had the flexibility of its own economic enormity. Your average engineer, however smart, however physically sturdy, could perhaps not be expected to understand this fact.

He thought about Elliot, of course. He thought, I'm so angry with that son of a bitch I'm almost happy. Then he thought, No, no. Leave it at that. Don't try to reason it through.

He thought, still later, Raul in the middle of a surprisingly impassioned speech about the superior quality of morning light in the bad parts of cities in the western world, I'd like another drink just now. And I might be able to swing that in future if I bring my own little bottle and pour it into one of those plastic snap-top coffee cups.

The producers finished hammering home their victory and left. Graham found a tuneless melody coming out of him, something that had been running through his brain alongside his other thoughts, and which now emerged humming. *Da da da da da. Dee de de de de.*

"You coming?" Zweigler said, poking his head back into the room with the charts and the plans and the rolls of drawings and the hooks where all the unused rain gear was now hanging. "Group pix. Crew and all. Let's go. Let's go."

Graham went out with a broad smile into brilliant sunshine, which was refracting through a million drips of water on the underside of scaffold cross members and along the bottom seam of steel skids that would guide the building into place over the new piles. The blue tarp was gone.

"Where's your brother?" someone was asking. The other producer. Or one of Gimble's people. Or both of them, because here came the question again. "What's happening with Elliot? No answer on his cell." Graham was moving through the site toward a viewing platform that had been built for observers and cameras and invited members of the press and local architectural community and that would now be used for the big happy family shot before the storm of hoist rigging began.

He smiled. He shook his head. He shrugged. He thought, Pull yourself together, man. Jesus. You don't need another drink after those first two an hour ago. Although he didn't feel guilty, not ashamed in the least, an unexpected insight having gripped him the day before. People down in this neighbourhood do it all the time. They wake up, they roll over. They check out the clock. And if it's after nine they know the Blue Eagle or the Orwell or the Princess will be serving. Then they go down and have a couple. Simple as that. He'd seen working men do this at their favourite Paris zinc bars without getting a second look. Little half-beers for the young guys.

A snifter of brandy if you were an old pro. Nothing moral in the breach here. Not even in the eyes of tourists hunched over their café crèmes and Let's Gos who just thought it was charming and local and who, if they were honest, probably felt a little ache inside seeing this unvarnished authenticity to which they had no access.

But why didn't they? Here came the insight for Graham, waking up on a pallet of blankets in the upstairs room of what everybody (even his brother) had been calling Story House lately, like it didn't have an actual street address. Like it had never needed one. That morning at seven-thirty, before any of the trades came in, Graham lay in Story House and thought, Why not charge up in the morning in the place called home and in an establishment where, if they didn't know your name precisely and if you'd be well advised not to use the bathrooms, nobody looked at you funny for the a.m. double rye and Seven? You could sit on a rickety bar stool, hump an arm over your pal in his cedar box and think about the unruly thing that life had become. It wasn't like you had to worry about kids. Not now. Not ever. And that was a simple matter of prophecy.

Graham laughed, thinking of it. His brother agonizing all those years. The stupid prick had been given the wrong fortune. The bad luck (he squeezed the box tight) belongs to me. And here he laughed again and ordered another drink and realized that the week before he'd missed his own fortieth birthday.

"Graham Gordon?"

Yeah, yeah fine. Where should he stand?

The photographer took Graham by the elbow and shuffled him into position, then moved himself back to the top of the platform. There they all stood for several seconds, squinting, smiling, wincing, doing all the things that people do in those seconds before they're forever captured doing only one shred of a thing: a half smile, a two-degree click of the eyeballs off centre, a finger to the rim of a nostril or an ear, a throat half cleared. Never a whole thing. Because that, still, was impossible to capture with photography.

Then they all lost themselves in the supernova of the flash.

Friday morning. Zweigler assessed the weather out of cracked eyelids from where he lay on the floor of his suite just in front of the living-room glass. Because of the hour—his alarm clock set to 4:00 a.m. in order that they could shoot the dawn—this required more a penetrating barometric sense of things than a strict visual appraisal. Zweigler sensed: high sky, bare licks of pale cloud and a gentle wind that was chunking the sea below. Piling the water against itself and releasing, again and again, in a stable and inexhaustible rhythm.

Zweigler was in a hurry. That scheduled sunrise was threatening even now to paint the east fringes of his horsetail clouds. But he lay naked and unashamed for a few minutes before rising, the sea and sky pinching him rather pleasantly in place. He was a specimen under examination. Held between the eternally steady thumb and forefinger of God. With his loves arrayed around him at some distance too. He could feel them out there. The corners of his triangle spread and ready, channelling impossible energy down to him.

On site, things were also poised and in place. Zweigler's heart thumped up a gear against all efforts to mitigate with slow breathing exercises in the car on the way over. Gimble and his men had performed magnificently. The readiness of the structure for movement was articulated like longing, clear even in this pre-dawn stillness. The excavation had been widened to accommodate the new footprint of the building. The new corner piles were in place, swung far out to the left and right. They stood darkly above the earth at the bottom of the pit and communicated readiness to receive: first the shadow and shape, and then, when footings and foundations were poured, the full weight of Story House. Long steel skids marked the path the building would move, rails lying across a trellis of new support cribs. But most dramatic of all, surely: the crane. A thin finger of impossible strength, gathering to its distant tip the cables running down to cross members under the east side of the building.

His camera operators were waiting. So too Gimble, the lift foreman and crane techs. But: visuals before actuals. Zweigler and the director huddled, then got everybody pointed in the right direction to capture the dawn as agreed. Then over to the engineer's shed, where Gimble and crew talked loudly and drank coffee. The engineer hoisted himself the short distance from sitting to standing, stalked over and poured Zweigler a cup. Handed it to him with a chummy pat on the shoulder.

"Late night?" the engineer joked. But they were smiling. All of them on the same side just then, the gale force of the day blowing through them all in one direction.

"Where's the architect?" Zweigler asked Gimble. "Where's the other one?"

Gimble shrugged. The other one had been nowhere in sight for days now. The architect. Well, that was different. "You want me to go wake him up?"

Zweigler listened, then went and found Graham himself. Top floor, back room. Pile of moving blankets. Still, he managed to look chicly ready for the day, rolling over and sitting up, hair pasted vertical up the side of his head, one leg of his impossibly creased Armani rolled up to his left knee in sleep.

"Good morning," Graham said, grinning. He was coursing through with some energy of his own.

Which pleased Zweigler, entirely and without reservation. He embraced this to himself, to his vision of events unfolding. He waved a hand over his shoulder to indicate that the Bolex operator should keep rolling. He handed Graham a cup of coffee he'd carried up from outside, thinking that the image—that first bleary sip, rendered on film and cut between the dawn and the first crank-over of the diesels that ran those cranes—would play like a mad prophet awakening to a day that he knew held either his absolution or his death by fire at the stake. He was only unsure, smiling crookedly, squinting toward the window, which it would be.

"Don't forget your box," Zweigler said to him, leaving.

They had light by seven. Dawn in the can. They had official crowds by eight, punctually as requested. People jumped to a schedule when filming was involved, Zweigler knew from experience, but he was still pleasantly surprised to see those invited file in at the scheduled hour. The art people and the architecture people who milled around the coffee tent, pulling parkas around suits against the morning chill. The community advocate and city administration people, who stood brown-toned and corduroyed by the curb, smoking last cigarettes. A lone provincial official, who had arrived by HeliJet that morning, who could not be separated from his pale, pre-election smile. The mayor last, climbing from a double-parked car and approaching the bureaucrats at the curb. Laughter ensuing, which caused Zweigler's lift-mounted camera to pivot over and zoom.

By 8:30 a.m. the observation stand was full, and Gimble was growing irritable keeping people back from the lip of the excavation. An announcement was finally made over a bullhorn, and people shuffled back down the flanks of the stand, while outside the high metal fences that circled the site, a dozen, then two dozen, then three and four dozen neighbourhood curious gathered. They leaned in, they strung fingers through the square grid of the fence and hung on their arms. The long pan shot down the inside of the fence, taking in the graffiti-covered hoarding across Mary Street behind them, would later render them like camp prisoners. A near-stock image of those on one side of a barrier, unable to fathom what lay without.

Or in this case, within. Something that Zweigler himself was taking some pleasure in not quite fathoming. And which, he was sure, was being not quite fathomed by all present in the same fashion. There had been some discussion of an announcement to begin it all. That Graham would say a few words, maybe even from the roof with amplification. But this had been abandoned for a simple printed handout instead. Zweigler's idea, who knew that a long, incomprehensible architecture speech would never make it into the film anyway and why, therefore, waste the time? So. On a single heavy stock folded sheet of paper instead: some text and a few line drawings, the barest sketches of idea. A rectangle showing the three original layers. Another cracked open. A third where the halves were opened fully. A final sketch on the back of the handout showed the helix alone.

To accompany these, Graham's words:

The new Zweigler Gallery and Museum of Packer
Gordon is a small footprint bearing enormous weight.
Today, as you look around the site, you see an often forgotten landscape. But these grounds represent the very
beginning of our city. The original site of growth, of gathering and community. In 1939, Packer Gordon made
what was then a youthful gesture full of hope. Gathering
together in himself all that had influenced his vision to
that point, all that had given structure to an imagining of
the built world . . .

There followed a description of his father's beginnings,
Avi Zweigler's great contribution to the project and a
summation of Graham's own ideas involving both the
radical altering and the humble leaving of found ideas.
The cracking of the building like a book. This material
climaxed:

> . . . because it is, on several levels, useless to attempt trib-
> ute to antique structures. It defeats us in our attempt to be
> real to what is no longer real. The longhouse, the double-
> helix stair, the white room stripped clean of adornment,
> all of these penetrated Packer Gordon's vision, but they
> cannot be returned as a direct sensation to any person
> entering the space today, at least not in the form originally
> envisioned. That form is gone. And so our Miesian ideal
> becomes not a space formed by an architect, nor an elab-
> oration in new materials, but a form made organic by items
> that penetrate and open the physical space. This includes
> the objects in it, his objects. But it includes also the light
> shafting through its various layers and new apertures.

It includes, ultimately, the events that unfold here over decades and lives.

Two cream pages on nice stock. A thing fiddled and fanned in the hands of the gathered crowd. Read quickly and tucked into purses. Folded and refolded. A thing so fragile and temporary in the hand that it quickly gave one the effect of having been a found object itself.

Somebody said, "Sound."

Someone else said, "Rolling sound."

Then, "Quiet on the set!"

Then, "We're rolling!"

Zweigler was hunched at his monitor. He whispered into his headset, "Okay, pan right three please on the crowd. Two, we're on the crane. One, stay with the roof line. Bolex, you're on Gimble and the architect. Okay? Let's do good, guys."

And high in the air, they had their first real movement. It flowed from smaller movement, invisible to the crowd. A nod from Zweigler at the control tent just in front of the engineer's shed, a word from one of Gimble's men into the headset frequency shared by the construction people, a thumbs-up from Gimble himself in the back alley and the tiniest wrist movement by the crane operator. And up there against the blue, the tip of the crane arm tightened as the rotors wound up slack from the cables, and the building very slowly, microscopically, with an intake of breath from the audience and a round of applause from those outside the fence, began to lift off the steel support members that had been run underneath it.

A subtle shifting. No visible space opened up beneath it. This lifting was instead a matter of shifted weight. That which had previously communicated its mass directly to the earth now did no longer. And it could be seen to lighten in the transfer of tension to the crane, in the expansion of the support cribs, now free of the building, even in the walls of the structure itself, which shuddered and squealed, as joints were realigned in ways long unfamiliar.

Zweigler held his breath throughout. Raul, some distance back from the control tent, standing on the back of an overturned wheelbarrow for a better view, smiled broadly and gave him a thumbs-up.

Breathe, he mouthed.

A few seconds of silence followed, as progress was assessed by Gimble and the hoist foreman, who both skirted close to the building in the rear, looking down the length of the skids. Murmuring.

"Two, please roll over to the Gimble huddle there. Bolex, stay with the architect." Zweigler heard himself speaking and was pleased to note authority and calm in these words.

Gimble had arrived at some positive conclusion and was back in the alley, talking into his headset to the crane operator, who gave a thumbs-up. The foreman then moved over to the east winches and spoke with the crew there.

"Two, on the winches please. One, close on the front of the building. This is it. Three, standby crowd."

The winch machinery came to life with a grind of mechanical teeth and a high electric whine. Again a tautness developed in advance of action as cables connected to the side of the structure (through the walls and harnessed to the side columns) lost their slack and hummed with tension. Then, with a low scrape of large metal on large metal, the move began. East pulled away from west.

A crack of light appeared. Layers of flooring were exposed. Cracking could be heard, to be sure, masonry pieces falling and the tinkle of a window breaking. But in all, it held firmly to Graham's vision and Gimble's promised delivery, opening very slowly but steadily. The negative yawning where it was previously positive. An emptiness forming at the core of something previously solid.

Good crowd work here, Zweigler noted. The reaction in the front row seemed one of real pleasure, smiles, surprised laughter. They'd known what was coming, still the execution amazed. Graham's book metaphor had been the right one, Zweigler thought. It was just like that. The new information on display was to be found on the revealed surfaces within. But something in the space between the pages, as well. That first crack, that first sensation. With a book, Zweigler associated this with a smell. Something long closed, now exposed.

"Three, can you find the mayor? Two, good. One, zoom to the top if you can get the angle. I'd like sky behind. Right, good."

Again a pause, this one more stable. The winches were powered down. Gimble talked with this foreman and crane operator again. They were open about six feet at this point, just a fraction of the distance the east side would have to skid. A process that would then be duplicated on the west side the following day. But the crane operator now touched his headset and nodded, triggering down his lift arm a fraction to return some of the weight of the structure to the supports.

The invited crowd shifted on its feet. The one outside the fence made general crowd noise: cheers, jeers, impatience. The mayor—found by camera three—turned and smiled, waved.

Zweigler said, "Bolex, please follow close here. And two, I need you to track them until they go up."

Graham moved toward the rear of the building where a man-lift was parked, neck down to the alley pavement. Camera two revealed him in princely calm. Unshaven, true enough. Haggard and unwashed. But setting his foot in the lift, letting it carry him upward with the Bolex, up out of the shadows at the rear of the building and into the midmorning light, cedar box pinched tightly under his right arm, he looked every inch the inheritor. The quiet repository of received wisdom.

He climbed over the rear parapet and onto the gravel. The Bolex followed. Here Graham took measured steps forward to the very front of the building, where the opening was widest and was, finally, visible in full to the crowd.

Someone on the far side of the fence called out, "Jesus Christ. Su-uperstar . . ."

"One, tight. We need to see the box," Zweigler said. "Three, medium on the front. Can we try to get the pipe being hoisted. Okay, here it comes."

The plan was simple enough. Two of Gimble's men would lift a forty-foot length of PVC pipe up to the eaves. The lower end would be placed down into a trench that had been dug deep in the excavations below the crib. Graham would step to the top end of the pipe and with the help of an aluminium funnel—there was a low breeze—he would pour the ashes down into the trough of the new foundation.

Raul was motioned for Zweigler's attention. He gestured, *What's up?*

Zweigler mouthed, *Wait for it.*

Worth waiting for, at least the first few steps that proceeded perfectly against the scripted line. Gimble's men lifted the PVC, which spindled up into the air and into place against the side of the building. They got the butt of it down into the pit and passed the top over to Graham, who rested it against the parapet. He inserted the funnel, which glinted in the hardening sunlight. Then, turning and reaching down, he retrieved the box, got it up to the lip of the funnel and began to pour. At which moment, it seemed quite obvious from the ground, somebody or something unexpected appeared on the roof.

Zweigler couldn't exactly sequence these events until he looked at the film later. As it happened in front of him that morning, it was a bit like trying to follow a poorly edited silent film. Graham began to pour. And although Zweigler could hear the granular ash coring down the pipe, making its way to the ground, all else was silent. He could see Graham's face very clearly, a tight shot now available to him on the monitor, and a most unfortunate expression too: a kind of maniacal half laugh combined with what could have been an allergy or asthma attack. Face red, breath coming in gasps, eyes streaming with tears. Nose running too.

"Christ," Zweigler said. "One, wider please. The guy doesn't have a hankie?"

Which was when Graham stopped, sharply and unpleasantly distracted. He turned. His expression lost to all of them but the Bolex, which swivelled over with his glance to something arriving across the eastern eaves.

"Two? Two? Someone please show me what's happening on the east side here."

Two of course had nothing. A blank shot of idle winches.

"Ah shit," Zweigler said. But then his problem was temporarily resolved because the distraction came into full view. Elliot in black against a rising sun. Elliot with a long shadow across his face, but clean-shaven, his regrown head of hair combed and parted neatly. Elliot looking like a choirboy, approaching his brother.

"Ah shit," Zweigler said again, not sure entirely what about this tableau predicted shittiness descending. But certain nonetheless. "One, tight please."

But he was shouting now. Why was this? Zweigler still wearing his headphones. Still at the monitor. He was at once compelled to communicate his instructions across the air itself with no help from radio waves.

One could have gone in tight or not. Zweigler couldn't know. He was just then, as was everybody else present, distracted by developments up top. First an argument, the words of which nobody could make out, but which was readable as an argument from a great distance. Arms extended, palms up. Hands to hips. Fingers pointed. A stone was kicked. A hand touched an arm and was shaken off sharply.

Then a fight broke out.

Zweigler was still squinting up in disbelief. But these physical motions could not be misinterpreted. They were goddamn fighting. Elliot poised in an undeniable boxer's stance opposite Graham—*"One, tight on the architect!"*—who was himself down in some kind of sumo crouch. They were forming fists. They were swinging these in at each other. They were hitting each other, producing a sound quite unlike anything Zweigler had ever heard. The soft, wet insult of flesh to flesh. First Graham to Elliot. Then Elliot to Graham. They were taking turns. The abuse appeared to be governed by rules. And Zweigler was a helpless man watching this event unfold, helpless just like the last time he let a Gordon drive home the final nail.

He turned to find his partner. To read, in a glance, how badly this particular nail would hurt them all.

Raul was hugging himself. He was rolling from side to side. He was laughing. Zweigler caught his eye. His partner held his hands up. *What can you do?* At which moment Zweigler first processed the crowd noise. Inside the fence, laughter and groaning, cringing and wincing, but not one eye turned away. Outside the fence, what could only be interpreted as a celebration. The elected officials had vanished, of course, back to their cars and helicopters. But in the mouths of the people, that aggregate noise was one of intense approval.

Zweigler had a five-second window to enjoy a rebound in his mood. Enough time anyway to work his way through to an ending. They'd had their money shot. And now he was going up there, right this second. Going around the back and up the lift and across that roof. He was going to put a calm hand on each of their shoulders and gently but firmly separate them. He was going to say precisely one word: *Enough.*

TIMOTHY
TAYLOR

Which would be enough. He knew it. He knew the future. They weren't going to hug or reconcile or even stop hating each other. But they were going to stop fighting. They were going to finish up with those ashes, put

their father back down in the ground where he belonged. Dust to dust. And they were going to stand back, at that point, and let Gimble and Zweigler himself and the people on the payroll, all the people in the stands here too, let each of them do their jobs in moving Story House onto its final footings.

·And Zweigler was absolutely right in predicting this outcome, only absolutely wrong in foreseeing what sequence of steps would bring it about.

He took a final glance upward, then turned to make his way around to the alley. Only pulling his eyes off the roofline just that instant, he missed the long descent of the PVC pipe. The crowd saw it. He heard that peculiar exhalation of breath and throat noise. Something like: *ohhhhhrgggg*. He heard the pipe make impact too. It produced another sound he recognized: a science-fiction explosion sort of sound, a tubular *waang* followed by long, elliptical, metallic aftershocks. *Wowowowowow*.

And of course, he felt the pain too. Across his shoulder and up the side of his head. A dark sensation, a ripple of deep blue that moved downward through his body in waves and that was followed then by other strange effects. There was stickiness in his ears. There was a red veil over his eyes. His arms would not work. Auditory impacts too. He was listening to an angry world through several thousand gallons of inner-ear fluid. He was swimming. Submerged. And in front of him — perhaps as a result of losing his balance, he could not be sure then, and wasn't sure later either — the great building itself was slumping. That white box out of which had flowed all of his past, present and immediate troubles. His future ones too, he imagined, if he were to be granted a future. But that three-layered thing, all along the top edge of which a battle still raged, it was moving downward somehow.

Zweigler sat on the ground and shook his head. The PVC pipe, which was not heavy, had glanced off his ear, onto his shoulder and lay now across his legs. It wasn't heavy enough to pin him in place but quite irrationally, Zweigler felt he could not move. He heard himself calling out. Plain words at high volume. He looked up at the structure. Those two shapes still silently trading blows and scattering gravel up there against the blue. He pulled his headphones back in place over malfunctioning ears. Raul just now arriving to his aid, crouching, taking his arm. And Zweigler, clawing at the pipe, called out quite clearly, "Lift it! Lift it! Lift it!"

Behind the building, camera two would later return the results of this poor choice of words. Gimble had been smoking and frowning, exchanging glances with the hoist foreman. Then he put his hand up sharply to the side of his headphones. "*Lift it*. What the fuck?"

The hoist foreman squinted hard. He said, "Lift it?"

Gimble shook his head, then nodded. Still listening.

The hoist foreman turned and motioned to the crane operator: one thumb up. An unambiguous signal. And up went the building. Up went the crowd noise. Screams now. Quite definitely screams. Gimble was saying, "No, no, no."

The crane inched skyward. The winches howled to life and began to pull. The whole structure, as per procedures carefully thought out by Gimble in advance, began to grind toward the east, steel squealing against steel, wood members cranking along the rails toward their final destination. The book open ten feet now. Then fifteen.

Gimble was no sprinter, but he covered the ground to the crane in about three seconds. Thumb raking downward the entire way but failing to communicate with the operator whose eyes were quite rightly oriented upward. Only when Gimble was close, wrenching open the side door glass and screaming—something like "Drop that fucker down right now there are people up there!"—did the crane operator turn and see him, freezing in confusion.

Out front, Zweigler watched the building sway a moment, light actually visible under the lift support members. He was on his back again. Raul had helped him to a standing position a moment before, which had not been successful. Now he was down again, looking at a crack of sunshine opening under the building. The mechanical scream of winches coming from the far side of the building.

Then the building crashed downward.

It didn't hit the skids with enough force to break them. This point had to be made strenuously later to prevent the crane operator from taking all the blame, which he really could not fairly be given. Gimble, for one, had reached into the cab of the machine and pushed the operator's hand on the toggle. The crane releasing faster than he might have liked. Still, the skids did not give. There were cracking sounds. There was more of that distant tinkle of breaking windows to those listening closely, to those not yelling and storming for the Mary Street exit. But these sounds came from indeterminate places within the structure. They were hard sounds to work with, to use in developing a definitive strategy. They merely happened and were impressive in their own way, and then— in the seconds that followed, when the whole structure swayed but appeared to hold—seemed perhaps not to have been so important.

Graham climbed shakily to his feet on the rooftop. So did the cameraman, although without his camera. (The remaining crowd, largely outside the fence now, was calling out, *Get down. Get down.*) From behind the building, camera two recorded them climbing over the parapet and into the man lift, Graham and the Bolex operator. It recorded them descending to the alley pavement. But then things became difficult to sort out. Graham helped the cameraman out of the cage, then stood rigidly in place himself. He might have been registering the absence of either his brother or his father's camera, hard to say. But he hammered back the lever on the man lift, in either case, and soared back up again to the rear roofline. From there, without climbing back onto the roof, Graham could be heard to say quite clearly, "Gone."

Zweigler, maybe alone in the crowd, saw enough to know that Graham had been right saying so. Neither the camera nor his brother remained on the roof, because Elliot had by that point dragged himself and the old Bolex across the gravel and down through the steel reinforcing bars around the central stair column. Here he was beginning to make his way unsteadily toward the ground. The building, cracked open partway, might only have shown the sight to Zweigler. He might have been alone in watching Elliot go round and round—and regaining his senses while doing so, a looming awareness of things in precarious imbalance growing and growing—and therefore the only one to understand what it meant that the air was still full of mechanical screaming. The structure itself had been reseated, the crane had released its overhead tension. But with a man still inside the guts of the thing, somebody had forgotten to turn off those east-side winches.

That was when the support crib broke. In the middle of the excavation, no less. Almost directly under where Elliot was now descending. And it broke—engineers would later argue to agreement on this point—because the winch cables broke first. Loaded up to a stress point well past their five-times safety capacity, the strands of the cables separated and released, one by one, the sound like bullets passing through the higher octaves of a piano soundboard. And when a sufficient number of strands had done so, the cables all (magnificently, it had to be said) surrendered at once. A God-scale bowstring was released and they snapped in unison. The tension came off the east side of the building. The weight of the structure slewed radically to the west. And with this almost invisible motion (to the eye, the building hardly rocked at all) those support cribs at the centre of the excavation groaned in defeat.

The building leaned, then cracked, then shut tight the opening they had so artfully devised. From east to west, the open book closed itself and Elliot vanished from sight.

Now a more general pandemonium, forces unleashed, results unpredictable. People inside the fence were trying to get out. People who'd been standing on Mary Street were trying to get in. Zweigler's camera operators at the front of the building stood staring over their units, not filming at all. Raul was dumbstruck. And in front of them, for those who still cared to watch as the support crib gave out entirely, the east side of the building was leaning over so hard that it appeared to be climbing into the west. Force building and building, the whole structure starting to quiver.

Watching the tape later, somebody would compare this motion to a tidal wave hitting shore. Zweigler couldn't remember who, precisely. One of Raul's silk-shirted colleagues, no doubt. Somebody who had never seen a wave previously as anything but a recreational object off the Santa Monica pier. Still, a first view of something is on occasion the clearest.

Zweigler thought, It does look like a tsunami. It shuddered slightly, gaining size and strength, piling into a single gigantic thing. Then it rumbled, as something internal gave way. A floor beam breaking, something punching down through a layer that should not be punctured. And then all the composite forces that made the structure what it was intended to be spun away from one another and out of the envelope of feasibility entirely. Stresses spiked through capacities, strain points were reached and exceeded, plastic flow was accelerated dramatically, materials ceased functioning in any way that could have been envisioned. The building hit the shore. It stopped being a building. It cracked and schismed and broke apart inside. The roof descended through the chute of its walls. Remaining glass shattered in one exhalation, a last breath spraying itself outward in a cloud. And then everything folded in on itself in a long rattle, stretching out and sinking down until (it seemed to Zweigler) there was no structure, no elevation remaining at all. Only materials, elements and ideas at rest.

TIMOTHY
TAYLOR

NEW AUSPICIOUS

One

ELLIOT WEPT. ELLIOT PRAYED. FIRST TIME HE'D
done those two things together in ninety days. Not counting that, first time ever.

Elliot went swimming in the ocean the next morning
at eight.

It was the car that did all these things to him, 1973
Cadillac Brougham, bright red, with a set of black Texas
longhorns as a hood ornament. He noticed—tears coming
down, his prayer whispering away upward—that Kirov had

used rhinestones and white glue to write $K + L = Love$ in the centre of the steering wheel.

She said, from the back seat, "We get stopped by the cops, you might get these kids taken away."

Elliot breathed in and out. Recovered. He said, "Lucille, honey. They don't take your kids away for not using a car seat. They fine you. Got your belt on?"

She did.

"And which one do you have there?"

Louis, she thought. Malaya nodded in Elliot's rear-view. Deirdre sat in the passenger seat next to him. She was smiling.

"Okay, then just hold on to Louis. Malaya will hold on to Huey. Deirdre will keep a lookout for speed traps, and off we go."

Lucille said, more to herself than anybody else, "I've never been to a funeral before."

Elliot thought: Me neither, that I remember properly. Me neither, sober. Then he winced, because whatever unconscious physical things happened in his body in response to guilt still made his leg and chest hurt. Ninety days later. Ninety days since last tears, last prayers. Ninety days since lying on concrete for eighteen hours under the rubble of Story House.

More or less. All that day, all that night. He emerged into dawn again, dirty black from dust that had not been thought of, much less disturbed, in decades and decades. The floorboards released it. The broken columns and shattered beams. The walls did too. Pounds of dust, the ash of a flameless fire. He was stretchered up and out of a long path cleared through the broken timbers. He was loaded directly into an ambulance and, from there, sirened across town with great fuss and a surprising amount of press to the quiet of a serious-but-stable ward in St. Paul's Hospital. Broken bones, collapsed lung, multiple lacerations to the chest and face.

Some irony in these injuries, Elliot knew, although he didn't bother explaining it to anyone. Even to Deirdre, who showed up the next day with the twins. The miracle twins who were long past the scrawny pink infants he remembered, now grabbing every bit of tubing, any loose scrap of bandage and shoving it directly into their mouths. They gaped at Elliot. They smiled little two-teeth smiles when he puffed out his cheeks. They chewed on his knuckle when it was offered. Then reeled back to bury their faces in Malaya's neck when he tried to kiss them.

The unexplained irony was the height of the fall that caused all these injuries. About three feet, only Elliot knew. Because in the splintering, cracking, heaving and collapsing universe of 55 East Mary Street, he'd actually found some shelter. (This was all shortly following a series of strange happenings that he couldn't explain. Yes, they had fought. Yes, he had known they would fight. And yes, for a moment, Tapgol Park was unveiled in all its truth for the fact that he knew there in the rising morning sunshine that he wanted to beat his brother dead. But then God stamped his foot and the earth moved and Hell was released from below. And this he no more wished to understand than he wished to see his brother again. Which was to say, in only a very complicated way.)

In any case, after that, he had found a place of shelter within. Right at the foot of the spiral staircase, at the bottom of that steel cage they had constructed to protect its pristine dimensions. And while the building piled down on top of him, Elliot was able to crouch here and cover his head, and register only a precipitous darkening. That was all. His environment went from rooftop clear to basement dungeon in about thirty seconds. And when that process was complete he uncovered his head, opened his eyes, and saw that—while the Bolex Paillard lay smashed into useless bits at his feet—he was intact. He saw three steps leading down to a portion of the basement pad. All of it pressed right down into the bottom of the pit. But here a five-foot cube like a bell jar holding out the wreckage around him. He was hunched over, granted, broken beams pressed down low, but he was able to take a step. Then he tripped.

Down he went. Three stairs, one spiral-fractured tibia, a dislocated thumb and, on account of taking a rack full of torn-apart wall timber directly into the face and chest, the deep searing pain of rusty nail cuts and, more troubling still, a sense of his chest deflating. He was leaking air. He was gasping, bleeding, lying on concrete that (it came to him, in his pain) had been inexpertly slump tested and poured under the supervision of his father.

Fuckity fuckity fuck.

Eighteen hours. After the tears and the prayers, you could only reflect on death and prophecy. Item One: Tapgol was a crock of shit. *If I'm not careful I might cause this death.* Who nearly killed who here? Who was

lying under a ton of scrap?

Voices were calling down after less than twenty minutes. Not Graham's, he noticed. Official voices.

"Elliot, are you down there?"

"Elliot, if you can't speak or call out, try hitting a piece of wood near you."

"Elliot, it's Raul. I work with Avi. Hang in there, you hear?"

Hang in there. He liked that. They were going back in

time. They were zooming back to the beginning of things. He was corked on a mat somewhere not too far from this very spot, just up above him and over to the east a few feet. (Oh yes, Item Two: who had a track record of nearly dying on or near this spot?) People hunching down on top of him. Somebody with breathing gear. And his father right at his ear. Real or imagined, it didn't matter. While the cops and the firemen swarmed, he heard the words.

You hang in there, boy. You aren't done with this business yet. This business of building up a thing called you. You hear me? Going to build me a mountain, uh-huh. From a little hill. Oh yeah. Gonna build me a mountain, yes sir. Least I hope I will . . .

Strange. He felt sure he was now making that part up. Yet the words rang so clearly.

Elliot hammered on a timber nearest his left hand. Then he called out, but weakly. He said, "Look down. Look wa-a-y down."

Elliot looked way down into the driver's footwell. He spotted a lighter. Zippo clone marked with a bad fake Marlboro patch. He reached down, picked it up. He snapped the top open and lit a smoke from the pack he found in the glovebox, then handed the lighter back to Lucille. She looked it over.

She said, "I gave it to him."

$K + L = Love$. There was a nice simple equation for you.

He started up the car, wheeled into Hastings Street while the sun flashed in stripes across the faces in the rear seat. He imagined Kirov's face among them, next to Lucille, seeing them together like he remembered from the wedding. Cyrillic script up the small of her back and around his arm. The hennaed vows read, Kirov told him later, "Something like, I love you to death, you love me to death, we both love each other to death. Like that. Three halves of the same thing."

Elliot said to Kirov at the time, *One thing can't have three halves*. But the point was clear enough. In the entire world, anything plus anything was a degree more complicated than $K + L$, even equations that didn't involve what his own had lately.

Deirdre said, the week before, "Are you depressed?"

No, of course not.

She said, "I worry that you don't leave the house any more since all this happened. Mary Street. Kirov."

Well, Mary Street. What was there to be depressed about? So he was named in the lawsuit the city had filed. If anybody paid, it was going to be the cable channel. And they weren't anyway, because they'd win. The building fell down. Thirteen million people watched. Interested parties made gazillions of dollars. No one was hurt except him. So Packer Gordon didn't become any more of a household name. So Packer Gordon got maybe a little lost in the television show as presented. He was sorry about that.

Deirdre just stared at him.

And Kirov didn't have anything to do with anything.

Fine. So then she moved on to what was clearly the most important thing she had to say: "It's been three months since you got clear of your brother. If ever there were a time for you to have a little personal cultural revolution, now would be it."

He was holding Huey. And Huey, he'd just been thinking, was clearly going to be the trouble-prone leader of the two boys. Because while Louis lounged back under the colourful suspended toys of his Gymani, arms lolling to either side as he contemplated the world as he knew it, this one here had a good grip on a piece of Elliot's face. And using that as a handle, he'd managed to stand in Elliot's lap, knees leaning into his still-sore chest, and was just this minute trying to make out what could be accomplished with the knobs of the radio on the shelf over Elliot's shoulder. It was tuned to a basketball game Rico would have cared about deeply, but the thread of which Elliot had lost many moments before.

Deirdre, lovely Deirdre. She sat on the edge of the coffee table. Red hair spilling down. She took a finger and moved a strand off her cheek. She waited for him.

Sun flickering off their faces in turn. With each block, another thrown pattern of light from above. Something slowly resolving in that pattern, he imagined. Something slowly resolving.

"Let's have a funeral then," he said to Deirdre.

The church was smaller than Elliot had imagined. Somehow, in his mind, these spaces were all looming and long and imposing. They were puffed to twice the size required and smelled of self-righteousness. This one, not so much. It smelled, if anything, a little like ginger and fish sauce, sandwiched as it was between two Chinese restaurants. A bare white room with stacking chairs set out in simple rows. It had a cross hung centrally on the front wall, with a flanking Star of David and an Islamic Crescent in ecumenical but subservient positions. It had various banners hanging down the side walls. They said things like: Prayer Changes Things; I Have Seen The Light; and one showed what looked like a pigeon coming down out of a cloud that said simply Love Descending.

Kirov—who circumstances dictated could not be present either in the form of a body or as ashes—was in the room only as a presumption of death based on circumstantial evidence. Nobody whose clothes were found rotting in the trunk of a rented car parked behind fish totes at a packing plant on the waterfront could be expected to return. Yes, there had been a red felt cowboy hat, ditto spanky boots, a Swatch watch. *Swach.*

Details Elliot found crushingly sad.

Not Lucille though, who idled along as if the absence of his physical being prevented her from emotional response. Her expression lost. Her eyes drifting, hazy. She spoke to nobody but the kids, Elliot, Deirdre and Malaya. And then only in short non sequiturs or in the hummed lines of an old children's tune.

Mr. Rabbit Mr. Rabbit . . .

When he phoned Lucille about the funeral, she said, You mean like for closure?

Sure, Elliot told her. Like for closure.

Now he could hardly meet the eyes of the many people who'd decided to attend. Rico's various Orwell Hotel associates, of course. A trio of Uncles, who set down their flowers, bowed their heads to Lucille, then sat in the brilliant foliage of their own colours in the back row. A couple of Kirov's Russian friends who kept violent expressions trained on the floor. Dozens of other faces too. People Elliot remembered from the wedding so long ago. Many more he didn't.

Lucille hummed and sang next to him.

> *Mr. Rabbit, Mr. Rabbit . . . your coat is mighty grey . . .*
> *Yes bless God it was made that way.*
> *Every little soul must shine, shine.*
> *Every little soul must shine, shine.*

Louis leaning back, looking up at her like he understood perfectly. Elliot's tears threatening again now. Then receding. Threatening and receding.

Mr. Rabbit, Mr. Rabbit . . . your eyes are mighty red . . .
Yes bless God I'm almost dead . . .
Every little soul must shine, shine.
Every little soul must shine, shine.

Right to the end of the liturgy. The blank words of condolence. The reminder of things beyond. Right to the end of it all when the Uncles were swaying to their feet, one of them nodding in Elliot's direction and a busload of schoolkids spilled into the room. Obviously at the wrong place. Very obviously at the wrong place. Their teacher lost on the sidewalk out front, maybe looking at a slip of paper with an address that read 220 West Hastings, not 220 East Hastings. And who, in any case, could have had no idea what effect the children were having inside.

Down's syndrome, Elliot thought. Two dozen smiles and wide, wet eyes. And a whole lot of handshaking going on. Nothing Elliot could explain then, nor anything he tried to sort through later. But the kids were moving through the room and shaking hands. Loose grips, fingers splayed. *Hi hello. Hi hello. Hi hello.* Of course, nobody was refusing them. Everybody stood in place and shook the long parade of pudgy hands solemnly like the kids were royalty dropped in for a surprise visit. Rico's men. The Uncles. Even the priest, or the rabbi or imam or whatever he was, stood up there and shook twenty-eight hands with a big, dumb, honoured grin on his face.

And Elliot was flooded all at once with a memory: Kirov on stage that first time. Kirov who unequivocally did not want to fucking die. Kirov who was coming on stronger to Elliot precisely because of his resolute absence. A new power was his. To gather effect close to himself. To energize molecules and stir up reaction. To move people and things across the world and back. These forces had always been at work within him, but now, Elliot found himself fervently believing, they had been intensified.

Power in disappearance. He couldn't help but think at the same time of Graham, of their father, of the structure they had destroyed in their devotion. There was residual power in what they forced, through the sheer weight of their unchangeable selves, to disappear. Or thought of another way, perhaps it would be better stated: if it hadn't been for both of them, if their oppositions hadn't created the precise, unfailing energy that it did, what structure would ever have been erected?

Of course, if anybody had ever proposed such a thing to Kirov himself, he would have shrugged and arched his eyebrows, then let his face morph back uncannily to the very position it had been in before. *Who knew anything anyway?*

Elliot turned away from himself, physically turning from the front of the church and back into the nave. The Down's kids were still swarming happily. Elliot himself growing a significant degree happier. He began to shake hands. Up and down the aisle, he shook as many as he could in the time it took the teacher to burst in, apologizing, trying to restore order and herd her charges back out the door and into the bus and across town those critical five blocks that would return them to what she no doubt thought of as the safe side of town. Elliot worked the room in all the time this effort took her.

Hi hello. Hi hello.

Then, that teacher's world restored to balance (as he decided she would think of it), Elliot began what he recognized as the long process of doing the same in his own. He still had a few hands to shake among those left (the Uncles, others, not the Russians because they left), some kisses to give out too (one each for Deirdre, Lucille, Malaya, Huey and Louis). After that, he had only a simple two-step plan for the immediate future.

First: the Postum, for cheese omelettes, where Cleo took Deirdre's face in her hands, kissed both her cheeks. Then Elliot's too.

Second: straight home to straighten up. There was grass to cut and hedges to trim. There were stacks of paint cans in the garage that had been earmarked for use *on* the garage for approximately the past eight months. Flagstones to power wash. The list went on. He'd do all these things, preparing slowly and steadily and patiently the place that they'd built together. A big place with many rooms and windows, lots of grass to play on and a little piece of its own shoreline. A place where Lucille would be free to stay as long as she pleased, if she pleased. (And she did please.) A place where he would wait patiently for as long as it took for the next stage of his life to reveal itself.

A place where he would go swimming in the ocean each morning at eight.

This idea emerged fresh on first waking the next day, early. He stood, naked. Deirdre still asleep. He pulled on trunks. He walked downstairs and out onto the lawn and down to the rocks and dove right in. He paddled out a long ways, not a good swimmer, but responding as he believed one should to a genuine inspiration. And a good thing he had too, he thought, treading water and turning around, farther out than he'd ever been before. Because it was only from a distance, it was only standing offshore far enough that you knew you'd be tested on your return swim, that you had a reliable perspective on things: your position in the particular moment. The house. The sleeping family. The built life. And that perspective remained even if a light swirl of dizziness descended, which Elliot shook off, which he tried to ignore. Which he did successfully ignore for one minute, even two minutes. Treading water. Arms now trembling.

And then, which he could no longer ignore. Two distinct movements making it so. In the first, he thought of Graham. In what particular moment did his brother just then find himself? In the second, Malaya emerged with coffee on the deck and shaded her eyes to look out at him. And Elliot felt himself observed, her brow furrowing with concern, a silent calculation of distance being completed. And that reversal of views—he was being watched, in a place where he'd never been before, thinking about his brother—that seemed to slew his perspective radically again. Or, at least, that was the way he had time to frame his thoughts as dizziness avalanched down his arms and legs, as an old and familiar pain spumed upward into his brain, as the combination of these forces stripped away his vision, leaving him blind, in very deep water. A larger moment (he might have thought, were he still in a position to entertain such thoughts) sweeping up and over, consuming this particular one.

Two

GRAHAM GAINED ALTITUDE RATHER SHARPLY.
Ninety days after Story House, and he had somehow lost
his fear of flying. He waited for the drops of sweat to bead
at his hairline. None. He waited for the shakes. Not a
tremor. He closed his eyes—this test perhaps most critical
to him—and waited for the vision of a billion particles
floating outward from one another.

Not a bit of it.

He was climbing up out of the harbour—howling up,

the aircraft was old—climbing one loop of a double-helix stair, the wing hard over. He looked down through clean air calmly. The city comprehensible below. Its pieces identifiable and plain. Money, poverty, green, concrete, rowhouse, tower. Patterns and patterns, things designed. The built seam, that bit of business at the meeting place of sky and water.

Graham carried only a briefcase in which there were important papers and a single extra pair of boxer shorts. No other clothes. No fishing rod. His stay, he'd calculated, would last twelve hours and he'd happily return home in dirty clothes if she came with him.

They did a strange aerial manoeuvre on the way out that Graham could only put down to a slow air-traffic-control day. They headed out between the uprights of the Lions Gate Bridge, the normal takeoff pattern in a landward breeze. Then, up over the freighters at anchor, they jogged southwards in a loop that took them, surprisingly low really, directly back over the international airport. It was, for a moment, alarming. He visualized a heart attack at a radar console in the tower below. Somebody slumped in place while chaos mounted unnoticed in their headphones. Near misses. Planes spiralling toward the ground. He remembered from somewhere that the military term for a plane flying into the ground unaware of impending catastrophe was CFIT, Controlled Flight Into Terrain. But none of this caused his pulse to uptick even slightly, as it suddenly came clear to him that the air directly over any given airport was in fact quite safe. Things landing or taking off—that is, things that might be run into—were all about five hundred feet below them.

So they flew over the airport, his nose back to the window, eyes cast way down. Crossing a zone of utter calm. No danger for him staring down straight at the runway, blackened with its thousand skid marks, one each for a thousand screeching impacts that recorded the transition from inbound to arrived. And coming in now, from the east, just such an inbound object. Still flying, slung low to the ground, low enough almost to overlap its shadow, which flickered across the rooftops and power lines, the roadbed and the log boom. A shadow that went opaque and hopeful on the surface of the river, then hardened on the bright green grass under the runway lights.

It touched down with a faint puff of smoke, almost directly beneath them. Had they been at the same altitude, the collision would have killed all of them. One hundred and fifty or so of his people. The six of us here in this Otter, Graham thought, with its rattling side panels and the bellow of its single broad-bladed prop. But he wasn't thinking about redundancy systems or bailout-over-water procedures or what would be found in the survival kit, wherever it was stored. He was conscious of others in the plane, naturally. Four heavy-set men he could not quite place. All with the personalized fishing gear and the stories of past trips. All with the leader board sensibility that made the whole fishing enterprise tick. But something unpolished about them too. Black leather boots he did not associate with bankers on shore leave.

In any case, he was too busy to muse further on this as he contemplated the action below. The city at motion and at rest. The shape of it lining and cramming the delta. The way it fell astern and a different coastline was revealed. An endless and impossible seam up the western edge of this continent. Rocky and unforgiving. Marked by the white foam of a colliding sea, which could be appreciated as the underworld perhaps better from this altitude than from any other vantage. An underworld to which all debts were somehow owed. To which supplications could still be addressed.

Esther, he said, as they crawled up into the central coast, please be there. And, addressing the sea, he said this aloud. He caused two of the large men to shift in their seats opposite, to exchange raised eyebrows.

Esther, he went on, please be open to my proposal.

In his briefcase, folded into an envelope next to the boxers, was a strategic plan. These weren't documents with which Graham had a lot of prior experience, but he'd nevertheless prepared one himself over the course of the past few weeks. And he was proud of them. He was proud of thinking, he hoped, like Esther. Thinking in organized lines of inquiry and resolution, thinking through from goal to objective to tactic.

Esther, please recognize my efforts to make things right.

Goal One. An Effective Marital Team.

They were rattling now, Graham registered faintly, still looking down out the window to the play of sea and shore below. A rattle coming from somewhere under his feet. As

if a chain lashing something in place had come loose and was now trailing along the fuselage. They arced northwards, the Otter howl changing tone. A low roar gone just a shade higher, a degree more work taken on as it climbed up the side of the earth.

Goal number one, sounding cold on the page but held with hot conviction in Graham's heart just then, had seven objectives nested under it. *Am I really doing this?* he thought, leafing through the pages of the StratPlan

Workbook he'd found above the desk in Esther's den. *Well, yes, lacking anything remotely like a better idea, I suppose I am.* So: Honesty Day to Day, number one. Better More Regular Sex, number two. And so on.

Goal Two: Financial Stability.

Here Graham had fewer of the details worked out, understanding them to be complicated. Perhaps not more complicated than reinstating marital harmony, but less blue-skyable. Would Esther return to work? He didn't know. He wrote the idea under "tentative tactics," alongside his own reinvigoration of GS Design. Yes, with Fila. Although the item was footnoted to emphasize that she was moving back from Tokyo with a new husband.

A slight fudge. She wasn't moving back *with* him. But with him on the books. He'd be staying on in Tokyo. Fila said, *Don't ask.*

"But who is he?" Graham had been incredulous when first he heard. Fila, for her part, seeming more pleased with every degree his own voice rose. (The Otter engine, as if to make a point, was up two more tones of its own, which was odd, but certainly within the envelope of rickety nonsense he'd come to associate with ancient float planes.)

Well, he was a genius, for one. He'd been to Eton, Oxford and USC.

"Japanese?" Graham asked her.

Half Japanese, half English, half Cherokee Indian.

"How can he be half three things?" Graham asked. "Who goes to SouCal?"

He was criticizing the man's resumé, he realized.

Well, he went there as a student, Fila explained, so he could do a contract for Gehry without getting a green card.

Fine. "How tall is he?" Graham asked before flushing crimson. Had he just said that? Of course he had. That would be the only explanation for Fila's laughter.

He was about midway through the StratPlan when she'd phoned. Middle of the night, of course. She said, "Up with the lower angels, partner?"

He told her about thinking things through. About planning for the future.

"What do you have written down under the heading Personal Health?"

Sober sixty days, he told her. Running every day. "I'm trying to take back something I've let go a long time. And I mean Esther too."

"Speaking of whom," Fila said, "I'm getting married."

So they talked about that for awhile. Graham moving, in the space of fifteen minutes, from the bleakest, most murderous and fully automatic variety of jealousy to something like chummy support for this, his partner and new best friend. Because that's what they'd been all along, hadn't they? Best friends. Brother and sister, almost.

"Aren't you going to miss him? Leaving him there?" he asked.

"Hmm," she said, thinking. "And you?"

Well, he had plans, although Esther had complicated things slightly by not answering her phone lately and being no one place that anybody would admit to knowing. She wasn't even at the PFS, one person said when he called the club. No, they didn't know where she might have gone.

He went to see her father, in desperation. Phoned first, of course. "Dr. Lee, it's Graham Gordon."

"The increasingly famous Graham P. Gordon," said Dr. Lee.

"That was shortly after the whole fiasco," Graham told Fila. "And I wasn't, at that point, quite, if you know what I mean . . ."

"Sober?"

Precisely.

"Bit of excitement," said Dr. Lee when they met, the king of understatement.

Graham closed his eyes and rubbed his forehead. He accepted wine. He sipped, eyes closed. Opened them to find his glass almost empty. On the coffee table between them. *Architexture 4.04.* Cover story: "Why Things Fall Down—The Story House Meta-narrative."

Dr. Lee topped him up. His smile was of the I-still-like-you-but-have-no-stake-in-you variety. He asked, politely, "How is your brother?"

"Well," Graham said. "He's lucky he survived, anyway."

"Maybe you were lucky he survived," Dr. Lee said.

Maybe. On bad days, Graham hated himself for thinking, Maybe not. "I'm here about Esther," he said, coming to the issue bluntly. Speaking louder than he wanted to. Sounding less confident.

Dr. Lee shook his head.

"What's that mean?" Graham asked.

Dr. Lee raised his eyebrows.

"A head shake. Enigmatically raised eyebrows. No, you can't help me. Is that it?"

Dr. Lee put a finger in the point of his chin. He rubbed it in a circle. He said, "What shall I say?"

Graham drank wine again. He helped himself to the bottle. "Did you like my father?" he asked Dr. Lee.

"Truthfully," Dr. Lee said. "Yes. But I was rare."

"Why rare?"

"Because your father was extraordinarily egocentric. He had destructive self-regard. Careful people are wary of this type."

"Aren't you a careful man?" Graham said.

"Perhaps you should be more careful," Dr. Lee said. "Would you like to know an important detail about 55 East Mary Street?"

Graham, who had had several drinks before arriving, was quite sure that no important detail in the world would be more important than the one that he was about to share with Dr. Lee right this moment.

"I love your daughter," he said.

"Perhaps you do," Dr. Lee answered.

"Not perhaps. I love her. I love Esther."

"Graham, sit. Be comfortable. Drink if you want to. Your father always did. But don't stand in front of me like that."

"I love her more than I love myself."

Dr. Lee spread his hands. *Please.*

"I've loved her from before the time I was born. Story House was for her. Something complete. Something mine."

Fila asked him, "What important detail did he tell you?"

Graham rubbed his forehead in the Otter. He seemed to have a welt across the middle of it. A mark of some kind. He wondered where he'd picked this up and how it was he had not noticed it before. Then he started, sharply, looking up from the strategic plan that lay open in his lap. The briefcase open on the seat beside him.

Less chatter in the cabin than previously.

Goal Three: Children. Now this would require courage, after all they'd been through. Graham listed eight options under this heading, but his throat tightened on reading the first. *One, we get lucky.*

"I don't like that," said one of men across the Otter's aisle.

Graham looked at him. The man cracked a grin. A genuine expression of camaraderie followed by a wag of his head to the window. Graham noticed only with that motion that under the man's yellow golf shirt he had tattoos on his neck.

Graham looked out. They were descending. No doubt about it. The Otter engine up two, three more notches, screaming now as if it were under really radical stress. As if it were being mechanically garrotted.

"Tell me," Fila said. "This really important detail."

He resisted and the moment was lost. She was full of so many other things to tell him. Contacts in Tokyo. People they had to follow up with. A small museum expansion. An apartment bid in Kyoto. She was full of ideas about how they should return to something more purely architectural.

"You know, Lark was pretty good to you," she said. He enshrined the ideas. He published the line drawings. They ran a shot of the building collapsed down into the hole, sure. (One taken before his brother was rescued too, something Graham knew from the time code in the corner of the photo.) But Lark had spun the article in the most ingenious and favourable light imaginable. In "Story House," dreams outstripped the willingness of human beings to live them. Ideas grew lighter than air and were brought down to earth by more mundane forces.

Graham wasn't exactly exonerated. He was, however, placed on a mountaintop alongside rarefied savants, idiot and otherwise.

We need to use that, Fila was telling him. That strange momentum. Playing to your strengths. Branding, you know, it had its moments but became a bit production-oriented. Did he agree with her? Did he think that was true?

He was failing just in talking to her. That was the truth. He was thinking about sleeping with her again. "When are you back?"

In the fall. Jesus.

"I need to know," she asked him, her cadence, her delivery, dropping in the windup before a real question.

Anything. Ask me anything. "Go ahead," he said to her.

"Is there any chance," Fila asked him, voice like a thread of spun sugar, "in the opinion of whoever you're talking to legally, that is . . . that you might be sued over the whole 55 East Mary Street thing?"

When people were impressed by what he'd done, they referred to the whole incident by the title of the break-away success television show it had spawned: *Story House*. When they worried for him, it was only an address that could be found on legal surveys.

Graham laughed aloud, aware now that the bulky men in their leather vests and slightly anomalous private-label English fishing gear had stopped talking entirely. It was strange how this sudden drop in cabin noise made him hear all at once what they had been discussing: boast-worthy fishing experiences and their relative cost to acquire. One in the group, just at the moment of conversation vaporizing, had been in the middle of confessing that he'd never fished the Spey.

"Holy shit," said someone.

To the window again, Graham saw they had descended through the altitude which transformed the water below from a large anonymous thing called an ocean into a continuum of individual waves. They stood out singly. Some taller than others. Some thicker. Some more flecked with foam or more likely to part and accommodate the impact of a collision.

This was a large and slatey expanse of individual waves. And the nearest land (Graham craned his neck around) was receding rapidly to the stern. Graham was just computing uselessly in his head if he thought they could wheel about from here and make it to the sheltered water near land in the event of real trouble—deciding it was probably iffy touching down on the high seas with what appeared to be ten-foot swells—when the pilot arrived at the result of his own calculation and drove the aircraft into the steepest bank Graham had ever endured.

They were standing on a wingtip. They were all floating about the cabin like paper waste. Graham was yelling. And just as a brown nylon fly-rod tube swam down the aisle and struck him behind the ear, he heard the pilot say a word you never like to hear at any altitude very far above or below sea level.

Motherfucker!

Down they went, fast and steep. Falling, really, for an alarming number of seconds before the pilot found a flyable straight line pointing back the direction they had come. A string of curses coming out of the cockpit the entire time. Impressive military cursing aimed at the engine and the control surfaces, the pedals and the stick, jointly and separately. Thirty seconds, maybe sixty seconds passing before Graham even noticed that they were now gliding. No engine at all.

The large men did not scream or call out or pray through any of this. They only complained. "Sweet Fucking Jesus

Murphy Christ," said one. "We are going to be seriously late."

And there were other comments to this effect. But now the pilot, having finished his abusive appeal to the mechanical beast wrapped around them, was directing instructions back over his shoulder with a barking cadence that commanded attention even with these guys. Diction that recalled precisely his military experience (air transport, Kosovo, other places). He said, Gambling men would bet they were not making the beach. Life vests were an excellent idea. Suck your ass cheeks together and brace. Start now, no point waiting. See you in the water. Conditions likely chilly thereafter, but no cocksucking sharks.

There was more, but Graham couldn't listen. He was thinking instead, The reason this isn't happening, or won't, is that people who spend their lives worrying about air incidents never go down in crashes. Yes, Esther would dispute the point for lack of supporting statistics. People who went down in crashes were generally far too dead afterwards to complete surveys. But Graham had to respectively disagree with the smartest person he'd ever met in his life before. Just this once, he was going to be right. And that certainty would not be abated by the fact that his biology disagreed with him strenuously. His teeth were chattering uncontrollably. He had wet himself in a flood of fear he hadn't even felt arrive. Yes, that was his own mess and smell down there. And crying too.

Still, belief was a choice, wasn't it?

Sit, Dr. Lee had told him again.

Esther? he asked aloud. Provoking no smiles from anyone else in the cabin, because there seemed to be more distracting noise around them all with the engine off than there had been with it on. Quieter noise, to be sure. But of an intense, low and consuming register. The big men were talking urgently. They were considering an impending event that was most decidedly unplanned.

Esther, Esther.

And now Fila leaned in. Growing insistent. "What important detail did he tell you?"

"I love her with all of my heart. I love her more than the world. I love her in a way that no God can be loved."

Sit, Dr. Lee said. And of course, Graham collapsed as Gordon structures do. His own giving out onto a long, modular, black-leather couch that had been designed specifically for this house. They fit together perfectly, the place and that couch. They were right, in the location where they had been placed forty years before. Still absolutely right, and no reason to think about moving either of them.

"What about you?" he asked the sea. "Maybe you want to say something?"

The sea could be observed to break at the leading edge of its waves. Foam licking down the crests and laughing in the troughs. It was deep green sea. It was full of life. And they were banking down steadily now toward that life. Toward the deep. That seam of island lying directly ahead, either out of reach or make-able, depending on the gambler.

Dr. Lee said, "I wonder. Are you a gambler? You know poker?"

A shrieking sound in the ears now. One of the large men having calmly walked to the rear of the plane and opened the hatch. Here he was throwing out suitcases, one by one. Graham looked back, registered the action. Then forward again. What did it mean anyway? Somebody's shit falling into the drink.

Here was some vintage Lark: *The play of interior and exterior as designed was complex but pleasing.*

As designed. Okay. Goal Three, Children. Options exhausted.

1. Natural luck
2. Semen wash and assisted injection
3. In vitro
4. ICSE

And this despite the fact that at no point in the structure as visualized by the father (and revisualized by the sons) would this complexity ever be relieved. It runs wall to wall through each of the original layers. It defines space. And so great is the resulting tension . . .

"Sons," Lark wrote. Who could fault the man. It had been both of them, hadn't it?

Dr. Lee said, "You know bluffing?"

Goal Three, Children. Options still available.

5. Adoption
6. Sperm donation

Fila said, "You've got to be joking."

No joke. Lost it in a card game. His son's inheritance. Or both of his sons. Or his first-born. Packer Gordon had apparently never been absolutely clear on this point in conversation with Lee. The good doctor only knew that it had been the old man's intention to pass it along to someone, that they might finish it as they pleased. Until, that is, he came up against a well-played two pair eights over fives.

"Bluffing means playing like you have better," Dr. Lee said. "Your father went to the showdown with Jack high."

Well, of course he had. And that's why Graham planned to say to Esther: The key to any strategic plan (he'd stand back to say this, admiring what would be a beautiful tan by now) . . .

No, start again. The critical point was. . . .

7.   Sperm and egg donation with surrogate carry
8.   Kidnapping (just kidding!)

. . . that no strategic plan was an attempt to change the past. That much was a given. The StratPlan was merely a frame that bore the unpredictable weight of what was to come. He was trying to build something here. For them.

Why was he unable to build something for them?

Dr. Lee said, "You have to forgive. That was your father's problem too. No forgiveness in him."

Esther, please forgive me. He was wholly engaged on the topic of forgiveness now. Water streaming past now. Straining upward toward him. To hold him. It wanted Graham Gordon, that water did. It wanted him like the soul of something that had missed him a long time.

Forgive me for sleeping with Fila.

Forgive me for enjoying it so much.

Forgive me for crying when I learned she was getting married.

"Forgive, forgive, not *ask* for forgiveness." Dr. Lee shook his head. "Your father asked for forgiveness plenty of times. He asked my forgiveness about ten times. When we were in Korea together he got into bed with my cousin's girlfriend, I ever tell you that?"

Why? would have been a good question to throw in there. But Graham hadn't thought to ask it.

"Elliot," he said aloud. And he actually clenched his hands in a gesture of prayer, doing so, waiting for something to come. Which it did, in a fashion. Nothing quite like forgiveness, the asking of or giving of it. But a flash awareness of linked lives. Of inextricability. A chain connecting them even as they fell together. And another sense. This one of how all efforts to separate from each other would be forever overthrown. Graham could strike Elliot from his thoughts and Elliot could do the same. And still, just before sleep, just on waking, at all moments of imbalance, he would feel that tremor. His own existence leaning into that of his brother.

As he did now, looking up sharply, imbalanced by shouts from the front of the cabin. A celebration underway. Jubilation. And a great spluttering, roaring sound that was nothing less that glory itself. The sound of victory.

The pilot was yelling. "Whoo-hoo! Whoo fuckin hoo!"

There was a hand under Graham's seat. That was the sensation. An enormous hand that caught the plane and lifted it. And that hand, Graham allowed himself to believe, was his father's. Reaching back from beyond the laughing grave. Spreading the distance between him and the water, just as if his only intention were to keep them safely apart. They rose with this new force from below. For one, two, three seconds. Maybe five total. Because on about the six-second mark, the engine threw a rod.

Graham—who had little experience with engines, but who was living in the viscous, slow-moving soup that was time just then—could actually see the slender push-rod come out of the Otter's aluminium nose cone through a clean bullet-sized puncture wound and whistle away into space. And he understood, immediately upon seeing this quite beautiful sight, that in order to sail away into grey air in just that fashion, the rod would have had to punch through quite a bit of other critical structural stuff first. Starting with the engine block.

All was serenely quiet again. Everything once again in slow descent. Then faster. All along the windows on either side, a black curtain of oil spraying back over the fuselage and slowly obliterating the view.

And fair enough that they should go down blind, Graham thought, his open briefcase now disgorging paper.

Goal Four: Building A New House Together.

Fair enough that he should be conscious of nothing but a storm of white laser-printer paper, winging about like very large snowflakes, then growing smaller, like rain, like mist, like the hundred thousand shards of a dream from long ago. That moment of creativity with the never-quite-rendered perfection that was supposed to follow. Fair enough because . . .

But he lost the rest of that thought.

Three

.

ESTHER SLEPT ON A BEACH, OUTSIDE HER TENT. And there she had a dream. In that dream, a bird came flying in across the bay and began to circle slowly. When it came near to her, she could see that it was, in fact, half man half fish half bird.

Stop. *How can you be half three things?* Esther asked the creature.

Oh God, it said, flying by and away again in a big arc. *One of those.*

One of those what?

One of those hyper-rational types.

All right. Go ahead with the dream.

You're giving your own dream permission to continue?

Esther rolled over to her other side, something a sleep specialist once told her she'd been doing for years right through all her nightly cycles, and which would explain why a low-level fatigue had begun to creep up the length of her days.

Yes, Esther said.

The half man half fish half bird landed on the beach and came toward her. It was more manlike up close. Old manlike, in fact. Dressed in sweatpants and a T-shirt. Trim but aging. The old man/bird creature said, *All right then. Here goes.*

What's your name?

The more-manlike-than-ever creature rolled its head back and stared at the sky.

Am I not allowed to ask questions? Esther said.

Ask, ask. Can I stop you?

What's your name?

What's yours?

Esther, you know that.

How would I know that?

Esther didn't know how it would know. She'd just

assumed. *Well, I told you.*

I don't tell my name to anyone. You have to guess.

Oh, you're like a riddle bird.

A riddle bird, the creature said. *What the hell is a rid-dle bird?*

You know, like a bird from a legend or whatever.

Or whatever. Listen to you, the creature said. *Anyway. As it happens, I have a short message.*

Andrew.

What about Andrew?

Your name. Is it Andrew?

My name is not Andrew. Not Bill. Not Charlie.

I'm a member of Mensa, you know.

Congratulations, the creature said. *And why are you telling me this?*

Andrew, Bill, Charlie . . . You're trying to get me to do the alphabet.

Oh. Am I.

David? Derek? Dilbert?

Ha.

Keep going?

I'm not playing this game with you.

Esther rolled over again. *Fine. Your message.*

Somebody starts low, somebody starts high . . .

I told you. Riddle bird. Like in myths. This is funny.

You think myths are funny?

A lot of the time, yes.

You want to hear this or not?

Esther nodded.

Somebody starts low, somebody starts high, but both end up in the water.

End up in the water like drowned?

I don't have all the details. Like wet, though. That's for sure. You decide.

I decide?

It's your dream.

That's it? You've come all this way to tell me the dream turns out any way I want?

Who said I came a long way?

Or whatever.

One other thing.

All right.

This is the advice part of the dream.

Go.

Get up. Now.

What? Esther said, not rolling over or moving at all. *I'm comfortable here.*

Seriously. You should get up.

Why?

Because someone's coming.

That's your advice. Get up? Not: give more money to the Burn Unit. Or: work harder on your personal relationships.

Well, sure. Both those things too.

Oh, great. Yann. Yves. Yorrick.

But the creature had taken flight by now. It was circling at a height of about ten feet, round and round, red in the face and looking like it was preparing for a moon shot.

Please. One more question.

You have only seconds to ask it and I'm out of here. And don't bother with the name. Maybe I'll visit you when you're ninety and tell you my name.

Okay then, where do you live?

Hey, the creature said with a smile. *You're good.*

So? Tell me. Peter, Paul, Patrick. Your name starts with P. *I have this hunch.*

But now the birdman was flying for real, circling enormously, throwing off huge gusts of wind with his wings and buzzing in so close over Esther's head that she had to curl up in a ball on the beach so as not to be blown away and into the sea herself.

"Tell me," she said out loud. And doing so caused her to roll again, farther down the beach. This time almost to the wet line of the rising tide.

The waves pulled back, way down the flat pebbly beach. Then they crashed in, running, running, pouring across the stones and over the clam beds, up around the musselled boulders near the entrance to the harbour. All the way to Esther's shoulder, where the water splashed up and into her clothes, down her neck. And she was sitting up then, quickly, sharply, gasping, spitting. Crying out.

The wave was now pulling back again, readying itself for another run. She would have to stand, right quick, if she didn't want to get wet again. But she stayed where she was just a moment longer and pretended that she could interpret the words of the sea, babbling over those pebbles in their long retreat. Washing away around the musselled rock. An answer to the question she had asked in her dream.

She listened hard. She thought, maybe, she heard something like:

w h y n o t a s k t h e b r o t h e r s?

Esther woke up on the beach. Somebody was indeed arriving.

"Okay," she said aloud, scrambling. Checking her clothes. She was dry. The tide mark still down where she had calculated it would be. Her tent still safely high and dry. The little deck area she'd built out of driftwood, ditto.

A Zodiac. One of the dock kids driving. The green pennant was flying. Still, the dream gripped her.

She poked her head into the red glow of the tent's interior. She grabbed a water bottle full of stream water. A handful of PowerBars. She withdrew from the beach at a hurried crouch, into the low brush, into the higher brush, only standing when she hit the very faint trail that lead from here up to the ridge line. And even on this trail, she still ran with her back bent. Her neck involuntarily lowered, looking over her shoulder. To see and not be seen.

Esther had ledges from which to look at the sea. Esther had caves in which to hide supplies. Esther had a freshwater spring and bottles in which the water could be stored. Esther had thirty days under her belt away from a mattress which wasn't what people at the PFS normally came here to do.

"Where you going?" the club manager had asked her.

At first she wouldn't tell him. Then he became very angry. And so striking was this reaction that she relented. They didn't want to bother her. They only needed to make sure she wasn't dead on any given Tuesday or Friday. So. Twice weekly a Zodiac came down and buzzed the bay where she was camping. If there wasn't a green streamer flying off a stick placed in a high and visible location, somebody was coming ashore.

"What do I fly when I finally catch a king?"

Two greens, the manager said with a smile.

Two greens it was, from day one onward. No point lying and saying that her first hook in pulled up a big one. But her third or fourth hour out that day, squinting into the midday sun, she smelled the change in something (again, no point pretending she knew what it was). She hooked one at thirty pounds with dime-store coho lure, no herring bait at all. She released it. Then a big boy. Maybe forty, forty-five pounds. Then another thirty. She kept one fish all day and not a king at all, which would have been too much meat. She kept the ugliest-looking rockfish she'd ever seen, one pulled up so fast its guts would have burst and there'd be no point throwing it back anyway. Fish over the fire that night, sparks flying up into the blackest air imaginable. And an absolutely hollow feeling within. The sea still teemed. Or it teemed again. Forever. Temporarily. Who was to say? Did she feel good about it? Esther asked herself. Not particularly.

Because she wasn't here for the fish any more. Graham. Sure. Time to think about Graham. But her training defeated her here too. After stewing and mulling and considering options, what did she arrive at? How did she prepare to decide on that one? She said to herself, When he inevitably comes up to try reasoning with me, I'll listen to what he says.

That was it. Her father, naturally, bemused and unhappy. "You're not thinking anything crazy about staying up here permanently, are you?" he asked her one weekend when he'd flown in. "These people are lifers. Hard-cores. Here we paid for the big education and you're holed up with a bunch of Norwegians."

She never even answered.

"Your architect is a loon, but a loon with certain markings."

"What does that mean?"

Dr. Lee made a flapping motion with his hands. "He flies pretty good. He managed to collapse a building in front of millions of people, and still he moves on to bigger things."

She'd read the local news stories. She'd talked to people at the firm right after it happened, right around the time she was trying to hand in her resignation.

"I won't accept," her senior partner said.

"Well," Esther answered. "You will eventually. So who fucked up?"

He thought the engineer had fucked up. Had she seen any of the TV series? It was amazing, he said.

A point of view with which the producers agreed too.

"You know, I'd just about had it with this whole game," he said, in the confessional way that former clients did after engagements that ended better than expected.

Esther saw the L.A. area code. She popped open the phone. "Avi Zweigler. Still hard at it."

"Esther Gordon-Lee," he returned. "Do you have any idea what you missed?"

Zweigler was on to a new thing by this point. He blasted through a description, bored of it obviously, but unable to pull out on account of the money now flowing in his direction. He used to have to seduce money, he told her. And he'd been good enough at that. But *Story House* had vaulted him into the class of people who didn't even have to do that much. Money came to them.

"Still up Stone Canyon?" she asked him. But she needn't have, because she knew he was. Some prisons are maximum security. Others are custom-built for one occupant and impermeable.

Zweigler said, "Ah . . . which brings me to a question."

No, emphatically, she didn't know where he was. If he didn't answer at the house or on his cell, he was doing just as her father predicted: flapping his wings slowly and flying way.

Zweigler didn't press the point. He only said, "And where are you, then?"

On a beach, she answered. Which provoked an enthusiastic response. Good for her that she should reward herself with a bit of tropical downtime. She smiled on her stony beach, looking out into the bone-freezing waves of the deep North Pacific. "Exactly," she said.

Now she breathed evenly and watched the Zodiac approach. It was pulling slowly around the sunken ship in the small bay. Esther, who had by now very thoroughly surveyed this half-submerged object, at first going only as close as ten yards in the tricky surrounding kelp beds—could have reported that it was safe to power by at any speed you wanted at the distance the Zodiac was taking and in the present tide. But she had observed in herself the tendency to caution around the hulk, the unnatural impulse to slow in the shadow of a thing so enormously defeated. One hundred and seventy-five feet. Drawing twenty-five feet when it was buoyant. A decent and deep-seaworthy fish packer from a time before such vessels became cost-inefficient for their medium size. Keel put down in Korea or Taiwan, she guessed. It would have been around for duty through the Korean War, the Vietnam War. It would have seen a lot of sea before this final trip. Overseen by snakeheads and other assorted crooks and thiefs. Suffered through by the great mass of hopefuls who had paid their money for the right to cram her holds. East to West and then no more.

She bobbed around it for days, trying to make it out. She memorized its dimensions with her eyes. She imagined its internal structures. The lay of its passages. Where the bridge lead down to the galleys by ladder. Where the wide inside spaces were. Where the engine room lay aft. She visualized it, day after day, even eventually coming close enough to touch its flank. And on one of those days, she couldn't place how long this had taken, she had worked her way down the starboard stern, that quarter most dangerous for being nearest the rocks, and hand over hand in an ultra-low tide that would not be repeated for another year, she found at last the name. It was riding low on the stern, still below the waterline. Painted over black so as not to be seen.

She had tied the Zodiac—dangerous lunacy this—to a broken piece of cable coming off the deck. She'd gone overboard into the kelp bed, paddling closer, now touching the ship with her hands, feeling the letters one by one.

New Auspicious.

It had both panicked her and elated her to know the name, a confluence of feelings better avoided when swimming in a kelp bed. She had to fight the impulse to thrash away, to leave the Zodiac behind. Instead, hand over hand up the hanging cable. Her forearms quivering. Back into her little boat. And then she was racing to the shore. She was writing the name in the sand and filling these with stones, high above the watermark, where they would not be washed away. She was running through the bush, looking now for evidence she had not had the courage to look for previously. And finding it soon enough, strewn through the bush along a rough line leading from the beach to the nearest hilltop. The first impulse of the shipwrecked being, of course, high, high land.

A rusted-out space heater. A cheap Styrofoam cooler. A spilled box of cooking utensils: bowls, chopsticks, a Sterno stove. A bag of rice long emptied into the mouth of the forest by the time Esther found it. Each grain carted away by ants. Each grain now grown into generations of future ants and, through them, out through nature's impossible web of interconnections, into the very trees that swayed solemnly above the rotting burlap bag.

And graves too. These she found much later, after her searching had slowed. After she had carried back all the artifacts in the forest and arrayed them along the beach above the name in the sand. A museum that grew quickly, then more slowly. Then, when she had combed the forest dozens and dozens of times, stopped growing at all. What was left of *New Auspicious* now laid out to be examined, to be judged there in plain view of both the high hill and the water. She walked around the display daily, maybe touching a chopstick, or fingering a piece of textile, faded and torn. Imagining from what sort of garment, wrapped around what sort of person, it had originally come.

Then graves. After which she stopped combing the forest. Stopped looking for anything. Three only. Marked by stacked stone cairns. She didn't need to dig them up to know the story here. One medium-sized. Two much smaller, one on either side.

She climbed back into the Zodiac after finding them. She circled the wreck once entirely, a final time. She went mad for some time, sleeping two nights away from the beach in a thicket of broom. Waking up shivering, lips cracked, frightened.

Now, lying on a ledge she called Day 12 for when it was first discovered, a place she had used for lying naked in the evening sun, her two green streamers flying high and proud, she watched as the dock kid piloted the Zodiac slowly to the beach, eyes flickering from her camp to the face of the forest. Wondering where she was.

Not alone, either. Esther could now see that there was another person in the boat. Not her father. Not her husband. A woman.

Esther went down the trail to the beach again. She walked slowly, in no hurry. And when she came out onto the sand, she saw that only the woman had come ashore, climbing out of the Zodiac in the shallows.

This woman had beautiful red hair. She didn't look familiar. But then, in her expression—she was looking down at Esther's *New Auspicious*, marked in the sand, and reflecting a kind of grief, to be sure, Esther only unsure at that moment just how far and wide the ripples of this grief had spread — it became apparent that the two of them were about to know one another extraordinarily well.

Acknowledgements

Special thanks to:

Jane, first and always.

Craig Doyle, whose work inspired me.

Trevor Boddy, Tim Collett, Pat West, Neil Minuk and Rui Nunes who each gamely answered questions about architecture.

Lea Williams, from the incomparable Railway Club in Vancouver, for giving me her own signed copy of *The Architecture of Erikson*.

Gordon Miller who showed me his diagrams of Kiusta. And Dr. George MacDonald, whose book *Haida Monumental Art* was invaluable.

Kevin Reynolds and Richard Peltc who taught me whatever I've managed to learn about boxing. And Chris Elgin, with whom I have sparred countless rounds.

Arjun Basu and Charlene Rooke, whose assignments have a way of staying with me.

Also, for their advice and assistance in various areas: Dr. Dylan Taylor, Anthony von Hahn, Steven Galloway, Diane Martin, John Eerkes-Medrano, Deirdre Molina, Scott Richardson, Scott Sellers and everybody else at Knopf Canada/Random House of Canada Limited, Dean Cooke, Suzanne Brandreth and the Canada Council for the Arts.

TIMOTHY TAYLOR is the author of the bestselling novel *Stanley Park*, which was a finalist for the Giller Prize. It was selected by the Vancouver Public Library's "One Book, One Vancouver" program. He is also the Journey Prize–winning author of the short-story collection *Silent Cruise*. He lives in Vancouver.

A NOTE ABOUT THE TYPE

The principle text of *Story House* is set
in Electra, designed in 1935 by William
Addison Dwiggins. A popular face for book-
length work since its release, Electra is
noted for its evenness and high legibility
in both text sizes and display settings.

BOOK DESIGN BY CS RICHARDSON